"Intelligent and lingering...
Cade's Rebellion is a smart, memorable story of clashing cultures."
—*Clarion Review (four stars)*

Cade's Rebellion

Edward Sheehy

First published by Dog Ear Publishing
4011 Vincennes Rd
Indianapolis, IN 46268
www.dogearpublishing.net

ISBN: 978-1-4575-6024-8

This book is printed on acid-free paper.

Printed in the United States of America

For Emma and Jack

1

Forward Operating Base Scorpion
Iraq, 2005

The remote village was accessible only by Thunder Road, a stretch of unpaved road cratered by countless improvised explosive devices. Everyone hated that route. A real white-knuckler. As the counter-IED specialist, Staff Sergeant Jack Cade trained the *jundi*, Arabic for "soldier," on techniques for the detection and disarming of the explosives. Homemade bombs were easy to make and easy to hide—in a dog carcass, a baby carriage, or a garbage heap.

Explosives could be artillery shells and mortar rounds duct-taped together in containers filled with nails, ball bearings, or rocks. "Trust nothing," Cade taught the jundi. "Assume *nothing* is safe." The Humvees, equipped with electronic equipment, could jam remote activation signals—but that equipment wouldn't detect trip wires, pressure plates, or timers.

Cade stood with Grif in the back of the briefing room. He watched Grif arch his eyebrows—the barest acknowledgment that they were about to traverse the most treacherous road in Iraq. The two sergeants fist-bumped—a gesture communicating: *I got your back, bro.*

After the briefing, the jundi and members of the US Army Military Transition Team dispersed into preassigned squads packed into three troop carriers. The Iraqi commander led the convoy. Cade's Humvee brought up the rear, Grif riding shotgun, the boom box blasting Drowning Pool's "Let the Bodies Hit the Floor."

Fifteen kilometers from the village, the convoy ground to a halt. A spotter reported an unidentified object by the side of the road about fifty yards ahead. Cade leapt from the Humvee and jogged to the front, the clink and clack of full battle rattle announcing his arrival. He directed the jundi team to sweep the area with handheld Minehounds—like metal detectors on steroids. Their ground-penetrating radar was able to detect both metal and non-metallic bomb components. Other members of the patrol formed a perimeter to protect the sweepers from sniper attack.

The jundi scoured the roadside, looking for any unusual sign of disturbance: footprints, cut foliage, misplaced rocks, anything out of place—just the way Cade had trained them during long hours in the classroom and in the field—covering everything from circuitry to construction to camouflage. "Think like an insurgent bastard," he'd preached to the jundi. "That way you will have a better idea, a sixth sense, of where to detect and defeat IEDs." He had let that thought sink in, before adding: "Success is mandatory."

Cade waved to signal the jundi to fan out when the familiar jolt of pain hit him. An electric sting radiated from his neck and shoulders and raced down the neural pathway of his right arm. An internal combustion of intense agony. According to an Army doc, the sixty pounds of gear Cade had lugged over three deployments had ruptured the soft cushion of tissue between the vertebra in the cervical spine—or in layman's terms, a herniated disc. The jolt often left his arm numb, barely able to hoist an M-4 rifle. So far, he'd successfully kept the symptom hidden from anyone. His fingers found a Percocet and he swallowed it dry.

Up ahead, a Minehound-wielding jundi radioed that the roadside object was a slab of tire tread, most likely blown off a tractor-trailer. Further investigation revealed no evidence of a booby trap. Relieved, they returned to the convoy and continued down Thunder Road on heightened alert. The convoy entered the village from the north and halted. The jundi deployed into three squads, each with a US advisor. Squads swept the village west to east, checking for contraband weapons and interrogating the occupants for any intelligence on insurgent activity.

Cade's squad, including Malik and Zaid, entered home after home. He remained outside. An American presence in the home was considered an insult. Residents would clam up. Some jundi wore ski masks to avoid recognition and retaliation.

Thirty minutes later, the block was swept clean. No arms found and no intel collected on insurgent activity in the area. Cade's squad regrouped next to a white Nissan pickup loaded with plump green watermelons. Malik sliced one open and passed around juicy red chunks. When Cade stuck out his hand, Malik scowled and turned his back—still angry about Cade's near fatal mistreatment of two jundi. He'd caught the men not paying attention during a field exercise to locate mock IEDs. An unforgivable lapse of focus that could cost lives. Cade punished the men with an order to run laps while carrying a sandbag. The jundi had collapsed in a close call with heat stroke. Malik had sworn in Arabic and English that Cade would be brought up on charges as soon as the patrol returned to FOB Scorpion.

Zaid saw the poisonous looks that passed between the two men. He carved a melon slice for Cade. Cade nodded and squatted against a cinder block wall, shaded from the scorching sun. He chomped down on the succulent fruit, the Percocet kicking in. A crackle of radio static pierced the stillness of a village baking in a 120-degree oven. An emaciated dog snuffled by searching for scraps. After a final bite, Cade tossed the rind to the mutt.

At the same time, a boy, maybe nine or ten years old, approached from the south end of the street. Zaid held out a slice, but the boy ran to a whitewashed concrete house two doors down from the Nissan. A few seconds passed. Then a man appeared in the shadowed doorway. He peered at the jundi in their desert camo and wraparound ballistic shades, laughing, smoking, and spitting melon seeds.

In that instant, Cade saw the device in the man's hand.

2

C ruising down Washington Avenue and ready to flick off-duty, Cade spotted a businessman on the corner, arm and index finger extended. One more fare, why not? He steered left to the center lane, ready to slide over to the curb, when an unmarked blue minivan suddenly swerved in front of his cab, nearly clipping the front bumper. The minivan lurched to a stop, and the businessman stepped through the sliding door. Cade glimpsed the Uber insignia taped to the windshield. An illegal street pickup. *Son of a bitch!* He jerked the wheel to the right, and screeched to a halt behind the minivan. He grabbed a tire iron from the trunk and ran up to the driver's window. "No way, man," Cade screamed, and pointed the tire iron toward the backseat. "Get out of the car, buddy. This pickup is against the law." The passenger's eyes widened. The businessman reached for the latch, but before he could exit, the driver floored the accelerator, and the minivan squealed through a red light and vanished in the rush-hour crush.

Left standing in the curb lane, Cade sputtered obscenities. A panel truck driver leaned out a window. "Move your cab, asshole." Cade faced the truck driver, but held his fire and got back in the car. A revenge fantasy flared involving the tire iron and the minivan's windshield. As an independent cabbie, he struggled to compete in a market dominated by well-financed fleet operators. Now, he also had to contend with Uber drivers with their smart apps chipping away at his profits, and on his turf. The freelance drivers were not bound by the same regulations and inspections as a licensed taxi. Totally unfair. If only he could exterminate all private driver competition, his finances would improve immensely.

Still fuming, he headed back to the Glebe Valley apartments. As always, he parked the Green Flash in a far corner of the lot to avoid dings. A quick chamois cloth wipe-down removed the road grit. Even in summer twilight, the old Checker cab's emerald-crystal metal-flake powder-coated pearlescence dazzled. The Green Flash had generated local buzz. FM jocks asked listeners to call in sightings of the glittering vehicle. The result: a growing following of loyal customers. The thought of how close the Uber driver had come to hitting his pride and joy reignited the smoldering rage.

Cade extracted a few envelopes from the mailbox inside the entrance, then climbed to a third-floor apartment. Cooking aromas of cabbage and curry seeped beneath the doors lining the hallway. Inside, he tossed the mail on the coffee table, grabbed a beer from the kitchen, and popped a tab of oxycodone to dull the chronic shoulder pain exacerbated by sitting eighteen hours in the cab. A cockroach skittered across the cracked Formica countertop. The window air conditioner wheezed a trickle of coolness into a sweltering room reminiscent of scorching summers in Iraq.

Flopped on the sofa, he rolled the cold bottle across his forehead before taking the first swig of the day. His eyes rested on the IKEA bookcase—the sleek Scandinavian lines contrasted with the ratty sofa and other post-divorce detritus. His eyes settled on the white fire safe resting on the bottom shelf of the bookcase. From behind the family Bible, he retrieved a key. Stashed among Army discharge papers and family keepsakes was a notebook encased in a protective archival pouch. He flipped through the sketches and stanzas. Just the touch of the rare possession was reassuring when money was tight, which it always was. Perhaps it was time to cash in the notebook. He returned it to the pouch and the fire safe and slid the key behind the Bible.

The mail consisted of the usual junk and bills, except for one yellow envelope with large block letters: Public Notice. He ripped it open and scanned the contents. *Goddammit!* Throughout the long hours of fighting traffic and dealing with rude passengers, the one thing that kept him from going insane was the thought of swinging by the salon for an impromptu hookup with Cassandra. He hadn't seen her in two days. A carnal craving diverted his attention momentarily from the public notice.

He moved to the bathroom, ran a brush through an unruly thatch of red hair and beard, brushed his teeth, and rolled deodorant under each arm. Getting back in the cab after a long day to attend a public meeting was not his idea of a good time, whereas a rendezvous with Cassandra was but a short stroll down the block. Back in the living room, he drained the beer—the oxy's relaxing embrace taking effect—and headed for the door.

* * *

Inside the packed school gymnasium, Cade crushed a few toes on his way to an empty chair mid-row. He scanned the room for familiar faces, but the crowd, with fresh haircuts and leather briefcases, resembled more closely the business fares he picked up at Reagan National. The women wore suits and heels. At the podium, a man in his mid-thirties wore a tailored suit and struck a pose of casual authority. His blond-brown hair swept back with the gelled wet look.

The man hushed the crowd and introduced himself as Mick Finn, Senior Vice President of Development for Urban Renaissance Partners. Finn's PowerPoint opened with a history of the Glebe Valley apartment property dating back to the Civil War era of freed-slave camps. A century later, the thirty-acre apartment complex had attracted returning veterans and defense workers with government jobs at the Pentagon and in DC. With the exodus of bureaucrats to the suburbs, low-wage workers claimed the apartments. Today, five thousand residents, more than two-thirds from Central America, called Glebe Valley their home.

Next, Finn hyped an array of luxury townhomes, flats, and condos, and a rejuvenation of the retail strip along Washington Avenue. An added benefit: the project's close-in location. "A mere ten-minute commute to the district."

Cade thought: *Maybe at three on a Sunday morning, you idiot.*

The strain of a long day, and the Uber driver encounter, had exacted a huge toll. A throbbing behind his eyeballs signaled the onset of another migraine. For unexplained reasons, the oxy had no effect on his chronic headaches. Rivulets of sweat soaked his collar and armpits. Cade struggled to focus on the sales pitch, but when Finn said that PUD meant "Planned Urban Development," he wanted to scream. PUD also stood for his diagnosis of peptic ulcer disease due to an overuse of painkillers. Maybe the PUDs were related.

He learned another new word, equally obnoxious: *rebranding*. Apparently, Glebe Valley lacked cachet. A poster board on an easel displayed an architectural rendering entitled The Glebe at Cub Run. He bristled at the pretentiousness. Everybody referred to the complex as the Valley. Until now, he never cared or wondered what a glebe was. Now it was *The* Glebe, as if the meaning should be obvious to all. And the pathetic excuse for a creek behind CVS, the one that flooded the soccer fields every time it rained, that was Cub Run?

Finn clicked a remote. The computer-generated architectural visualization opened with an aerial shot of the plat—a superimposed yellow border outlined the parcel boundaries. From the high-altitude angle, the camera's eye swooped down to street level and panned the aging apartments, crosscutting to chain-link fences, rusted swing sets, and barren courtyards. The scene froze on a frame of the apartments shot through a shattered windshield.

Then magically, the apartments transfigured into stately brick-front townhomes, with sidewalks and trees. A matched pair of elegantly designed mid-rise buildings materialized, with ground-floor retail below five floors of glass-walled apartments.

The video showed a micro-cluster of upscale retail and sidewalk cafes taking shape. In a blink, check-cashing walk-ups and dollar stores resolved into galleries and trendy boutiques. Cassandra's Unisex Hair Salon & Psychic Palm Advisory shape-shifted into a wine-and-cheese shop. Jiffy Lube gave way to a magnificent pedestrian plaza with public sculptures, a farmer's market, and an arborvitae-ringed poetry corner tucked outside a bookstore. Lampposts strung with gaily colored destination banners luffed in a summer breeze. Audience oohs and aahs punctuated the smooth jazz score fused with a bass line of electric funk.

Kenny G elevator music. Cade hated it.

The migraine shifted to his temple, like an auger drilling a hole in his forehead. The overhead fluorescents flashed like heat lightning—an aura warning of an intense episode. His right leg pumped with pneumatic energy. He'd just witnessed an animation of a neighborhood demolished and resurrected into something unrecognizable. Iraqi villages reduced to rubble never reassembled to the saccharine riff of an alto sax.

The video ended, but not so the throbbing of the icepick in his skull. "Bullshit," Cade yelled, stumbling out of the tightly packed aisle, upsetting a folding chair in the process. He threw the chair across the hardwood floor with a loud clatter and headed for the door. In the parking lot, he heard his name as he hurried toward the cab.

"Cade! Wait up."

Luis Guzmán jogged toward him. Luis lived in the Valley and managed the Chapelita Community Center. Backlit by the yellow light spilling from the gymnasium door, his stocky frame vibrated with dark energy.

"Can you believe that guy?" Luis said. "What are we gonna do?"

Cade fumbled for his keys. "Who's we?" He pointed to the gym. "Didn't you hear? It's a done deal. A lost cause." The migraine blurred his vision; colors bled together and muddied the sharp angles and rounded contours that distinguished objects from people. A bad time to be behind the wheel. "FUBAR!"

Luis returned a quizzical look.

"Fucked up beyond all recognition. Never mind, can't talk now, Luis." He cranked the ignition, threw the gearshift into reverse, and slammed the Green Flash right into the back of a black sedan.

Shit!

Cade yanked the selector into drive and sped toward home before it morphed into a goddamn PUD!

3

"*Y*ou missed the turn!" shouted the man in the backseat. The black Dodge Charger screeched to a halt in a lane of traffic. The Charger commenced making a U-turn in the middle of the road, straddling the center line, blocking traffic in both directions, when a horn blasted from an oncoming vehicle. The three men in the car confronted a dazzling green taxi cab with a scowling red-bearded driver mouthing unpleasantries.

The Dodge continued the U-turn, and when the driver's side windows were abreast, the Charger driver spat on the cabbie's door and peeled away. Halfway down the block, the Charger's headlights went dark, and it made a sharp turn down an alley and came to a halt behind the service entrance to Kim's Drycleaners. Seated in the backseat, a man with a purple bandana tied around his forehead gripped a machete between his knees. The Condor blade measured eighteen inches of high-carbon stainless steel—the finest manufactured in El Salvador. Before setting out, he had clamped the tool securely in a vise grip. Then, using a double-cut file, he'd honed the blade to a razor sharpness. As a finishing touch, he wiped the blade down with an oil-moistened cloth. A reflection from the fluorescent light cast a silvery thread down the center of the edge. He scraped the blade across his forearm. The hairs lifted cleanly. Perfect for shaving, he mused, tapping the blade ever so lightly against the soul patch sprouting beneath his lower lip.

Reeking Dumpster smells of rotting meat triggered a brief wave of nausea. The driver cut the engine. A soft ticking marked the seconds. The front seat passenger pulled the slide back on a Glock 9 with a seven-inch suppressor barrel, and released the safety. Suddenly, the security light over the alley door to Wings & Things illuminated the Charger, flooding the car's interior with light. The three men froze. A silhouetted figure tossed a black garbage bag into the Dumpster, lit a cigarette, then squatted on his haunches.

Soul Patch tightened his grip on the machete. The smoker exhaled a cloud of smoke and seemed to fix his gaze on the Charger's chrome rims. Up ahead, Kim's delivery van partially blocked the view of another figure, this one in a hooded sweatshirt, approaching a Ford Mustang with tinted windows.

"There he is," the driver whispered.

Soul Patch shifted his attention to the hooded figure. He tapped the shoulder of the man who held the Glock and pointed to the smoker. Ready to spring, he reached for the door latch, when the smoker suddenly flicked the cigarette, turned, and reentered the restaurant, shutting the door behind him. The block of light disappeared, plunging the alley back into darkness.

Soul Patch slid out of the car, blade in hand. He crouched behind the van, eyes locked on the hooded figure standing next to the Mustang. The figure withdrew a packet from the sweatshirt pouch and passed it through the Mustang's window. From inside, a hand returned a fold of bills. Transaction complete, the Mustang moved down the alley, turned right on Washington Avenue, and disappeared.

The hoodie turned toward a rusted Toyota Corolla. Sprinting between cars, Soul Patch raced up behind the hooded figure, sneakers slapping on the pavement. The figure spun around as the blade came down hard on his left shoulder. The hoodie screamed and fell, his back against the car. The attacker glimpsed the face of a kid, no more than sixteen or seventeen years old. He grabbed the kid by the hair and pulled him forward, spread-eagled on the pavement. Soul Patch screamed, "¡Cabrón!" as the Condor slashed the victim's neck. Breathing hard, he sucked air and spun around, the blade twitching for another strike. His eyes darted side to side, searching for any sign of a witness. As blood pooled on the asphalt, he'd never felt more alive.

Soul Patch retrieved the roll of bills from the kid's hoodie. He grabbed the Krylon spray paint and scrawled "2-O-2" across the car. The

"2" stood for the second letter of the alphabet—the graffiti tag for Brothers of Blood. A *placa* to mark the territory and warn others—*mi barrio!*

To enter another gang's territory showed profound disrespect. A slap in the face. Any intrusion constituted an insult of the highest order, requiring immediate payback. To look the other way labeled you as a punk, and for a *líder*, that amounted to a death sentence.

Not unlike the battles for market share he'd studied in the prison college business courses. A refried customer base of wastoids and tweakers would not attract the revenue he needed to keep up with emerging market segments, create brand value, and drive revenue. The latest synthetics from Thailand were expensive to import for discriminating millennials. Grossing a hundred thousand a month was decent, but not great, for such an affluent region. The pressure from up the chain to move more product and boost profits never stopped. And as the pressure increased to expand distribution, so did the risks.

Success on a nine-figure scale required control of the supply chain from production to consumption, which then led to dark web retailing, complete with customer reviews and same-day delivery. Not hanging with a bunch of dumb fucks knocking off low-level street runners who just got off the late shift at Wendy's.

Back at the Charger, the driver scowled at Soul Patch's blood-soaked jeans and shirt. "Ditch those in the trunk, and use the trash bags." Clad only in boxer shorts, he slid onto the backseat, the leather cool on his thighs. His lips curled as a business course expression came to mind, coined during an era when the robber barons controlled the supply chain of goods and services and underpriced their products to drive out rivals. He studied his bloodied hands: *cutthroat competition.*

As the Charger pulled away, he turned for a final glimpse of his handiwork. He expected retaliation. They would be coming at him hard and fast. And he would be more than ready. Because he'd gladly do it again if another *bastardo* encroached on BOB's turf.

4

*L*ate and stuck behind an infinite dotted ribbon of red brake lights, Mick Finn drummed the steering wheel with his fingers. *Come on, move it. Move it. Christ, people, learn how to drive.* To make matters worse, the drive-time DJ reported numerous fender-benders due to windshield glare from the bright sunshine.

The community meeting last night had run late. People lingered to ask about pre-construction financing and custom build-outs. And what about Big Red, the tall guy with the flaming hair and scruffy beard, rudely interrupting a pitch to a roomful of prospects and throwing a chair on his way out? Real class.

Idiots like Big Red were a pain in the ass, an obvious crazy from the Not-In-My-Backyard crew. Antigrowth complainers who whined about increased traffic, light pollution, and everything in between. They filed lawsuits, tying up some projects for years. Except Glebe Valley residents didn't own a damn thing, much less a backyard. *They were renters, for crying out loud!*

Besides, the company offered an extremely generous relocation package. The company deserved thanks, not an insult, from the likes of Big Red. If push came to shove, Finn planned to bump up the relocation bonus, maybe throw in lights for the soccer field. Then the few disorganized NIMBYs would fold in a heartbeat.

His cell phone chimed. An incoming text from Beth Daniels, the chief financial officer: *Where are you? The pipeline meeting started without you.* Finn replied: *Traffic, twenty minutes max.* Robert Oliver would have to wait. Besides, what else did the old boy have to do? When the current CEO of Urban Renaissance Partners declared a need for an immediate sabbatical to rediscover his life's true path, the board had enticed Robert

Oliver, the retired founder and former CEO, to take a break from racing hot air balloons and return on an interim basis. Now Oliver beamed in from London once a month to babysit US operations—video conferences that Finn hated more than sitting in traffic.

Finn was running down a mental to-do list—phone calls, emails—when a truck in front moved forward, then slammed on its brakes. His split-second reaction avoided a rear-end collision. Heart pounding, eyes closed, he inhaled and exhaled deeply while counting to eight. Calmer, he reopened his eyes to the sight of black exhaust spewing from the truck's tailpipe. Finn smiled, thinking how the noxious fumes reminded him of his first, and only, in-person meeting with Robert Oliver—his last interview in a hiring process that had dragged on for two months.

He had been working for a real estate development company out of Dallas when the headhunter called. A global company needed a senior VP to take over the Eastern Division in North America. The recruiter knew Finn had received an award for a master planned community on the Florida coast, a seaside buffet of quaint cottages and picket fences—*cottage* being a misnomer of epic proportions, as many of the so-called cottages listed for three mil. The exclusive community included a town center and specialty shops featuring artisanal olive oil costing more than the California wine that Finn had stocked at home.

From Phoenix to Poughkeepsie, urban villages were the hottest trend in real estate. Everything old was new again. People wanted to reconnect, rediscover, reimagine. Talk to their neighbor over the back fence. Bicycle to the ice cream shop. Stroll to work, shops, and theaters. Sidewalks—what a concept!

He had sat outside the executive suite waiting for the receptionist to give the signal. The opportunity of a lifetime loomed on the other side of the door. He fretted about shaking Robert Oliver's hand with a sweaty palm. When the receptionist nodded, he wiped his hand on his trouser leg and entered the suite.

During the interview, Oliver mostly boasted about his achievements. Never asked Finn a single question. In the end, Oliver stuck out his hand and said, "Welcome aboard." Finn admired Oliver's visionary (and moneymaking) genius—despite a deserved reputation for being something of a windbag. At cocktail parties, Oliver pontificated on the decay of cities at the drop of a cheese ball. Another lecture on the new urbanism would send him over the edge.

Traffic started moving; a fender-bender had cleared to the side of the road. The dashboard clock read nine-fifteen as he rolled the black Lexus into a reserved spot near the Ritz Carlton entrance. He scrambled through the concourse connection to the Galleria Tower, cursing the traffic, formulating a plausible excuse.

The penthouse suite of Urban Renaissance Partners (ticker symbol URP on the New York Stock Exchange) offered a sweeping vista of two hundred million square feet of suburban sprawl. The massiveness stretched west toward Leesburg, inching ever closer to the pristine borders of Milltown, a settlement of Quakers in 1740, now a small enclave of wealthy preservationists residing in colonial-era townhomes and farmhouses. To Finn, Northern Virginia looked less like an edge city and more like a malignant growth blocking traffic arteries and oxygen flow to the brain.

Finn entered the boardroom and eased into a chair next to Beth Daniels. She faced the drop-down screen, going over numbers with Oliver.

"Beth, remind me about the financing package," Oliver said.

"A syndicate with deep pockets, led by Jacob Grossman, owner of the Washington Nationals."

"Football?" Oliver asked.

"No," said Beth, "you're thinking of the Redskins. The Nationals are baseball. Lost to Atlanta Braves last night, by the way. I hosted some clients in our corporate suite. In any case, Grossman is a personal-injury lawyer. He inherited sole ownership of the club when his father kicked the bucket and made him richer than he ever imagined."

"Who else is in the syndicate?"

"That's good news. Grossman brought in Saint Andrew's Episcopal Church. He's on the board of trustees and knows their finances well. And as a bonus, Saint Andrew's owns an old strip mall along Washington

Avenue, a block from Glebe Valley. The parish needs cash fast. They've agreed to sell the mall to us. A definite win-win."

Oliver's eyes brightened. "Interesting."

To Finn, the involvement of St. Andrew's was more than interesting. The church's halo would shine all over this deal. Nestled in a sweet spot known as Hampton Hills, less than a mile from The Glebe at Cub Run, the parish occupied a prime parcel of real estate set among upscale older homes spaced neatly along tree-lined streets with sidewalks and parks. Real estate values were solid and appreciating. Although rich in history, Saint Andrew's desperately needed hard cash to jump-start a capital campaign for a new wing on the elementary school bursting at the seams with corpulent preteens. A subtle throat clearing signaled to Finn that Beth had finished her briefing.

"So, Mick," Oliver said with undisguised sarcasm, "glad you could join us."

Finn considered mentioning the windshield glare, but thought better of it.

"How about a quick three-sixty from your side?"

Finn spun to the screen and faced the high-definition, pixelated image of Robert Oliver. His narrow, angular face complemented a strong jaw and straight teeth. His coiffed silver hair spilled over the collar, although his eyebrows remained dark and bushy. Meticulously well-dressed in Savile Row tailoring, Oliver cut a dashing figure for a man pushing sixty-five. Lovely women a decade or two younger often accompanied him to charity events.

Like flipping a light switch, Finn reeled off an abbreviated version of the spiel he'd delivered last night. The Glebe at Cub Run would include a prototypical mixed-use development of upscale housing and Main Street retail. A faux Federalist style but with a hip urban vibe—a *new* old town. The drawings called for 900 luxury townhouses, 300 condos, plus upscale rentals. City code required a minimum of 250 below-market rentals set aside for existing tenants.

"How does the community feel about it?" Oliver asked.

Big Red flashed in Finn's mind. "Most of the community meetings have gone well. A little pushback at last night's meeting. Nothing major. The city wants the deal, but we have to kick in a relocation fund." Finn waited for the inevitable question.

"How much?"

"Don't know exact numbers yet."

"Remember, make them move in our direction."

Finn resented tips from Oliver on the art of negotiating. Time to change the subject.

"I met privately with the Planning and Zoning Commission. Non-committal, but very intrigued." Finn underplayed the P&Z's reaction, which had been effusive. When the P&Z viewed the architectural animation, they saw the mishmash of mediocrity transformed into a shiny new financial engine. Instead of property values depressed to the point of suicide, they envisioned a bright future with a long-term return on investment. A target demographic of empty-nesters, downsizers, and simplicity-seekers would breathe new life into a ravaged carcass of deteriorating apartments and shops.

Finn continued, "First P&Z public hearing is coming up Wednesday, week after next. We'll have the votes. The chairman wants more open space. Not a problem. Chamber of commerce is on board, too. We're going Zee 9, of course."

Oliver's eyebrows shot up.

"Zee 9," Finn explained. "Shorthand for the section in the zoning code granting special exceptions. We need a special exception to get around density limits."

Beth's lips pulled back in a tight smile. Finn's references to Zee 9 for a special exception had become an office joke for anyone needing an excuse. Running late for a meeting? Zee 9. Need a bump in a budget? Zee 9. Once, Finn had emailed Beth asking when the pro forma would be ready. Her reply shot back instantly: *Zee 9, asshole.* Beth could dish it out with the best of them.

"So, everything is on track," Oliver said.

"Well, there is one small thing," Finn said. "BOB."

Oliver peered over his spectacles. "I beg your pardon, Bob who?"

"B-O-B, short for Brothers of Blood," Finn explained. "Local street gang. They've tagged most of Glebe Valley with graffiti, marking their turf. MS-13 wannabes."

"MS-13?" Oliver said. "I'm not following you."

Oliver's questions about gangs were sidetracking Finn's presentation. But he had brought up the topic, so he was stuck with explaining it. "MS-13, aka Mara Salvatrucha. A gang with roots in Southern California. Former Salvadoran guerillas. Now they're into drugs, prostitution, extortion, murder, you name it. Machete is a favorite weapon. Up close and personal, if you know what I mean. Instills real fear in rivals."

Oliver coughed. Beth looked down at her notes. Finn dialed back the lurid imagery. "MS-13 chapters have gone viral across the country. Including Northern Virginia. A buddy of mine knows a cop on a gang unit. He says BOB wants to affiliate with MS-13. Police think they may be getting outside help."

"Is that a problem?" asked Oliver.

"Short term, until the police get it sorted out. Police suspect BOB in last night's machete attack behind a strip mall. A rival gang member, the Four Mile Kings. No firm leads. Police believe BOB is holed up in Glebe Valley somewhere, and the residents are too scared to talk."

"Will the incident affect our plans?"

Finn loved British understatement, but Oliver's comment exceeded even his cynical tolerances. A seventeen-year-old kid's head nearly decapitated. A brutal murder. Now Oliver referred to the *incident* as if someone had spilled soup on his tie. "Hard to say. Tenants are mad as hell at the mayor and the police. Community leaders are trying to calm everyone down."

In fact, the nonstop media coverage was diverting attention away from Finn's three-step visioning process designed to move the community toward consensus, commitment, and consent. Crime scene reporters interviewed the victim's grandmother, neighbors, friends, and teachers—an endless stream of stricken faces. They all said the same thing: He was a good boy, never hurt anyone. Must have fallen in with the wrong crowd.

The networks ran a crime scene reconstruction complete with animated avatars reenacting the murder in photo-realistic detail. Forensic experts opined on the angle of the slash and speculated that the assailant was right-handed. Defensive wounds indicated a struggle. Investigators reported that the striations on the skull were consistent with a cleaver or machete blade. Viewers learned more than they ever wanted to know about hacking trauma. *Give it a rest, people. One drug dealer murdered another drug dealer. For god's sake, let's move on.*

"And how will BOB react when they find out their precious territory is being sold and razed?" Oliver asked.

"Like everybody else, BOB can get in line to kiss my ass." Finn hated talking to the screen and wanted to return calls.

"Yes, Mick, I appreciate a firm position, but be careful. We need to close quietly. And on schedule. I don't want anything to interfere with our new prototype. I will have an importance announcement soon. It sounds like you may have disgruntled tenants already. I'm sure you don't want to add BOB to the Finn fan club."

"No big deal, Mr. Oliver. Once you approve the relocation fund, that'll cool everybody down."

"Good, I don't want any surprises on our rollout."

Finn stood, signaling his end to the meeting. "I can assure you, Mr. Oliver, no surprises on this one."

Relieved, he headed back to his office and returned calls and sent emails. By five thirty, his thirst demanded a happy hour. He texted Beth: *Zee 9 at Clyde's. Meet me.* He rode the elevator down to the concourse level. Approaching his sedan from the passenger side, he stopped short.

Anger rose in his gut as he ran his hand over a deep gash. Not there yesterday when he left for last night's Glebe presentation. Flecks of green metal-flake paint twinkled like emerald stars in a black Lexus night.

Columbia Rooms 1 and 2 of the Arlington Westin hotel were banquet set for five hundred hungry conventioneers. Rita Castro considered ducking out for a quick smoke, but people streaming in from the morning workshops rapidly filled the tables. The three-day conference offered a rich smorgasbord of topics for low-income housing operators. The seminar on eminent domain provided an excellent update on court cases around the country, as well as on tactics for negotiating settlements and compensation. Too often, profiteers used eminent domain to target racial and ethnic minorities under the guise of reducing "blight." A plague of takings in poor neighborhoods had inflamed outrage over property rights and constitutional safeguards. Communities fought back with the aid of law firms specializing in opposing condemnation.

Rita checked the change fee to fly back early to Miami, but a glance at the monitor outside the ballroom convinced her to stick around. The surprise replacement for the canceled keynote speaker was none other than Arthur A. Arthur—a tenants' rights firebrand and media darling. Defenders of unfettered free enterprise regarded Arthur as a formidable adversary, but prone to demagoguery. Rita had become an Arthur acolyte in college and an avid fan of his books and blogs ever since.

Rita noticed several network vans with microwave transmitters parked outside the mezzanine doors. On-air reporters and camera crews scurried into the ballroom, rigging lights and sound equipment. If the conference planners had hoped Arthur would draw media coverage, they were right. Police cruisers blocked off the circular driveway from two factions of college students, separated by yellow tape, brandishing signs and chanting things Rita couldn't make out.

Her urge for a cigarette break vanished. She found a seat near the front of the room. Off to the side, a skirted table arrayed with Arthur's books and DVDs did a brisk business as a sales agent slid credit cards through a reader.

A name tag hanging from a lanyard identified Brenda from Memphis in the seat to Rita's left. She recognized Brenda from the eminent domain seminar. How could she not? Six feet tall, Brenda wore a hot pink sleeveless dress, accessorized with matching earrings, lipstick, and nail polish. A short-cropped afro and oval face emphasized large eyes and full lips. A striking woman who radiated self-confidence and intelligence. During the seminar, Brenda had regaled her fellow attorneys with an anecdote about a devious eminent domain proposal in a Midwest capital rife with payoffs in smokeless backroom deals.

In a honeyed Tennessee lilt, she recounted how a proposed bill would have specifically defined the removal of blight as serving the public interest. The perverse result would have been that a municipality could simply declare a property to be blighted, but then shift the burden of proof onto the owners to show that it was not. "It's a shell game, pure and simple," said Brenda. The legislative sponsor and a developer had concocted a scheme to use "blight" as a cover to avoid legal scrutiny for taking property. Not to be outmaneuvered, Brenda unleashed a full-court press of homeowners onto wavering legislators. The story ended on a note of high drama, with Brenda in the starring role, testifying before a rapt committee that everyone in America has a *goddamn* right to remain in their homes until their last dying breath. The bill died on a voice vote.

Brenda reached for the bread basket and asked Rita, "Are you originally from Miami?"

With a name like Castro, Rita had expected the question sooner or later. Just once she'd like to see the expression on someone's face when informed that her father, Cesar, was the bastard half-brother to Fidel. Indeed, Brenda might choke on a breadstick if she learned that Cesar had fought alongside Raul Castro and had overseen the execution of hundreds of Baptista loyalists.

Then again, Brenda's liberal bleeding heart might hemorrhage to learn that Cesar had also helped break up corporate property holdings and redistribute the land to peasants and farmers. But disillusionment might set in if she learned that too many monetary assets had found their way into Cesar's pockets—so much in fact that he narrowly escaped to Miami in a cigarette boat as bullets whizzed overhead.

"My family is from Portugal," Rita replied as the clatter of forks and plates filled the room with an amiable din.

In between bites, Brenda said, "Did you see who the speaker is? I've seen Arthur on CNN. Boy, does he rile people up. This should be entertaining."

Rita smiled. Arthur didn't just rile people up. He straddled the line of direct incitement. The police presence made sense.

When the waitstaff had finished busing the tables, the conference director appeared on stage. After a few housekeeping announcements, she introduced Arthur A. Arthur. "Our special guest today is an associate professor of geography at the University of California, Berkeley. An academic from the field of geography may strike some as an odd choice for a housing conference. But for those who have followed Arthur's writings over the years, you know him as one of the foremost leaders on spatial justice and the rights of city dwellers."

The conference director held up Arthur's book, *Urban Rebellion: A Call to Action*. "Critics have derided his new book as Marxist claptrap for liberal elitists. A frontal assault on the United States of America as a capitalistic nation of liberty and freedom. But others celebrate it as a profound discourse on the equitable distribution of resources as a human right.

"Arthur's premise is quite simple," she continued. "The contours of spatial injustice are found in economic geography. Some spaces, like mountains and rivers, are permanent. But other spaces are shaped by their means of production and are easily manipulated. As evidence for his argument, Arthur deployed geographic information systems and econometric tools to document the spatial inequities of community assets such as housing, transit, grocery stores, schools, stores, driving distances to jobs—take your pick. The result is the clear-est proof yet of a *drastic and deliberate* concentration of the resources essential to societal growth, indeed human survival, into urban areas that favor the production and recycling of capital."

The conference director paused and allowed herself a polite chuckle. "I hope our guest speaker will forgive me if I attempt to rephrase that last line, make it less opaque." The director coughed into her hand, and proceeded. "The resources are concentrated in urban regions that preserve the status quo of the haves and the have-nots."

A soft murmur of voices rose from the audience. The director found a marker, adjusted her glasses, and read a brief passage: *You want proof of injustice, look at a map. Insatiable capitalism is the prime cartographer, draw-ing the lines and boundaries of power and wealth in cities across America.* She closed the book. "Without further ado, please join me in giving a warm welcome to Arthur A. Arthur."

Modest applause greeted Arthur as he walked on stage. A gangly six-foot-five, he sported black jeans, a tweed jacket over an open-collared denim shirt, and high-top Converse All-Stars. Brown hair flopped over retro-cool horn-rimmed glasses. A wireless microphone protruded dis-creetly from his collar. Despite a lanky physique, his voice projected a muscular tone of authority and righteousness.

Arthur touched a remote. The lights dimmed, and an image filled a large screen. "Ladies and gentlemen, meet Randall, sixty-nine years old, from Atlanta, Georgia. Not long ago, he received a notice to vacate his apartment to make way for Center City, a mixed-use retail and condo-minium complex. Let's hear Randall in his own words." A video clip rolled of Randall on a couch holding a cat.

"Tell you the truth," Randall drawled, "it's like living on borrowed time. I got a Purple Heart in 'Nam. Been on disability ever since. Money's kind of tight right now. I get my last month rent-free, so I guess that's something. But I don't know what I'm going to do."

From the darkened stage, Arthur said, "Let's go now to Charlotte, North Carolina. Millie Burton is ninety-one years old. She's lived in the Rock Ridge apartments for over fifteen years. Her apartments were recently sold to make way for The Boulevard, a new shopping and residential district."

The snippet opened with Millie sitting at a kitchen table surrounded by grandchildren. "I was in the hospital for a week with pneumonia. When Marcus brought me home, I seen this letter." Millie held up a piece of paper. "Said I had to be out in ninety days. When I asked for an extension, they said no. My lord, I don't know where I'm going to be living next." Millie hugged a young girl with cornrows and beads. "Maybe move in with my children. But I don't want to do that. I like my independence. It's either that or the street, and I'm too old for that."

"You see the pattern?" Arthur asked. "It's the same story in cities across the country. Low-income families, often entire ethnic communities, forced out of their homes and neighborhoods so developers can make a quick buck." His inflection dripped with indignation. "The endless pursuit of capitalistic gain is destroying America's cities. This is a profound injustice and a violation of human rights."

Rita thought of her father. Though he professed that capitalism corrupted the wealthy few to the detriment of the many, he had no compunction about investing his plunder in a chain of Arby's restaurants. He'd drilled the dogma into her head from his franchise on Ocean Drive, where she worked after school. The cedar aroma of his ever-present cigar enveloped her in a cloud as fragrant as expensive perfume—although her girlfriends gagged at the smell. Her father would pat her cheek and repeat the same musty bromide: "As brother Fidel says, 'Revolution is no bed of roses.'"

At first, Rita accepted her father's teachings. But as she grew older, and he opened more franchises, the contradictions became clear. He seemed comfortably nestled in roses. Maybe the unscrupulous lure of wealth had clouded her father's judgment. While Fidel may indeed have said revolution is no bed of roses, he also said that the revolution would end the private exploitation of housing.

Rita knew that critics used the term "social justice warrior" as an epithet of derision and scorn. But not so back in the early days of the Movement, when Fidel led an outmanned and outgunned guerilla force to victory against a military junta supported by US capitalists. Fidel, now *he* was a true social justice warrior. Rita loved her father dearly, but she would never sell out to the capitalists. Her curled fists dug sharp finger-nails into fleshy palms. She relaxed her fists just as Arthur again hit the remote.

"This, my friends," said Arthur, "is an ouroboros." A picture of a giant serpent devouring its tail towered over the audience. "One of humanity's oldest symbols. The eternal return. The perfect representation for the endless capitalistic destruction of our urban centers."

Arthur's voice boomed across the ballroom. "I ask you, where do we find the ouroboros today?" The picture of the serpent disappeared, replaced by a montage of monumental edifices to corporate wealth: banks, skyscrapers, and high-tech towers. "I'll tell you where it is," Arthur said. "The ouroboros is all around us, as we have just witnessed in Char-lotte and Atlanta and other cities across America. It consumes our cities in a never-ending cycle of capitalistic gluttony, feeding upon itself, until one day, it suffocates on its own vomit."

Arthur doffed his coat, revealing a shoulder holster and the butt end of a Ruger .45. Some attendees scurried toward the exits.

"Ladies and gentlemen," Arthur implored. "Brothers and sisters. Please do not be alarmed. The great commonwealth of Virginia, in its divine and constitutional wisdom, permits citizens to both conceal and open carry. I've survived many attempts to silence me. My family has been threatened. My computer hacked. My car fire-bombed. Those who dare speak truth to power must be prepared to defend the truth."

"Whose truth?" an angry voice retorted. "Yours?"

Catcalls and boos joined handclaps and whistles. Rita glanced around the ballroom. A schism in the audience crackled and buzzed like an electric current. A low-level thrum for now, but Arthur might spike the voltage at any second.

"Stay with me." Arthur's voice was soothing, placating the audience. He paced to the center of the stage, head bowed, as if gathering thoughts—or steam. The ballroom audience settled into an uncomfort-able silence, waiting. Slowly, Arthur rolled his denim shirtsleeves to the elbows. Damp spots darkened the armpits. Seconds passed. Then, with arms raised heavenward, eyes shut, Arthur roared with evangelical fervor, "A ruinous cancer; that's what it is! Lewis Mumford, the twentieth century's great chronicler of urban civilization, said we must bring *life* into the city so that its poorest inhabitants will have a chance to touch and feel the earth."

A smile spread across Rita's face. Arthur's raw passion for justice touched a nerve. His metaphor was right on the money. Grave violations of a basic human right had spread like cancer in communities across the country. The cancer must be excised and eliminated at any cost. Rita wanted to stand and applaud.

"Imagine," Arthur continued, "a *right* to simply touch the earth." He spun in the other direction, his arms outstretched as if beseeching a higher power. "People not only have a right to touch the earth, but they have a right to the city built upon *that* earth. The cry for justice shall be heard!"

A murmur rippled through the audience. Rita shifted in her chair and saw two cops standing inside the ballroom doors. The shouts from the college students seemed louder, more insistent.

The next image on the screen displayed a long shot of a sprawling complex—a three-story redbrick apartment complex. "No interviews yet for this one," Arthur said. "It's under the radar for now, but just wait. And it's just a few miles from where we sit. Glebe Valley is home to over five thousand low-income tenants."

Arthur hit the remote, and the face of a distinguished older gentleman filled the screen. "Meet Robert Oliver. Founder of Urban Renaissance Partners. His projects have displaced tens of thousands of families all over the world. Now he has his sights set on Glebe Valley. This man," Arthur cried, pointing an accusing finger at Oliver, "is the snakehead. And it must be cut off!"

A collective gasp rose from the audience. Brenda gathered her briefcase and looked at Rita. "I've heard enough. You?"

"I'm staying," Rita said.

A crash of glass, then loud, strident voices startled everyone. Arthur reached for the Ruger. The food service doors flew back, and two dozen college-age students rushed the ballroom, hooting, "Free markets! Free markets! Free markets!"

The students had foiled the barricade through a side entrance. The news media would later identify the protesters as members of the Young Entrepreneurs Club, a campus club dedicated to launching future business leaders into the stratosphere of a laissez-faire economy.

Hotel security and police charged into the room and herded the students out. Rita watched as the entrepreneurs, news media, and police packed the corridor so tight the clot could only move as a single organism to the custody buses idling outside.

Back inside the ballroom, Arthur had left the stage. The conference director apologized for the disruption and said the afternoon workshops would begin on time. Rita wandered over to the table selling Arthur's books. She bought an autographed copy and tossed it in her bag. As she headed toward the exit, she glanced over her shoulder. On the screen: the ravenous ouroboros.

6

*C*ade drove past the Chapelita Community Center countless times a day. The end-unit building sported a three-story mural depicting the struggles and heroes of the Chapelita people.

In the lower left quadrant of the mural, a peasant woman with a sack slung over her shoulder confronted a man in a military uniform. Behind her, white grave crosses dotted a barren hillside. Above the yellow rain gutter running to the pavement, two men in suits outside a factory brandished a fistful of greenbacks. Moving left to right, construction workers maneuvered an iron beam dangling from a crane. Women stood shoulder to shoulder: a doctor in a white coat, a field worker, a mother holding an infant. Even Rosie the Riveter and her flexed biceps made a cameo appearance.

Further down in the right sector, workers of all nationalities grasped hands across a brick wall in a show of solidarity. The radical depiction of workers united in a common bond apparently discomfited local nativists. Once, Cade happened by to find the mural vandalized with spray-painted slurs. Scaffolding went up that afternoon, and volunteers restored the mural within a week.

Cade swung into the lot and entered the back door. Inside, a small office held two gray metal desks and a photocopier. Five computer stations lined a back wall. At one desk, Luis Guzmán sat hunched over the *Washington Post* sports section, coffee mug anchoring a corner.

Cade read the headline upside down: *Nationals Drop Two to Phillies.*

"Nats suck, huh?"

Luis's eyes remained fixed on the newspaper.

"I came to apologize. That guy last night pissed me off. Didn't mean to take it out on you."

"Yeah," Luis said, still looking at the paper. "You made your point about taking the relocation money. What got into you last night? Throwing a chair like that?"

Cade looked away. "I get bad headaches sometimes. Feels like I'm going to explode."

Luis's head came up. "You all right now?"

Ignoring the question, Cade surveyed the office. "This place is deader than a Nats fan club. Where is everyone?"

"It's early. Computer lab starts at ten."

"So why did you ask me last night what we were going to do?"

"Look, it's easy for a single guy to take the money and run," Luis said. "Not so easy for families to pack up and move. Affordable rents are hard enough for one person to find in this area, much less five thousand."

Cade shrugged.

"Yeah, well, not everybody feels that way." Luis walked to the coffee stand and refilled his mug. "I got a call today. From a woman who defends tenants from losing their homes."

"Who?"

"A lawyer. Rita Castro, from Miami."

Cade frowned. "What does Miami have to do with Glebe Valley?"

Luis set the mug down on the newspaper, sloshing coffee over the Philly shortstop who had hit a walk-off homer in the ninth. "I'm getting ready to tell you."

Cade held up his palms. "Okay, okay."

"Lot of Latinos in Miami; like Chapelita, only more. Rita helps tenants get organized. Pressure the right people. They blocked developers from tearing down an affordable housing complex, sort of like Glebe Valley. She's in DC for a conference. Heard about our situation from a guy named Arthur somebody. She asked around, and someone told her to call me. Says she'll help us fight a takeover by the developer."

"So?"

"So, I asked her to swing by, and she agreed. I want someone else to hear what she has to say. See if she makes sense."

"And?"

"I'm simply asking you to listen to what Rita has to say. A few minutes of your time. *Por favor.*"

Cade cringed at the thought of listening again to someone talk about fighting a takeover—resurrecting memories of training the jundi to take over the fight for their homeland so American forces could withdraw. At least that was the theory from the generals on high. But to grunts on the ground, the situation looked like a soup sandwich—a sloppy mess. Everywhere you looked, a sect, tribe, or militia fought for control over a neighborhood, a village, or a god-forsaken piece of dirt in a scorched earth hellhole. Extreme turf wars, where every fucking lunatic carried an AK-47 assault rifle. Headlines back home had already declared the war lost.

"Sounds like a soup sandwich if you ask me," Cade said.

"Soup sandwich? What's that, another Army expression?"

"I don't care what this woman—"

"Rita."

"I doubt whatever *Rita* has to say is going to make much difference. I'll think about it."

"Don't think too long. Rita's only in town a day or so." Luis scribbled a number on a piece of paper. "Call her. Set up a time to meet here."

Cade stashed the paper in his shirt pocket, stood, then sat back down. "Hey, can I ask you something?"

"Shoot."

Cade propped his arms on the edge of the desk. "Do you know what the hell a 'glebe' is?"

7

Cade inched the cab forward in the drive-thru lane. At the speaker, he ordered a breakfast sandwich and pulled up to the second window. The kid with the sandwich sack gawked at the metal-flake luminosity of the Green Flash.

"Hey, DeShawn. Check out this car, man!"

Another teenager, one with a low fade and a gold tooth, appeared at the window.

"Damn!" DeShawn said with a wide grin. "That's what *I'm* talking about!"

The two teenagers high-fived and threw in a large fries, gratis. Cade waved and then pulled into a shady parking spot. He fished Rita's number from a shirt pocket. Probably a waste of time, but as a favor to Luis, he made the call.

A woman answered. "Yes?"

"Rita Castro?"

"Who is this?"

"Jack Cade." He blew on his coffee. "Luis gave me your number. Said you talked to him about the Glebe Valley situation."

Silence, then: "I'm sorry, who are you, again?"

Cade resented her tone, intended or not, that made him sound like a telemarketer. *Who am I? Who the hell are you?* "I live in Glebe Valley, same deal as Luis. I was at the developer's presentation the other night. Luis said you could help. He asked me to call you and set up a meeting. That's all I know."

A pause, then he heard what sounded like a loud sigh.

"Okay. Meet Luis and me at the Chapelita Center today at four."

"Rush hour is my busy time."

"I'm busy too. I'm flying back to Miami today." She clicked off.

Cade lowered the coffee into the cup holder and turned left on Jefferson Highway toward the nearest hotel. Ten minutes, that's all he'd give Rita Castro. For Luis, *por favor.*

* * *

At 3:20 PM, Cade dropped off three soldiers at Marine Corp Base Quantico, south of DC. A hefty fare plus a generous tip from the jarheads, but thirty miles now lay between him and his four o'clock with Luis and Rita. Luckily, traffic on 95 North moved at a steady clip, unlike the bumper-to-bumper mess exiting south out of DC.

Cade raced from one lane to the next, whipping around cars and trucks. When he cut in front of a semi, the air horn blasted his eardrums. At exactly 4:05, he pulled into the Chapelita Community Center. Inside, seated at a desk, he found Luis and a thin woman eating submarine sandwiches. She wore blue jeans, a T-shirt, and Nikes. Auburn hair in a tangle of curls framed large brown eyes under finely drawn brows. An olive skin tone glowed like a natural tan. Her T-shirt logo advertised the Miami Marlins.

Luis waved him over. "Meet Rita Castro."

Cade faced the woman. "I'm Jack Cade. We talked on the phone."

Rita wiped her mouth with a napkin and extended her hand.

"Rita's a legal aid lawyer," said Luis. "Also, she works for a tenants' co-op in South Florida. Fought a developer down there. She got the residents involved. Pressured the city council. Turned it around. Know what I'm saying?"

Cade lifted his shoulders.

Luis looked to Rita. "Tell Cade what you told me."

"Luis has the basics right. Essentially, a developer approached the city with the idea of condemning a public housing complex of six hundred and fifty units, mostly low-income, working-class families. We organized the community, identified leaders, and stroked the media." She approached a map of the metropolitan area above the coffeepot and pointed. "We're about here, right?"

"Bingo," said Cade.

31

"We framed our story to the media like Goliath versus David and people of color. A community under attack. We fought to hold on to our culture and history. Gentrification displaces local workers." She looked at Luis. "You understand gentrification, Luis?"

Luis nodded.

Rita studied the map. "We're pretty close to DC, right?"

"Five miles to the district line," Cade said.

Rita's finger circled the District of Columbia. "DC is one of the most gentrified cities in the country. Rents are skyrocketing. Poor folks are driven out. Next, vultures swoop in and redevelop the neighborhoods for upper middle-class professionals. DC's black population has dropped dramatically in recent years. Latinos in Glebe Valley are next."

Cade yawned, stretching his arms.

Rita paused. "Am I keeping you awake?"

"Long day. Go on. I'm listening."

Her gaze shifted to Luis. "Gentrification is just another word for economic eviction. Developers grab communities by the neck and cut off the air supply." Her hands strangled an imaginary victim. "Then they turn a profit on the undervalued land in hot markets, like Miami and—" Rita caught Cade thumbing a text message.

"Okay, that's it." Rita scowled at Luis. "I got better things to do. Good luck, Luis. You're going to need it. I'm calling a cab."

"Hey, I drive a—" Cade started to say.

"Wait a minute, wait a minute," Luis said, tugging on Rita's arm. Then to Cade, "Can you put that damn phone away?"

Cade slid the phone into his pocket. "Sorry."

"Sorry, my ass," Rita said. "Why are you even here?"

"Luis asked me."

"That's it? You're doing us a favor by blessing us with your presence?"

"Ease up, Rita," Luis said. "Cade has experience in these sorts of things. That's why I invited him."

Rita tilted her chin at Cade. "Yeah, what kind of experience?"

Luis looked at Cade. "Can I tell her?"

Cade wagged his head.

Rita's expression soured. "Yeah, right. Did you hear anything I said so far?"

"A developer wanted to condemn a public housing project. Economic eviction. Gentrification. Blah, blah, blah."

Rita jerked her thumb in Cade's direction and said to Luis, "Smartass, huh?"

"Sorry, Rita. Cade don't mean any disrespect." He glared at Cade. "Do you?"

"No disrespect," Cade said, holding up four fingers. "Scout's honor."

Luis touched Rita's arm. "Hey, it's great of you to come over before your flight." He eyeballed Cade. "Please go on."

Rita set down her shoulder bag. "I'm telling this as a favor to you, Luis. As I was saying, developers in hot markets like Miami—and now Alexington—are drooling over infill parcels like Glebe Valley. The developers talk a good game like they're going to clean up a blighted area. But what they do is push the tenants and workers out to the distant burbs, away from job centers and transportation, cutting them off from their culture and community. Scattered like debris from the demolition of their homes.

"Once the tenants are isolated, any grassroots threat to their power is gone. The city and developer hold hands and build shiny new retail and housing. URP gets rich off selling condos to wealthy clients, and the city gets an increase in property taxes. Sound familiar?"

Luis furrowed his brow as if diagraming the transactions in his head.

"It's a shell game," Rita explained. "Don't you get it? The banks lend URP money to build the Glebe. The same banks turn around and lend money to yuppies to purchase the condos. Banks take a cut from both ends. URP takes a cut. The city takes a cut." Rita spun her finger in a circular motion. "Capital is recirculated. And then the cycle begins again. Like a snake eating its tail."

"A snake eating its tail?" Luis asked.

"The symbol of a snake eating its tail represents a never-ending cycle, the beginning, and the end. The eternal circulation and accumulation of capital in the hands of a few will destroy Glebe Valley, and other communities just like it."

The mention of a snake reminded Cade of the "snake eaters" in Iraq—US military special ops forces trained to go after Islamic extremists and terrorists.

"Buddy of mine is a snake eater," Cade said. "I could give him a call."

Rita stuck her finger on the map, the speck representing Glebe Valley. "You know, I don't know which is worse, Cade. Your ignorance or your don't-give-a-shit attitude. Right now, Glebe Valley residents are the only thing standing in the way of URP. Their modus operandi is to get folks to move quickly and quietly. Throw them a bone—relocation expenses and lease termination bonuses. Most are too scared to speak up for fear of reprisals. They take whatever is offered and get out." Cade felt Rita's gaze drilling into him. "The only way to break the cycle is to cut off the head of the snake."

Cade returned a blank poker face.

"So, what you should do is educate folks. Let them know they have a say in what happens to their community: educate, mobilize, advocate."

Luis glanced at Cade. "See, that's what I'm saying. Get folks educated, mobilized."

Cade shifted attention to Luis. "Where are you going with this?"

Rita broke in. "I'll tell you where it's going. There are tenant movements across the country: New York, San Francisco, LA, Atlanta, Miami. We got to fight to take back our homes. Block by block."

She swigged a water bottle. "The movement is about educating tenants about an important principle: people have a fundamental right to the place they call home until our last dying breath. And that place is not just the four walls of an apartment."

Rita walked over to the window and looked out on Washington Avenue. "The place we call home is where our culture flourishes. Am I right, Luis?"

"Absolutely," Luis said. "Chapelita is our home."

Rita turned. "The point is we have the right to decide how the city adapts to our needs. Not the other way around. URP doesn't get a free pass to move people around to fit its capitalist agenda." Rita spat the word *capitalist* like a turd from her mouth.

Cade noticed perspiration above Rita's lip. Clearly amped, perhaps delusional, maybe both. For a moment, he imagined her as a whacked-out panhandler trolling a traffic island for spare change. "So, if this shit is going on all over the country, why are you so concerned about what's happening here?"

Rita eyed Luis first, then Cade. "We have to pick our windows of opportunity. The Glebe is still at a stage where intervention can turn things around. But if you wait much longer, the window will close. Besides, Urban Renaissance Partners is the big fucking deal. Robert Oliver is the founder and former CEO. Claims he's on a mission to save civilization by rebuilding cities. Early in his career, he was all gung-ho to build affordable housing in reclaimed urban wastelands. Then somewhere along the line, he went off the rails and became all about the hard cash. Now he comes in with lots of high-sounding rhetoric and investor equity, then cashes out and moves on to the next deal. Funny thing, the people living there never share in the bounty. If we can stop URP in Glebe Valley, it'll be a huge victory for the movement."

Cade had no interest in any fucking movement and wished Rita would stop using that word.

"What about this guy Finn," asked Luis, "who did all the talking at the gym the other night? Where does he fit in?"

"Finn is an Oliver lackey. Just in it for the commission."

"How do you know so much about URP?" Cade asked.

Rita hesitated, then seemed to choose her words carefully. "Trust me; I've been following their exploits for some time. All over the world, in fact."

"Say we take on URP," Luis said, "what do we do next?"

Rita snorted. "Get your ass in gear. Did any of you bother to read the zoning notices plastered all over the city? The first public hearing is

Wednesday, week after next. I've read the preliminary staff report to the P&Z."

"P&Z?" Cade asked.

"Planning and Zoning Commission. I've looked at the city's master plan. The city wants this deal, bad. It looks greased. But it's not a done deal yet. The public hearing is to approve URP's application for a Zee 9— and before you ask, that means a special exception from certain zoning requirements."

"Zee 9," said Luis, making sure he heard it correctly.

"Zee 9," Cade repeated, because the words had zing.

"Yeah, Zee 9," said Rita. "There's still time to do something to stop URP in their tracks. But understand, if you take on URP, be ready for what comes back at you. Big bucks at stake here. URP has the muscle to back up their plans."

"What kind of muscle?" asked Cade.

"The kind that can kick your ass. I don't know about you, but I wouldn't want to move so a bunch of downsizing suburbanites can live like urban bohemians. Fuck that shit!"

Fuck that shit! Cade smiled to himself. Finally, a battle cry that made sense. He would happily lead a million-man march under that banner. Rita swore like a sergeant. Obviously passionate about the movement, whatever the hell it was. Though a bit on the thin side, Rita appeared fit. Possibly a runner if the Nikes were any indication. Her gestures suggested a feline quickness and independence.

Rita returned to the chair. "The only things I hate more than URP are the marketing idiots they hire. Have you seen the signs?" Rita flapped her elbows like a wounded duck. "The Glebe is coming! The Glebe is coming! Sounds like the goddamn plague."

Cade stifled a laugh. "Well, since you know so much about URP and Zee 9, why don't you stick around and get things organized?"

"Because I'm from Miami. Glebe Valley needs someone local they can trust. Someone with a stake in the future of Glebe Valley. Guys like Luis—and you."

"Yeah, well, Luis maybe," Cade said. "He's got city connections."

Luis's twisted his lips. "Uh, well, the Chapelita Center has a grant from the city to run an after-school program. I can't piss off our funding source. I've got to keep a low profile."

Puzzled, Cade squinted at Luis.

Then, almost as an afterthought, Luis jerked his thumb at Cade. "But my man here has organizing experience. C'mon, man, let me tell her."

Cade relented. "Tell her whatever you want."

Luis rubbed his hands together. "All right." He turned to Rita. "A few years ago, Cade here organized a cab drivers' strike—"

"A long time ago," Cade interrupted.

"Shut up," Luis barked good-naturedly. "I'm telling the story. I'm a new driver at the time with Metroland Taxi, Cade too, but we didn't know each other at the time. The cabbies complained about everything: low pay, long hours, and management keeping too much of the cut. Credit card fees were killing us too. The owner overcharged us for insurance. Everyone concerned about safety after a driver got robbed and murdered."

"He should never have been in that neighborhood," Cade said.

"So, what happened?" Rita asked.

Luis told Rita how the drivers would complain and complain, but the owners just ignored them. "Then one day, out of the blue, Cade comes up with a plan. He tells the drivers to make up a list of grievances; then he arranged to have the cabbies meet up at the dispatch office the next day with homemade signs, *Justice for Taxi Drivers*. Pretty amazing considering most of them could hardly speak English."

"I don't get it." Rita's eyes blazed at Cade. "*You* stepped up to lead the strike?"

Luis responded before Cade could reply. "We didn't know it then, but found out later; he'd served in Iraq. Training soldiers or something. What were you, a captain?"

"Sergeant," Cade mumbled.

"Whatever. I don't know what got into him, but he takes charge of the whole deal, starts giving orders to the men. You should have seen him. The next day, fifty drivers showed up and signed a petition. Cade's

standing on a picnic table with a bullhorn." Luis looked at Cade for confirmation. "Remember?"

Of course, he remembered. He'd started a call and response through
a bullhorn, and the cabbies had joined in. The pace picked up with the
decibels:

Lower the lease!
Stop the greed!
Lower the lease!
Stop the greed!

Cade took over the story. "I had my back to the office when the dis-
patcher suddenly bolted out and knocked me off the picnic table. Took
ten stitches to close the gash in my head."

"Son of a bitch!" said Luis, pumping his fist in the air.

Really into it now, Cade recounted how he'd raised himself off the
ground, blood gushing from his scalp. "I drove my fist into the bastard's
balls. He doubled up, and I jerked my knee under his chin. Broke the
sucker's jaw. He went down for the count. Someone called the police."

"True story," Luis said.

Rita looked first to Luis then Cade. "Was that the end of it?"

"Hardly," Cade said. "A news van showed up the same time as the
cops. It made the evening news. My bloody shirt, the drivers' protest
signs. The *Washington Post* followed up on the plight of the local drivers."

"Excellent," said Rita.

"Long story short," Cade continued, "the attorneys for Metroland
sent a letter to all the drivers agreeing to our demands: shorter hours,
lower lease payments, and a larger cut."

Luis picked up the thread. "A month after we got the letter,
Metroland got bought out by a large fleet operator. All of the cabbies
who signed the petition were laid off. They called it downsizing. A lot of
blood and sweat for nothing."

Rita noticed Cade looking at the floor. "Is that how you see it, all for
nothing?"

The plight of the cabbies had struck a sympathetic chord that had
been sealed off since the deaths caused by the IED attack. Hell, some of

the drivers, refugees from the Middle East, even resembled the jundi assigned to his squad on that fateful day. Scrounging for a better life for themselves and their families. Painful reminders. In the end, though, the cab strike had vaporized into dust, just like the explosion in the desert. Fighting URP sounded like one more hopeless mission that he didn't need.

"Tell you the truth, I don't care anymore," Cade said. "After I got laid off, I went independent and blew my savings on a Checker cab. Rebuilt the engine and splurged on a custom paint job, to set me apart. An emerald-green metal flake with glow-in-the-dark paint pearls. You need shades to look at it. I call it the Green Flash."

Rita smirked. "Isn't the Green Flash a superhero?"

"Not a superhero." Cade waved his hand dismissively. "It's an optical phenomenon. The sun sets over the ocean, and—bam!" Cade's hands flew apart like an explosion. "A green flash of light. I saw it once in Hawaii, on my honeymoon. My wife and I were hiking the Na Pali coast—"

"Hey," Luis cut in. "Can we get back to Glebe Valley? The point is you have experience organizing. Come on, man. You can do it." He looked to Rita for encouragement. "Am I right?"

Rita rolled her eyes.

"I can do whatever I set my mind to," Cade said. "I just don't see the point."

"Don't pay any attention to him," Luis said to Rita. "What's our next step?"

"My next step is on a plane," Rita said. "Your next step is to make up your mind about who's going to get this thing off the ground. Then convene a tenants' meeting. Tell them what's going on. Get them to show up in numbers next Wednesday at the public hearing."

"And do what exactly?" asked Luis.

Rita rooted around in a large tote bag and handed a checklist to Luis. "Read it, out loud."

The two-page checklist consisted of assignments with spaces for names, cell numbers, and email addresses. Luis cleared his throat and read:

Decision makers
Speakers
Police liaison
Press communications
Signs and Banners
Marshalls and Peacekeepers
Jail support team…

Rita interrupted, "That's enough. You get the idea."

"Jail support?" asked Luis, shooting Cade an anxious glance.

"Don't worry, Luis," Rita said. "Just covering all the bases. You probably won't need it. I can bring in some people to help you organize if Mr. Green Flash can't get off his butt. Nobody's going to get hurt." Rita grabbed her tote bag and looked at Cade. "Any chance you're going back to Reagan?"

Caught off guard, Cade muttered, "Uh, sure. Let's go." Cade and Rita said good-bye to Luis and left the community center. Outside, the Green Flash dazzled in all its sunbaked brilliance.

"Whoa, nice ride, Cade. You weren't kidding." Cade caught her staring at the cab's dented rear bumper. "Fender-bender?"

"Have to be more careful what I back into."

"You and me both. Look, I apologize for being too rough on you in there."

"No big deal. Like I said, I don't see the point in wasting a lot of energy on something that in the long run isn't going to make a difference."

Rita tossed her carry-on into the back and slid into the passenger seat. Cade turned off the meter. Her profile showed off a strong jawline and long, upswept eyelashes. "You a Marlins fan? I noticed your shirt."

Rita stared out the window.

"Just saying, the Nationals are playing home against the Marlins the Saturday after the zoning hearing." They passed the exit ramp for rental car returns. "So, I'm thinking, maybe you could fly up for the zoning hearing next week and catch a game while you're here." He glanced at Rita. "A friendly rivalry, so to speak."

"Thought you said you were hiking with your wife," Rita said without looking at Cade.

"Divorced, eight years ago. I'm not on the rebound if that's what you're thinking."

Rita cracked a smile. "Believe me; that's not what I'm thinking. I'm not flying up for a baseball game if you and Luis don't have your act together for the zoning hearing. Make up your mind about that first."

They passed a sign for passenger drop-off.

"I've been in real firefights. I'm not intimidated by URP."

Rita laughed. "Glad to know you're not intimidated. Does that mean you're in?"

Cade stopped in front of the departure drop-off. "Didn't say I was in or out."

Rita grabbed a book from her bag. "Read this. Make up your mind about whose side you're on." Then she retrieved her carry-on from the backseat. "You have my cell. Call if you need help." She extended her hand for a shake—dry and firm—then gave his hand a bonus squeeze. She stepped onto the wide apron that fronted the curbside check-in and disappeared behind sliding glass doors.

He stared at the doors. A horn blast drew his attention to a car blocked by his cab. An orange-vested traffic attendant waved at him to move.

Rita's words and body language back at the Chapelita Center had communicated aggressiveness, as if spoiling for a fight with URP. And all her bullshit about snakes and capitalists and a movement. What was that all about?

An airport police SUV pulled up behind the Green Flash. "I'm going, I'm going," Cade shouted, his mind's eye conjuring an afterimage of Rita Castro, when the engine warning light blinked red.

8

A stagnant air mass hung over Washington DC like a Dixie fili-
buster. Cade inhaled a lungful of the humid soup. He'd been
driving since 5 AM and had listened to three of the twenty-nine CDs of
the *Don Quixote* audiobook left behind by an absentminded passenger.
A stomach growl signaled time for a break.

Cade and a lot of cab drivers often ate at the Waffle Shop. Cheap
eats twenty-four/seven. The restaurant occupied a triangular building,
with one side bordering Washington Avenue; its sharp angle
reminded him of the prow of a ship. The Waffle Shop appeared
poised to punch through the crust of an asphalt sea. Floor-to-ceiling
windows afforded patrons an excellent view of the street action, while
a curbside bus stop presented a change of scenery with each discharge
of passengers and diesel fumes. Inside, nine swivel stools faced the
counter. A row of cracked red vinyl booths lined the view to the
avenue.

Cade sat at a stool nearest the door. The smell of fried onions
seeped into every pore. He glanced at the baseball game on the TV above
the door—the Nats losing to the Mets. A handwritten note taped to the
cash register announced that the restrooms were for use by customers
only. Laminated signs decorated the walls and depicted platters of food
in garish colors: *Mita de Pollo Asado; Con Frijoles; Arroz o Papas; Plantanos
Fritos.* Saturday afternoon and the diner showed as little life as the Nats
down six in the first inning.

"Just coffee, Miguel," Cade said to the counterman as he swiveled to
face the avenue. A young woman at the bus stop held a squirming toddler while she checked a cell phone with her free hand. He glanced at his
watch for the third time since he sat down.

Luis entered the diner and slid onto the stool next to Cade. "I got tied up. You called?"

"Yeah, I talked to Rita on the drive to the airport. I wanted to clear up a few things."

Luis ordered scrambled eggs in a tortilla and coffee. His face soured when he glimpsed the score of the Nats game. "Yeah?"

"All that talk about rounding up tenants. Getting them down to the Planning and Zoning hearing. You acted gung-ho, but then you say you can't do anything because of a contract with the city? You've told me yourself that that contract has been shrinking for years. So that's bull-shit."

Luis looked down as if studying the placemat, avoiding eye contact. Then he turned and gazed out the window.

"Why don't you get a friend from uh…" Cade hesitated, "*your* community to take the lead? Folks are more likely to listen to—"

Luis spun toward Cade, eyes ablaze. "Don't worry about that. *Hermanos* from *my* community will step up big-time when the time comes. Right now, we just need you to get this protest off the ground by next Wednesday."

Miguel came over to pour fresh mugs of coffee. When Miguel returned to the grill and was out of earshot, Cade changed the subject. "And another thing. Did you notice how Rita looked at me funny when I asked her how she knew so much about URP? What's up with that?"

Before Luis could respond, Miguel slid a platter in front of Luis, reminding Cade of his stomach growl.

"You know, all the times I've been in here, I've never had the waffles. Hey, Miguel, how about fixing me up a stack of your world-famous waffles."

"No waffles today," Miguel muttered over his shoulder.

"What?" Cade feigned shock. "How can the Waffle Shop not have waffles? Never mind. Just give me whatever Luis has."

Luis slurped the hot coffee. "I checked on Rita after you guys left. Called a buddy, Hector, in Miami. He works in public housing, knows Rita. She's well respected in the community. Also, she has a low tolerance for anyone who doesn't believe in the movement as much as she does."

The word "movement" again. There had been all kinds of political movements in Iraq—a new one every day. Demonstrations and protests that often turned violent, with hundreds arrested. He gave up trying to make sense of any of them. He wanted no part of any movement.

"Well, I got a low tolerance for fanatics," Cade said.

"Rita's not a fanatic, just a hard-ass. Recruited out of law school. Worked for a top firm in Miami. After two years, she walked away to work in a legal aid office. Eventually, she took over as head of a tenants' co-op, making a third of what she used to pull down."

"Why would anyone throw away that kind of money?"

"Ask Rita. All I'm saying is, she has a good rep. Hector says she's smart and tough, and known to have a mouth on her. Just don't put her in front of a reporter."

Miguel arrived with Cade's order. He dug in while Luis continued. "Look, I didn't mention something yesterday, with Rita around."

Cade bit into the tortilla and motioned for Luis to continue.

"There are a lot of things happening right now. The machete murder, mainly. Families are keeping kids at home, not sending them to our summer camp. People just as soon take the relo money and move. Go where it's safer for the kids. A lot of fear. Might make it a tough sell to get people to stay and fight. To top it off, the Watchdogs called ICE the other day. They hauled off two young men minding their own business at the Git 'n Go."

"ICE?"

"Immigration and Customs Enforcement. I saw a woman banging on the van as it pulled away. Folks are afraid to come to the center, wondering if they'll get picked up next." Luis's face twisted into a scowl. "I hate the fucking Watchdogs."

Cade had read about the Watchdogs in the *Glebe Gazette*, the local merchant rag for mattress discounters and journalism interns. The Watchdogs began as a klatch of neighborhood moms walking kids to the bus stop before they stopped by the Git 'n Go for coffee laced with hazelnut creamer and a quick check of the bulletin board for tear-off slips of babysitter services.

Wary of the furtive looks of the day laborers congregating by the Dumpster, the moms expanded their civic duties to include a watch rotation from a car parked safely across the street. They looked on in disgust as the men urinated behind the Dumpster, discarded trash on the pavement, and whistled at the young girls returning from school. The Watchdogs called in nuisance complaints to a police department overwhelmed with crimes of a higher priority.

Before each shift, the Watchdogs traded possession of a clipboard, binoculars, a camera with a telephoto lens, and a yellow-highlighted copy of the United States Constitution. A binder on the passenger seat contained photos of men known to hang out in the parking lot. Rumors circulated that each Watchdog possessed a concealed carry permit. While the Watchdogs were careful not to break any laws, their countless reports to the police were a constant source of aggravation in the Chapelita community.

"They've got guns, like a damn militia," Luis said, a little too loudly. At the mention of guns, the man on the next stool swiveled toward Luis as if hoping for some hot gossip. "Mind your own business," Luis growled. Startled, the man drained his coffee and left.

Luis leaned into Cade and lowered his voice. "One of these days a Watchdog is going to shoot someone."

Cade scratched his beard. "Oh, they're just housewives, Luis. Don't get paranoid. Besides, if folks are too scared to come out in the open, why are you so eager for me to lead a protest?"

Luis finished off the tortilla, stared straight at the mirror behind the counter, and caught Cade's eyes. "Because part of me thinks it's the right thing to do, and you're the only guy I know who is halfway smart enough to do it on short notice. *Comprende?*"

About to respond, Cade paused when Luis's cell phone chimed. Luis said a few words in Spanish. "Visitors. Got to go." Luis wiped his fingers and threw down some bills. "*Mañana.*"

Cade watched Luis cross the street to the Chapelita Center. Something was holding Luis back from organizing the tenants, but it was not his shrinking city contract. Maybe he was scared to stick his neck out, afraid it might get chopped off. He got awful touchy when asked about other Latinos coming forward to lead the protest. Probably lashing out to hide the fact that he didn't have the guts to lead the fight himself, promising instead that unnamed brothers would take up the gauntlet. Despite a hot-blooded temper at times, Luis was a real softie at heart.

Cade pushed the platter away and rubbed his temples. The more immediate thought of finding another apartment pushed aside worries about leading a protest fight. Moving outside the city limits would mean losing his housing subsidy—the only thing now keeping his bank account above water. The subsidy had cost him a sizeable payoff to a friend of a friend of a cabbie, who in return had moved Cade to the head of a five-year waiting list. The ill-gotten subsidy came with a twinge of remorse since he knew of families in far more desperate straits than him. But in Iraq, payment for special favors was standard operating procedure. Nearly anything a soldier desired could be obtained on the black market: drugs, laptops, weapons, cell phones, electronics—even a newborn baby. Although why a soldier would want a baby was way above his paygrade. But there it was. After a while, the twinge had receded into an occasional flare-up.

Besides the loss of the subsidy, relocation figured to be a major hassle. Glebe Valley's proximity to major airports, hotels, and tourists ensured a steady stream of business. Uprooting to the burbs would upset a critical balance of cash flow and convenience.

Admittedly, he'd grown comfortable with the seedy "chicness" of the neighborhood. A block from the Waffle Shop, the new microbrewery at the Lucky Strike bowling alley offered an exquisite IPA with which to drown his sorrows. One lonely evening last week, long past midnight, he had sought the company of other reprobates by paying a small cover to enter the back room of Tommy's Tattoo and Piercing Parlor. There, on a makeshift stage under a black light, two naked young women, inked head to toe with ultraviolet dyes, undulated and moaned in tantric ecstasy. A Tibetan peep show next door to an all-night pizzeria. A slice of low-rent nirvana.

Even better, his long dry spell, bordering on monk-like celibacy, had finally ended. Things had started to click with Cassandra. The first time he'd laid eyes on her was at the Waffle Shop when she'd breezed in to take out. Her brightly colored caftan reached sandal tops encrusted with jewels and stones. Raven hair pulled back in a tight bun gleamed with perfumed oil. A chocolate complexion glowed with lotions of aloe and jojoba. When she gave Miguel the order, her Caribbean patois rose and fell like birdsong. Intrigued by the exotic creature, Cade initiated a conversation that led to drinks at the Alamo.

Over a third Cuba Libre, Cassandra confided that her real name was Betty Vegas and that she'd emigrated from Trinidad. She took Cade's right palm and traced his heart line. The tickle of her polished nail uncorked a torrent of blood rushing to his groin. She identified the shape of an X that crossed his lifeline. A warning sign, she said, but not something to worry about now.

Cade didn't worry about it since he didn't believe it. They hit it off immediately and had been hooking up on a semi-frequent basis ever since. When in the neighborhood, Cade always made it a point to swing by the salon to get his love line extended. A move, however, might snuff a promising new spark in his life.

On the other hand, the recent machete murder behind Kim's Drycleaners had freaked the neighborhood out of its collective mind. Maybe not a bad time to relocate. Mentally, Cade tallied the pros and cons of moving as his gaze returned to the bus stop. The young woman holding the toddler was gone, swept away by the Pentagon 10A.

* * *

Officer Corrine Rodriguez had groused when Detective Sergeant Paul Nichols of the Northern Virginia Gang Investigative Unit said he'd pick her up in thirty minutes. Not a polite request, more like an order. At five-foot-six, she felt dwarfed sitting next to the Hulk in an ill-fitting gray suit.

"Sorry for the short notice," Nichols said. "We got a lead on the gangbanger involved in the machete murder. Figured you could help."

Corrine eyed Nichols's bald head and wondered if he shaved it every day. "Where are we going?"

"We're going to talk to Luis Guzmán."

"You think he's mixed up in the machete attack?"

"Not Luis," Nichols said. "His son, Enzo."

Enzo had gotten into trouble a few years ago, but Corrine had lost track of his whereabouts, and Luis never brought him up in conversation. The son Luis did boast about was Javier. He had a full-ride soccer scholarship to the University of Virginia, plus he coached the U-9 boys' soccer team in the police summer league. A good kid.

"What makes you suspect Enzo?" Corrine asked.

"Last year, I busted three BOBs. You know, the Brothers of Blood?"

Corrine shot Nichols a look that said, *Do you think I'm stupid?*

Nichols smiled. "So, the BOBs pled to beating a rival to death as punishment for disrespecting one of their homies. After that, the gang dispersed, went into hiding. Until the machete attack on a rival drug dealer. Word on the street is that BOB has a new leader and muscle from New York."

"So where does Enzo fit in?"

"Five years ago, Enzo was busted in a Virginia Beach house. Cops found two hundred pounds of weed, eighty thousand in cash, and a couple of .45s. Four of the dudes with priors got the max. Enzo had no record and pulled five years. A few months after he entered Portsmouth Correctional Center, the state selected the joint to pilot the Virginia Prison College Program."

"I've heard of that," said Corrine. "We had a graduate speak to our at-risk kids."

"It's supposed to prepare ex-cons to reenter society. Help them get a job. Enzo enrolled in the program. Turned out to be a real eager beaver. Portsmouth said they'd never seen anything like it. He completed courses in computer programming and business software applications in record time. Seemed to have a real knack for it. Said he planned to start up his own business once he got out of Portsmouth."

"Impressive," Corrine said. "Considering his father never completed high school. But that still doesn't explain Enzo's connection to BOB."

"I'm getting to it," Nichols said. "Portsmouth officials were proud of Enzo's accomplishment. They asked Enzo to visit other correctional facilities and inspire more inmates to participate. Enzo rode the state prison circuit: Red Onion, Indian Creek, Greenville, Cold Spring."

"Not a bad gig."

"When Enzo's time came, the parole board took note of his goodwill tour and academic achievement. They lopped off the last two years of his sentence."

"So that's the good news," Corrine said. "What's the bad?"

"Some bad actors also saw potential in Enzo—" Nichols swerved to avoid a woman wearing earbuds and staring at a cell phone as she stepped off the curb. "Jeezus Christ!"

Corrine waited a beat until Nichols calmed down. "You were saying something about bad actors."

"Oh right," Nichols said, shifting back to the conversation. "There's a small MS-13 clique in Portsmouth. They keep them in a segregated block of the prison. But they still control a lot of action on the street. They suck up the local gangs when it suits their purposes. Think of it as a franchise, like Burger King. MS-13 provides the locals with assistance and connections. In return, they take a big cut of the profits. After I busted the three BOBs, the Portsmouth clique wanted a new man. Someone with smarts, for a change. They gave Enzo an audition."

"What kind of audition?"

"If he ran the clique and made money, his reward would be 'getting jumped' into MS-13. It's like hazing into a fraternity. Only instead of a butt paddling, the homies beat the shit out of a new guy for thirteen seconds as a reward for proving his loyalty. Except if he fucks up, the beating doesn't stop until he's dead—and then dismembered."

"So, you're saying that you think Enzo is running BOB while auditioning for a job with MS-13. Then why talk to Luis? He hasn't seen or talked to Enzo in years."

"We're aware of that. We have reason to believe Enzo is holed up in Glebe Valley waiting for the heat to die down. Enzo's estranged from his father, but he might get in touch with his younger brother, Javier. The kid used to visit his brother in Portsmouth."

Corrine drew her lips into a thin line. "Is Javier in danger?"

"Not if he's as smart as everybody says he is," said Nichols. "We just want Javier to let us know if Enzo contacts him. We want to put BOB out of business, permanently."

Nichols stopped for a red light. Across the street, on the side of a building, the unmistakable tag for BOB: a multicolored swirl of inter-locking numbers—2-O-2—that popped out like 3-D.

"Wild style," Nichols said, pointing toward the wall. "Originated by SID88, a notorious Bronx subway tagger. Fell under the wheels of a moving train. Rookie mistake. Why don't you call it in? You're just encouraging them."

"Because it wasn't there yesterday," Corrine said. "I'll phone it in."

"Gangs will do anything to protect their turf."

"Like the machete attack behind Kim's Drycleaners?"

Nichols's jaw clenched.

Corrine looked at the side of Nichols's bald head—his mangled right ear looked like a dog's chew toy. They passed the Glebe Valley apartments. As the community liaison officer, she received a rent-free apartment. She'd seen the notices of the planned sale and wondered if she would get another free apartment somewhere else. If not, she might have to moonlight as a rent-a-cop, or maybe double up with her sister, or—

"You were looking at my ear," Nichols said.

"What? Uh, no, not really, I just—"

"That's okay. Hell, in eleven years with the gang unit, I've been punched, shot at, knifed." He pointed to his ear and laughed. "And bit."

Corrine stared out the window and mulled ways to trim her budget to afford a higher rent.

"Hey, why don't you swing by our offices? Find out everything you want to know about BOB. We've got new software. It predicts the points of competitive outbursts of gang violence along territorial boundaries. Remind me to show you the algorithm."

"I can hardly wait," Corrine said. "Turn here."

Nichols pulled in and parked next to the Chapelita Community Center mural. A note taped to the door read: "Back in ten minutes."

"Give Luis a call," Nichols said. "Let him know we're here."

* * *

As Luis crossed the street from the Waffle Shop, he saw Officer Corrine Rodriguez in an unmarked car next to a broad-shouldered man in a suit, his shaved head the color of polished ebony. "Hey, Corinne, what brings you here?"

Corrine introduced Detective Nichols. "Can we go inside?"

Luis unlocked the door, and the trio entered the small office.

Inside, Nichols took over and rehashed that the police were still looking for the man who killed the drug dealer and the connection to BOB.

Nichols eye-checked Corrine, then continued, "We have reason to believe that members of BOB are hiding out in Glebe Valley. We have the complex under surveillance. But it could take a lot of time before one of them comes up for air."

Luis waited for it.

"So far the tenants have not been very cooperative with my men. Nobody is speaking up if they know anything. People fear reprisals. But to get these dudes off the street, we need everyone's help."

"Yeah, so?" said Luis.

Corrine stepped in. "May I, Detective?" She turned to Luis. "The police have reason to believe Enzo is involved in the machete attack."

"I haven't heard from Enzo in three years," Luis said, his expression impassive.

"We think he may try and contact Javier, for help."

Luis crossed his arms. "No way Javier is involved with Enzo."

"I didn't say Javier is involved," Nichols said. "But he did visit his brother every month in prison. They must be close."

"Javier didn't have anything to do with the machete attack," Luis snapped.

Corrine stepped in front of Nichols. "We're not saying he did, Luis. What Detective Nichols means is that Enzo may reach out to Javier, you know, brother to brother."

"Then what? Javier gets busted as an accessory?"

Nichols started to speak, but Corrine caught his eye. "If Enzo contacts Javier, tell Javier to call me. We'll take it from there. Right, Detective?"

"Absolutely. We just want to talk to Javier about—"

"I'll talk to Javier. Leave him to me," said Luis.

"Excuse me," said Corrine. She moved Luis away from Nichols. "You have my personal cell number, Luis. Call me anytime."

Nichols handed Luis a card, and the two police officers left the center. Luis watched the unmarked car pull out of the parking lot. His hands balled into fists. Enzo had been a happy kid, bright and popular in school. He brought home report cards with notes from his teachers. Luis read English well enough to understand that the teachers considered Enzo to be a smart kid, but not well enough to help him with homework.

Javier had no sooner started walking when Enzo showed him how to kick a soccer ball. The two boys were inseparable, at least until Enzo started hanging with the older boys in the park. Luis warned him to stay away from the teenagers, but working three jobs meant he wasn't around much to keep an eye on him. The street kids showered Enzo with the attention a young boy needs, filling the void Luis left by working eighty hours a week. Most nights he returned home late, exhausted, the kids already asleep. He'd look in on them, snug in the same bed, and his eyes would well up.

The changes in Enzo happened gradually: his taste in music, clothes, and the practicing of hand signals. The street kids offered Enzo something he could not get at home—a sense of belonging and status. And later, access to drugs, money, and the young Latinas attracted to the thug life. Enzo reminded Luis of a young boy who joins the Army and returns home as a hardened soldier.

He understood the appeal all too well. Like the camaraderie he'd felt in the Salvadoran Army. Young men barely out of their teens granted a license to unleash unspeakable violence upon the enemies of the state. The soldiers became a force to be feared and respected. It dawned on Luis that Enzo reflected a version of his younger self.

The door opened again. "Hey, Luis, you left your sunglasses at the Waffle Shop," said Cade.

"Toss 'em on the desk."

"I saw cops leaving. What's going on?"

Luis slumped in his chair, holding his head. "They're asking about Enzo."

"Enzo? I didn't know he was back. What's he doing now?"

Underneath the desk, Luis kicked the wastebasket across the room. "How the fuck should I know? What are you, another goddamn cop?"

Cade held up his hands in mock surrender. "Ease up, man. I'm on your side."

"Sorry. Got a lot on my mind right now." Peering up, he added, "Speaking of which, did you make up *your* mind about this zoning protest thing?"

"I said I'd give it some thought."

"You do that, man." Luis ran a hand over his face. "But don't wait too long."

* * *

After leaving Luis at the Chapelita Center, Cade drove for several more hours. By ten thirty, when he finally dropped off two executives at the Marriott Courtyard, he called it a day and returned to the apartment. Too wired to sleep, he headed to the kitchen for a beer.

Back on the sofa with a Corona, he clicked on the tube. Two hundred channels and nothing on. He muted the audio to a WWII movie. A silent squadron of fighter aircraft soared over enemy territory. A pilot in a helmet mouthed wordlessly into a radio transmitter.

World War II made a hell of a lot more sense than the mess in Iraq. Back then, at least you knew the enemy by their uniforms. In Iraq, one day he'd be killing the bastards, and by the next morning he'd be handing out MREs to their widows and kids.

A car backfire snapped Cade back to a soundless barrage of machine-gun fire from a German Messerschmitt hitting a US fighter plane. Black smoke poured from the fuselage as the aircraft plummeted to earth in a silent death spiral.

Cade clicked off the screen and headed to bed. He lay in bed and rewound the past few days, a crazy splice of jump cuts, close-ups, and long shots like the WWII movie: Finn's slick presentation, hitting a car in the parking lot, Rita's hand squeeze, Luis egging him to organize the tenants, cops looking for Enzo, figuring out an apartment move, and where things were going with Cassandra. It was all too much, like a constellation of images aligned in an imaginary pattern visible only to him.

Loud salsa music from the apartment below lulled him into a troubled sleep. Alone on a desert highway, he registered a premonition—a ferocious threat, everywhere but nowhere, deceptive as the heat waves rippling up from the blistering asphalt. He ran and ran, but gained no separation from the unseen menace. His parched throat was unable to summon help. The scene suddenly shifted, and now he stood in a long hallway facing a door. The threat was now behind the door exerting a relentless pressure. Cade threw his weight against the door. But the pressure grew and grew until he could no longer contain it. The door flew open to the remains of a headless jundi corpse. Cade screamed and woke to slats of broken light thrown across tangled bedsheets.

9

$\mathcal{A}$fter three cups of Sumatra Gold Roast on an empty stomach, Cade's head buzzed with more questions than answers. He'd left Finn's presentation early because of his migraine and had missed important details. His curiosity piqued, he wanted to see firsthand what the city had in store for Glebe Valley.

He booted the laptop and searched for the Planning and Zoning Commission. A click on the P&Z site brought up the staff reports. He opened the link for The Glebe at Cub Run. Up popped URP's application for a special exception per Section 9 of the zoning code. *Zee 9!* Rita had called URP a bunch of capitalist bloodsuckers, but Cade couldn't tell it from the P&Z report—a morass of regulatory minutiae covering everything from signage to sewage. He clicked a tab and zeroed in on the project narrative. The P&Z spiel sounded eerily like Finn's pitch. They were on the same page all right. No wonder Rita considered the deal greased.

The zoning application narrative began with a vision for The Glebe at Cub Run: a smart-growth niche community enriched with historical references and coherent design. Cade grunted. *A vision!* A hallucinogenic word, often a distorted version of reality. Once he had a passenger, a hyper-social young man wearing a baby-blue suit with a matching shirt, vest, and tie, on his way to present a motivational speech at a convention of air-conditioning contractors. The man, with extremely large teeth, leaned over the bench seat and asked him if he had a personal vision statement. "You know, something that gives you a powerful mental picture of what you want your life to become."

And at that exact moment, what Cade desired most in life was a security partition, so he wouldn't have to listen to a salesman in a butt-ugly suit. However, the question did trigger a vision he had once, on

Christmas Eve, right after a nasty firefight. He'd decompressed behind the latrines, sprawled across a mound of sandbags, with a fifth of Jack Daniel's and a cigarette spiked with opium. In the fading light, he beheld a white winter sun burst forth shafts of pure light, painting the underbelly of the clouds purple, orange, and blue—like a soft flannel blanket swaddling the infant Jesus. In his altered state, he imagined a host of herald angels singing, *"Glory to the newborn King."*

But no improved streetscapes appeared in that majestic vision. Cade sighed and plunged deeper into the labyrinthine passageways of Zee 9. Finally, he reached the end of the vision statement: The Glebe epitomized a fully realized micro-urban village parachuted into a dream infill location along the Eastern Seaboard megalopolis that stretched from Boston to Miami. Just turn on the fountains and *voila!* Instant old town! Or rather, a *new* old town.

A discussion, buried deep in the narrative, described the relocation of existing tenants of the Glebe Valley apartments. A map showed a thirty-mile radius of comparable rental units and vacancy rates, concluding that the market could absorb most of the low-income residents.

Absorb!

Cade winced at the use of the word. His neighbors likened to a spill to be wiped up with a sponge. So dehumanizing. No wonder Rita cursed the bloodsuckers. But the P&Z saved the best for last—the cherry on top. The city deemed the Glebe to be consistent with the city's master plan. Salvation at the end of a shovel!

Glory to the newborn King.

Too bad. Cade didn't believe in a master plan, or divine intervention for that matter. But there it was, his fate forever intertwined with floor-area ratios and floodplain management. Rita had nailed it. The city wanted this deal bad.

He followed a link to URP's website, clicked on executive staff, and found a headshot for Robert Oliver, founder and former CEO of the company. A headline banner teased Oliver's rumination on a breakthrough in urban planning: *emotional communion.* A hundred-fold magnification of deeply embedded attachments to one's home and community. Advancements in brain-computer interface would complete the circuit between individual identity and the community. A rising wave of techno-amplified social interactions in commerce, governance, and culture would birth the next generation of smart cities around the world.

Dumbfounded, Cade shook his head. Strengthening the bonds of a community while at the same time displacing five thousand residents. What a concept. The small font on the screen strained his eyes. He retrieved a pair of reading glasses and returned to the sofa with the book Rita had shoved in his face at the airport, *Urban Rebellion: A Call to Action.*

The jacket photo showed a bespectacled middle-age man with a do-it-yourself haircut, squinting into the California sun. The blurb mentioned Arthur A. Arthur's position as an associate professor of geography at the Univerisity of California, Berkeley. When Cade had been in school, geography had been about finding state capitals on a map. At Berkeley, however, geography assumed much grander dimensions.

Arthur taught graduate courses on the influence of spatial constructs on urban politics and social change. He also wrote a paper about the geo-political ramifications of urban encroachment on South American bee pollination and crop yields, although that seemed more a sideline than a primary focus.

The tough slog through the interstices of urbanization and the concentration of capital tested Cade's focus, but he plowed ahead through dense thickets of syntax and followed Arthur as he traced the roots of spatial justice back to Henri Lefebvre, a French intellectual. Coincidentally, Lefebvre drove a taxi in Paris during the 1920s. Cade felt an instant kinship with a cab-driving philosopher.

His own philosophy of being—a moment of existential clarity—recently dawned on him while deadheading past *The Reserve*, a gated community in the far western exurbs. The privacy wall along the highway resembled the HESCO barriers that had fortified Forward Operating Base Scorpion. Heavy-duty blast walls provided a modicum of security for those on the inside, yet also conveyed a message of apartness from the populace they were sent to protect.

When he finally returned to the States, it was as if a personal security perimeter warned all who approached him to keep away. Driving by the walled estate of *The Reserve*—with privatized security and one-way tire shredders—he realized that he was now the outsider, a cab driver with few friends, little money, and a sketchy future. But why stay on his present path? Take charge. Make a fresh start. Be who he wanted to be, not what other people expected of him. Nothing prevented him from turning the Green Flash around and heading west toward unfenced horizons. Nothing, save the terror of jundi ghosts unbound by horizons—fenced or otherwise.

The fresh start fantasy vaporized soon as Cade read that Lefebvre had also fought with the resistance movement against the Nazi occupation of France. A cab driver *and* a guerilla fighter. Now Cade liked Lefebvre even more—he was a fighter, not someone who cut and run when the going got tough. The French Resistance claimed modest success in sabotaging rail lines to disrupt the flow of German supplies to the front lines. Cade filed the idea away in case the time ever came to slow the blitzkrieg of advancing bulldozers on Glebe Valley.

Long after the war ended, Lefebvre published *Le Droit a la Ville* (Right to the City). The gist being that underpaid urban dwellers (*citadins*) didn't just rent a place to sleep, eat, or work a minimum wage job; they *inhabited* the city. And with that came certain rights to the urban space, including a say in the investment decisions by developers. If you just showed up at a zoning hearing, you were already too late. But, apparently, Rita didn't think it was too late.

Cade snorted when Arthur posed a rhetorical question: Should we do less for city dwellers who suffer habitat destruction than we do for pandas and sea turtles? He thought of a fish kill earlier in the summer in Cub Run, the stream behind the Glebe Valley apartments—hundreds of dead mackerel washed up along the muddy banks. An investigation confirmed that storm water runoff from a construction site had caused the kill.

Whether *citadins* or critters, it didn't matter. The same crew drove the steam shovels that destroyed habitats the world over. Clearing the land for more hotels, more condos, more shopping malls, more, more, more. To what end other than the infinite accumulation of capital?

Like a snake eating its tail.

Arthur outlined the three keys to not being run over by the bulldozers: resistance, objection, and disruption. Delays are costly to developers, and losses can quickly run into millions of dollars. Delay and disruption were excellent tools to bring the opposing party to the negotiating table.

But Rita's bluster about opening new urban battlefronts constituted some radical shit, asserting the right of Glebe Valley tenants to remain in their apartments, taking on the banks and developers. On one hand, it sounded righteous; on the other, a recipe for trouble. If it was anything like his doomed fight to unionize the drivers of the Metroland Taxi Company, that's when the fights broke out and the cops showed up.

A tension knot bulged in his neck. He rubbed his eyeballs and set the book down. He'd be out on the street soon if he didn't start making plans to move—plans that required searching for new digs in his nonexistent price range. Time he couldn't afford. And the Green Flash needed bodywork to repair his self-inflicted damage in the gymnasium parking lot. Maybe he should move west and start over. Either way, he needed a quick infusion of cash. His mind wandered to the notebook stashed in the fire safe.

Stretched out on the sofa, he massaged the muscle tightness in his neck, closed his eyes, and reimagined Rita's hand squeeze at the airport. Her T-shirt and tight jeans suggested an athletic leanness. A daydream of nimble foreplay was interrupted by a soft rap on the door. He squinted out the peephole, opened the door, and smiled. "I was just thinking about you."

Cassandra stepped past him, a firm set to her jaw. "That's not the vibe I'm getting."

"I'm surprised, that's all. I wasn't expecting you."

"I saw your cab in the lot. You left your watch at my place." She held out the cheap Timex.

Cade strapped the watch to his wrist. "Thanks."

"So, what's going on?"

"Not much, I was just leaving as a matter of fact."

Cassandra turned and ran her slender fingers along the dusty bookcase, then bent at the waist and waved her hand around the white fire safe. "I get a vibe, like you've been thinking about it. What's in the safe?"

Cade shifted on his feet. "Just some old Army stuff."

"Right." She walked over to the coffee table and picked up Arthur's book. "*Urban Rebellion.*" She arched an eyebrow. "You reading this?"

"Somebody left it in the cab. I was just looking at it."

She moved in close and held both his hands. "I'm getting all kinds of weird vibes in here. So, let's try again. What's really going on?"

Embarrassed by his noticeable tumescence, Cade slipped his hands out of her grasp. "Okay, you got me. You really want to know my secret?"

Cassandra locked eyes with Cade. "I want the truth."

He gently nudged her toward the bedroom.

A complicit smile spread across her face. "That's not a secret."

He held an index finger to his lips. "Wait and see."

* * *

Cade opened one eye and checked his watch. He'd dozed off after the romp with Cassandra. Now she was gone, and he was late. He needed the Flash to make some cash. In the bathroom, he splashed cold water on his face and brushed his hair and beard. He descended the three flights of stairs and walked toward the Green Flash in the far corner of the lot. Drawing closer, he saw two shirtless men installing a small billboard on a grassy wedge. One worker swung a four-by-four post and smashed it against the passenger side door of the cab.

Cade ran the last twenty yards. "What the hell are you doing?"

"Relax," said a muscled man with a blond ponytail and a pronounced brow ridge. "It was an accident."

Cade couldn't fathom the disrespect for private property as splendiferous as the Green Flash. He ran his hand over the deep crease. First, the rear bumper dent—okay, that was clearly his fault. But now this. His pride and joy was taking a beating. A line in the sand had been crossed. Cade erupted. "You're going to pay to have this repaired."

Ponytail turned his back, and Cade spun him around. "You don't leave until I get your name and who you work for."

"I said it was an accident, pal. Call your insurance."

Cade chest-bumped his adversary. "I ain't your pal. Look—"

That's when a right hook clocked Cade on the cheek, followed by a four-by-four post rammed into his gut. He buckled at the knees, down for the count.

* * *

Cade rolled onto his back. Shock waves rippled through his head and torso. Ponytail and his buddy were gone. He rose on one elbow, transfixed by the billboard the men had erected. The four-color rendering of the new condo complex was identical to the one Finn had displayed at the community meeting. The banner across the top screamed like a banshee: *The Glebe is coming!*

Retreating to the apartment, he collapsed on the couch. His ribs ached. Painful just to breathe. The welt under his eye bloomed purple and black. He washed an oxy down with a Corona. Back in the bathroom, he frowned in the mirror. "Time to choose a side, bro."

* * *

Cade arranged the meeting for the Applebee's at the corner of Washington Avenue and Bonaventure Street—the fringe end of the Glebe Valley business district and the transition zone to the upscale environs of Potomac. Founded in the late nineteenth century, the town once bordered the sprawling maze of tracks and freight cars of the Potomac Railroad Yard. In its prime, the yard had been a major hub for northbound and southbound freight—over one hundred trains a day steamed past, carrying goods up and down the Atlantic coast. Modest bungalows, built for railroad workers making $700 a year, now went for $700K—and up.

Inside, his old buddy Grif sat at the bar, watching a baseball game on a flat screen, a frosted mug on the counter. He wore a polo shirt with the Volvo logo over the left breast pocket. Bluish veins popped out of his forearms from the iron he still pumped.

Cade had watched the first Gulf War on CNN with Grif in his parents' basement. The laser-guided bombs blasting bunkers and vehicles resembled the video games the two boys played. Tracer rounds streaked across a sky bathed in a luminous green light by a night-vision camera. When the second Gulf War rolled around, it was their honorable and patriotic duty to serve and fight.

After a second tour, they were assigned to a Military Transition Team charged with training the Iraqis to be infantry-ready combat soldiers, fully prepared to make critical decisions on the field of battle. A way to give the Iraqi people a sense of hope and control over their destiny. Seeing the results in the jundi who completed the boot camp had been a source of pride for Cade. In the beginning, he'd felt a sense of accomplishment and of a contribution to a great and worthy cause—until it all went to hell on a hot, dusty patrol.

Cade snagged the stool next to Grif. "Hey, man."

"Hey," replied Grif, eyes glued to the game. The hitter got caught looking, and the Nats went down in order at the bottom of the seventh. Grif signaled the bartender for two beers. Cade added a shot of Jack Daniel's.

Grif eyed the boilermaker. "Little early, isn't it? Laying off the oxy, I hope."

After the IED attack, Cade had suffered chronic back pain. The Army doc prescribed opioids. After his discharge, he'd found a passenger who kept him supplied. But he had his self-medication totally under control. Cade slugged the shot and half of the beer. "No problem. How's it going?"

"Fine." Grif peeled his eyes away from the screen and turned to Cade. "Hey, what's up with the Ray Bans, man? You going Hollywood?"

Cade removed the shades to reveal the shiner under his right eye.

"Whoa." Grif whistled. "What happened to you?"

"You know the apartments where I live? A company plans to tear them down and build condos. I got into it with some construction jerks. They dented my cab."

"Uh oh, bad move," Grif said, shoving beer nuts into his mouth. "How's the Flash?"

"Just a flesh wound."

Grif's eyes went back to the screen. "Is that what you wanted to talk about?"

"Sort of, but also about a lawyer from Miami. She asked a buddy and me to get residents to show up at a zoning hearing. Try to stop this company, or at least slow it down."

"She?" Grif's attention shifted back to Cade.

"Yes, *she's* a lawyer."

"Shit." Grif drew out the expletive as if it had sixteen syllables. "Man, lawyers are bad news."

Cade laughed. "Relax, hoss. Anyway, the developer may push back. You never know. Feathers get ruffled, tempers flare, maybe somebody plays too rough. I'm going to help out."

"Are you kidding? Why bother?"

Cade lifted his shirt to reveal a large blot of purple skin.

"Holy shit. How'd that happen?"

"Same guys that gave me the black eye."

Grif frowned. "So, *that's* your reason?"

Not his *only* reason, but Cade didn't feel up to the task of elucidating Arthur's thesis on spatial justice when confronted by powerful forces of privatized tyranny. Maybe after a few more boilermakers.

"Goddamn right it's *my* reason," Cade said. "And if I see them again, I'll kick *their* asses. In the meantime, whatever I can do to fuck up plans for the Glebe, that's what I'm gonna do."

"That's cool, bro," Grif said. "You always were good at leading a mission."

"Didn't work out so well the last time."

"Don't blame yourself, man," Grif said. "Article 15, remember?"

Of course, Cade remembered. The "27 Articles" of T. E. Lawrence, aka Lawrence of Arabia, summarized the Englishman's approach to dealing with Arab armies during the First World War. The articles were required reading for the advisors in Cade's Military Transition Unit. The articles so well known, all you had to do was say a number, and instantly everyone knew what you were referring to. Article 15 was an exculpatory favorite: *Do not try and do too much with your own hands. Better the Arabs do it tolerably well than that you do it perfectly. It is their war, and you are there to help them, not win it for them.*

But it had felt like a personal failure to Cade. He had been the counter-IED specialist, the man the jundi counted on to keep them safe. Back at FOB, the Army trainers ate meals with the jundi. He got to know the men personally and knew the names of their children and what they did before the war. He had worked hard to earn their confidence, and he'd thrown it all away. His judgment had been clouded—and not for the first time, either. Whenever he pictured the jundi sharing the watermelon, an inner voice admitted that the Percocet might have relaxed his guard for just a moment—a moment when he otherwise might have warned the men away from the truck.

"Hey, I'm talking to you, man," said Grif. "You want another round?"

Cade refocused. "What? Uh, no."

Grif tapped his mug against Cade's. "*Insha'Allah.* Hey, that reminds me, remember that time on the firing range?"

Cade cracked a wry smile. "Article 12."

Article 12 referred to the time when they were supervising the jundi recruits on the firing of the PKC-47 machine gun. Grif had sidled up to Cade, with more pent-up energy than usual. He'd been showing a jundi how to aim the weapon properly to increase the chances of hitting the target. The jundi waved a dismissive hand, and muttered, "Insha'Allah." *If God wills it.* "In other words," Grif had said, "if Allah wants your bullet to hit the target, it will hit the target." They laughed, and quoted Lawrence Article 12: *Cling tight to your sense of humor. You will need it every day.* Ever since then, the two friends bantered Article 12 to express good-natured cynicism of anyone who put their faith in a god to spare the bombardment of a village or favor their team to win a Super Bowl.

"Look, if you need a hand with this protest thing, call me," Grif said.

"Thanks. The zoning hearing is Wednesday, week after next. I'll let you know."

"I'm worried about you, bud," Grif said. "Maybe you need an X-ray or something."

"Ribs are a little sore, but I'm fine."

"You don't look fine."

"You don't look so hot, either." Cade threw down a ten and headed for the door.

"Hey, man," Grif called, eyes back on the screen.

Cade turned and looked at the back of Grif's head.

"It wasn't your fault."

10

*A*fter leaving Applebee's, Cade called Luis to say he was all in on the tenant protest. Since the project would also demolish the retail shops in the strip mall along Washington Avenue, he figured the shop owners had a stake in the fight as well.

Cade pulled into the lot fronting the shops. Dandelions sprouted in the cracked pavement. A twelve-pack of dingy storefronts clung to life support, awaiting a cash transfusion. Brown wrapping paper covered the windows of two vacant stores. Hand-lettered signs advertised everything from payday loans to plantains.

Before driving to the mall, Cade'd composed a message at a FedEx office. He wrote a few lines, crumpled the paper, started over, crumpled another sheet, then stared off into the middle distance, his brain on lockdown.

What would Rita say? She'd probably go for the jugular with a black and red caricature of a capitalist vampire sucking the lifeblood out of the Chapelita community. Too extreme. He needed to touch hearts, not rip them out.

For some buried reason, a thought came to mind of the Muslim woman he'd encountered next to a pile of debris. A few minutes previous, the apartment house had bustled with life; then it smoldered in ruins from an attack of mortars and RPGs. Twisted strands of rebar poked out of slabs like arthritic claws. Bodies lay buried under a shroud of concrete dust.

Between sobs, the woman tore at her clothing. Then her grief turned to anger. She directed a stream of vicious utterances toward him. Veiled head to foot in a black chador, the woman evoked a sorceress casting a spell.

Luckily, Glebe Valley hadn't been reduced to rubble, yet. Cade scratched out a few lines and paid a clerk to format the message as a flyer and run a hundred copies on screaming neon orange paper stock. He examined the finished product:

SAVE CHAPELITA!

Our Homes! Our Right!

We are the people of Chapelita.

We have a right to the community we call home.

We reject the displacement of five thousand people from Glebe Valley.

We reject the theft of our homes by Urban Renaissance Partners.

Listed across the bottom: the date, time, and location of the public hearing on the zoning application. Contact information for the Chapelita Coalition for Justice included a phone number and email address for jcade1450. He'd invented the coalition name to give the protest an appearance of street cred.

Cade began at the left end of the mall with the Sunshine Mercado. The aisles were narrowed by stacks of flour sacks and crates of fresh produce. Fresh tilapia rested on ice chips in the glass case. Arrayed behind the cash register were stacks of Juicy Fruit gum, condoms, and motor oil. An old man tended the register—a ragged fringe encircled his bald dome. Cade introduced himself and explained the circumstances of the zoning hearing and the effort to organize a protest. The man reared back at the sight of Cade's bruised eye. The shopkeeper excused himself to wait on a customer with a basket of mangos and peppers.

"I'll just leave some flyers," Cade said. "Maybe stuff them into the grocery bags, okay?" Cade chalked the grocer up as a definite maybe.

Next in line, a Salvadoran bakery. The aroma of fried plantains and strong coffee met him at the door. Customers sat at tables squeezed into a tiny space between the takeout counter and the wall. A blackboard menu announced the day's specials. Cade pitched the owner, a pleasant middle-aged woman by the name of Delores, who wore a white cotton blouse and a colorful peasant skirt. Instead of a promise to attend the protest, she gave Cade a hug and a takeout bag with a large coffee—on the house. He took that as another maybe. Once out the door, he tore into the *pupusa* stuffed with cheese, beans, and pork and washed it down with the strong Salvadoran brew. He wiped his mouth, making sure no crumbs caught in his beard.

Next up: a tax preparation office. A silver bell jingled as he opened the door. Two empty cubicles carved up the small space. Three yellow plastic chairs lined the wall, fronting a fake wood veneer counter. A plastic tray on the counter held a stack of business cards for Everhard Tax Preparation Services, Earl Everhard, CPA. Cade called out, "Hello, anybody here?"

A flush of water sounded from a bathroom in the rear of the office. A door opened, and a middle-age man walked toward the front counter. Dressed in a white short-sleeve shirt with a brown tie and brown slacks, Earl Everhard greeted Cade with a wide smile. "Anything I can help you with today?"

By the time Cade explained the protest at the public hearing, Earl's smile had faded. As president of the chamber of commerce, Earl informed Cade that the chamber supported the project a thousand percent.

"A thousand percent, eh?" Cade said. "Even though you'll lose your business?"

Earl spread his arms. "Lose this office you mean, not my business. I've got an option on office space in the new development. Condo owners are going to need tax services."

Cade studied Earl. The Glebe at Cub Run represented a golden goose for a cash-strapped city, plus a guaranteed revenue stream for Everhard Tax Preparation Services.

"If I were you," Earl cautioned, "I wouldn't waste time getting folks riled up at a zoning hearing. URP is offering a generous relocation package. We don't want to jeopardize that. And I understand they're willing to spruce up the soccer field, maybe add some lights."

Anger rose like bitter reflux in Cade's gullet. Earl's doughy face begged to be punched.

"The relocation package is a joke, and you know it. Dangle a few bucks in front of hard-working people, and they'll go quietly, is that it?"

Earl's face hardened. "I don't think you fully understand how this development is going to benefit the community. URP has worked very closely with local businesses. It's a win-win for the city. Look, if you want my advice—"

Cade slammed the door on his way out, the silver bell tinkling sweetly in his wake.

* * *

Earl Everhard's smug expression caught in Cade's craw like a chicken bone. His civic boosterism was conveniently aligned with his tax preparation business. A sweet deal for everyone except the tenants of Glebe Valley. He needed to vent before visiting the other shops. Cassandra's Unisex Salon & Psychic Palm Advisory shop beckoned from a few doors down.

When he walked in, a young woman with dreadlocks was sculpting an intricate Lakers logo into a boy's scalp. "Is Cassandra around?" Cade asked.

The stylist's eyes remained focused on the logo. "She's finishing a webcam reading. She'll be out in a few minutes."

Cade grabbed a celebrity magazine and parked in the salon chair next to the boy. He'd almost caught up on a pop diva's colonic cleansing ritual when Cassandra appeared. She flashed a radiant smile when Cade stood. Then her expression changed.

"Oh, my god. What happened to you?" She rushed up, examined the ugly bruise under his eye and then grabbed his palm. "Come, please!"

Cade followed Cassandra into the backroom office of the salon. The webcam on a laptop screen showed an empty chair behind a desk. On the wall, a multicolored tapestry depicted the energy chakras in the human body.

Cassandra motioned Cade to sit. She pulled another chair to face him, knees to knees. "Your aura is like a sunspot," she explained. "A black splotch against a yellow radiance emanating from your electromagnetic field. You've got blockage."

"Is that anything like constipation?" Cade teased.

Cassandra responded with a gentle love slap. "Why do you come here if you don't believe?"

"Because you believe. And I believe in you."

Cassandra smiled. "We'll see. It so happens a black spot in the aura indicates an area of intense magnetic activity. In your case, I sense feelings of unreleased grief and guilt."

"You're probably reading migraine leftovers."

Cassandra held his face between her hands. "No, a physical disruption would be more reddish. Could be connected, though. I am sensing something powerful, an inward struggle perhaps. Ring any bells?"

"After you left my apartment, I got into a fight with two construction workers. A guy punched me, and another guy jammed a four-by-four into my chest." Cade lifted his shirt and showed off the contusion beneath a gauze bandage around his rib cage.

Cassandra's eyes widened at the sight of the discoloration, lightly touching it as if sensing a vibe. "I don't understand. Why would they do such a thing?"

"One of the construction jerks got careless and put a huge crease in my cab's door."

"So, what did you do?"

"I politely informed him he had to pay for the repair, and he disagreed. No way I'm going to let some SOB walk away from that. You have any idea how much it costs to repaint green metal flake?"

Cassandra pushed her chair back. "Sometimes I think you care more about that cab than me." She cast an appraising look. "Or maybe someone else. I sensed it when I was in your apartment. I'll ask one more time, is there something you're keeping from me?"

Cade fumbled for a response. His Rita daydream sprang to mind. The road had forked into relationship territory. Landmines everywhere. Step lightly, men. The hazards of dating a psychic. "The Flash pays the bills," Cade countered, "but she ain't near as pretty as you." He rubbed his bruised cheek. "Besides, those dudes work for the same company that plans to tear down Glebe Valley—and this strip mall, by the way. Aren't you worried?"

"Answer *my* question first."

Cade groaned as he let his shirt drop. "I'm sorry, what?"

Cassandra walked to her desk and closed her laptop. "Never mind." She sat down in her high-backed chair. "I'll miss my regulars..." Her voice trailed off for a beat, then bounced back on a high note. "But I can set up a new salon anywhere."

"Anywhere, huh?" Cade thought she sounded surprisingly upbeat. He handed her a flyer. "I'm trying to round up folks for a zoning hearing. We could use your support."

Cassandra barely glanced at the flyer, then set it aside. She shuffled papers as if there was some importance to the sequence in which they lay on her desk. A strand of hair had strayed from her tight hair bun, and she became preoccupied with putting it back in place.

"Did you hear what I said?" Cade repeated.

Cassandra looked up with a distracted smile. She moved back to Cade and laid her hand across his forehead. "It's obvious you're worked up about this. A lot of negative energy. Something personal is going on. An eye-for-an-eye kind of vibe. I sense conflict in your future."

Cade put his mouth next to Cassandra's ear. "I've got some other energy that wants to get out, too."

Cassandra glanced at Cade's lap. "I don't need an aura to see that. You're like a damn tomcat. We close at six. I got jerk chicken in the back. Come by, and I'll heat it up for us."

"I'll bring the Red Stripe." He pecked her on the lips and felt better already, his blue vibe humming.

* * *

After he had left the salon, Cade completed visits to the remaining shops. The tally: five *we'll see*, three *definite maybes*, two *owners not present*, and one *no* (Earl). Cassandra was ambivalent, but he thought she'd slide over to the *definite maybe* column.

He drove around the block, stapling or taping flyers on telephone poles, bus stop shelters, and trees. Miguel gave permission to tape a flyer to the Waffle Shop window. Cade dropped off flyers at the public library and the Git 'n Go, then sped over to Glebe Valley and affixed flyers over the mailboxes in the entranceway of each building.

Two blocks from the apartments, a gray stone church squatted at the intersection of Washington Boulevard and Jefferson Street. Our Lady of Seven Sorrows. Guessing that many of Glebe Valley's Latino population were probably Catholic, he turned into the church lot.

He grabbed a handful of flyers and bounded up the steps two at a time. Inside, the vestibule loomed in deep shadow. Sunbeams split the clerestory windows. A series of small alcoves depicted each of the seven sorrows of the Virgin Mary. A rack of votive candles awaited a match and a donation.

A sign pointed to the basement fellowship hall. Three window wells, level with the parking lot, cast a grayish pall across the linoleum floor. Stacked against the wall were folded chairs and tables. A cluttered bulletin board held notices for youth ministries and math tutors.

"Are you looking for someone?"

Cade spun around. In the half-light, he made out a man of middle height in a white T-shirt and paint-splattered cargo shorts.

"Yes, I mean no," Cade said. "I just wanted to put up a notice about a protest to stop Glebe Valley from being torn down."

The slender man cloaked in shadow said, "By any chance, is your name Jack Cade?"

Caught off guard, Cade asked why he wanted to know.

"I was at the gymnasium the other night," the man said. "You made a rather noisy exit. It seems everybody has heard of the Green Flash. Jack Cade not so much. I asked around."

"I guess that's good news and bad news. Why were you there?"

"Many of our parishioners are residents of Glebe Valley. I wanted to learn more about what URP had in mind."

Cade turned his head. "Look, is there someone in charge here? Someone I can talk to?"

"You can talk to me. I'm Father Gustavo Romero, assistant pastor. Call me Gus." The priest extended a paint-flecked hand. "Our head pastor is on extended sick leave. Excuse my appearance; I'm painting the bathrooms." The priest reached for the flyer in Cade's hand and flipped on a light switch to read the notice. Cade got a better look at the man who appeared to be in his early thirties and wiry with an athlete's build.

"The Chapelita Coalition for Justice? Never heard of it."

"I made it up," Cade admitted. "Gives the impression there's an organization behind this thing."

"And are you doing this *thing* by yourself?"

Cade hesitated. "Well, a friend at the Chapelita Center is helping out."

"Luis? Luis Guzmán?" Gus asked.

"Yeah," Cade said with a trace of surprise. "You know him?"

"Sure, I know Luis. Good man. How do *you* know him?"

"We go way back."

"If you don't mind me asking," Gus said, a finger pointing underneath his own eye, "what happened to you?"

"I got into it with some jerks working for URP."

"Drew first blood, eh?" Gus chided. "Tell me more about this Chapelita Coalition for Justice. What kind of justice do you have in mind?"

"The basic kind, I guess. I live in the Valley too and I don't like getting pushed around. Maybe others feel the same way." Cade pinned a flyer to the bulletin board. "How about you, Father? What kind of justice are you looking for?"

Gus motioned Cade to a small room next to the fellowship hall, a kids' playroom with crayon drawings taped to the walls. He grabbed a thermos and poured two mugs of coffee and pointed to a chair. "Let me ask you something. Just how much do you know about the residents of Glebe Valley and the Chapelita community?"

Cade sipped the mug. "They're neighbors. What else is there to know?"

Gus seemed to weigh the answer. "Well, then you know a lot of the folks around here are from El Salvador, right?"

Cade nodded. "Yeah, of course, I guess. So?"

"So, you live *in* the community, but you're not *from* the community. Just saying it might help to know more about them if you want to rally them to a cause."

"Actually, I'm just pinch-hitting as a favor to Luis until next week and then someone else takes over." Cade paused, then added with a sly smile, "Maybe you?"

"Hold on." Gus raised his hands. "I'm new at the parish. Got a lot on my plate just now." He looked down at his paint-spattered shorts and added with a sheepish grin, "And on my cargos. I must be mindful of the archbishop looking over my shoulder, making sure I don't screw up while our pastor is recuperating from heart surgery. But I will definitely help out."

It occurred to Cade right then that everybody's got an excuse why they can't lead the protest. First Rita, then Luis, now Gus. Everybody except me. I'm the sucker.

"I promise to make this quick," Gus said, and before Cade could object he plunged ahead. "For starters, did you know Chapelita is the name of a small village on the coast of El Salvador? And that during the civil war, thousands of Salvadorans fled the massacres. Quite a few from Chapelita made it to the States. Some landed here and rented apartments in Glebe Valley. They set up small shops, restaurants, a lot of the businesses you see in the neighborhood. They felt homesick, so they named their new neighborhood Chapelita. Even painted the mural on the side of the community center to remind them of their country."

Cade sighed. He could already tell that any hope of making the church a quick stop was fading fast. "I know the mural," he conceded. "I drive by it every day."

"Well, then you know that the mural depicts a scene from the civil war in El Salvador."

Cade squirmed. "I'm fuzzy on the details."

"Details are important."

Cade checked his watch. "Okay, but can you speed it up? I've got to be on the meter during rush hour."

"*No hay problema.* Besides, the bathrooms need a second coat. I'll tell you about my father, Reuben. It will give you an idea of what the war was really like." And with that, Gus launched into a story about his father, a factory worker in the garment district of San Salvador, a devout Catholic, and how he walked to church one day and found the bodies of fellow factory workers stacked in front of the doors—limbs and faces cut off with machetes. Gus's hand shot up as if marking the height of flood-waters. "A real buzzkill for mass attendance."

"Tough stuff," Cade said, recalling the time his patrol encountered an Iraqi forensic team exhuming a mass grave. The technicians, wearing face masks and protective blue gowns, measured, catalogued, and pho-tographed brown skulls and bits of bones arrayed on a plastic sheet above the ditch. Ragged shreds of clothing clung to skeletal remains. A fibula attached to a running shoe. Preserving evidence for justice that would never be meted out while families kissed the dirt and wept.

Gus continued the story of how Reuben eventually found a safe house where a Jesuit priest offered Catholic mass. The priest denounced the crimes of the government, which oppressed the poor. Indeed, the very cause of their poverty was itself a sin. The government's actions con-demned most Salvadorans to miserable lives of sickness and poverty. And that cause, to nobody's surprise, traced back to a corrupt political system.

"Political corruption, who'd have thought," Cade cracked. "But that was a different situation. From now, I mean."

Gus raised an eyebrow and told how the Jesuit priest exhorted Reuben and the men to stand up for their rights. "The government paid lip service to land redistribution. They held out false hope to keep the campesinos and factory workers from joining the leftist radicals. In the end, they evicted the farmers and turned over their land to rich coffee barons and corporations." Gus paused. "Sort of like the promises of lease termination bonuses and relocation expenses to keep people from protesting too loudly. Sound familiar?"

"Keep going."

"So, the priest tells them it is just to fight back against a corrupt gov-ernment that murdered, raped, and stole from its people." Gus raised his arms. "Liberation! The road to Salvation."

Cade stared at Gus. He'd picked up Bible thumpers before and knew best to ignore them. But this clergyman sounded different. A genuine anger simmered beneath a boyish exuberance.

"What's the matter?" Gus asked. "You never heard of *jus ad bellum?* A just war? Thomas Aquinas?"

Cade rolled his shoulders. "Never heard of him. I've heard of Thomas Martinez."

"Who is Thomas Martinez?"

"Plays third base for the Nats. Power hitter. Bats cleanup."

"Never heard of him, either." Gus retorted with a smile "Thomas Aquinas, on the other hand, said there were three things for a war to be just: right intention, right cause, right authority."

"The three Rs," Cade mumbled.

"You should be writing this down."

"Why?" Cade asked. "Is there going to be a quiz?"

Gus grinned and made a throwaway gesture. "You never know when there could be a test." He resumed the story of how the Jesuit priest told Reuben and the men that they must do something about the security forces snatching men, women, and children off the streets, never to be seen again—*los desaparecido*—the disappeared.

Cade had heard it before, different war, different place. Women came to the FOB Scorpion perimeter fence topped with razor wire to stick photographs of a husband or a son or a daughter, hoping the Army would help to find them. "I get it. I served in Iraq."

Gus's expression shifted. "Oh, I didn't know you were a vet. We have a vets group that meets here once a month." Gus indicated the fellowship hall. "Maybe you'd like to—"

"Father, Gus, whatever, I don't have the time to—"

Gus backed off. "Just thought I'd mention it." Settled on the edge of a desk, he recounted how Reuben started going out at night to secret camps where the guerillas taught tactics and how to handle weapons. After one meeting, Reuben headed home when he heard the rumble of trucks approaching the village. Reuben hid in the shadows and watched soldiers search each house. They brought the men out at gunpoint. The women and children were forced to remain inside. The soldiers asked the men where they were hiding the guns.

"They begged for their lives." Gus held up his hands as if in surrender. "We're farmers, not guerillas. It didn't matter. They stood them against a wall and shot them in the head. One soldier yanked a man's head up." Gus's flat hand went up and down in quick succession. "Chop, chop, chop."

Cade adopted the middle-distance stare he'd acquired from seeing too many brothers-in-arms cut down by bombs and rockets.

"Then they set fire to the houses." Gus's voice cracked. "When the women and kids ran out, they shot them too. Reuben watched a soldier toss a baby into the air and catch it on a bayonet." Gus made the sign of the cross.

Cade lowered his eyes, repulsed at the memories of dismembered children who had picked up bombs disguised as toys. How could men inflict such unimaginable evil on fellow human beings? "Pardon me, Father, but—"

"Gus, remember."

"Take me back to what this has to do with the people getting kicked out of Glebe Valley."

Gus studied a child's drawing of a stick family holding hands outside a house with trees and birds and a smiling sun. "Once again, we are confronting sin. Only this time URP is the oppressor, conspiring with the city to go after the homes in Glebe Valley. The times are different, but the results are the same. The Glebe land grab is just the latest in a long line of insults to the dignity of the people of Chapelita. I can't stand by and watch it happen again. Jesus Christ stands with the people of Chapelita."

"So, you're on board?" Cade said.

Gus placed his left hand on Cade's shoulder. "The Lord says do justice and deliver from the hand of the oppressor him who has been robbed. Jeremiah, chapter twenty-two, verse three."

"I'll take that as a yes."

"One more thing." Gus reached into his cargo shorts and pulled out a small leather-bound journal with an embossed gold cross on the front.

"I write things down from time to time, pieces of scripture, ideas for future sermons. Folks in this parish find solace and inspiration in the Bible. You never know. Might come in handy someday."

Cade pushed it back. "No, really, I can't—"

"Please, take it off my hands," Father Gus insisted. "I have ten more in my room."

Cade slid the journal into the back pocket of his jeans. "Let me ask you something personal, if you don't mind."

Gus smiled. "Go ahead."

"Just wondering, why did you become, you know—"

"A priest?" Gus added. "Unfinished business, perhaps. What Reuben could not accomplish through the war I thought maybe I could help through reconciliation. I ministered at a local church in San Salvador for three years. Even visited the real Chapelita. Mountains slope down to some of the most beautiful beaches along the Pacific coast you've ever seen. Excellent surf, by the way, at El Cuco."

The shift from massacre to surf confused Cade as if Gus had flipped channels from news to sports. "You surfed while you were there?"

"Are you kidding? Let me show you something." Gus led Cade down the hallway to a storage closet. "I don't have room for this in my rectory apartment." He unlocked the door and, with a showman's flourish, exclaimed, "Check this baby out!"

Inside the closet was the biggest surfboard Cade had ever seen—tall as a redwood.

"Nine feet four inches. A Dewey Weber Performer, very rare. Best nose rider ever made." Gus thrust out his arms and bent at the knees. "El Cuco was perfect for beginners like me. Surf's a little mushy, but you get the occasional hollow barrel, good for two hundred yards or more. I surfed in the morning, built a school during the day, then celebrated mass and mojitos on the beach at sunset. I was in the zone, man. Can't wait to go back."

Cade gaped at cans of Mr. Zog's Sex Wax.

"It's not what you think." Gus laughed. "It's wax for the board. Best stuff around."

Watching him lock up the longboard, Cade figured Father Gus to be more free spirit than holy spirit. Back in the playroom, Cade's gaze lingered on a buxom blonde in a red swimsuit and high heels.

"She likes to surf too," said Gus.

Cade stammered, "What?"

"Malibu Barbie."

He laughed to hide his embarrassment. "Not my type. You know something, Father, I drive for a living, and right now I ain't making a dime."

"Call me Gus. Save the Father bit for confession."

"Not going to happen."

"That's what they all say."

The windowless room lacked fresh air. Cade craned his neck in search of a fan. Instead, his gaze landed on a crucifix above the door.

"Nobody was spared."

"Excuse me?" Cade said. Gus had flipped channels again.

"Nuns and priests. Just like the Jesuit who inspired the villagers to fight back. Eventually, the government came after them, too. I visited the garden where six Jesuit priests were gunned down at Central American University in 1989 by a unit of the Salvadoran Army." He locked eyes with Cade. "A unit, incidentally, trained by the US military. The government claimed the priests were rebel sympathizers. The Army tried to blame the FMLN for the murders."

"FMLN?"

The Farabundo Martí National Liberation Front, a coalition of guerrilla groups that banded together to fight the government. "Unlike the Chapelita Coalition for Justice, these guys were the real deal. Guerillas, rebels, insurgents—whatever you want to call them."

Cade gritted his teeth. In Iraq, he was instructed that the insurgents were Saddam loyalists carrying out brutal attacks against the citizenry. But the insurgent label was a vague descriptor and didn't make it any easier to pick the enemy out of a crowd. In the end, insurgents could be good or bad, depending on which side of the war you were on. Either way, blood ran in the streets.

"Only these rebels had money and guns from Castro," Gus added.

The Castro name clicked. Fidel backed the Salvadoran rebels. Rita Castro was supporting the Glebe Valley tenants, many from Salvador. Castro a common name. Probably stupid to even think about a connection.

Gus continued, "After murdering the priests, the Army left behind a sign that read *'Victory or death'* to try to frame the rebels. They accused the FMLN of executing the spies who turned on them. Nobody believed it, of course. The guerrillas demanded the equitable distribution of the land. The United States cried Marxism. First Cuba, then El Salvador, Nicaragua, and soon all the dominos in South America would fall to the communists. Ring any bells?"

Cade connected the dots between the equitable distribution of land and spatial justice. Maybe Arthur A. Arthur was an insurgent, too. Why not? It seemed to be trending. "I get what you're saying," Cade said. "But I'm just trying to rally people to show up at a zoning hearing. We're not dealing with bodies in the street."

"Maybe not," Gus said, "but we're dealing with people's lives all the same. There may not be another opportunity, to turn things around, I mean."

Cade bit his lip. There were no do-overs in Iraq either. No second chances. No forgiveness. How could there be? There was nobody alive who could forgive him even if they wanted to, which they didn't. Forgive yourself, the chaplain had said to him. Really? How does that work? You fuck up big-time and then forgive yourself. Good luck with that. Whatever *it* was that manifested itself in his night terrors wasn't about to forgive him, not for a second.

"Are you all right?" Gus asked. "You zoned out for a second."

"A slight headache, that's all."

"I've got some aspirin if—"

"Naw, I'm fine, fine."

Gus eyed Cade. "Anyway, to wrap it up, Reuben fought with the guerrillas until he got sick of the bloodshed. He fled to the United States and ended up in Akron, remarried, and raised a family. Including yours truly."

"Is he still in Akron?"

"Passed away last year. Lung cancer."

"I'm sorry," Cade said, standing. "Look, I gotta go. I'll be in touch, soon. If you need to reach me, my info is on the flyer." Cade gave Gus a quick handshake and hurried out of the basement, relieved to be back in the fresh air and sunshine.

Stumbling upon Father Gus in a church basement had been a stroke of good luck. He'd bring an avenging God to the coalition team to bat cleanup, a power hitter. How could they possibly lose?

* * *

Cade drove for a few more hours and then hurried back to Cassandra's salon for the promised dinner, anxious to tell her about his meeting with Father Gus. The "Closed" sign hung in the window. He rapped lightly, but no one answered. He turned the unlocked door and entered the darkened salon. A yellow light drew him to the back office.

Two wine goblets sat on a small lacquered table, along with a flickering candle. Cade sniffed sandalwood incense. Cassandra emerged from the shadows wearing a black sleeveless shift that reached to her bare feet. Her arms encircled his neck as she pulled him toward her.

"Ouch!" Cade cried. "Look out for my ribs."

"Oh no, I'm sorry. I forgot." Cassandra gestured to a large pillow. "Sit."

Cade gingerly lowered himself to the cushion and opened a bottle of chardonnay icing in a mop pail. "And I *forgot* to bring the Red Stripe."

Over the next hour, they ate jerk chicken, drank wine, and talked. Cade told Cassandra about Father Gus and showed her the leather journal with the embossed cross. Despite Gus's encouragement, he lamented that the fight against URP seemed hopeless. Mick Finn had the deal locked up.

Cassandra lifted a goblet to her lips. "Coward."

Cade flinched. "What did you just call me?"

"Not you, Finn." Cassandra laughed. "He hides behind URP's money and lawyers." She patted his arm. "You should have seen the expression on your face."

Relieved, Cade gazed at Cassandra at rest upon the pillow in a lotus position, her shift gathered in folds. Candlelight shadows danced upon the walls. Maybe it was the interplay of wine and incense, but for the briefest of moments, he would have sworn she levitated.

He told Cassandra about how Earl Everhard was pushing the chamber of commerce to support the new development and how he planned to benefit from the new project by moving his tax prep business to the new Glebe retail space. "What a sleazeball."

Cassandra looked at her wine goblet.

"What's the matter? You don't agree Earl is a sleazeball?"

The yellow flame cast Cassandra in a chiaroscuro of light and shadow, her features a contrast in strength and vulnerability. "I need to tell you something. I'm moving the salon."

"I know. You mentioned that earlier. Where to, out to the burbs?"

She held Cade's eyes. "I have a lease option on the Glebe. It's a great opportunity, I can't pass it up."

Astonishment blanketed Cade's face. "What? I don't believe it. I *can't* believe it. You're siding with Earl?"

"I must think about my future, too," Casandra said softly, almost a whisper.

Cade shifted position on the floor and stared at the ceiling, hands laced behind his head. "I don't get it; how can you possibly afford to move in there? From what I'm hearing the rents will be sky high."

She raised her goblet. "I'm doing okay. I picked up a new sideline, psychic stock picks. I already have over one hundred subscribers." Cassandra leaned forward and whispered, "You wouldn't believe the money pouring into the cannabis sector. Get in now while prices are low."

"Thanks for the tip. How much do I owe you?"

She slid down next to Cade. "Don't be angry." Her hand roamed gently across his chest. "Do you think *I'm* a sleazeball too?"

"Definitely not." He continued staring at the ceiling.

Her hand reached his belt buckle. "We can still be friends, can't we?"

"I guess."

Cassandra snuggled close. "Also, gold will hit $5,000 an ounce."

He reached over and snuffed the candle. "Careful of my ribs."

* * *

Hours past midnight, Cade dropped Cassandra off at her apartment in Glebe Valley. Back at his place, he decided on a quick email check before bed. When he logged on, he grinned. "Holy shit!" He had 135 unopened emails.

11

*T*he London headquarters of Urban Renaissance Partners occupied a palatial town mansion once owned by Sir Albert Oldcastle, a member of Parliament in the eighteenth century. The house fronted Saint James Square in the heart of the West End district. Robert Oliver faced a window overlooking forty-five acres of leafy commons, the equestrian statue of William III barely discernible through the canopy of green.

And just a few blocks away, the offices of Shipton & Shipton, a niche architectural firm that specialized in parking garages, where he'd started his career designing concrete storage boxes for cars. After a few dreadfully tedious years, he returned to Cambridge and received a Master of Philosophy degree in urban planning.

Around that time, a Cambridge professor told him that the New Labour Party needed people from many disciplines to think about innovative ways to redevelop old industrial sites and abandoned warehouses. A hodgepodge of politicians, city planners, artists, social activists, and business leaders attended the meetings. People tossed around words like rebirth and revival without embarrassment. The conversation turned to new democratic institutions leading the way toward more inclusive planning, design, and growth. A grand synthesis of capitalism and community-led partnerships breaking down the barriers of exclusion: poverty, education, jobs. Nothing less than a compassionate rebalancing of the social compact—not right wing, not left wing, but a Third Way. They toasted, drank, and slapped each other on the back. The urban renaissance movement was born.

Oliver had felt genuinely alive for the first time in his life. He was riding the exhilarating crest of social change. He volunteered to work *pro bono* on reclaiming a decrepit portside warehouse for new housing for citizens struggling on the edge of destitution. But it soon became clear that *pro bono* consulting would not pay the bills for his ambitious start-up firm. He justified the need to bulk up the private equity side of the business for a few years. Then he could afford to rejoin the march to an inclusive urban renaissance. But as the commissions and investments poured in, the return to inclusivity kept getting postponed.

And now, with URP on the verge of a quantum leap in urban development, it was more important than ever to keep the private equity spigot flowing. But the confidence of the Glebe's financial partners could be at risk due to a low-life rotter dragging the name of Urban Renaissance Partners through the mud.

Oliver held a printout of an email from Bill Ashpole, the attorney representing Saint Andrew's on the strip mall purchase. At the top, the flyer read SAVE CHAPELITA! Underneath, the time and date of the zoning hearing and a telephone number and email address for jcade1450. Oliver recalled Finn's smug assurance of no surprises on the Glebe project.

But the irritation with Finn did not stop there. The rhetoric on the flyer was all too familiar. The right-to-remain crowd. The malcontents were cropping up all over the world, like mushrooms after rain. Now the parasites had spread to Glebe Valley. Goddamn freeloaders. Living off the contributions of others. Nothing but Marxist redistributors.

He'd heard reports that their poster boy, Arthur A. Arthur, had besmirched his name at a conference in Washington, DC. Even had the gall to call him a bloody snakehead while projecting a picture of a snake eating its tail. Balderdash! Arthur was nothing more than a parasite himself, a damn anarchist, egging people to buy his books and oppose development projects while he sat back and collected the royalties. Right to remain—socialist rubbish. And why the hell didn't Mick Finn keep him abreast of these developments?

Oliver hit speaker on the desk phone and pushed a button.

A woman responded, "Yes, Mr. Oliver?"

"Margaret, book me a flight to Dulles Airport."

"Yes, Mr. Oliver. When would you like to go?"

"Tomorrow. And call the local office. Tell Finn to be there when I arrive."

* * *

Mick Finn had a 1:00 PM appointment with the city attorney. The office, located in a municipal monstrosity, commemorated Virginia's forty-ninth governor, Elbert Lee Trinkle. The merciless concrete bunker with gun slit windows stuck out as a classic example of brutal brutalism.

Inside, he saw the locals lined up in front of three bulletproof transaction windows paying fines. Finn mused: no doubt for loitering and public urination. The sooner these miscreants vacated Glebe Valley the better. A sign pointed right for the courtrooms, left for city offices. He found the outer door for the city attorney, Stephen S. Slegg, and walked in. Behind the counter, a young receptionist read a fashion magazine.

"May I help you?" she inquired, not looking up from the magazine.

"Name is Finn. I have a one o'clock with Slegg."

"I'll let him know you're here."

Finn checked email. Nothing new in the last ten seconds.

"You may go in now," the receptionist announced, her eyes fixed on a mascara ad.

Finn opened the interior door to the private office. City Attorney Stephen S. Slegg stood by a bookcase. Rail thin with an unfortunate comb-over, Slegg's suit hung loosely on a bony frame like a coat hanger.

"Mick," he said without cheer, "what brings you down?"

"This," Finn said, holding out the orange flyer.

Slegg gave the flyer a cursory glance. "So?"

"So, they're all over the neighborhood. Some jerk is planning a rally at the zoning hearing next week. Coming on top of the machete attack, we don't need more negative media on Glebe Valley."

Slegg slid a periodical into the bookcase. "Well, there's nothing I can do about it." He walked back to his chair and propped his feet on the desk.

"Zee 9, remember?" Finn said evenly. "It's called a *special* exception for a reason. Do something *special*." He withdrew a newspaper from a leather briefcase and pushed it toward Slegg. An envelope peeked out of the fold.

Finn's eyes roamed over Slegg's law school diploma from Prairie Schooner University, which paled next to his pedigree from the University of Chicago Law School, along with double masters in real estate law and finance. It pained him immensely that the progress of the Glebe rested in the hands of a hookworm from PSU. "I'm sure you can figure out a way to keep things running smoothly."

Ignoring the newspaper, Slegg removed his steel-rimmed glasses and commenced cleaning the lenses with his silk tie. "Did it occur to you to find out who jcade1450 is before you came here? Did you try the phone number?"

Finn returned a blank expression.

"You didn't, did you? Look, Mick—"

Finn jumped up. "No, you look, Slegg. URP has $500 million riding on this zoning application. Not to mention a sizeable tax base for a city hemorrhaging money. I expect *you* to find out who the hell jcade1450 is. And don't let some bullshit Coalition for Justice create a disturbance. Bring in extra security. Do whatever you have to do to make sure we get approval."

Eyeing the edge of the envelope, Slegg said, "It's in everyone's interest to make this go smoothly. I'll do my best."

"I don't want your best." Finn snapped the briefcase shut. "I want it done." He walked out, leaving the inner door ajar.

* * *

Slegg shut the interior door and thumbed the stack of hundreds inside the envelope before dialing Sheriff Donnelly's cell.

"Donnelly here."

"I need you to find someone for me."

"Name?"

"Not completely sure," Slegg said. "Can you get it from a phone number? I need a full background."

"Give it to me."

Slegg relayed the number on the flyer. "Keep this between us. And if it will help connect a name, his email handle is jcade1450."

12

*F*inn hunched over the staff report from the Planning and Zoning Commission, checking and double-checking every ordinance, deed restriction, and site requirement for The Glebe at Cub Run. The intense preparation helped him anticipate any eventuality, including anything that jcade1450 and his minions might throw at him.

He'd dealt with NIMBYs before, even the more extreme types—the CAVE dwellers: Citizens Against Virtually Everything. He'd received letters of support from the chamber of commerce, distinguished members of Saint Andrew's Episcopal Church Board of Trustees, and of course, many well-heeled neighbors in Hampton Hills.

And if more ammunition was needed, he had a back pocket of concessions ready to go: *Why yes, we would be happy to include an apartment locator service. Yes, we'll sponsor a résumé writing class. Yes, we'll donate green space. Yes! Yes! Yes!*

Nothing left to chance, including the token of appreciation he'd hand-delivered to Slegg with instructions to keep the riffraff from disrupting the zoning hearing. Putting aside thoughts of jcade1450, Finn rehearsed responses to any question the P&Z or opponents might hurl his way, paying close attention to pacing and pauses for dramatic effect.

When the eventual displacement question arose, he would tout the generous package of relocation expenses and termination bonuses to free the tenants of the worry and anxiety a change of residence can cause. Highly trained customer-centric "move managers" would coordinate the myriad details from move-out to move-in (with emphasis on *move-out*).

Locked and loaded, Finn could reel off the Glebe's advanced design features: respect for historical precedent, high-quality architectural aesthetics, and affordable housing set-asides. All backed up by URP's guarantee of environmental sustainability, complete with rain gardens and eco-friendly building materials. A green dream come true. The Glebe at Cub Run would be a total immersion experience, elevating the mind and body connections of the urban lifestyle.

Moving from aesthetics to the practical, Finn knew the numbers by heart: the jobs created, traffic counts, and most important to the P&Z, the additional tax revenue the project would generate. The deal would soon be sitting on Robert Oliver's desk with a bow. Zee 9, baby!

Finn rubbed his eyes. The desk phone buzzed.

"There's a Sheriff Donnelly here to see you," said the receptionist.

Irked at the interruption, Finn snapped, "So, escort him back."

"He'd rather you came out to the desk."

Finn hung up. *Christ, now what?*

The sheriff wore a tight-fitting khaki uniform and had blonde hair styled high and tight in a military cut. Finn extended his hand. "I'm Finn."

The sheriff placed a manila envelope in Finn's outstretched hand.

"What's this?" Finn smirked. "A summons?"

"Just delivering a package." The sheriff turned toward the elevator bank. Finn waited until the doors hissed shut before he extracted a thin folder with a business card from the city attorney's office. Slegg had come through quickly, and with an impressive courier to boot. Maybe Slegg could be counted on after all. He carried the file back to his office. Inside the envelope, a single sheet of paper with neatly printed information:

John Mortimer Cade – aka Jack

Residence: Glebe Valley Apartments, Building 5, #301

Divorced. No children.

Police record: Assault and battery charges pressed by the Metroland Taxi Company involving an attempt to unionize the cab drivers. Charges dismissed. No priors.

Sole proprietor of the Green Flash Taxi Company.

Military service – Staff Sergeant, United States Army, Military Transition Team, Forward Operating Base Scorpion, Iraq. Three deployments.

Awarded the Purple Heart and Bronze Star.

Court-martial—Bad Conduct Discharge.

Finn puzzled: bad conduct discharge? What the hell was that all about? A driver's license photo showed an unsmiling man with a shock of red hair and a lumberjack beard. A spray of brown freckles dotted a narrow face with a sharp nose protruding at an acute angle. *Big Red!* Finn instantly recognized the jerk who had disrupted the community meeting and thrown the chair across the floor.

A light rap on the office door drew Finn's attention. "Come in."

CFO Beth Daniels entered and made herself comfortable in a chair. Her nylons swished as she crossed her legs. "Guess who's coming to dinner?"

Finn rubbed his face. "I'm not in the mood, Beth."

"Robert Oliver. Flying in tomorrow. Word is he knows about the Glebe protest, and he's not too happy he didn't hear about it from you."

Finn looked out the window, suddenly worried that Oliver planned to fire him personally. Put on a big show. Intimidate everybody in the office. If word got out on the street that Oliver had canned him, he might be too radioactive to catch on with another top-tier firm.

"Nothing I can do about it now." Finn sighed.

"Just a heads-up." Beth slid the door shut as she left.

Finn shifted his attention back to the photographs in the envelope. Another glossy photo showed Cade leaning against a green metal-flake cab glowing with the radiance of a million tiny suns. Exactly like the metal flakes he'd found on the front bumper of his black Lexus sedan. Finn stared at the photograph. "Paybacks are hell, Sergeant Cade."

13

*R*ibs newly sore after the workout with Cassandra, Cade felt too wired to sleep. More than three hours had passed before he finished replying to all 135 emails requesting information about the zoning protest. Neighbors, shop owners, total strangers expressed gratitude that someone had stepped up to lead the community.

The old excitement of planning a mission returned: *Plan, Prepare, Execute.* Only this time instead of a house-to-house sweep, the mission meant rallying folks to hang on to their homes. Not all that different from the jundi he trained in Iraq—like Zaid.

With a slender build and a neatly groomed mustache, Zaid had looked more like a clerk than a soldier. But he was always eager to tell his story to anyone who would listen. And one morning, Zaid told it to Cade at breakfast at FOB Scorpion with Malik listening in. Cade chewed as an interpreter translated.

Zaid called himself a Marsh Arab. For generations, his family had planted a small rice plot in the lush marshlands that lay between the Tigris and Euphrates rivers along the southern border with Iran. Called the Garden of Eden, the marshlands became a haven for refugees escaping persecution by Saddam Hussein. In retaliation, Hussein drained the marshes and burnt the village where Zaid's family had lived for many generations. At the end of the story, the interpreter turned to Cade. "Zaid says he wants to rebuild his marsh home someday. But right now, he just wants to kill the bastards who wiped out his village."

Some of the emails Cade had just read had expressed a similar sentiment about the URP bastards. He walked over to the bookcase and pulled out a paperback. Tucked between the pages was a photograph of Cade, Zaid, and Malik leaning on a Humvee, weapons at their side, shit-eating grins spread across their faces. This was the good-natured, easygoing Malik before they had their falling out over the jundi Cade'd ordered to run laps in hundred-degree weather. Malik had a degree in electrical engineering and spoke English. When Zaid finished his sad story, Malik had pressed a small square of cloth into Cade's hands. The cloth displayed horizontal bands of red, white, and black. Green Arabic script ran across the white middle band. Cade recognized the Iraqi flag. He fingered the green script and asked, "What's this mean?"

"*Allahu Akbar,*" Malik said. "It means God is greater." Pointing to the flag, he said, "The black band stands for oppression, overcome by blood, which is the red band. The white stands for Iraq's bright future."

Cade pocketed the flag while making a mental note to pick up a soccer ball for Malik's son. Lawrence Article #16: *Never receive a present without giving a liberal return.*

Malik continued shoveling in the hash browns and added his two cents to Zaid's story. Malik's family had had a farm, too—south of Baghdad. One day the insurgents camped on his family's land. A tank leveled their house. The insurgents dug up the fields and planted mines. Now the family could no longer grow anything on it. Malik had joined the Army to avenge his family's honor.

Cade turned off the computer. Malik and Zaid had lost family homes. A tragedy, but only a drop in the ocean compared to the tens of thousands of Iraqis who lost or fled homes, destroyed during the war. Squatter camps sprang up on private property without sanitation or water. Hot, dry winds carried the stench of burning excrement. On patrols, he'd passed makeshift homes built of mud and tin. Families camped in tents on traffic islands. The jundi complained about corrupt officials conspiring with bankers to drive the squatters out and redevelop the land.

The Army, as usual, had the exact right slang for it—SSDD. Same shit, different day. Like Salvadoran *campesinos* evicted from farms coveted by rich coffee barons; or Finn unzipping his fly and piss-marking Glebe Valley for development. SSDD.

Cade had taken the liberty of telling everyone to rally at the Chapelita Community Center an hour before the hearing. The Planning and Zoning Commission met in an office located a few short blocks away in the Elbert Lee Trinkle Municipal Building. Only one minor detail remained. Luis's permission to use the Chapelita Center.

* * *

Luis convulsed awake at the image of feral dogs gnawing bloodied corpses. The damp bedsheets were a tangled mess. His cell phone chimed: 2:03 AM.

He answered, listened for a moment, then grumbled, "No, absolutely not, forget it."

"Who is it?" Angie asked, her voice muffled by a pillow.

"It's Cade. Go back to sleep." Luis carried the cell to the sofa in the living room. Venetian blinds threw trapezoidal bars across the parquet floor. "You should've checked first before you promised a hundred people to show up at my center."

"A hundred and thirty-five to be precise," Cade said.

"I've got GED classes scheduled at that time. And no way we can get that many people in the center. Fire marshal would be all over my ass."

"Come on, Luis," Cade pleaded. "I let you drag me into this thing. Where am I supposed to hold a rally for over a hundred people?"

"Nobody dragged you into anything," Luis said. "And why the hell are you calling me in the middle of the night to spring this on me?"

Cade backpedaled. "Sorry, man, I got carried away with the emails. Are you in on this protest thing or not?"

"I can't talk right now. Call me tomorrow." Luis ended the call and moved to the bathroom. In the mirror, he saw the faded tattoo on his right biceps: an angel brandishing a flaming sword, with the words underneath *Escuadron de la Muerte*. Death Squad. Making the Chapelita Center ground zero for the protest rally would be risky. The spotlight might spill over onto him, with reporters asking too many questions. Finding things that didn't need to be found. Such as, where was Luis Guzmán on the evening of November 16, 1989?

* * *

The cool November air blew across the face of seventeen-year-old Private Luis Guzmán huddled in the back of a pickup racing toward the campus of the Central American University—one of four troop-laden vehicles speeding through empty streets. Gray clouds scudded across the night sky, hiding the waning gibbous moon. The trucks skidded to a halt at the entrance to the campus. The soldiers jumped out amidst a clatter of rifles. An officer barked an order to proceed to the pastoral center.

Fifty soldiers surrounded the low-slung, whitewashed residence. On command, the men started pounding on the doors and windows and walls, clamoring for the priests to come out. Luis watched as a man opened the front door. Officers and soldiers barged in, pushing the man aside.

An officer ordered Luis to stand guard outside the door. He heard shouts from inside the dwelling. A few moments passed, and five middle-age disheveled men filed out at gunpoint. An order came for the priests to lie face down in the rose garden. A zephyr from the west carried a scent of jasmine and honey.

Five shots rang out in quick succession. From inside the residence, Luis heard a woman scream, followed by more gunshots. The final toll: six Jesuit priests executed, along with the housekeeper and her sixteen-year-old daughter.

Angie called out from the bedroom, "Luis, come back to bed."

Luis shook off the memory. "In a minute." In the kitchen, he poured a glass of milk. He recalled a newspaper article a year or two ago about one of the officers involved in the executions. The officer was deported by immigration officials from his home outside Los Angeles. The man had been living a respectable life with a wife and kids and a job at an auto parts store. Not so different from the quiet life Luis had built in Chapelita after narrowly escaping the Truth Commission investigations.

Now things seemed to be heating up again. Rita's inflammatory language about fighting capitalist oppressors. In the Army, Luis had been on the side of the government, destroying the leftist opposition. Except now, with Rita and Cade, it seemed like he was on the side of the guerrillas. Not wanting to keep Angie awake with his thrashing, he opted to stretch out on the sofa. Headlight beams swept across the ceiling. He desperately wanted to talk to someone who would understand the events of that terrible night. Someone who could keep a secret. But who?

* * *

After calling Luis, Cade searched the dirty shirt pile to find the scrap of paper with Rita's telephone number. If he was going to walk point, then he damn well wanted backup. He could count on Grif. Luis seemed oddly hesitant. Father Gus might turn the protest into a religious revival. Rita had experience and said to call if help was needed.

He punched the numbers. The call was about to go to voicemail when a drowsy voice answered, "Hello."

"Rita, it's me, Cade."

Silence.

Cade thought he heard the snap and click of a lighter. "Glebe Valley? The Green Flash?"

"What time is it?" she asked.

"Zero two three zero," Cade answered with military precision.

"What the hell time is that?"

"Never mind. Good news. I've got a rally planned for the day of the Glebe hearing. A hundred-fifty RSVPs and counting." A stretch, but Cade figured the promise of a big turnout might get her attention. "Haven't got a location nailed down yet, but Luis and I are working on it. Shouldn't be a problem." It was *already* a problem. "You were a great inspiration to Luis and me. I thought you might like to be here in person for this one. You know, maybe say a few words."

Cade pictured the orange tip of a cigarette, gray smoke shooting from Rita's nostrils like contrails of jet exhaust.

"Maybe. I have to check on a few things first."

"No problem." Then he sweetened the offer. "Hey, remember the Marlins are in town the Saturday after the hearing? Playing a double-header with the Nats. My treat. What do you say?" He told himself that inviting Rita to a baseball game was strictly an enticement to join the protest. Technically, it didn't count as a date. Even though he didn't believe in Cassandra's psychic powers, he had to admit she had uncanny intuition. The risk that she would pick up an unfaithful vibe was a toss-up. What the hell, he needed the help.

"I'll let you know." Rita hung up.

Disgusted, Cade threw the cell on the sofa. He must have sounded like a hard-up school boy. Rita radiated sexual heat—like his ex-wife Lisa when they'd first met. He'd spied her at a bar outside Fort Pickett, Virginia—a cue stick in one hand, a Bud Light in the other. Faded blue jeans tucked into Western boots of python snakeskin. Her camisole rode up in the back as she leaned over the table and banked the three ball in a side pocket. Dirty blonde hair buzzed around the ears in faux hawk fashion projected a rebellious streak— outlaw country meets punk rocker—an edgy combo that went well with Waylon on the juke. Six months later they were married. It was fun for a while when all they did was party and screw. But after he deployed, he changed, becoming consumed with day-to-day survival while Lisa yammered on and on about a woman in the next cubicle who wore too much perfume. He began to realize how little they had in common. Sometimes he wondered if he knew her at all. On their webcasts, he learned to be patient and nod, the distance between them not measured in miles.

When he finally made it back to Virginia, the welcome home sex was hot, like when they'd first dated. But then his reliance on painkillers and booze led to stupid fights over meaningless slights. The more time they spent together, the more he wanted to be alone. He lost interest in sex, save for the occasional soapy release in the shower. At first, Lisa was patient and understanding, but Cade was relentless. He criticized everything she did—from the food she cooked to the money she spent.

When the meds ran out, he didn't refill. Lack of sleep increased his irritability. Then came the migraines. He was miserable, and so was Lisa. Hungover one morning, Cade called her a selfish bitch. With tears streaming down her cheeks, Lisa screamed, "Can't you just love me for who I am?"

Cade shot back, "Well, who the fuck are you?"

One night, he returned home after a binge and found Lisa had moved out. Clothes, cosmetics, everything—gone. Wedding album pictures lay shredded and scattered like leaves across the floor. A week later, the divorce papers arrived in the mail. He crumpled the lawyer's letter and roared with such blasphemy that it startled the neighbors.

The old memory rattled Cade with remorse. He headed to bed. His mind wandered to a more recent and pleasant encounter—his date with Cassandra. The candlelight and wine. The synchronization of hips. Something beyond the occasional hookup was taking shape. Something solid, maybe permanent. However, Cassandra's ability to read emanations was like a damn polygraph. His aura would spike off the charts if he attempted to explain a ballgame with Rita as a business expense. He'd worry about that later. For now, he closed his eyes and relived the evening with Cassandra in glorious high-definition detail.

* * *

Rita stubbed the cigarette in the ashtray on the nightstand. Never for a moment had she thought Cade would step up and organize the zoning protest. But the son of a bitch had rounded up 150 people. Or so he said. She'd call Luis in the morning and verify. But on the off-chance Cade was telling the truth, she hit autodial.

Tomás answered on the first tone. "Wassup, babe? Booty call?"

"You wish. Heads-up. I may need you to fly to DC on short notice."

"What's happening in DC?"

"Robert Oliver is wrapping up another deal here. Need you to be ready."

"I'm ready now."

"I'll say when. There are a few loose ends. A local guy, a cab driver no less, is organizing a protest. And get this, the poor jerk has a crush on me."

"Hmmm, I'm jealous. How about I do him for no extra charge?"

"No, he might be useful to get us close to Oliver. I can work him to our advantage." Rita tapped another cigarette from the pack. "This time, we're going to cut off the snakehead for good."

* * *

Cade nursed a third Jack Daniel's and Coke on the rocks. On the muted TV above the bar, the Nats were losing to the Braves 4–2 in the thirteenth inning. Other than a nearby couple at a table, the place was dead. Tuesdays were always slow at the Alamo.

Rita had said she would call today, but that was twenty-two hours ago, so technically the day was not over. Call if you need help, she had said. *Total bullshit*—the Jack Daniel's taking hold. Well, he would do it without her, with help from Luis, Father Gus, and Grif. Fuck Rita. And fuck the goddamn Marlins.

Behind the bar hung portraits of the Alamo's heroes: Bowie, Travis, and Crockett. He imagined how the rebels must have felt: outmanned, outgunned, ready to die for Texas independence, but praying for a miracle. A slab of pine, engraved with wood-burnt lettering, displayed the last words of Lieutenant Colonel William Barrett Travis from a letter smuggled out to the People of Texas & All Americans in the World: *Victory or Death.*

Victory or Death—again. Father Gus had said the Salvadoran Army tried to make it look like it was the rebels who murdered the six Jesuit priests by forging a sign that read *Victory or Death.* What was it about men who cast their fate in such stark choices? How about a negotiated settlement? Less bloodshed. Cade raised his glass and toasted Travis and the boys.

But he was still angry at himself for calling Rita in the middle of the night, sounding needy, like he couldn't pull off the protest without help. "Fucking moron," Cade said to no one.

At the other end of the bar, Tony toweled glasses. "Talking to your invisible friend again?"

Cade flipped Tony the bird and feigned interest in the baseball game. A commercial break teased the local news coming up. The machete logo behind the newscaster signaled the lead story was still the savage attack that took place a few blocks down the street.

Tony walked to Cade's end of the bar. "How goes it?"

"Not bad."

Tony looked up at the Nats' pitcher. "Is he the fucking moron?"

"Huh? What? No. Are you kidding? What have they lost now, like thirteen games in a row?"

"Fourteen after tonight. The Nats are chasing the '61 Phillies' record of twenty-three consecutive losses."

Cade tapped the empty glass. "I wish them luck."

Tony mixed a fourth JD and Coke. "So?"

"So what?"

"So, who's the moron?"

Cade sipped the drink. "Me, I'm the fucking moron."

"What's new about that?"

Cade smiled, then laid out a condensed version of events with URP, the city, and his efforts to round up folks for the hearing.

"Yeah, I heard about the project," said Tony. "Near where that kid got hacked."

Cade nodded.

"It's hard enough to get people to come out on a weeknight," Tony said. "Now a frigging gang has practically driven everybody off the street. Business is down. Can't the cops nail this guy?"

"They don't know who they're looking for, I guess."

"That's not what I hear. A guy in here the other day says the cops know exactly who done it."

"What are you talking about?" Cade asked. "I ain't heard that on the news."

"They're keeping it quiet. You know the guy who runs the Chapelita Center?"

"Luis? Course I know him."

"His son, Enzo. Police figure him for the machete murder."

Now Luis's anger over the cops asking about Enzo made sense. Cade's first thought had been a parole violation. Enzo was in a whole different league of badass. "Who told you this?"

"A guy. Does it matter?"

Cade slugged the JD and laid down three bills. "I'm out of here." The couple at the table was gone. On a slow night at the Alamo, with no reinforcements in sight, he was the last man standing.

"Watch yourself driving," Tony warned with a wave.

Cade returned a left-handed salute. "Victory or Death."

A glance at the TV showed the final score: Atlanta 4, Nationals 3.

* * *

Cade squealed onto Washington Avenue, barely missing a car parked at the curb. He swerved into the oncoming lane and then jerked the wheel back. He had things to do: call Luis in the morning and buck up his friend, take his mind off Enzo; get that red warning light on the dashboard checked; swing by Cassandra's.

He cranked up the volume on his cab-driving anthem: The Doors' *Roadhouse Blues* and sang along with Morrison's voice, ravaged by cigarettes and booze, "Keep your eyes on the road, your hands upon the wheel"—until rudely interrupted by blue and white lights flashing in the rearview mirror.

Shit!

Cade pulled to the side of the road, the cruiser on his bumper. He switched off the ignition and watched a darkened figure in the rearview. *What the hell is he doing? Probably running a check on my tags. Maybe it's just a taillight or expired plates.*

At last, a woman officer swaggered up to Cade's window. Her duty belt displayed a holster and firearm, ammo pouch, flashlight, baton holder, handcuffs, pepper spray, electronic control device, and walkie-talkie.

Cade's first thought: *Why do cops need all this shit?*

His second thought: *Christ, I have to piss.*

"License and registration, please."

Cade popped the glove compartment. "It's in here. Hold on, Officer."

While Cade's fingers roamed the glove box, the officer asked, "Do you know why I pulled you over?"

Cade had a clever comeback, but played it straight. "Yeah, I guess I might have been going a little fast back there, huh? Kind of late though, not much traffic."

The officer carried his license and registration back to the cruiser. Cade's bladder was ready to burst. All he could think was: *How long does it take to write a goddamn speeding ticket? Jeezus, could you possibly move any slower?*

She returned with Cade's license and registration pinned to a clipboard. "Have you been drinking tonight, Mr. Cade?"

Here we go. "Well, I had a beer or two," Cade lied, wondering if that fourth JD and Coke had pushed his blood alcohol level into the abandon-all-hope tier of DUI. His license would be suspended. Plus, a fine he couldn't afford.

"Please step out of your car, Mr. Cade."

Cade exited the cab. "You see, Officer, I can explain—"

The officer walked around the cab, aiming a flashlight in the cab interior. "What's that on the backseat?"

Cade followed the flashlight beam to the flyers. "Oh, that? Just some notices I've been handing out today."

"May I see one please?"

Cade opened the rear door and handed the cop a flyer.

"I've seen these all over the place. Are you jcade1450?"

"In person." Cade managed a tight smiled while clenching his pelvic muscles, his hope for a warning waning.

"This business about the Chapelita Coalition for Justice. By any chance do you know Luis Guzmán at the community center?"

For the first time, Cade noticed the nameplate on the officer's uniform shirt: *C. Rodriguez.* Her hair was pulled back in a tight bun, like Cassandra's. But this woman was more square and compact than Cassandra, like she could drop and give him twenty on command. "Yeah, Luis and I are working together on this protest."

"You and Luis, huh?" Officer Rodriguez handed Cade his license and registration. "Okay, Mr. Cade. I am going to let you off with a warning. This is a nice neighborhood with a lot of kids. Know what I mean? Don't let me catch you again, because I guarantee I will put your ass in jail and impound this green piece of shit. We clear?"

"Yes, sir. I mean ma'am. I mean officer. Thank you—"

"And Mr. Cade—"

"Yes?"

"Tell Luis he owes me big-time."

14

*L*uis looked around the empty church. Dust motes floated in the stained-glass light of Our Lady of Seven Sorrows. A cloud of guilt clung to his head like a damp fog. Last night's nightmare of wild dogs. The arrest of a former officer in his unit. Bad omens. The confessional curtain parted, and an old woman shuffled to a pew to recite a good act of contrition. Next in line, a young girl, not yet a teenager, inched forward, as if to the gallows, and disappeared into the darkness. A few minutes passed, and the young girl reappeared, head bowed, as she slipped past Luis. *No turning back now.* Luis entered the booth and bent to the hard-wooden kneeler.

The screen slid back and Father Gus said, "Confess your sins that ye may be healed."

"It's me, Father. Luis."

"Hey, Luis. How are you doing?"

"You should know," Luis said. "I just saw you at the Waffle Shop."

"Of course, of course," Father Gus hushed. "Welcome, Luis and keep your voice down. All of us have sinned and come short of the glory of God. He who confesses and repents his sins shall know the mercy of God."

"I'm not here to confess, just talk."

"We can do that in my office."

"I'd rather do it in here. Vow of secrecy and all that."

"All right, then. What's on your mind?"

Luis hesitated. "Let me ask you something. You spent some time in Salvador, right?"

"I served a ministry there for three years."

"So, you know about the war?"

"Too well, I'm afraid."

"I know it too. I was in the Army, long before you arrived. All this talk about fighting URP. Someone said Chapelita is going to be a battleground."

"Who said that?"

"A lawyer, from Miami. Not important. The thing is, it stirs up a lot of old feelings. Things I never told anyone, not even Angie."

"What kind of feelings?"

"When I was in the Army, we…did some bad things. Things I'd like to forget." Luis's eyes adjusted to the dim light, and he could make out a checkered grid of Father Gus behind the privacy screen. Only the width of an aluminum mesh panel separated the priest's face from Luis's. The intimate proximity to another man made him uncomfortable.

"Jesus Christ died for our sins that we may be saved."

"Yeah, well, you must understand, my family was dirt poor. My father grew sugar cane on a small piece of land and sold it for a few centavos. Never enough to feed six kids. Do you know what it's like to always be hungry?"

"Not like you did, Luis. Please, go on."

"I had an uncle, a captain in the Army. One day he comes to our house in a jeep with a bunch of soldiers. He says we've got one day to get off the land. A new owner needed our fields for a coffee plantation. My father begged. We had no place to go. The government didn't care. Then my uncle tells me I should join the Army and get regular meals. I take a half a second to make up my mind"—Luis snapped his fingers—"and before you know it, I'm in a truck with a rifle and a full belly."

"How old were you at the time?" Father Gus asked.

"Sixteen. There were a lot of kid soldiers in my unit. Boys grabbed off the streets and forced into the Army. It was always the poor ones who got snatched. Does my age make a difference?"

"I was just wondering. What is it you wish to confess?"

"Talk, remember?" Luis reminded, "just talk. So, one day my uncle tells me that the peasants are hiding the guerrillas and that they are fighting against reform. He says the reforms will help the farmers and factory workers. What do I know; I'm just a dumb kid."

"You were away from home for the first time, and scared. So, what happened?"

Luis coughed and struggled to find the right words. "My unit scouted the villages for guerillas." His voice trailed off into an inaudible mumble.

"Speak up, Luis. What happened?"

"I said there was this time when my captain ordered me to shoot a skinny kid who was about the same age as me. He had no shoes and was wearing a New York Yankees cap." He smothered a nervous laugh. "Some crazy shit, huh?"

"Go on."

Luis's mouth was dry. He sucked in a deep breath and continued, "Anyway, the captain said the kid was suspected of aiding the rebels. He ordered me to shoot him. The kid was crying. I couldn't do it."

"God bless you, Luis. What a horrible situation. What did you do?"

Luis peeked around the curtain of the confessional. Ten people now stood in line, waiting their turn for absolution. At the head of the line was a grizzled old man resting on the fold-down seat of a walker. His face betrayed a wry smile that made Luis think he had overhead everything. Vow of secrecy or not, Luis was taking a calculated gamble in coming here. He turned back to the screen and lowered his voice, a sob welling up in his chest. "So, the captain points a pistol at *my* head and says shoot or be shot. Now *I'm* crying. So, I raised my rifle, closed my eyes, and pulled the trigger. Someone handed me whiskey. The soldiers cheered my first kill. It was the worst day of my life. But there were more days like it to come. A lot of nights I can't sleep. Sometimes, it's hard for me to look at Javier and not think of the young boys I—" Luis paused. "Well, I needed to talk to someone."

Silence.

"Yo, Father," whispered Luis. "You still in there?"

"Yes, I'm still here. You know you were lied to, Luis, don't you? You know that, right?"

Luis shifted his weight, his kneecaps screaming. "I believed what the Army told me. They said the rebels wanted to take money away from the landowners and divvy it up, so everyone gets a piece. But my uncle said that is not how democracy works. He said the guerrillas were scum and that we must destroy the rebellion."

"You realize though that the guerillas were fighting for the peasants, like your family, and the others who were run off the land."

"Sure, I do—now," said Luis. "But this company is trying to kick us out of Glebe Valley, and we're trying to stop it. It's strange, it's like I'm with the rebels this time."

"I prefer what Saint Timothy calls us," Father Gus said. "Soldiers of Christ."

"Whatever. What's funny is that instead of just running us off, URP is offering us a fat bonus to move. That ain't so bad, is it? Democracy is crazy."

"That's not democracy; that's bribery."

Luis laughed. "Same thing!"

"Shhhh, keep your voice down, Luis. And no, it's not the same thing. Micah tells us, 'Woe to those who plan iniquity. They covet the fields and houses and seize them. They defraud people of their homes and rob them of their inheritance.' It's not the Glebe development that's the problem. It is the oppression of the poor by URP, in league with the city government—*that's* the problem. The struggle of the working class *is* the struggle for justice. Do you understand what I'm saying?"

Luis shrugged. "In Salvador, those with the power decided what justice was. Anyway, I'm having second thoughts. What's a protest going to accomplish? We have no real power."

"We fight the injustice of an evil force with the power of the Lord on our side. Matthew tells us the Lord comes not to send peace, but a sword."

Luis considered that. "Will a machete work just as well?"

"No jokes, Luis. The sword represents the divine truth. That which gives us the power to fight injustice. Have faith in our efforts to stand up for the people of Chapelita. I'm glad you came in today to have a little talk. Now others are waiting. Go in peace."

Luis coughed again. "Wait, uh, there is maybe one more thing. You remember those Jesuits shot at the university?"

"Of course, I've visited the garden where the soldiers executed the priests."

"Well, that was *my* Army unit. I didn't do any shooting. I swear. But I am worried. ICE deported an officer involved in the shootings not long ago. They're still looking for us. Could be a bad time to be sticking my neck out at a public rally." Luis rubbed his sore kneecaps. "Know what I mean?"

"Most of the soldiers who carried out the murders have been identified or tried. Also, there was a general amnesty granted to both sides. I doubt anybody is looking for you."

"I don't know. It feels like it sometimes."

"That's because you're still troubled by your actions, my son. Are you truly sorry in your heart for the deaths you caused?"

"Of course."

"Do you promise the almighty Father never to repeat those actions ever again?"

"Yeah, yeah."

"Then I absolve you of your sins in the name of the Father, the Son, and the Holy Spirit. Give thanks to the Lord, for He is good. Go in peace and sin no more."

"Wait," Luis stammered, "I didn't *confess* anything."

"It's a gift from our Heavenly Father, Luis. Just accept it."

"Amazing."

"Yes, the Lord's mercy is amazing."

Luis's swagger returned. "See you at the rally?"

"Count on it. And, Luis—"

"Yes, Father?"

"Our Father in Heaven is merciful and forgiving. Those on earth not so much. My advice, stay out of Salvador."

Before Luis could respond, the screen slid shut.

As soon as Luis stepped outside the church, he called Cade. "Sorry I was a little grouchy last night when you called. You can set up in the parking lot. We've done it for concerts. It's the best I can do."

"It'll be hot as hell outside," Cade groused. "Why the change of heart?"

"It's a gift," Luis said. "Just accept it."

15

*T*he countdown was on. The flyers advertising the rally shouted from every lamppost, telephone pole, and flat surface in the neighborhood. A few more email inquiries had trickled in. If only half showed up, that would be eighty-five people. Half of a half was forty, give or take—Cade would be satisfied with that. But if they came to the rally, would they stick around and go to the zoning hearing? A big if.

Cade swung the cab into the Chapelita Community Center lot to check with Luis on the setup for tomorrow's rally. When he entered, Luis was sitting next to a teenage boy, earbuds implanted, tapping a computer keyboard.

"Javier is organizing my files. He knows more about computers than I ever will."

Cade greeted Javier with a smile and a wave.

In the back of the room, two young boys kicking a soccer ball sent an errant shot off the wall, careening into the table holding the coffeepot.

"Okay, guys, take it outside," Luis said to the boys. "When does practice start?" he asked Javier.

"Right now, I'm done." Javier stood and unfurled all six feet, two inches of his lanky frame. He wore black soccer shorts with three white stripes down the side and a yellow T-shirt sporting a green crest with five blue stars arcing over the top. Beneath the crest in green capital letters: BRASIL. Javier grabbed a net bag filled with soccer balls and walked toward the door. The young boys followed behind like ducklings.

"Great kid," Luis said. "Going to the University of Virginia on a full-ride soccer scholarship."

"Terrific," Cade said. "Look, sorry I woke you the other night. I was anxious to get back to everyone with information about the rally. I appreciate the parking lot." Cade paused. "Although inside with air-conditioning would be better."

"Same answer, no. Make sure you tell the police you're holding an event in the parking lot, okay? You don't need a permit. Just a courtesy. Don't forget."

"I won't forget. Speaking of police," Cade said, "I ran into a friend of yours last night."

Luis tilted his head.

"Officer Rodriguez. I left the Alamo on a full tank of Jack Daniel's. She saw the flyer about the rally. She let me off as a favor to you. Said now you owe *her* big-time. What's that mean?"

Luis laughed. "Corrine pulled you over? She should have thrown your ass in jail. She's our community liaison officer. She helps work things out if somebody gets in trouble with the cops. Why'd she think I'm involved with you?"

Cade wrinkled his brow. "I may have mentioned it."

Luis rubbed his chin. "Of course! Corrine lives in Glebe Valley, too. The city gives her a rent-free apartment there. She read the flyer and figured you were trying to stop URP from kicking her out too. She gave you a break. Now you owe *me* big-time."

"Put it on my tab."

"You don't have a tab. So how many are you expecting?"

"Tell the truth," Cade said, "I have no idea. Fifty?"

"Remember what I told you. Folks have a lot of stuff on their minds now," said Luis. "Don't be surprised if you only get five."

16

*E*velyn Everhard's shift as a cashier ended at the Super Giant at 3 PM. Ten minutes later, she was already lounging on the sofa of her home in Warwick Village, a complex of 600 post-World War II row houses lining the hilly streets of what had once been the sprawling estate of Frank Hume—a Confederate spy during the Civil War. Evelyn's house offered a view of the Washington Monument as well as of jets making the final descent over Gravelly Point at the north end of the runway at Reagan National Airport.

She drank sweet tea and had time for a half hour of *Ellen* before driving to her Watchdog post across from the Git 'n Go. A two-hour shift and she'd be home in time to whip up spaghetti for Earl and Jenny, before they returned from soccer practice.

Warwick Village was one of the few affordable neighborhoods inside the beltway for a family scraping by on two incomes. A decent starter home for young families if they didn't mind the renters who didn't give a darn about upkeep and garbage pickup. Worse, the renters parked too many cars on the scarce number of spaces, triggering shouting matches and suspiciously flat tires. To Evelyn and Earl, the renters with uncounted non-family members under the same roof were a drag on property values. Last week, Social Services had discovered ten Salvadoran men sleeping in the basement of one house. Up-and-comers shoulder to shoulder with the down-and-outers.

And there was more reason than ever these days to be on guard around the neighborhood. The machete attack, of course, but also the day laborers hanging out at the Git 'n Go. Hard faces looked at Evelyn as if *she* was the outsider. That's when she and Kathy founded the Watchdogs—patriotic citizens protecting the community from illegals mooching off taxpayers for free schools, free health care, free housing, and free food. Once on trash night, Evelyn startled a man stealing her recyclables. Time to draw the line. And the line was right here, right now.

Evelyn pulled her Subaru wagon up behind a white Yukon SUV. Kathy walked back to greet her. "How's it going?"

"Not bad. Feet are killing me, though."

"Tell me about it." Kathy stocked shelves at the Costco in Pentagon City. She had the Watchdog checklist in hand. "Not much going on this afternoon. Too hot for Pedro, I guess." Pedro was the Watchdog's nickname for the day laborers. Kathy handed over the holstered Smith & Wesson .22 caliber pistol with a ten-round magazine.

"Got your concealed carry permit?" Kathy asked.

"Right here." Evelyn patted her purse.

"Enjoy," Kathy said. "Hey, why don't you bring Earl and Jenny over Saturday? We'll grill something. Keep it simple."

"Let me check with Earl. He's been busy lately at the chamber of commerce. This big Glebe project he's working on with the city. I'll give you a call."

Kathy waved as her SUV slipped into the southbound lane on Washington Avenue. Evelyn glanced at the few cars in the Git 'n Go parking lot. A lone Latino man sat on the curb near the Dumpster, sipping from a brown paper bag. She plucked the camera bag from the backseat.

Evelyn zoomed in on Pedro: hair buzzed to the scalp, scraggly wisps of a mustache, and a clump of chin whiskers as coarse as broom bristles. And my god, the tats. Barbed wire on his neck and arms, spiderwebs, and undecipherable hieroglyphics. And what was that, a single blue teardrop under his left eye? What the heck did that signify?

Evelyn scanned the plastic sheets in the binder containing photographs of other assumed illegals. No match. She had to get this guy's photo. Kathy would be proud.

"C'mon, Pedro, look this way." Through the lens, Evelyn saw the man look directly at her—crooked teeth bared, his mouth contorting itself into angry shapes she could not hear. "That's it, Pedro, hold that pose." She depressed the shutter, and the motor drive fired off four quick frames. The image disappeared for a second, then came back into view as Evelyn realized Pedro was crossing the street, headed toward the car.

She raised the window and locked the doors, running through her options: Ignore the threat, and he'll go away? Not likely. Abandon her post? Forget it. Call 911? Hell, no! She was a Watchdog! Evelyn mouthed words to the advancing man. "What's your deal, Pedro? What are you going to do, huh?"

Pedro circled the car, sipping from the paper sack. He screamed obscenities. Evelyn felt her car bounce. Pedro's foot was on the front bumper, rocking it. She pulled the Smith & Wesson from the glove box, keeping it low and out of sight. She slammed in a clip and flipped off the safety.

Pedro moved to the rear of the car. Evelyn twisted to follow his movement. The bottle in the brown sack shattered against the hatchback. *Was that a gunshot?* She aimed in Pedro's general direction and pulled once, twice, three times. The rear windshield exploded. Screams rang in her ears.

* * *

Javier was pitching soccer balls to a new goalie when the shots rang out. He ran toward the Git 'n Go. Two police cruisers, a fire truck, and an ambulance were on the scene as he sidled up to a big-bellied kid slurping a strawberry slushie. "What's going on?"

"Watchdog shot a dude."

"Dead?"

"Naw, got away. Cops looking for him."

Javier hurried back to the Chapelita Community Center and burst in the door. "Shooting at the Git 'n Go!"

Luis was watching an instructional video. At the sight of Javier's wide-eyed expression, he yanked off the earphones. "What did you say?"

"Shooting at the Git 'n Go!"

"When?"

"Just now," Javier said. "A Watchdog shot some dude. There's like a million cops."

Luis speed-dialed Officer Corrine Rodriguez.

"I'm on the scene," Corrine answered before Luis could say a word.

"What's going on?" Luis demanded.

"A Watchdog says a day laborer attacked her. Claims she fired in self-defense."

"Anybody hurt?"

"The suspect may be wounded. The Watchdog got his photograph. We'll get him."

"While you're at it, take away their guns."

Corrine paused. "They got permits, Luis."

"Screw permits," Luis said. "The Watchdogs are a menace. I'm telling you, Corrine, if the cops won't protect us—"

"And I'm telling you we're handling it, Luis."

"What's going on with the crowd?"

"Angry, but under control. Could use some cooler heads. Any chance you can swing by?"

"I guess. Someone said I owe you big-time."

"Wait, what? Who said—"

Luis slammed the phone down.

"What did she say?" Javier asked.

"Find Father Gus. Tell him to meet me at the Git 'n Go. Now!"

17

*C*ade couldn't move forward, couldn't move backward. Landlocked in every direction. Nothing to do but sit and wait in the taxi-holding ramp at Reagan National Airport. He counted twenty-three cabs lined up in front of the Green Flash leading up to the yellow stripe that read "100." One hundred and twenty-three cabs ahead of him waiting for the next influx of flights to dump passengers at the terminal. A lull in the action on a miserably hot July afternoon.

Cabbies gathered in clusters, smoking and talking in hushed, conspiratorial tones. Some read newspapers, others caught shut-eye. Cade listened with half an ear to the sixteenth CD in his *Don Quixote* audiobook—the scene where Don Quixote asks Sancho to whip his own bare bottom a few hundred times to break the spell upon Dulcinea. When the narrator, with arch inflection, recited Sancho's line: "Now that I've been sitting on a bare board, does your worship want me to flay my bum?" Cade's laughter drew quizzical glances from the other drivers.

He paused the CD, then picked up where he left off in Arthur A. Arthur's book, *Urban Rebellion: A Call to Action.* Cade carefully examined the colorful graphics that mapped the inequitable distribution of community assets such as housing, transit, grocery stores, schools, stores, and driving distances to jobs. All community's assets could be plotted and correlated with dot density charts, hot spot analysis, and zones of indifference.

According to Arthur, the inequality of asset allocation was a gross injustice. An erosion of the social compact. Spatial justice required opposition to the forces of inner-city exploitation. Like an advancing conflagration, a backfire would snuff the all-consuming scourge of voracious capitalism. The cleansing blaze would rebalance the unequal distribution of assets. Just as a forest regenerates after a fire, so does rebellion create the conditions for dormant seeds to germinate and give rise to new growth and justice.

He flipped back to the jacket photograph of Arthur, the geographer who inflamed Rita's passions. His sunken eyes and hollow cheeks presented a cadaver-like appearance. A grim countenance, and by the looks of his gaunt expression, hungry for retribution if the cries for a fair share were not met. An academic egghead, a movement leader, and an unabashed agitator. Cade mulled this strange brew until the cell buzzed.

"Did you hear the news?" said Luis.

"What news?" Cade said.

"A Watchdog shot a day laborer at the Git 'n Go."

Cade glanced out the windshield. Two Nigerian drivers stood chest to chest, exchanging heated words.

"Not a lot of details yet," Luis continued. "Police think the laborer may be wounded. A young girl got cut by flying glass. Nothing serious. Folks are blaming the cops for letting a Watchdog shoot up the neighborhood. Father Gus and I went over to cool things down, for now."

"Everything under control?"

"It ain't over, if that's what you mean. Coming on top of the machete murder and the immigration bust, it's like I told you, folks are crazy mad right now. Got other things on their mind besides a zoning protest."

Cade threw Arthur's book onto the front passenger seat. *Goddamn Watchdogs!*

"One more thing," said Luis. "I talked to Father Gus. He mentioned the two of you are working on this protest rally thing together. Why didn't you say something to me?"

"Hadn't got around to it yet. Things are moving fast."

"Real fast, apparently. The archbishop got wind of it, and he's not too happy. Gus has been reassigned to a parish in Bismarck, North Dakota. I guess he's not spending enough time tending his flock around here."

Cade had been counting on Father Gus to lend canonical credibility to the protest. Now he was being hustled out the door. Something didn't smell right. "What can I do?"

"I don't know," Luis said. "But you better figure something out. Otherwise, your rally is going down the toilet."

The Nigerians poked fingers in each other's chests. Other drivers perked up at the prospects of a fight. A tight circle formed around the two men, the spectators taking sides, placing bets, rooting for one driver or the other.

"I'm kind of boxed in at the moment," Cade said.

The drivers argued loudly in a foreign language, although an occasional "fuck you" could be heard. A shove and a punch coming any second. Cade thought of the recent taxi riots in Paris, and remembered the tire iron in the trunk if things got out of hand.

"Your call, amigo."

Cade hung up just as two airport security guards came running and wedged themselves between the Nigerians. The circle of drivers quickly dispersed to resume being bored.

Cade keyed the ignition. Immediately the cabbies thought the line was moving and started toward their cars. He backed up an inch, pulled forward, backed up, and gradually worked enough clearance to pull his cab free of the taxi in front and head for the emergency exit out of the ramp. He followed the airport access road to Route 1 and headed south to Glebe Valley. He glanced over at Arthur's book, *Urban Rebellion*. The black and orange subtitle like a rallying cry: *A Call to Action*. It was time to set a little backfire of his own.

18

*T*wo hours after the Git 'n Go shooting, Luis's cell chirped a Cuban club tune. He recognized the number for Officer Corrine Rodriguez.

"We ID'd the Git 'n Go guy," Corrine said. "Dude was camera shy for a reason. We ran the photo the Watchdog took and got a hit. He ain't no day laborer. Name is Rafe Velez, aka Macho Nacho. MS-13 out of New York. Nasty piece of work. Likes knives. Cut up his girlfriend pretty bad. Outstanding warrants. He may be our machete guy as well. We connected Velez to the MS-13 clique in Portsmouth Correctional Center."

"Where Enzo did his time," Luis said.

"Exactly. When we find Velez, chances are we'll find Enzo. Detective Nichols's task force is combing the area. Just wanted to give you a heads-up."

"Whatever. Enzo is on his own. Now, what about the Watchdogs? Are you going to get them off the street, too? And take away their guns? Bad enough folks are getting screwed out of their homes. Not a lot of trust that the city is looking out for our welfare."

"I hear you, Luis. I'll talk to the Watchdogs. But real estate ain't my jurisdiction."

Luis shot back, "Well, it sure as hell is ours."

* * *

Gridlocked on the beltway, Finn listened on the radio to a pair of sports jocks debate the fortunes of the hapless Nats—losers now of sixteen straight. At the newsbreak, the lead story reported that the man the police had picked up was the man who was alleged to be involved in the shooting at the Git 'n Go and a possible link to the machete attack.

Finn checked his cell and saw the appointment with Oliver for later in the afternoon. The prick was flying all the way across the Atlantic just to fire his ass. All because he didn't tell him about a piddling protest rally led by a dimwit cab driver. He might never find a gig as sweet and remunerative as URP. Unless, of course, the protest didn't go off as planned.

Finn turned off the radio and voice-activated the car phone. After six tones, it went to voicemail. "This is Finn. Call me back."

After being stuck in traffic for the better part of an hour, Finn's mood was dark as he walked past Ann's cube. Her manicured nails held out a pink message slip. "He returned your call. Very rude. Cut me off."

He carried the message slip back to his office, hit speakerphone, and dialed.

A man's voice answered, "Ashpole."

"This is Mick. I need your help." Finn waved to Ann outside his office, pantomiming drinking from a coffee cup.

"You sure do, pal," Ashpole said. "The trustees at Saint Andrew's are nervous if they should stay in this deal with URP. The Git 'n Go shooting has stirred up things. Bad time for Saint Andrew's to be putting the squeeze on small business owners at the shopping center. Maybe we should hold off on the zoning application. Wait until things cool down."

Finn reached for his stress ball emblazoned with the Washington Nationals logo. Risk-averse trustees manifesting typical investor anxiety—a little bump in the road and suddenly everyone wants to bail. Not unlike the market jitters that triggered overreactions on Wall Street and led to sell-offs and crashes. But investing in the Glebe was nothing like the stock market. Real estate in the metro area was a no-brainer. But if Saint Andrew's bailed, the syndicate financing package could unravel. "Calm down, Bill. No need to panic. Everything will be fine. But I need a small favor."

Ashpole said something, but all Finn could hear was a metallic announcement: *Metroliner service to Baltimore, Wilmington, Trenton, New York, and Boston. Departing Track 8.*

"Cut to the chase, Mick. I gotta run."

"Your firm handles criminal defense, correct?"

"The best."

"Can you give me a referral?"

"Why, are you in trouble?"

"Not me. For someone else. And one more thing. I need to be in the room when the attorney sees the client."

"Not so fast. The client must give permission for you to be present. Who are you so anxious to talk to?"

Finn scrolled his email while listening to Ashpole. Oliver was demanding an immediate status update on the Glebe as soon as he arrived. "Rafe Velez."

A pause.

"Isn't he the guy connected to the Git 'n Go shooting? Where are you going with this, Mick?"

"Just calming the waters for your trustees, Bill. Trust me. Now refer me to your best guy and relax."

"I'll get back to you." Ashpole hung up.

Ann came in and set a mug of coffee on the desk. Finn hated asking Ashpole for a favor. And the bastard had been rude to Ann. He threw the stress ball at the floor-to-ceiling window.

Ashpole.

Asshole.

19

*T*he stairwell to the maintenance room stank of beer and urine. A gray metal door sealed the world off from the tapping of a keyboard. Enzo perched on a bar stool while his computer rested on a closet door supported by two stacks of cinder blocks. Of the five utility rooms scattered throughout the Glebe Valley complex, the maintenance crew heeded his threat that this one was strictly off-limits.

Borderline claustrophobic, he resented that Butcher had insisted on bringing a weight bench with a set of barbells into his already cramped makeshift study. On the plus side, except for the hum of the fluorescent lights, the confined space was a conducive environment for concentration. And he needed to concentrate. The online course on risk management was a bitch. Only six more credits to finish coursework for a BS in Forensic Business Intelligence, an emerging field that combined financial transaction analytics and informatics to trace criminal activity in the age of Big Data. His business plan would make the FBI acronym sweetly ironic. His dark web business model would minimize risk associated with bloody turf wars, DNA residue—and witnesses. Technological innovation had progressed significantly since the demise of the Silk Road—an early adopter of dark web drug retailing. Today, thanks to encryption algorithms, vendor and buyer anonymity was virtually impenetrable. Gross revenue projections of five hundred thousand dollars a week were not unrealistic.

Managing risk to maximize reward was the crux of his nascent enterprise. Risk identification, risk analysis, upside risk, downside risk, risk mitigation. Every decision, every action, every investment hinged on a careful assessment and weighing of multiple complex and interconnected risk factors. Even now, while constructing a matrix risk profile for a case of financial fraud, he wrestled with the risk posed by Nacho, now in police custody. What an idiot. Drinking in a parking lot and going after a Watchdog in a parked car. Cops everywhere. And here he was, holed up in a stinking basement, scurrying back to the apartment at night like a rat from a Dumpster. His own risk score was in the high double digits. He needed an exit strategy, fast.

He wiped sweat from the keyboard. The utility room was not much larger than the six-by-eight-foot cell he'd occupied in the Portsmouth Correctional Center. A real shithole. The prison college program had been a lifesaver. Javier wasn't the only one with brains in the family.

Hardly a day went by when he didn't regret getting hooked up with the dropouts in the Virginia Beach bust. He'd seen up close how machismo on steroids shriveled brains and testicles to the size of raisins. He swore never again to follow men too dumb to find their ass with a mirror on a stick.

Despite inmate taunts, he'd completed the certificate programs in business software applications and computer programming in two years with a 4.0 GPA. The suits running Portsmouth marveled at his exemplary behavior and academic accomplishment. They sent him on a tour to the other Virginia prisons as an ambassador for second chances. Enzo could sell it because he believed it. After all, he'd spent hundreds of hours staring at a cellmate's upper bunk mattress practicing the creative visualization skills taught to successful executives at Google, Apple, and Microsoft.

The goodwill tour paid off in spades. The parole board cut two years of his sentence. After only a few weeks on parole, an MS-13 emissary had shown up at the halfway house. A *líder* wanted Enzo to run the Brothers of Blood clique in Northern Virginia. A recent bust had decimated the leadership ranks. As an added incentive, if he hit financial targets, he was assured of an opportunity to affiliate with MS-13. The first step on his way to vision actualization. The next thing he knew, Nacho and Butcher had shown up at his door. New York muscle, only this time Enzo was calling the shots.

But to really expand and hold territory, he was going to need more muscle than Nacho and Butcher and some weekend warriors playing gangbanger on Saturday nights for the chicks and coke. That fact became more evident when the *líder* sent word that a rival gang, the Four Mile Kings, were moving product on their turf. Even the gang name was an insult, laying dubious claim to a tri-county region that included some of the wealthiest zip codes in the country. And the Kings wanted it all to themselves. The order had come to send a message.

Enzo's hand slipped to the machete. The Condor had performed well last week against the punk behind Kim's Drycleaners. The adrenaline rush returned—the thrill of the kill and dominance over a weak adversary. It filled him with an overwhelming sense of power and confidence. He also knew the Kings would retaliate, and an all-out war would require a much bigger and better armed clique, and fast.

But news reports of the teenage victim showed a sweet-faced kid about the same age as Javier. At times, his murderous fantasies replaced the drug dealer's face with that of his brother and triggered a disturbing chill. He hefted the blade and inspected the weapon with a cold, appraising eye—as if the reason for the odd reflex might be revealed on the razor-sharp edge—when a text message chimed. A minute passed, followed by two quick knocks on the maintenance room door. Enzo stowed the machete and opened the door to a heavily muscled man with a shaved head and wearing a tank top and baggy jeans.

"Hot as shit in here, 'Zo," Butcher said. "Whattaya doing?"

"Working where it's quiet and keeping out of sight. Not blasting music in the apartment like you. Why don't you just hang out a sign?"

Butcher lay on the weight bench, wrapped both hands around the barbell, and pushed up 225 pounds. "Came to tell you something."

Enzo glared at Butcher's tats spreading out of the tank top like a Technicolor oil spill. A macabre gallery of demons, barbed wire, and a four-color Virgin of Guadalupe spread taut across the canvas of his massive lats and traps. A single teardrop under the left eye signified Butcher had snuffed a con in prison. Enzo hated tats. They hindered movements in public and made identification way too easy. He'd warned Butcher to at least wear a long-sleeved shirt during daylight hours.

"Tell it," Enzo said.

Butcher bounced the barbell on his pecs, rocked it back in the crutch of the weight bench, and rose to a sitting position. He reached into his back pocket and handed Enzo a crumpled orange flyer. Enzo scanned the notice for a protest rally, then tapped the laptop keys and searched the name of the developer. Up popped nine hundred hits for Urban Renaissance Partners.

The home page displayed links for a mission statement, client list, and a photo gallery of urban village projects from around the world. The link to the executive management team brought up a photo of Robert Oliver, URP's founder—a billionaire business executive— a man with a vision.

The banner quote across the top of Oliver's photo promised the next generation in urban living: *Emotional Communion*, an evolution of spatial relationships nurturing the deepest feelings of home and community. He scrolled to current projects, found The Glebe at Cub Run, and muttered, "Fucking bullshit."

Butcher glanced up from the weight bench.

Enzo tapped again and up popped a headshot for Mick Finn, Senior Vice President of Development. Butcher expelled loud airbursts as he curled sixty-pound dumbbells, his biceps bulging like small boulders. Pungent body odor filled the cramped room.

A few more clicks and Enzo pulled up Finn's bio. Real estate attorney. Big shot developer. This was the asshole planning to raze the Glebe Valley apartments, kick BOB out from their turf, and ruin his dream of affiliating with MS-13.

The dumbbells thudded on the concrete floor. "What'd you find?" asked Butcher.

Enzo picked up the machete. The carbon steel caught the light of the fluorescent bulb. He swung the blade so close to Butcher's nose that he jerked back in reflex.

Enzo laughed. "Find out about this Chapelita Coalition for Justice and who the fuck jcade1450 is. Comprende?"

Butcher nodded. "Then what we gonna do?"

Enzo tapped the blade against the screenshot of Mick Finn. "The first thing we do is cap this muthafucking lawyer."

20

*C*ade occupied a Waffle Shop booth and signaled Miguel for a refill. After escaping from the holding pen at Reagan Airport, he had called the troops for an urgent meeting. Outside, a 30 percent chance of thundershowers hammered the awning over the windows. A torrential downpour smothered windshield wipers. Headlights cut the sodden gloom of an old-fashioned gully washer.

Luis ducked in the front door and took a seat opposite Cade. "It broke loose just as I started crossing the street." He wiped his face with a paper napkin. "You said you had a plan?"

"Wait until we're all here."

Father Gus arrived next, holding a large golf umbrella over his head. He wore a white guayabera shirt draped over neatly pressed jeans and honey-colored huarache sandals. Along with two-day beard stubble, the overall effect was more GQ dope dealer than a man of the cloth. He appeared untouched by the storm. He slid in next to Luis.

Within minutes, Grif dashed into the restaurant, wet hair plastered to his scalp. He grabbed the open seat on Cade's side of the booth. "Whose idea was this?"

"Gentlemen," Cade said to Luis and Father Gus, "meet Grif, an old Army bud of mine. Now that we're all here, I'd like Luis to bring us up to date on the shooting you've no doubt heard about."

Luis recounted the events at the Git 'n Go that led to the police picking up Rafe Velez as a suspect. Cade noticed that Luis omitted mention of the police looking for Enzo. Luis said anger in the community was boiling over against the Watchdogs, the police, and Immigration. Coming on the heels of the machete murder, a lot of tenants planned to take the relo money and get the hell out of Dodge.

Cade looked at Father Gus. "Luis says you're shipping out."

Gus responded with a wide smile. "Archbishop O'Malley feels my services are needed elsewhere, and Bismarck North Dakota is about as far elsewhere as you can get. However, I'm taking time off before I go." He pulled out a quarter. "Heads I surf, tails I hang with you good fellows at the Waffle Shop."

Cade snatched the coin in midair. "It was tails. Seriously, I don't get it, Gus. Why does the archbishop give a shit about a pissant like you? No offense."

"No offense taken. I didn't get it either at first, so I asked a priest friend who works in the archbishop's office. My friend saw the paperwork that showed Saint Andrew's is selling syndicate shares to the Catholic Diocese of Northern Virginia."

"Syndicate shares?" asked Luis.

Grif jumped in. "A syndicate is like a bunch of real estate investors."

"But get this," Gus continued. "My friend saw an interesting name on the syndicate roster. Jacob Grossman."

Everybody with a pulse in the DC area knew the name of Jacob Grossman, the hated billionaire owner of the Washington Nationals.

"Son of a bitch," Cade groused. "Grossman trades our best pitcher, and now the Nats are losers of seventeen straight."

"Eighteen, as of last night," Gus said. "It gets better, or worse, depending on how you look at it. My friend also said that Grossman is a trustee at Saint Andrew's, who just happens to own the shopping center across the street. Which is part of the development deal along with Glebe Valley."

"You lost me," said Grif. "What does any of this have to do with the Church transferring you to Bum Fuck North Dakota? Pardon my French, padre."

"I think I get it," said Cade. "Saint Andrew's sells syndicate shares to the Catholic Diocese of Northern Virginia. In return, the archbishop agrees to protect their investment from an upstart priest at Our Lady of Seven Sorrows conspiring against the zoning approval."

Father Gus laughed and pointed at Cade. "Bingo! Give that man a cigar."

"So, the Catholic Church is essentially cashing in?" Grif said.

"Wouldn't be the first time," Father Gus said. "The Glebe is going to make a lot of people a lot of money."

"The Glebe," Grif said with disgust. "I'm sick of hearing about the Glebe. What the hell *is* a glebe?"

"It's a duck," Luis said.

Father Gus wagged his head. "You're thinking of a grebe."

"Stop it, you morons," Cade laughed. "I bothered to look it up. Back in the day, a glebe was a chunk of land the Church of England gave to a local parish. Most of the area we now call Glebe Valley"—Cade motioned toward the flooded street—"was once part of the original glebe the church granted to British missionaries in the Virginia colony. The big idea was to bring religion to the heathens."

A flash of lightning illumined the darkened street. The Waffle Shop lights flickered.

"Who are you calling a heathen?" Grif wisecracked.

"You, you frigging bastard," Cade shot back with a grin. "Eventually, the glebe became home to Saint Andrew's Episcopal Church. Over time, Saint Andrew's sold off most of the glebe, but hung on to a valuable strip alongside a road used by farmers to bring goods into DC." Cade jerked his thumb against the rain-smeared window. "Saint Andrew's stands to make—"

A crack of thunder rolled across the sky like artillery fire. As if on cue, Father Gus said, "They grind the heads of the poor into the earth and thrust the humble out of their way. Amos 2, verses 6 to 7."

Grif lifted one eyebrow. "What is that supposed to mean?"

Cade winked. "I'll explain it to you later."

"Well, do you have a plan or not?" Luis asked again.

"So happens, I do," said Cade. "Everybody and their brother knows we're planning to show up at the P&Z hearing—the archbishop, URP, Saint Andrew's. They're all expecting us, and no doubt ready to deflect our assault. Am I right?"

Grif twisted a smile. "Like an enemy expecting an attack."

"Precisely," Cade said. "We need a diversion, a feint to get past their defenses."

"Great, but how are you going to get people to show up in the first place," said Luis. "Like I said, it's less hassle to take the relocation money and split."

The thunderstorm ended as quickly as it began. Tires hissed and sprayed the wet streets.

"I've thought about that too," Cade said. "We have a lot of work to do in a short amount of time." Over the next twenty minutes, he laid out the logistics and the assignments. Nothing left to chance. Just like a mission in Iraq. Plan. Prepare. Execute.

* * *

The cell buzzed just as Finn pulled into Starbuck's drive-through lane, desperate for a double shot of espresso before heading back to the office.

"I got a defense attorney for your boy, Velez," said Ashpole. "First-rate guy, Bobby Simmons. He's on his way to meet Velez now. If you want to be in the room, you better hustle. Remember, Simmons is on your tab. He bills at seven hundred per."

"Thanks for the two-minute warning."

"Don't mention it." Ashpole hung up.

Finn swore under his breath, then eased the Lexus out of the drive-through and into a rare slipstream of green lights and made it to the Elbert Lee Trinkle Municipal Building in record time. The jail annex loomed as a malformed appendage grafted onto the backside of the building like a dowager's hump.

He found Bobby Simmons in the waiting room without any trouble. At six-foot-seven, he stood out like a weed in a manicured lawn. His unlined face retained a certain youthfulness, although a touch of gray at the temples hinted at the early forties. Finn surmised his suit must have cost at least three billable hours. He extended his hand. "I'm Mick Finn."

"Bobby Simmons."

"Bobby Simmons?" Finn struggled to remember how he knew that name. "Wait, didn't you play for Duke?"

"North Carolina."

"I knew it. Drafted by the Celtics and—"

"Until I busted my knee skiing at Breckenridge."

"Cool," Finn said, then, "I mean, too bad." He shifted to business mode. "You're Velez's attorney. Make whatever deal you want, I don't care. I just need five minutes to talk to him, okay? Can you get permission for me to join you in the room?"

"Stand by," Simmons said, and walked over to a cop at a desk behind a Plexiglas window. He disappeared through a door and reappeared a few minutes later, waving to Finn to join him.

When they entered the interrogation room, Velez slouched in a chair at a steel table bolted to the floor, his bandaged left arm in a sling, his right wrist handcuffed to a ring in the wall. Blue and green tats covered every inch of visible flesh on his hands, arms, and neck. A blue teardrop hung suspended under the right eye. Black stubble and scabs pockmarked his scalp. The personification of a murderous, thieving, cut-throat bastard—not unlike previous adversaries attired in pinstriped suits he'd sat across from at negotiating tables. Finn felt right at home.

"My name is Mick Finn. This gentleman is Mr. Bobby Simmons. If you want him, Mr. Simmons will act as your lawyer. He comes highly recommended. He'll get you the best deal you're likely to get, better than a public defender. But that's for the two of you to decide."

Velez's hooded eyes registered no interest.

Finn continued, "But I'm here to offer you a different deal. I will give Mr. Simmons five thousand dollars to hold for you. All I ask in return is that you deliver a message to your boss and ask him to call me. If you deliver the message, and your guy calls, you get the cash. Easy money. No call, no money. Simple, huh?"

Velez ignored Finn.

Finn slid a business card on the table. "Tell your boss to call my cell by five o'clock. One minute past and the deal is off." Finn motioned toward Bobby. "I'm sure Mr. Simmons will let you use his phone. Right, Bobby?"

Simmons's eyes looked up from his smart phone. "Sure, why not."

"Take the offer, Mr. Velez," Finn said. "What have you got to lose?"

21

*A*fter meeting with Velez, Finn was heading to the office when his smart phone vibrated. It was Beth Daniels, URP's chief financial officer. "Guess who just walked in, asking for you?"

Finn's grip on the steering wheel tightened. "He's early. Tell Oliver I'm on my way."

Beth explained that Bill Ashpole had emailed Oliver a copy of the protest flyer for the zoning hearing. Oliver was unhappy he'd not heard about the protest from Finn. Ashpole had also hinted that Saint Andrew's might pull out of the syndicate due to the bad publicity surrounding the incidents in the neighborhood—the machete murder and the Git 'n Go shooting. If Saint Andrew's withdrew, then Deutsche Bank might get nervous. The whole syndicate deal could collapse.

"Oliver is wondering if you're on top of things," Beth said.

Finn imagined his hands around Ashpole's throat. "Do me a favor, Beth, stall Oliver until I get there." Ashpole had gone over his head to Oliver, knowing it would upset the old man and get him thrown off the team. Retribution no doubt for the time Finn bested Ashpole on a long-ago merger deal. Now Ashpole had Oliver screaming for his scalp. Plus, a voicemail from Earl Everhard at the chamber of commerce hyperventilating about Cade papering the neighborhood with the same damn flyer. He pounded the wheel.

Thirty minutes later, Finn stepped out of the glass elevator that opened onto URP's penthouse lobby. The receptionist said, "He's in the boardroom."

Finn entered and found Robert Oliver seated at the head of a long, polished table with Beth Daniels and five URP vice presidents. A single sheet of paper and a large book lay on the table in front of Oliver.

He motioned for Finn to sit. The last thing Finn wanted was to be stuck in a meeting when the call came from Velez. He grabbed a seat across from the vice president of marketing. The young VP presented a chinless profile. Add thirty years and a bad comb-over and he could have passed for the twin brother of City Attorney Stephen S. Slegg. Another headache. Slegg had his thumb on the scale as to whether the Glebe zoning application got approved. But his nonchalance toward Cade's upcoming zoning protest was disturbing, essentially telling him it was his problem while pocketing a down payment for services not yet rendered. *Note to self: Light a fire under Slegg's ass.*

Oliver opened the meeting. "Thank you, ladies and gentlemen, for coming together on short notice. I flew overnight because of recent events that are casting an unfavorable light on the Glebe. I want everyone to leave the room today clear on one important point."

Finn checked his watch. The five o'clock deadline loomed. Maybe he'd acted too cocky, and Velez's boss wouldn't call. Although the real problem might be if the boss did call. His half-baked idea to get Cade out of the picture and use the Brothers of Blood as a cover was a calculated risk. Second thoughts about missteps and foul-ups clouded his focus as Oliver droned on about human ecology—mankind's collective interaction with the environment.

"Imagine the Renaissance period of the 15th century," Oliver said, "the period that gave us da Vinci's *Mona Lisa*, Gutenberg's printing press, the discovery of new continents and planets—a fountain of creativity in the arts and sciences." Oliver spread his arms wide. "Indeed, a veritable explosion of patronage and commerce that gave birth to capitalism!"

Finn's jaws clenched. Oliver was in full professorial mode. Finn checked his cell for a voice message from Velez but instead saw a text from Beth with a frowny face emoticon: *Get me out of here.*

Oliver caught Finn staring at his cell. "Mick, are you following this?"

"Sorry, Mr. Oliver," Finn said, red-faced. "I'm expecting a call from the Planning and Zoning Commission."

"Yes, well, this is important too. Try to keep up. This meeting is for your benefit as well."

He pocketed the cell, his face a mask of faux concentration.

Oliver eyed each VP in turn, then raised up the book *The City in History*. "The eminent scholar on urban civilization, Lewis Mumford, once wrote that the destiny of cities was to further the *emotional communion* of mankind's consciousness." His index finger tapped the tome for dramatic effect. "The magnification of all dimensions of life—from technological advancements to civic engagement to creative expression. The unification of mankind's inner and outer life."

Finn resented the thought of sitting through another of Oliver's boring disquisitions. He expelled a large sigh, a little too loudly, and drew the attention of the chinless vice president, who returned a glare of admonishment.

"This, my friends," Oliver said, "is the manifesto for the urban renaissance that guides our company to this very day. We cannot let a few inconsequential obstacles," and here Oliver looked squarely at Finn, "or *people* impede the fulfillment of that destiny."

Oliver walked over, stood behind Finn, and rested his arms on the seat back.

Finn tensed, recalling the scene in *The Untouchables* when Robert De Niro, as Big Al Capone, walks behind a row of tuxedoed gangsters carrying a baseball bat, each man nervously wondering who was going to get his skull cracked. He looked at the other VPs, ready to spring at the slightest whoosh of air in his direction.

"Allow me to put this in a less grandiose context. We are all familiar with the proliferation of smartphones, smart cars, smart houses. All these applications, in one form or another, integrate information and technology to improve the efficiency of the services and devices that we use in our daily lives, from controlling the thermostat to providing real-time updates on traffic conditions, water consumption, you name it. Indeed, smart house technology can already make lighting adjustments to match one's circadian rhythms," and here Oliver paused a beat, then added with droll British delivery, "or even tell you when to change the cat litter." Titters of appreciation arose for the boss's game attempt at humor from the senior staff seated around the elongated table.

"But so far, the smart data, no matter how advanced or sophisticated, still requires an old-fashioned brain to analyze and make sense out of it—until now."

Oliver tapped a button, and a white screen descended from a slot in the ceiling. A slide graphic appeared showing a horse and buggy next to a Lamborghini. "Some of you may be familiar with the term 'disruptive innovation.' It's a new way of doing things that shakes up a marketplace with a competitive advantage. Think about how automobiles replaced horses as transportation or how the computer disrupted the market for typewriters, and you can imagine the magnitude of disruption that can occur.

"For some time now, the Urban Renaissance Partners Foundation has been funding research into brain-computer interface—BCI for short. Our sponsored team at the California Institute for Advanced Neuroscience Research has achieved a powerful disruptive innovation. We now have the BCI to create a home and work environment that organically amplifies the brain's cognitive functioning. A neurofeedback loop, if you will, that continuously improves performance across multiple dimensions the more you use it. Think of the progress feedback loops can make by expanding the horizons in the arts and sciences and our democratic institutions—building blocks for the cities of tomorrow. Smart cities of the future will enhance psychic wholeness and connectivity across the urban landscape. The Glebe at Cub Run will be the prototype for the first holistic integration of mind and body and the built environment."

Oliver touched a remote and a rendering of The Glebe at Cub Run replaced the previous slide. Then, a digital animation of twirling stars dropped in from the four corners, spinning and pulsing multicolored lights. The stars formed beneath the rendering and resolved into letters spelling out: Psycho Unified Life Style Environment. Next, a musical score immersed the room in full-on surround sound—a new-agey electronic synthesizer chord built to a momentous climax synchronized to the digital resolution of the logo: PULSE *tec*.

As the last synthesized note faded out, the VPs sat stunned and mute, their blank expressions indicating they had no idea what to say about what they had just witnessed, except for Finn, who thought it was a tad cheesy, although on a scale of one to ten, a definite eight—but still not enough to make up for Oliver's self-congratulatory bombast.

Oliver pointed to the screen and, in a voice filled with pride, broke the fragile silence. "PULSE *tec* is our brand name for the new brain-computer interface." Continuing the showmanship, he lowered his voice to a stage whisper, and added, "All of us here"—he swung his arm to encompass the entire boardroom—"are on the cusp of a quantum leap in human ecology. Indeed, an urban renaissance, light-years beyond what we thought possible a few decades ago. Mumford would be proud."

Thinking, or hoping, Oliver's presentation was over, Finn joined the VPs in a round of polite applause. Instead of taking a bow, Oliver picked up an orange flyer and thrust it inches from Finn's face. "Let me ask you something, Mick. How much do you know about this Chapelita Coalition for Justice?"

Based on the report from Slegg, he knew that a cab driver by the name of Jack Cade was behind it. And that Cade had been court-martialed for an unknown reason. And that Cade was the son of a bitch who had dented his Lexus. Beyond that, not much else.

Before Finn could open his mouth, Oliver pounced. "Well, I'll tell *you* something about them. They're left-wing radicals, bloody anarchists. Their goal is to maintain the masses in poverty and blight, so they can stoke the flames of discontent to advance their socialist agenda. It was that old Bolshevik, Lenin, who said, 'Worse is better.' He meant that as conditions for the poor became worse—chaos, crisis, discord—the more likely it was they would start a revolution.

"Groups like this have been around for a while. Different names in different cities. A franchise of sorts. Oppressed third-world workers coming together against greedy developers displacing low-wage workers from their homes. Does that sound like the Chapelita Coalition for Justice to you?"

Beth and the VPs cast their eyes down. Finn was flying solo on this one.

"I'm not quite sure," Finn started, "but I intend—"

"You *intend?*" Oliver snapped. "URP is on the cutting edge of redefining man's relationship to the city, and you *intend* to do what? Sit around with your thumbs up your ass?"

Finn winced at the insult. *Fire me, you prick. I don't have to take this shit from you. As soon as I get out of here, I'm calling Langstrom at the CRG Group.*

Oliver crumpled the flyer and pitched it toward a wastebasket, missing. "Have you ever heard of Arthur A. Arthur?"

"I've been busy," Finn shot back, ready to walk.

"Well, Google Arthur sometime," Oliver said. "Your friends with the Chapelita Coalition for Justice consider him to be their guru of sorts. Open your eyes, Mick. There's more at stake here than just a damn zoning approval. We're talking about an international movement that is antithetical to everything URP stands for. Not just the Glebe, but all our projects around the world. Political demands cleverly disguised as a call for dialogue. But make no mistake, they are nothing but Marxist malcontents."

Oliver's British accent projected intellectual authority with dramatic flair. The old boy was laying it on thick. The cell in Finn's shirt pocket vibrated. The caller's name and number blocked. "I'm sorry, Mr. Oliver," Finn said, standing, "but I've got to take this. It's the P&Z."

Before Oliver could object, Finn was out the door. "This is Finn."

A man said, "Bring the money to me."

"Who is this?"

"The fuck you think it is?"

Finn shut his office door. "I need confirmation."

"Fuck you."

"No, no, just tell me this, did your homie Velez mention a lawyer?"

A pause, then, "A black dude."

Black dude, close enough. "Okay, okay, that's cool," Finn said. "Here's the deal. Simmons will hold the money for Velez, then—"

The voice cut in. "No, here's the deal, motherfucker. Drop the money tonight in the Dumpster behind the Git 'n Go. Three o'clock."

A late-night rendezvous at the Git 'n Go was not a smart choice for a first date, but it might be his only chance to connect. "Wait, you're Velez's, I mean Nacho's boss, right? I'll bring the money, but I want five minutes to talk. That's the deal."

Silence.

"Hello?" Gone. He must have been Velez's boss. It was a gamble, but if it paid off, Cade and his crew would be history. Finn checked his watch. Against his better judgment, he returned to the boardroom. When he entered, Robert Oliver walked up to him. "Everything okay with the P&Z?"

Still thinking about the 3AM meet-up, Finn hesitated. "Huh, what? Oh yeah, fine. Everything is fine."

"So, what do you think?" Oliver asked.

"What do I think about what?"

"About that damn Coalition for Justice!" Oliver barked. "Bloody hell, Mick, what do you think I'm talking about?"

Finn scrambled. "I agree, the Coalition is totally corrupt. In fact, I was just talking to an associate about how to deal with them."

Oliver's face darkened; then he threw an arm over Finn's shoulder. "Now look, we need to move quickly. That means we need a solid green from the P&Z." Oliver tightened his squeeze on Finn's shoulder. "Understand?"

Finn flinched. The old man had a surprisingly strong grip. "Perfectly. Don't worry, Mr. Oliver. I've got it under control."

"Yes, I've heard that before." Oliver relaxed his hold. "The Glebe will be my legacy, Mick. Too important to be bogged down with the trivial demands of leftist layabouts. Wouldn't you agree?"

Oliver's left eyebrow twitched. As a weekend poker player in Atlantic City, Finn recognized an obvious tell. The stakes had just gotten higher. "Absolutely, Mr. Oliver."

"Good answer." Oliver leaned in with a conspiratorial smile. "Now tell me how you're going to deal with this jcade1450 fellow."

22

A single light pole cast the Git 'n Go in a fold of shadows. Finn checked the dashboard clock: 2:58 AM. A driveway led to the Dumpster behind the building. He exited the Lexus with a brick of bills tightly wrapped in a black plastic garbage bag. Gravel and broken glass crunched underfoot as he crept behind the convenience store. A cut chain-link fence created a shortcut from the convenience store to the Glebe Valley apartments. Paper trash and food containers littered the asphalt. A Dumpster lid stood open. Rotting garbage fouled the air. He looked around, placed the brick on top of an egg carton, and hurried back to the car to wait for whoever showed up so he could make his pitch.

From ten feet away, the remote fob opened the door locks. The lights flashed twice, and the dome light brightened. Finn saw the goddamn dent in the rear quarter panel that Cade's Green Flash had inflicted. As he reached for the handle, a black Dodge Charger lurched to a stop alongside his Lexus. A man jumped out and pressed an object against his neck. Muscles convulsed and cramped as he collapsed in a heap. Electric shocks of pain twitched and jerked his limbs uncontrollably. A sensation of being dragged followed a wave of nausea before he blacked out.

Gradually, a swirl of indistinct shapes solidified into boilers and water meters. Overhead, a fluorescent light fixture hummed. A weight bench in the corner of the small room held a barbell with two large iron plates on either end.

At a makeshift desk, a man on a barstool wore jeans, a white T-shirt, and ASICS running shoes. Mid-twenties, medium height, with a lean-muscled build. Jet-black hair swept back accentuated a high forehead and an aqualine nose. Jade green eyes reflected a cat-like deviousness. A wisp of beard—a soul patch—sprouted under the lower lip.

A touch-screen notebook rested on the desktop. A row of textbooks lined the floor. Finn scanned the spines: Finance, Global Risk Management, International Banking. On the desk lay the orange flyer from the Chapelita Coalition for Justice. When Finn moved, a jolt of pain shot through his neck and shoulders. Out of the corner of one eye, two men lurked in the shadows of the small room.

"You wanted to talk?" Soul Patch said. "Talk."

Muscle control had returned to his arms and legs, though his limbs felt exhausted. Some autonomous function in his brain flipped on the familiar spiel. "My name is Mick Finn, and I work for a company developing the Glebe Valley apartments—"

"Cut the bullshit," Soul Patch shouted. "What do you want?"

What Finn wanted was to get out of the room alive. He could see now that contacting Velez had been a huge mistake. But here he was, in a high-stakes throwdown. Put up or shut up. Gesturing toward the flyer, Finn said, "There's this guy, Cade, screwing up our plans. Help me discredit this Coalition, and I'll give you a second payment. Twenty thousand total. Enough to relocate somewhere else."

Soul Patch seemed to ponder this offer, then spoke in Spanish, and a pair of hands yanked Finn to his feet. A delayed muscle cramp wobbled his legs. He thrust out a hand to steady himself on the weight bench. He noticed the notebook screen displayed his headshot and bio from URP's website.

Soul Patch followed Finn's eyes. "Yeah, I know all about URP. Projects all over the world. Aggressive pipeline. Solid investor backing. The Street pegs URP as a strong buy."

Though still groggy, Finn was stunned at the gangbanger's spot-on assessment.

Soul Patch clicked on a link, and a pop-up of the Glebe appeared. "Oh yeah, and let's not forget the Glebe," he said with undisguised sarcasm, "an emotional communion of civic and cultural dimensions."

Finn looked down at his shoes. "It's a concept."

"A concept, huh?" A flash of metal creased the air in front of Finn's face. The machete blade hovered at his jugular. "I've got a concept for you. How 'bout I mail your fucking head to Oliver? Maybe URP will up the price, eh?"

A warm wetness suffused his underwear and blotted his khaki trousers. He gulped with embarrassment.

"Look at that!" Soul Patch shouted to the other men. "Bitch better not piss on my floor, motherfucker!"

Humiliated, and reeking of urine, Finn screamed in his head, *Focus!* A gangbanger who knew about Wall Street ratings? Soul Patch was not the usual smash-and-grab punk. He glanced again at the textbooks and shifted tactics. "Okay, okay, let me put it another way. Looks like you've got a supply chain operation here. From what I hear, drugs, prostitution, extortion. A highly mobile customer base with high-risk modalities. Your finances need a secure enterprise platform. Dark web, impossible to trace. Am I right?"

Finn detected a flicker of light in Soul Patch's eyes that quickly extinguished.

"I know IT guys who can set you up." Even as his Adam's apple bobbed against the blade, he managed his best deal-closer smile. "You know something? You have that same hungry look as Steve Jobs." He glanced around the small room. "Although Jobs at least had a garage."

Soul Patch moved the blade from his throat and tapped a few strokes on the keyboard. He barked an order in Spanish. The men released Finn's arms and huddled with their boss. Then one man turned and sucker-punched him in the gut, doubling him over and onto his knees.

By the time he caught his breath, only Soul Patch remained in the utility room. On the desk lay a Glock 9 with a seven-inch silencer barrel. Soul Patch threw the crumpled flyer at him. "Twenty thou won't cut it, motherfucker. I want fifty, and something else."

Finn's stomach heaved, ready to vomit. "What is it?" he gasped.

Soul Patch picked up the handgun, aimed it at a paint can in the corner, and pulled the trigger, the muffled explosion like a popped balloon. The empty can kicked up in the air and ricocheted off the wall. The notebook screen showed Robert Oliver at number five on the Forbes list of the top one hundred billionaires. The Glock swung around so that Finn was staring down the snout of the silencer.

"I want a job with URP."

23

*L*uis watched an angry traffic cop in a yellow safety vest wave a long line of vehicles away from the Chapelita Community Center lot and in the direction of CVS for overflow parking. He'd cautioned Cade to give the police a heads-up about the rally, but clearly he'd forgotten. Maintaining good relations with the police was important. Pissing off the cops was a bad way to start a rally.

On a portable stage, the acoustic mariachi band from the Alamo switched to electric and jammed a hot salsa riff while hips swiveled in the heat. Food trucks sold fish tacos and snow cones. Kids pulled wagons loaded with ice chests selling bottled water and soda pop. A summertime crowd, chattering and laughing. The vibe more street festival than zoning protest. Watching his community enjoying the music and laughing moved Luis with a deep sense of love.

In a nearby tent, volunteers from Our Lady of Seven Sorrows handed out peel-off stickers that read *No Zee 9* and *Save Chapelita*. Twenty rows of folding chairs split by a center aisle spilled onto the pavement. A bucket brigade passed more chairs hand to hand from a storage room. Neighbors lined up ten deep to sign a petition listing URP's transgression against the residents of Glebe Valley.

When Cade moved to his side, Luis frowned. "You forgot to notify the cops like I asked."

"Oops, my bad." Cade turned away, quickly. "I'll be back. Gotta check security."

With Cade gone, Luis started to call Officer Corrine Rodriguez to apologize for not tipping her about the event when Father Gus, shades down, sidled up. Nagged by second thoughts about his non-confession,

Luis put the cell away. "So, Father, you know that thing I was telling you about in private?"

Father Gus slapped Luis on the back. "Vow of secrecy, remember?"

Just then, the conga player ripped a percussive groove backed by a screaming samba lick on lead guitar. Luis leaned close to Father Gus's ear. "Yeah, yeah, I trust you. But what I was going to say is, the reason I wanted Cade out front on this protest thing? I didn't want to draw a lot of attention to myself. But after our talk, I don't feel so, I don't know, shy about things."

A senorita in a bandeau top shimmied in front of Father Gus, who watched her get swallowed by the crowd.

Luis elbowed him. "Did you hear what I just said?"

Father Gus lifted his shades and smiled. "I heard you, brother."

Cade held up five fingers to the bandleader. The quartet finished with a blistering flourish to a round of enthusiastic claps and whistles. Cade hopped up onto the stage. At an elevated height, he was eye level with the multicolored mural wall of the Chapelita Community Center.

Up close, details appeared he'd never noticed from afar. The arm patch on the uniform of the soldier confronting a peasant woman depicted an angel with red eyes holding a flaming sword. Underneath the angel were the words *Escuadron de la Muerte*. Legible names appeared on the white crosses dotting the brown hillside. Gus's tale about the peasant massacre sprang to mind.

In the front row of folding chairs, seven teenagers wore lime-green T-shirts advertising *Oscar's Excellent Landscaping*. In an eighth lime-green T-shirt sat a middle-aged man with a full head of salt-and-pepper hair and a bushy mustache. Muscular arms folded across his chest. Cade guessed the man to be Oscar.

Familiar faces popped out of the crowd. A Korean couple from Kim's Drycleaners. The two guys from the apartment below him who played the loud music. Miguel from the Waffle Shop. No sign of Cassandra, though.

Javier stood off to the left side with the Chapelita Cougars dressed in blue and white soccer uniforms. Cade jumped off the riser and walked over. "Appreciate the Cougars' help with the signs."

Javier smiled. "Maybe all this attention will get us some sponsors for new uniforms and equipment."

"If this goes the way I think it will, you might get a really big sponsor." He bumped fists with Javier and then noticed Luis pointing to his watch. He nudged Javier. "Showtime."

Luis and Father Gus joined Cade on stage. Luis tapped the microphone. The amplified thumps settled people down. "¡Hola! Thank you, everyone, for coming out on such a warm evening. And how about a big round of thanks to our sponsors for the signs and stickers and T-shirts and fans."

The crowd responded with polite applause.

"I know it's hot, so we're going to get right to the reason why we are here. I want to introduce a good friend of mine. You may not know him, but you have probably seen his Green Flash taxi cab around the neighborhood. He has something to say about what's going on with Glebe Valley. Please welcome Jack Cade." Luis lowered the hand mike. "Give 'em hell, amigo."

Cade wiped the sweat from his eyes. A new day and a new mission. He surveyed the assemblage of friends and neighbors and began. "Hello, friends. My name is Jack Cade, and I'm sick and tired of people telling me where I can live and where I can't."

Scattered claps and shouts.

He launched into the basics: URP's plans to raze the Glebe Valley apartments, to be replaced by high-priced condos and townhomes. The strip mall across the street reconfigured into upscale boutiques and restaurants selling authentic Salvadoran crafts and cuisine that none of them could afford.

A wave of groans and epithets crashed upon the stage.

"Exactly right, my friends. URP plans to exploit your culture for every dime they can squeeze out of it." In a show of solidarity, Cade patted the shoulder of Father Gus and Luis.

"And that ain't even the worst insult. URP is going to throw us a few bucks to make sure we move out quickly and quietly. They call it a relocation bonus. Yeah, a bonus for URP, that is. It's a cheap way to move thousands of residents in a thousand directions. And once we are spread out, our political power is diffused."

The crowd booed and jeered.

Cade waited for the uproar to subside. "URP needs zoning approval to proceed with the deal. In a short while, just a few blocks up the street"—Cade pointed northbound on Washington Avenue—"they'll be asking the Planning and Zoning Commission for a big favor. A favor that says the rules don't apply to them."

The mike squealed with feedback. Hands clasped over ears. Cade grimaced, then continued. "You know what they call this favor? They call it Zee 9. A section of the zoning code that smart lawyers manipulate for rich clients. Not for folks like us that *live* here. It means URP gets a *special* exception, so they can kick us out."

Catcalls erupted from the crowd.

"I know where I'd like to kick URP," Cade shouted, really into it now. Laughter burst from the audience. "Say it with me: *No Zee 9! No Zee 9!*"

The throng echoed the refrain: *No Zee 9! No Zee 9! No Zee 9!*

Then, from across the street, Cade heard another chorus. From atop the stage, he saw a dozen women wearing T-shirts with the Watchdog logo: a German shepherd superimposed over a red, white, and blue flag motif. Their signs read, "Day Workers Go Home." "Protect Our Borders." "Enforce the Law." A woman with a bullhorn led the Watchdogs in a rousing cheer: *USA! USA! USA!*

Cade faced the Watchdogs, pumping his hands upward, egging the crowd to shout louder: *No Zee 9! No Zee! No Zee 9!*

USA! USA! USA!

No Zee 9! No Zee 9! No Zee 9!

USA! USA! USA!

Two traffic cops closed ranks to restrain the two groups from converging. Cade looked around frantically for Luis, then spied him in the middle of the street, shouting at the Watchdogs, "Put down your guns."

Cade leapt off the stage and pushed through the crowd.

"A Watchdog almost shot a little girl," Luis screamed at the woman with the bullhorn. The woman outweighed him by fifty pounds.

"Look, Pedro," she sneered, "go back to Mexico, where you belong."

"¡Perra estúpido!" Luis shouted, sending an inadvertent speck of saliva onto the woman's chin.

Her face flushed red with heat and anger, the Watchdog reared back and spat in Luis's face. Before Luis could react, a man in a brown tie and short-sleeve shirt jumped in front of the woman. "You started it," he said to Luis. "You heard her. Go back to Mexico."

Luis wiped his face and took a step forward when a hand on his shoulder yanked him back. Luis spun around and hissed at Cade, "Stay out of this."

Cade recognized the woman with the bullhorn from her picture in the newspaper. Evelyn Everhard, the Watchdog who'd winged the day laborer at the Git 'n Go. His gaze shifted from Evelyn to the man shielding her from Luis. Earl Everhard, from the tax preparation office.

Earl's eyes widened at the sight of Cade next to Luis. "You're with him?"

"Damn right, I'm with him." Cade grabbed Earl's shirt collar and drew him close enough to smell garlic on his breath. "You're a real piece of work, Earl. You got the chamber backing the Glebe and a sweet deal for your new office, but that's not enough for you. You have to come down here with these idiots and insult your neighbors, too."

"Watch your mouth, mister," Evelyn said. "Watchdogs stand for law and order. Must be a new idea for your illegal friends."

Earl's eyes bulged as Cade's grip tightened on his shirt collar

"You're killing him!" Evelyn dug her nails into Cade's hand. He yelped and released Earl. Father Gus pled for folks to go back to their side of the street. The Glebe Valley folks slowly retreated to the parking lot, while the cops herded the Watchdogs further away.

Father Gus hopped on the stage and called for everyone to remain calm. "Do not allow them to provoke you." He repeated his message in

Spanish. After a few minutes, the crowd settled into a rough idle, clearly rattled by the confrontation. Cade retrieved the mike from Father Gus.

"Folks, listen to Father Gus. Save some of that energy for the hearing. But we must act fast and smart. As I was saying, the other side has lawyers and lots of money—"

Before Cade could complete the sentence, an outbreak of voices, still riled from the brush with the Watchdogs, bawled and vented.

"Ain't nothing you can do about it," said a man in the third row.

"Take the money before it's gone," said another.

"Why wait to get hacked by gangbangers."

The outrage was going viral, spreading exponentially.

"Why don't the cops bust them?"

"Folks know who done it, but don't want to say."

"Scared of retaliation."

"ICE picked up Arturo last week."

"The Watchdogs called it in."

"Screw the Watchdogs."

The conversation was going south in a hurry. Cade had taught the jundi that unfocused anger equalled wasted energy. He had to reel it in fast. "Everybody, please, listen." He paused. The crowd hushed. And just like that, his train of thought derailed. He forgot what he was about to say. He felt the stage sway and a slight dizziness as if he were teetering on a wire. Exposed on the stage, he was an easy target for an insurgent sniper. Then, just at the moment of duck and cover, it was as if Arthur A. Arthur's rage coursed through his veins.

Many in the crowd worked two or three jobs to pay the rent, with little left over. Now URP was moving in, taking over, and evicting residents from their homes and community. And for what? So URP could sell emotional communion bullshit to well-off chic geeks in search of a socially networked urban village with a low carbon footprint and granite countertops? What did Rita say: *Fuck that shit!*

What difference did it make if men hung around the Git 'n Go to pick up extra cash doing whatever shit job a contractor was offering that day? They weren't bothering anybody. Except maybe the Watchdogs, who resented their very existence. Damn xenophobes. Time to crush the snakehead.

Flushed with adrenaline, Cade raised the mike. "Forget the Watchdogs. Stay focused on *our* mission. We must stand together. A company that builds homes for rich people made a deal with the city. A deal that affects my life. Maybe yours too, or somebody you know. Oh sure, they've had a few meetings in the neighborhood. Mostly for show. But seriously, did anyone ask *your* opinion on what should happen with Glebe Valley *before* moving ahead with plans to demolish *our* apartments? Our voices must be heard."

In the first row, the middle-aged man with the bushy mustache in a lime-green T-shirt shouted, "Nobody asked me nothing."

A man in the next row answered, "Exactly, Oscar. People have jobs here, families, kids in schools. What are we supposed to do? Throw our stuff in the back of a pickup and move who knows where?"

A hundred faces looked to Cade for a response. "My friends, there's a fire advancing toward Chapelita. A fire fanned by URP. And the fire is burning everything in its path. If we don't act now, it will destroy our homes and community." Sweat dripped from his nose like a leaky faucet. "You know what firefighters do when a forest fire threatens people's homes?"

"Use a hose!" a voice shouted.

"Exactly," said Cade, "but what else? I'll tell you. They set a backfire to extinguish the fuel that feeds the fire. And then the fire burns itself out." Cade snapped his fingers for effect. "Just like that." He stooped down, knees cracking, and asked a young boy standing at the foot of the stage, "Do you know what happens *after* a forest fire burns out?"

The kid rolled his eyes and shied away from the microphone.

Then, a synaptic connection retrieved a passage from Arthur's book that amazed even Cade, whose short-term memory had been decaying at an ever-increasing rate since the IED attack. He straightened, looked over the heads of the gathered faithful, spotted Grif at his watch post on the far perimeter, closed his eyes, and recited as if reading from the page: "'After the destruction, the forest regenerates itself, and creates opportunities for new growth—'" he paused for a breath, then added, '"and justice."' His eyes opened to a woman with a mop of curly brown hair, wearing khaki shorts and a black tank top with a green and red screened portrait of Che Guevara. Cade caught himself staring at Rita Castro. Her white smile beaming from ten feet away.

Stunned that she'd decided to attend the rally after all, he beckoned her onstage. Tanned and lean, Rita bounded onto the stage. Silver hoop earrings danced with her every move. A touch of blush brought out her high cheekbones. A smoldering presence, like a flint set to tinder. Perfect for lighting a backfire.

He introduced Rita as a special guest and passed her the mike. She wasted no time ripping into URP with a vengeance. Callous corporate rapists, she cried, despoiling the Glebe Valley community.

Cade caught the eye of Father Gus, who seemed to shrink in his chair at Rita's impolitic harangue. Luis turned up his palms in a gesture of helplessness as if to say, "You invited her." But Rita was just getting warmed up. She belittled Oliver's affordable unit set-aside as an insult to the working men and women of Glebe Valley.

The steamy heat and excitation whipped the crowd into a lather. Rita curled her finger, and a woman in the crowd joined her on stage. To Cade's surprise, Rita introduced Delores, the woman from the Salvadoran bakery whom Cade had tagged as a definite maybe. Rita held the mike while Delores told how the bakery had put her two kids through college. "We will not be forced out of our homes and shops," Delores said. "I am going to stay and fight."

Rita kissed Delores on the cheek. "You hear that? You hear that? We're going to stay and fight!" A roar of support rose from the people. Like a a gaping maw, the crowd hungered for more—and Rita delivered. Hurling insults and derision at URP, she exhorted the assembled men and women to a fevered pitch under a sweltering sun. Drenched in sweat, she spread her arms and wailed, "What do you say, friends? Will you stand up for Chapelita?"

Nobody moved.

Rita repeated it again, louder. "Will you stand up for Chapelita?"

Finally, Oscar stood up, followed immediately by his green-shirted landscaping crew. And then another man in the crowd stood, and another, and finally everybody was on their feet.

"We are Chapelita!" Rita proclaimed, the microphone acoustics fuzzing her words. In response, the crowd responded in English and Spanish, "We are Chapelita!"

"I can't hear you!"

"We are Chapelita!"

"Louder!" Rita cried. "So they can hear you at city hall!"

The crescendo rolled and echoed like cannon fire. "We are Chapelita!"

On the edge of the crowd, Grif kept a close eye on the bodies packed in front of the stage from behind a pair of black steel-framed sunglasses. He had watched the yelling match with the Watchdogs and had been ready to jump in, if needed. But Father Gus had calmed the situation nicely, and now things were back on track, more or less.

Off to his right, the two traffic cops had staked out a shady spot under a locust tree for relief from the relentless sun. At this distance, the portable speakers distorted most of what Rita was saying. But when Grif heard the crowd roar, "We are Chapelita," he figured the speechifying was wrapping up.

Making a final sweep of the crowd, he saw a head that stood out. The man wore a knit cap pulled low to a pair of mirrored aviators. A purple bandana hung loosely around his neck. Grif eased his way through the crowd. Up close, Grif noticed the man had a tuft of hair beneath his lower lip. He wore a long-sleeved denim shirt buttoned to the neck and untucked over black sweatpants. The knit cap, long sleeves, and sweats made an unusual fashion statement in ninety-five-degree heat. The man in the knit cap scanned the crowd. His eyes landed briefly on Grif and then moved back to the stage.

Grif inched forward. The cops had moved from their shady spot and now stood next to their cruiser. Another man, also with a purple bandana and a shaved dome, appeared next to the man in the knit cap.

He wore an oversized North Face hoodie that reached to his knees. When the hoodie turned his head, Grif spied a single blue teardrop under the left eye. The tightly packed crowd made it nearly impossible to push through. A bystander jostled the cell phone out of Grif's hand. He bent to retrieve the phone among the tangle of legs, and when he straightened, the two men had vanished.

Cade was awestruck at Rita's performance. Her stories of past renter fights, approaching mythical status, told of heroic victories against insurmountable odds. Despair not! She threw out everything but *I have a dream*. No awkward pauses like his embarrassing lapse. His remarks had been the steak, but Rita sold the sizzle. The climactic ovation had brought the crowd to an orgasmic release of tension and fury. Hands reached up to congratulate her. Perfect timing for Father Gus to cast a spiritual gloss over Rita's rabble-rousing rant.

Cade stood next to Rita and raised her hand like a prizefighter. "I thought you weren't coming," he whispered through a tight grin.

Her high-beam smile zapped Cade like a bug light. Whatever righteous indignation he had felt for her not calling him crumbled. His knees weakened. He needed to move things along, and quickly welcomed Father Gus back to the stage. He wore the same white guayabera shirt over creased jeans as he had at the Waffle Shop, but now with a black pectoral crucifix hanging from a chain around his neck.

"Brothers and sisters," Father Gus began, "you have heard from our friends"—he gestured toward Cade and Rita—"how URP exploits our labor, then banishes us from our homes to the far regions of the county, and beyond. Separated from families and jobs, perpetuating the very conditions of poverty that we seek to overcome, contrary to all standards of human dignity and the will of God. The impoverishment of our community is a sin that must not stand.

"They say the new Glebe will transform a distressed community. That's all we are to them, a *distressed lot*. But what shall we call a development that produces economic wealth for a few but cares not for the development of the soul, the immortal life breath that connects us all to our ancestors and all of God's creation?"

"Tell it, Father," a voice shouted.

"Shame unto them who make unjust laws and use them to take away our homes and heritage. And so, I say to you, my friends, in the name of a just and moral Creator, we proclaim our right to Chapelita." Father Gus raised his crucifix. "In the name of the Father, the Son, and the Holy Spirit, may God bless our actions today and hear our cry for justice." He paused, then said, "Say it with me: Amen."

"Amen," the crowd thundered. Men and women signed the cross. Cade embraced Father Gus. "Hell of a sermon, padre." Then he faced the audience. "What's going to happen next is that we are going to take a short walk to the municipal center. The Planning and Zoning meeting begins promptly at five o'clock. Over by the tent, we have signs and T-shirts. Pick up one of each. What do you say, folks? Are you ready to march?"

Again, the crowd cheered. Cade jumped off the stage. Javier and the Chapelita Cougars manned the tables in the tent and handed out signs and yellow T-shirts emblazoned with SAVE CHAPELITA. At the far end of the table was a stack of noisemakers—empty soup cans filled with pebble-sized rocks and beans.

He found Rita engrossed in a confab with some local neighbors and elbowed his way in. He caught her eye, and she excused herself for a moment.

"How in the hell do you even *know* Delores, much less get her to talk on stage? All I got was a hug and a pupusa."

Rita's lips curled into an enigmatic smile. "I have my ways."

"Well, I'm glad you made it. They loved you. Look, I gotta talk with a few people. Can you march with us?"

"Are you kidding? I wouldn't miss it."

And without thinking of Cassandra or her polygraph vibe detector, he added, "Just a friendly reminder, the Marlins and Nats are playing a doubleheader Saturday. Can you stick around?"

Rita hesitated. "Let's see how the protest goes first."

"Whatsamatter? Afraid the Marlins might get beat?" Cade joked with a crooked Harrison Ford grin.

Rita's smile vanished. "My team won't fail this time. I guarantee it."

* * *

Red Top, Blue Top, Yellow Top, White Star, Black Diamond, Cherry Blossom, Freedom Flyer, and Majestic—cabs from throughout the metro area—lined the curb outside the Elbert Lee Trinkle Municipal Building. It took only a few calls for Cade to find drivers more than happy to return the favor for when he'd organized the cab strike.

Meanwhile, five blocks away, Cade, Rita, Luis, and Father Gus locked arms and led the marchers past the Waffle Shop and the Git 'n Go. They stayed on the sidewalk as two police motorcycles kept pace in the curb lane. Onlookers cheered and joined the throng. Kids on bikes rode alongside.

When they approached the municipal building, instead of heading to the main entrance, Cade directed them to form up along a rear wall near a fire door. He sent a text, and a few seconds later, Grif opened the emergency exit with a conveniently disabled alarm. Father Gus ushered the folks into the cramped stairwell and up two landings to the main level, while Cade and Luis walked around to the front of the building to meet up with Javier and the Chapelita Cougars. Luis directed each Cougar to stand alongside a taxi with a white placard in hand.

From the top step of the front entrance, Cade saw a woman in a Subaru with duct tape over a shattered rear window aiming a telephoto lens and firing away. The same square-jawed Watchdog he'd clashed with a short while ago. Evelyn Everhard.

He waved to the cabbies, held up his fist, and counted down: five, four, three, two, one. He yanked down his fist and, in perfect synchronization, the drivers hit the horns on their steering columns. The outburst, like a megaton of angry geese, drew city workers to the windows to check out the commotion.

* * *

A soft knock interrupted City Attorney Stephen S. Slegg's contemplation of an amendment to a special use permit to co-locate a frozen yogurt shop with a hot yoga studio—the *YO-YO*. A wild-eyed secretary stuck her head in the door. "You better come quickly!"

Slegg raced behind the secretary to the frontage windows. The cacophony of honking continued unabated. Then, as if on some unseen signal, a line of thirteen youngsters flipped over their placards and spelled out: SAVE CHAPELITA. Two police officers brushed past Slegg to join other cops on the scene.

"Cade!" Slegg yelled.

The secretary pulled back. "I beg your pardon?"

Ignoring the woman, Slegg ran toward the hearing room in the opposite wing of the municipal center.

* * *

With the cops preoccupied with the taxi ruckus, Cade and Luis hustled down the hallway to the stairwell exit. Cade cracked the door and saw the huddled masses behind Grif, who gave the thumbs-up. He widened the door, and the marchers filed out in an orderly fashion and regrouped outside the city council chambers.

"Okay, this is it," Cade said. "Follow my lead." He pushed open the chamber doors, and the group filled the hearing room. A wall of yellow T-shirts that read *Save Chapelita* confronted seven Planning and Zoning Commission members seated behind a curved mahogany desk. Behind the desk, a six-foot portrait of Elbert Lee Trinkle frowned upon the rabble with an expression of pinched constipation.

A smaller table occupied the gap formed by the U-shaped desk. At one end sat a woman presenting the staff report to the P&Z. Propped on an easel was the architectural rendering of The Glebe at Cub Run. At the other end of the table, in front of a binder organized with color-coded tabs containing the zoning application, contracts, notarized letters of agreement, site plans, certificates, and duly executed attestations of authenticity, sat a man whom Cade recognized as the speaker at the gymnasium presentation. Mick Finn.

A woman seated at the center of the large table banged a gavel and called for security. She instructed a clerk to notify the police outside assisting with the cab riot. Five men unfurled a nine-foot banner: *Glebe*

Valley Is Our Home. Father Gus and others held up hand-lettered signs that read: *We have a right to remain* and *I can't afford $2000 for Apt.* Cade led the protesters in a chant: No Zee Nine! No Zee Nine! No Zee Nine!

Adding to the racket, the protesters shook soup cans filled with pebbles and beans. Cade gave a hand signal for quiet and then, in a voice loud and clear, read the petition:

"We are the people of Chapelita.

We have a right to remain in our homes and community.

We *reject* the displacement of five thousand people from the Glebe Valley apartments.

We *reject*—"

Cade didn't get a chance to finish. A man wearing a yellow *Save Chapelita* T-shirt over a long-sleeved denim shirt pushed his way to the front. He wore a knit cap and mirrored aviator sunglasses. A purple bandana covered his mouth and nose. His right hand leveled a Glock. Rita was closest to the gunman. She grabbed the man's wrist and spun him around, as the first shot rocked the chambers. The gun shot triggered a panic.

P&Z members dove beneath the desk. A stampede mashed at the chamber's door. Rita grappled with the gunman. Cade shoved bodies out of the way and got the shooter in a neck hold. Rita bit down hard on the shooter's wrist. The man screamed and kneed her in the stomach. Cade wrestled the man to the desk, scattering Finn's binder and papers. He wrestled with the assailant just as the gun discharged a second time. The man in the knit cap and purple bandana slithered away from Cade's grip.

Police reinforcements entered from a side door. A baton under his neck yanked Cade backward to the floor. Another set of hands restrained his wrists in plasti-cuffs. From out of nowhere, Grif appeared, punching the cop straddling Cade. Other cops overpowered Grif in a hail of body blows.

Behind the mahogany desk, the scowl of Elbert Lee Trinkle changed not a bit, shot though he was between the eyes. The cops pulled Cade toward a side exit. He glimpsed the body on the floor in the white guayabera shirt. One hand clutched a black crucifix, the Son of God nailed to a raft in a red sea of blood.

* * *

The protesters flooded out of the building. Luis stood at the foot of the entrance like a log dividing a river of humanity. A cop told him no one was to leave the premises until identified by a police officer. No sign of Cade, Rita, Father Gus, or Grif. Cops herded Luis and the protesters together for identification and statements. The police produced a composite sketch of the shooter based on the description of several panicked witnesses—a sketch that showed few discernable facial features under a knit cap, sunglasses, and a bandana.

The news media reported that Father Gus had been shot, but his condition was unknown. It was almost 10 PM by the time the police released the protesters. Exhausted, Luis found Corrine talking to another cop. He motioned her away. "Can I talk to you for a minute? How is Father Gus?"

Corrine's thumbs hooked into her leather duty belt, her elbows flared to the side. She twisted her neck as if looking for someone. "I'm sorry," she said.

"You're sorry? What are you sorry for?"

She adjusted the duty belt on her ample hips. "Don't say I told you anything, yet. A public announcement will be made after the next of kin are notified."

Luis's mouth opened, but no words formed. The man to whom he'd confided his darkest secret had just taken a bullet to his grave. Cade and Rita's bullshit had provoked a nut job to shoot up the city council chambers. He should have grabbed the mike when he had the chance.

"What about Cade?" Luis asked.

"He's being held for questioning." Corrine headed toward the station, then turned. "So, Luis, why'd you get mixed up with a nut job like Cade in the first place?"

"What?"

"Preliminary records check. He was court-martialed for striking an officer. Shirking duty. If you ask me, the dude is wrapped way too tight."

A loner maybe, Luis thought, but Cade's heart was usually in the right place; it just took a while for his brain to catch up. He moved away from Corrine to comfort a young woman holding an infant.

* * *

Luis called Angie to let her know he was on his way home. While passing the Alamo, he decided on a quick one to unwind from the day's ordeal.

Behind the bar, Tony watched the late news rerun the cell phone video from inside the council chambers. The video feed jerked and jumped with the pandemonium. The audio picked up the first shot, then a grainy view of a man holding a gun, then blurred chaos.

"Pacifica and a shot of Cuervo," Luis snapped. "Make it a double."

Tony set him up. Luis downed the shot, followed by a long swallow of beer. After a satisfying belch he pointed to the television. "Look!"

The police sketch of the shooter filled the screen. The knit cap pulled down low. The mirrored aviators, the bandana covering the chin and mouth. Viewers were urged to call the tip line with any information.

"I take it you were there," Tony said, eyeing Luis's *Save Chapelita* T-shirt.

"What a disaster."

"Heard a priest got shot. Any word on his condition?"

He wagged his head, recalling Corrine's admonition to stay quiet until the police made a public announcement. His finger tapped the empty shot glass.

Tony poured a refill. "What's gonna happen with all that protest shit?"

Luis threw back the double shot. "Nothing. It's over."

"Don't give up so quick," said a middle-aged man in a lime-green T-shirt crouched over a beer at the end of the bar.

Luis smiled. "Oscar, you mangy dog. You made it out."

"Yeah, the cops know me and my crew. They cut us loose early."

Luis carried his Pacifica and shot glass to the stool next to Oscar. The newscast had moved on to sports and the Nats' nineteenth loss in a row.

"Any word on Father Gus?" said Oscar.

Luis leaned into him. "Don't tell anyone where you heard this, okay? Father Gus is dead."

"Dead!" Oscar exclaimed, prompting Tony to turn from the television and look at them.

"Keep your voice down," said Luis. "It hasn't been announced yet."

"Aw, man."

Luis clinked his bottle against Oscar's mug. "To Father Gus."

A minute passed, maybe two. The men studied their beers. Luis signaled Tony and held up an empty shot glass. The Cuervo warmed his empty belly. He'd not eaten anything since lunch.

"Slow down, Luis," said Tony as he poured another double.

Luis slugged the golden agave. "The shooter better hope the police find him before I do." He rolled up his sleeve to show Oscar the blue and red tattoo of the Angel of Death.

Oscar's eyes widened at the sight of the ghoulish reaper of souls.

Luis raised his arms overhead, as if gripping a sword with two hands. His words tumbled out in a boozy slur.

"Soy el ángel de la muerte.

Que Dios se apiade de tu alma.

Porque yo no."

Oscar laughed nervously. "Hold on, Luis. My Spanish is not as good as yours."

Luis rose off the stool, wobbling from the Cuervo. His face darkened as he assumed the executioner's stance, wielding an imaginary blade.

The smile disappeared from Oscar's lips.

Luis repeated in English the last words heard by so many condemned men who had once knelt at his feet:

"I am the angel of death.

God have mercy on your soul.

Because I will not."

24

*A*fter fifteen hours of grueling interrogation, the police released Cade from custody. No, he didn't want or need a lawyer because he had nothing to hide. During the ordeal, the detectives had poked and probed every incriminating incident in his life—starting with the court-martial for striking an officer, the fight with the cab company owner, his outburst at the URP presentation, the assault on Earl Everhard at the Watchdog rally. They found the construction workers who claimed he threw the first punch over a minor dent to his cab. The detectives painted a picture of an unstable man on a short fuse, prone to outbreaks of sudden violence. Confronted with the accumulated weight of his shady record, Cade began to doubt his own innocence. Maybe he *had* blacked out and fired the gun. Was temporary insanity an actual thing?

The detectives expressed cynical disbelief at his lame explanations, hoping to provoke a confession. As the hours of questioning dragged on, Cade had grown noticeably agitated and sweaty. A phantom ringing in his ears signaled another migraine. They'd even asked where he was on the night of the machete attack. He teetered on the edge of a nervous breakdown. Fortunately, cell phone video surfaced showing the man in the knit cap firing the gun before Cade wrestled it away.

In the morning, Cade walked out of the police station exhausted, angry, and hungry. He found himself walking in the direction of the Waffle Shop. At the diner, he grabbed a booth with a discarded newspaper. The front page carried the story of the shooting and his checkered background. A photograph of Father Gus with the angelic smile of a newly ordained priest accompanied the article. The recall of Gus's blood-soaked body unleashed horrific visions of gut shot soldiers.

The paper also leaked details of his interrogation. Was it paranoia or did the old man on a counter stool just give him the hairy eyeball? And the young couple in the booth who stopped whispering when he sat down—what was that all about? Even Miguel poured his coffee in silence.

Cade's finger worked a rip in the vinyl seat, picking out small pieces of the foam cushion. As the purported leader of the protest, the article also delved into his military record. He looked at the grainy photograph with the caption: *IED blast kills seven Iraqi troops; one US soldier injured.*

He remembered the blast, like being punched by a giant fist. The cinder block wall shielded him from the first blast wave of highly compressed air, but the secondary wave, the back blast, came rushing in to fill the void caused by the first wave. The back blast is the motherfucker: bladders explode, lungs burst, brains oscillate and swell before rupturing. Milliseconds after the concussive shock wave, he was hit with a downpour of gasoline and hot debris.

He heard screams and shouts, then a ringing in his ears. Dirt and blood filled his mouth. Dust and smoke blanketed the street. Orange flames licked the remains of the truck. An acrid stink of burning rubber and bodies sickened his stomach. A hellish nightmare.

He was dimly aware of being lifted in the air. His hands instinctively reached out to make sure legs and arms were intact. He raised himself up on the stretcher and saw two jundi drape a sheet over a charred and decapitated torso. Metal and glass crackled underfoot as the soldiers searched the rubble for body parts. He asked for water, and a canteen appeared.

His voice croaked, "Grif?"

A hand touched his shoulder.

"Gimme a cigarette."

Grif patted Cade's pockets. He pulled out a pack of Marlboros along with a piece of cloth with red, white, and black bands. "This yours?" said Grif.

Cade reached up for the gift from Malik just as the wash from the medevac rotor blades snatched the Iraqi flag from his grasp in a swirl of smoke and sky. Somewhere a cell phone chimed. He looked around the Waffle Shop, then realized that the chime was coming from his pocket.

"Where are you?" asked Grif.

Cade shook off the blast wave and filled Grif in on the fifteen hours at the police station.

"Did you see the paper yet?"

"I'm looking right at it. Where are you?" Cade said.

"I'm at home. I slugged the cop on top of you, remember? But my lawyer got them to drop the charge given the heat of the moment and my spotless record."

"Good for you. My record ain't so spotless."

"Bullshit," Grif said. "You ought to sue them for slander. Seriously, how are you holding up?"

Cade massaged his temples. "I'm okay."

"You don't sound okay. Let's meet for lunch. You had nothing to do with that priest getting shot. Tell them to interview me. I'll set them straight."

The words stung. Once again, Cade had lived while another man lost his life.

Grif said, "I'll call you when I'm leaving. The usual place. You copy?"

"Copy that." Cade glanced down at the paper. A sidebar told the rest of his shameful past: *Protest Leader Blamed PTSD to Avoid Combat.*

After the IED attack and a brief recuperation from his injuries, he'd returned to Fort Carson in Colorado Springs. Intense headaches split his skull. He had difficulty remembering dates and places. The doctors referred Cade to an Army psychiatrist, but he'd refused to go, fearing the stigma of a weak-minded wimp.

Depression set in, then binges on beer and opioids. His hygiene slacked off—days went by without a shower. He showed up for muster in a rumpled uniform and beard stubble. A second offense. The captain barked an order to square away his slovenly appearance. Hungover, Cade swung a right hook to the officer's chin.

The military police charged him with multiple offenses, all variations on the theme of intent to inflict grievous bodily harm on a superior officer. His court-appointed attorney, newly minted from the Army Judge Advocate General program, was some fresh-scrubbed kid six months out of law school with a backlog of cases. He thumbed Cade's medical file.

"Don't even think about PTSD as a defense. The Army doesn't like that diagnosis. Too many slackers are trying to con disability payments. Plus, it can expose the Army to lawsuits for malfeasance. Hire a civilian attorney, if you can afford it. But if you ask me, you'd just be throwing your money away. Court-martials have a ninety percent conviction rate for a reason."

The kid checked his watch, one of those cheap plastic things sold in the commissary. "Court-martials are not like trials in the outside world." He met Cade's eyes. "In the Army, the judge and jury already believe you're guilty. Otherwise, you wouldn't be sitting there."

In the end, despite a Purple Heart for wounds suffered in the IED attack, Cade found himself on the receiving end of a bad conduct discharge. They might have just as well branded a giant *M* on his forehead: Malingerer.

The newspaper didn't come right out and say it. The inference was enough. Instead of a champion for the Glebe Valley tenants, another picture emerged—Cade the unstable coward. What would Cassandra think of him now?

Miguel refilled Cade's mug and noticed the gaping rip in the booth and a pile of foam padding. "What the hell are you doing?"

Still lost in the court-martial morass, Cade threw down a ten and bolted for the door.

* * *

Reporters ambushed Finn in the condo garage: *Did you see the shooter? Are you going through with the Glebe Valley project?* He stiff-armed the microphones and drove away. At the office, he shut the door and refused to take calls. The flat screen tuned to the midday news cycle. He channel surfed every few seconds. All the stations ran a loop of the cell phone video inside the municipal chambers. The gunshots, a jerky crush of panicked protesters fleeing for their lives.

The media was on both sides of the story. A *Washington Post* editorial praised the tenants and workers who defied the corporate exploiters. Father Gus was a martyr for the cause. More to Finn's liking was a conservative pundit's condemnation of Cade and the socialist protesters for instigating the violence that claimed the life of an innocent priest. Cade's court-martial added fuel to the gossip and speculation. Bloggers belittled him for shirking his duty. The allegations discredited him and, by extension, the motives of the protesters.

Not that Finn cared about any of that. Soul Patch had called demanding an extra ten thousand for his trouble. But the gangbanger was only supposed to disrupt the meeting, not kill anyone. Finn agreed to smuggle him out of the basement pissoir. Keep a low profile, Finn warned, until he could make other arrangements. Ever the ingrate, Soul Patch growled, "Get me a fucking job, and I'll decide where I want to live."

The demand was absurd. *How the hell am I supposed to get a gangbanger a job with URP?* But the machete blade at his neck had not been an idle threat. The thing to do now was to call Slegg and get the zoning application back on track.

The screen now showed live coverage of the Watchdogs carrying signs and parading in front of the Git 'n Go. After shooting a wanted felon, Finn figured the Watchdogs would keep a low profile—but here they were, claiming that the criminal's assault on Evelyn Everhard proved their point: illegals not only mooched public benefits, but they constituted a dangerous element. In comments to a reporter, Evelyn insinuated that the courthouse shooter was likely a disgruntled day laborer. The Watchdogs demanded that the city immediately shut down all pickup spots.

Finn muted the television. He was about to call Slegg when his cell buzzed. The readout indicated Sandra Howell, the attorney representing the Kaplan brothers, owners of the Glebe Valley apartments. For a second, he considered not answering. "Hey, Sandy, what's up?"

"The Glebe Valley sale is off," Sandy said, crunching ice chips in Finn's ear.

Finn clicked off the screen. "I'm sorry, Sandy, what did you say?"

"The sale is off, Mick. The complaint is being couriered over."

"Slow down. What are you talking about?"

"Zoning nonconformance, failure to perform, et cetera."

"Acts of God, we had no control over the shooting," Finn protested. "Besides, we'll countersue for breach of contract."

"Whatever," said Sandy.

Finn heard a burbling sound like someone sucking a beverage through a straw, and the grate of more ice chips. "We don't have to win," Sandy said, "just drag out the suit until your investors get tired of seeing their money tied up in litigation and watching public opinion swing our way. The syndicate will pressure you to settle. We'll get damages and attorney fees. You're going to lose, Mick. It's just a matter of when. Tell Oliver to cut his losses on this one."

Finn snapped a ballpoint pen. "Look, Sandy. We can work this out. I'll get the zoning app rescheduled. And bump the purchase price."

"You don't get it, Mick. This deal was supposed to go through quietly. Now the Kaplans are taking serious heat in the media for selling the property to URP. This mess is hurting their community relations image big-time. The sale is off." Sandy hung up.

Finn screamed, "Shit!"

Ann heard the expletive and stuck her head in the door. "Everything okay, Mr. Finn?"

Finn met her look of concern. "Sorry, I just got the estimate on the bodywork for my car. I'm okay." Ann withdrew with a puzzled expression.

Oliver would fire him for sure if he heard that the Kaplans had canceled the Glebe Valley sale. Maybe he could shift the blame and make Slegg the sacrificial lamb. He called Slegg with the news from Sandy and the likelihood of a protracted legal battle.

"Take a breath, Mick," Slegg said. "Sandy called me, too. I already have Plan B." Then, like an ovipositor wasp, Slegg inserted two words in Finn's ear to feed and hatch.

"I like it." Finn smiled. "Clean and simple. Let's do it." After hanging up with Slegg, he called Oliver, determined to give him the news first before he heard it from Ashpole. London was five hours ahead of DC. He imagined the afternoon sun deepening the shadows in the cornices and columns of URP's mansion headquarters.

"Yes?" Oliver's tone was sharp, impatient.

"I've got news," said Finn.

"Don't waste my time."

"First the bad news. The Kaplans are backing out of the Glebe Valley sale. Bogus claim with no merit. Essentially caving because of bad PR. We could counter for millions in damages and fees. But a suit could take years to litigate."

"Goddamn it, Mick. You know the Glebe is our next-gen prototype."

"Now the good news." Finn uttered the same two words that Slegg had given him, and from thirty-seven hundred miles away, he swore he heard the slithering emergence of a new wasp larva.

25

*A*fter ducking out of the Waffle Shop, Cade drove for a couple of hours to take his mind off the clusterfuck of the past twenty-four hours. He picked up a fare at the Pentagon, a trim man in a suit with military-styled hair. On a Pentagon tour, long ago, he'd learned that the government originally built the defense agency on swampland known as Hell's Bottom—a crime-ridden slum populated by ne'er-do-wells, freed slaves, prostitutes, and mosquitos. When the government needed more land to expand the massive fortress, more than 150 families faced eviction from their squalid homes. Echoes of Glebe Valley. Some things never change.

Stopped at a light, Cade glanced at the vehicle in the right lane, then screamed at his passenger, "Get down!"

Stunned at the outburst, the man swiveled to look for the threat. "What is it?"

Sweat poured down Cade's face. His heart thumped like a big bass drum. A white Nissan pickup idled in the next lane. "Uh, sorry, man," he stammered. "Thought I saw something. Never mind."

"Look, I'll just get out here." The man leapt from the cab without paying.

The light turned green. A car honked. Cade covered his face and wept.

* * *

When Cade entered the Waffle Shop, he found Grif scarfing down a platter of carne asada with beans and rice.

"I couldn't wait, so I went ahead," Grif said.

Cade slid in on the opposite side of the booth. The rip he'd made earlier had been patched with duct tape.

Grif looked up from the plate. "You all right? Eyes look a little red."

Cade recounted the incident with the white pickup. "I thought it was going to explode. I'm losing it, man. I can't stop thinking about Father Gus. He gave me this." Cade pulled out the journal with the gold-embossed cross. "He said I might find a use for it someday. Then the paper runs a bullshit article about me faking PTSD. Bloggers calling me a loser traitor. Cassandra's not returning my calls. Other than that, everything's fine."

Grif paused in mid-chew. "Cassandra? She that psycho chick?"

"Psychic, not psycho." Cade waved to Miguel and ordered an everything burger. "Migraines are killing me."

"Don't beat yourself up," Grif said with a mouthful of food. "The police will find the shooter." He pointed to the sliver of metal on Cade's carabiner key chain—shrapnel retrieved from his leg. "Still hanging onto that, I see."

Cade managed a rueful smile. "My lucky souvenir. Keeps me safe, or as safe as can be."

"Better than the souvenir we got from that bar girl in Bangkok," Grif said, almost choking on the flank steak. "Remember her?"

Cade snorted. "I remember the penicillin shots."

Miguel set a platter in front of Cade: a double bacon cheeseburger with a side of fries smothered in brown gravy.

"Man the defibrillator," Grif said.

"Comfort food. I need all I can get right now."

"Have you heard from Rita?"

"No word. We got separated at the shooting. Cops won't tell me anything." Cade pushed his plate away.

"Whatsamatter?" said Grif. "Not enough gravy?"

Cade looked out the window. "There's something I haven't told anyone, not even you, about the IED attack." He scratched his beard. "You see, when—"

Grif's attention shifted to the woman standing next to the booth. "Speak of the devil."

Rita, standing tall in tight blue jeans and a sleeveless blouse, slid next to Cade, her leg pressed snug against his.

"Figured I'd find you two here. Don't you ever think of checking out Denny's for a change?"

"What happened to you?" Cade said.

"Cops thought I might have some DNA between my teeth from biting the shooter's hand or under my fingernails. Had to hang around for some swabs and questioning. How about you?"

"I'm okay," Cade said, working the burger.

"The newspaper is a load of crap," Grif said to Rita.

Rita touched Cade's arm. "I'm so sorry about Father Gus. But you stopped others from being shot."

About to speak, Cade was cut off by Luis taking the seat next to Grif.

Cade looked at Grif. "You didn't say it was going to be a party."

Grif shrugged. "Should have gone to Denny's."

Luis signaled Miguel for coffee. "I just found out there's going to be a service for Father Gus the day after tomorrow at Our Lady of Seven Sorrows. The archbishop is going to say the mass. The mayor, city council, a lot of bigwigs will be there."

"Wait a minute," said Grif. "Didn't Gus tell us he saw paperwork at the archbishop's office? Something about the diocese getting syndicate shares on the sale of the strip mall to URP?"

"Interesting," said Rita. "It makes sense that the diocese would want to protect its investment. Transfer Gus before he got the tenants fired up and screwed the sale. Now Gus is out of the picture, and the diocese keeps the syndicate shares. A twofer."

"Hold on," Luis said. "Are you suggesting the bishop had anything to do with the shooting?"

"Nobody's saying that," said Cade. "Gus wasn't the shooter's target. The gun went off when I swung him around. I think he just wanted to disrupt the protest, not kill anyone."

"I don't get it," said Rita. "Why would a shooter show up at city hall with cops all around?"

"Money," said Cade.

"Money? Who'd pay him to shoot up a meeting?" asked Luis.

Rita waved her hand in the air. "Somebody who wants to discredit the protesters as troublemakers and clear a path for the Glebe to sail through."

Then, as if all were struck by lightning at the same instant, the foursome blurted the name in unison. "Finn!"

"Of course," said Cade, slamming his hand on the tabletop. "That's why the shooter wore one of our Save Chapelita T-shirts."

"*Hijo de puta,*" Luis cursed.

"I've got some news, too," Rita said. "I ran into an attorney at the courthouse. Someone I met at the housing conference. Word on the street is that the Kaplan brothers are having second thoughts about selling the apartments to URP. They're getting hammered in the press. My source says the sale is off the table. Indefinitely."

"That's great!" said Cade, high-fiving Luis.

"Slow down," cautioned Rita. "My source also says the city and URP have a new arrangement, and it doesn't require the sale of the apartments, at least not in the usual sense."

"I don't get it," said Luis. "No sale means no deal, right?"

"Not exactly," Rita said. "It means the city doesn't need the Kaplans to sell the Glebe Valley apartments to URP. They're just going to take them."

"Take them? Like stealing?" said Luis.

"Like stealing," Rita said, "only it's called eminent domain."

The three men returned blank stares and waited for the explanation.

"Eminent domain," said Rita. "Legal speak for taking land from one owner and giving it to another owner when it will serve a public use."

"Stealing land?" said Luis. "We fought a civil war over that."

"*Kelo v. City of New London.* Supreme Court said economic growth through private development is a permissible public use."

Luis shook his head. "I don't believe it."

"Believe it," Rita said. "The city will claim Glebe Valley is blighted, and then turn it over to URP so they can develop the land and claim it's a public-use taking. The Kaplans will get compensation, but probably not as much as a sale on the open market."

"Blighted?" Luis said. "Sure, the place needs fixing up—"

"It's more than that," said Rita. "The city will probably cite fire code violations, overcrowding, deterioration of the buildings, illegal drug activity, increased police calls. Whatever they have to say to justify that Glebe Valley poses a threat to the public welfare."

"Incredible," said Cade. "The city just waves a magic wand and overnight it's unsafe for thousands of people to live in the Valley? That defies common sense."

"It's not about common sense," Rita said. "It's the law. And it's happening all over the country. Some communities are fighting back with litigation and injunctions."

Grif broke in. "Lawyer talk for big bucks."

"You're right," Rita agreed. "Litigation costs money."

"Which we don't have," Luis said.

"Maybe," said Rita, "but my friend at the courthouse also told me about FRED."

Cade twisted in the booth to eyeball Rita directly. "Fred who?"

"F-R-E-D," Rita spelled. "Federalists for the Repeal of Eminent Domain, a legal defense foundation. They defend ED cases all over the country. They're considered the best."

"So, what will FRED do for us?" asked Luis.

"Honestly, I don't know yet. I've got a meeting in their office tomorrow to find out." Rita pressed her leg against Cade's. "You interested?"

Cade hesitated, then felt a stir in his boxers. "Uh, sure, why not."

"I doubt FRED is going to work for nothing," said Grif.

"Which means we must keep the pressure on the city and URP while we figure something out," Rita said.

"How do you plan to do that?" Grif said. "The protest didn't work out so well."

A glum silence fell over the foursome.

"I got it," said Cade, holding up a tine speared with a French fry. "Let the archbishop do the mass gig for Father Gus. I'm guessing there's going to be plenty of media coverage."

"Yeah, so?" said Luis.

"So, let's give them a second service to cover."

"Who gets shot this time?" Luis asked.

Cade winced. "Not a funeral, Luis. A memorial service. All nice and peaceful and out in the open. Two services. Double the coverage. Double the pressure on the city and URP. Buys us some time while we talk to FRED."

"So, who's in the coffin?" Rita asked.

"Nobody," Cade said, lifting the burger. "Just break out Mr. Zog's Sex Wax."

After the trio of friends departed, Cade commenced sopping up the burger remains when two men entered the restaurant.

"Well, if it isn't Sergeant Chickenshit."

Cade considered the face of a tall man with a blond ponytail standing next to a muscular companion in a filthy tank top. The cretins who had defaced the Green Flash and rammed a post into his rib cage. *"Kesafat e goh!"*

Ponytail sneered through yellowed teeth. "What's that, some camel fucker talk? Say it to my face in American, boy."

Cade knew the translation as "You dirty piece of shit." But what he said was, "It means walk away, friend—while you still can."

Ponytail nudged his friend. "You hear that? Sergeant Chickenshit says walk away." He spread grimy hands on the table. "We want this booth. *You* need to walk away, *now.*"

Cade cracked his neck and rolled his shoulders. Instinctively, his right hand slid down to cover his sore ribcage. His brain registered the knife next to his plate.

"I read how you let six men die while you hid behind a wall," Ponytail said. "Real fucking hero."

Outwardly, Cade appeared unfazed by the insult. His breathing remained steady, his mind solely focused on what was about to happen.

"What's a matter, Sergeant Chickenshit? Nowhere to hide now?"

The close quarters of the diner would restrict his options and movement. Speed and overwhelming force would be a necessity, just like he taught the jundi—emotional detachment coupled with pure aggression. No rules of engagement, only survival.

"Last chance," Ponytail said.

Cade laid both hands flat on the table, for leverage, ready to push up.

Ponytail turned to the diner customers. "Hey, everybody, look who's here. It's Sergeant Chickenshit!" Then he spun and grabbed Cade by the shirt collar, yanking him out of the booth. Cade came in low and jammed a heel palm hard under Ponytail's chin, rocking him against a counter stool. Ponytail screamed as he bit down on his tongue. The companion in the tank top lunged for the knife. Cade grabbed his wrist and wrenched it high behind the man's back until it cracked.

Cade heard Miguel yelling at him to stop. A woman screamed.

Ponytail swung wildly, his fist glancing off Cade's temple. Cade threw his bodyweight behind a jab to Ponytail's throat. The man staggered, hacking and wheezing.

Tank Top rammed Cade in the gut. Cade wobbled backward, bracing his fall on the counter. He brought his boot up into the man's balls and watched the man crumple.

From behind, Ponytail wrapped Cade in a bear hug. Cade seized a pinkie and bent it back until it snapped. The man hollered and released him from his grasp. Cade snap-kicked his shin, buckling Ponytail's leg, then crushed his instep. A head-butt sent Ponytail sprawling against the door, blocking a couple trying to enter. The fight was over in ten seconds.

Miguel pushed Cade away. "Outside, now!"

"Hey, Miguel," Cade called, popping the last bit of burger into his mouth, "you should have the garbage picked up more often around here—it attracts rats."

26

*U*RP leased a corporate suite at the Ritz Carlton for out-of-town executives on extended travel. A ground-level concourse lined with expensive boutiques and eateries connected the hotel to the Galleria Tower housing URP's penthouse offices. Finn had told Ann to reserve the suite for a client coming in for a week.

The client awoke at ten in the morning. He opened the French doors to the master bedroom and padded naked across the plush carpet to draw back the curtains on a bright sunny morning. In the near distance, a conveyor belt of cars and trucks shuttled around the beltway encircling the District of Columbia.

Anger over the screwed-up shooting bubbled to the surface as did a desire for revenge at being run off his home turf and forced to lie low. The police stakeout of the Glebe Valley apartments made a return to business-as-usual highly problematic. His dream of a lucrative dark web drug enterprise verged on collapse. And to make matters worse, the MS-13 clique felt betrayed by Enzo's sudden disappearance with drug profits and had ordered his execution. Fuck. Fuck. Fuck.

Enzo closed his eyes. The highway hum cut through the summer haze and carried him back to a simpler time—his first assignment with an earlier incarnation of the Brothers of Blood, most of whom now were either dead or in prison. As a seven-year-old, he was a *pee wee* in the parlance of the street. An older boy had ordered him to go and get some chips. When he protested that he didn't have any money, the boy sneered that you don't need any money, dumbass. Chastened, he'd walked down the street to the Git 'n Go. Pretending to browse the candy bars, he nervously waited for a chance. When the counterman ducked into the back room, he snatched a Pringles can and a liter of orange soda.

Unfortunately, his escape route was blocked by a wide-bodied woman entering the store. In attempting to squirm past her, he dropped the plastic bottle, spraying soda all over the floor. The high heel of the woman's shoe slipped in the sticky ooze, toppling her backward, half in, half out of the door. The counterman's shout froze him for a second. Terrified of being caught, he scrambled over the belly of the shrieking woman and ran all the way back to the corner hangout. Out of breath, he proudly handed over the purloined Pringles. In return, the older boy praised his actions in front of the other homies and rewarded him with a five-dollar bill.

The memory of sweet delinquency brought a smile to his lips as he stepped into a shower stall of slate and glass. Sixteen jets of steam and hot water zapped the tension from his body. Afterward, he wrapped his body in a luxurious cotton robe and ordered Eggs Benedict, a pot of coffee, and a triple-shot Bloody Mary. While he waited for room service, he clicked on the wall-mounted screen.

Morning talk show hosts blathered about recipes and summer fashions. The newsbreak reported that the police were still searching for the machete killer. He muted the sound and dialed the number on the business card. The call went to voicemail. He left a message and hung up. He shook a cigarette from a pack and stepped onto the balcony. The humid muck formed instant perspiration. Another shower would be needed.

As spacious as the suite was, he felt confined. Not like the dank maintenance room, but his movements restricted nonetheless. He'd have to shelve the plans for a dark web drug business, at least temporarily. For the time being, the more attractive and less risky alternative was a six-figure position with URP. Hunker down in the bowels of a corporate bureaucracy until he could build up his bank account and get things set up again, next time as a sole proprietor independent businessman.

In the robe's pocket, he felt the pebbled grip of the .45. Finn had better call back. With a job offer. And soon.

27

*O*n the drive to the offices of the Federalists for the Repeal of Eminent Domain, Cade had to listen to Rita drone on about how land seizures were used against politically weak communities—particularly those with high concentrations of minorities, like in Glebe Valley.

"Robin Hood in reverse," Rita said with contempt. "The city takes from the poor and gives to the rich. Nothing but state-sponsored thievery."

As they drew closer, she filled Cade in on FRED's executive director, Charles Wimberley. He had served as solicitor general representing the United States before the Supreme Court. When his political party lost the presidency, he landed a job with FRED. Wimberley was a property-rights warrior on a single-minded mission to push back the encroachment of government.

Cade found curb space three blocks from the redbrick row house. The address was a short jog from the Library of Congress and in the middle of the Capitol Hill Historic District. The Federal-style house had a gabled roof with dormer windows. Next to the door, a medallion signified its construction in 1805. A polished brass plate announced the offices of the Federalists for the Repeal of Eminent Domain.

Cade lifted the eagle's beak knocker and rapped twice. The door opened to an obese man in a gray suit. His paunch strained the buttons of a crisp white shirt.

Rita said, "We have an appointment with Charles Wimberley."

"I am Charles Wimberley," the man announced in a deep baritone. He stepped aside to allow the couple to enter an elegantly appointed foyer. An oriental rug covered hardwood floors. A crystal chandelier hung from a high coffered ceiling framed with crown molding.

Wimberley gestured toward the living room. Rita and Cade sat on the sofa, while Wimberley lowered his bulk in a leather wing chair. Remodeled as an office, the dining room off the kitchen contained a large executive desk with three computer monitors. A flat screen covered one wall. Shelves of neatly stacked law books filled leftover space.

"Let me first say that I am aware of the unfortunate demise of Father Gustavo during the recent unpleasantness. My sincere condolences." Wimberley cleared his throat. "My associates did a preliminary workup on the proposed taking of Glebe Valley. It is an absolute desecration of the Fifth Amendment to the Constitution." Wimberley's index finger pointed upward. "And must not, nay, *will* not stand."

"Nay!" Rita seconded, nudging Cade.

"Nay," mumbled Cade. "So, you'll take the case?"

"Of course, we'll take the case," Wimberley said, wiping a handkerchief across his brow even though the air-conditioning was going full blast. "We must stand up to corporate thuggery. Otherwise, no man's home is safe." His gaze remained fixed on Rita.

"That's great," Cade said. "When do we start?"

Wimberley looked at Rita while talking to Cade. "As soon as you come up with the retainer."

Cade leaned over Rita to get in Wimberley's line of sight. "I thought sponsors underwrote FRED."

"Indeed they do," Wimberley said, tilting on one buttock and then resettling, like the shifting of so much ballast. "But cases like this can run for years on appeals and are expensive to litigate. FRED can underwrite a portion of the expenses, but we ask our clients to make a good-faith commitment as well. The sanctity of one's home must be preserved at all costs, as I am sure you agree; otherwise, you wouldn't be here." He adjusted the knot in his tie. "After all, we're partners in a historic battle, are we not, Mr. Cade?"

"Just how historic are we talking about?"

"We generally ask for an initial retainer in the range of a hundred thousand."

Cade whistled.

Wimberley smiled. "You are retaining the best legal team in America with expertise in eminent domain. Pretrial motions, filings, research, depositions can burn a hundred thousand in a heartbeat. You do want to win, don't you, Mr. Cade?"

"Yeah, of course, it's just that—"

Rita kicked Cade under the coffee table. "He means we need to discuss the retainer with the Kaplan brothers—the owners of Glebe Valley."

"Yes, yes, of course. But don't tarry. My sources tell me the city intends to use quick-take authority. Cuts the length of time for condemnation to a matter of weeks. It means we need to hit the city hard." The corner of Wimberley's mouth turned upward. "Before they've had time to pull their pants on, eh?" His jowls jiggled at the small jest.

Cade shook his head in disbelief. He felt out of place in an elegant office where a high-powered lawyer mentioned a hundred-thousand-dollar retainer as if it was chump change. Grif was right. Lawyers were bad news. He looked at Rita to gauge her reaction, then had to remind himself that she, too, was a lawyer.

"We understand the urgency of getting a decision from the Kaplans," Rita said. "We'll get back to you shortly."

Squaring himself in front of Wimberley, Cade asked, "How confident are you we can win?"

Wimberley's chest swelled. "My good man, it was none other than James Madison, a son of Virginia, the Father of the Constitution, who wrote the Fifth Amendment—"

"What I'm asking is—" Cade began.

"—clause against the unjust taking of property."

"—what do you think of our chances?"

"No guarantees," Wimberley huffed. "But I can tell you this: FRED will do everything in our power to stop these thieving bastards from stealing the homes of the patriotic citizens of Glebe Valley."

Fed up with this pompous windbag, Cade joined Rita on the front stoop.

"Just come up with the retainer, Mr. Cade," Wimberley said, filling the door frame. "And leave the rest to FRED."

* * *

Rita parted company with Cade at the FRED row house and taxied back to the Howard Johnson motel in Crystal City—the cheapest lodging close to the airport. Decades ago, the area south of Reagan National Airport was a ramshackle collection of used car lots, concrete mixing plants, and low-rent motels. As time went on, the land became increasingly valuable. Almost overnight, developers successfully constructed the most nondescript urban landscape in America. The result was that Crystal City looked less like a place to live and more like a place to pass through.

HoJo's nostalgic architecture, complete with a cupola and a useless weather vane, clashed with the adjoining monochromatic glass and steel boxes. Rooms along the three levels opened onto cement walkways overlooking the highway leading to Reagan Airport. Ice and vending machines hummed noisily at the end of each stairwell. Rita raced up the steps to her room on the mezzanine level, slammed the door shut, and called Sandra Howell, the attorney handling the Glebe Valley sale for the Kaplan brothers. She dropped names of a few high-profile lawyers to establish her bona fides and in less than a minute downloaded her conversation with Wimberley and FRED's track record in fighting eminent domain takeovers.

"It's a slam dunk, Sandra," Rita said. "And the media will love a story of the Kaplans fighting for the underdog tenants. Their favorability ratings will go through the roof."

"How much?" Sandra asked.

"How much what?" Rita said.

"Legal fees. How much?"

"The FRED Foundation will pick up most of the litigation costs—except for a small retainer."

"How much?"

"FRED is the best legal defense in the country against eminent domain. An investment, really. The Kaplans will get more brand value and earned media from this fight than if they hired the biggest PR firm."

"*How much?*" Sandra demanded.

"A hundred thousand, up front."

"Forget it. We'll settle for fair market value, less hassle."

Rita clenched her jaw. Everything was riding on getting Oliver to the negotiating table, away from his private security bubble, to have a shot at completing the mission. "Sandra, wait. What if the Kaplans don't have to put up their own money? Then would they let FRED defend them?"

"What are you driving at?"

"Let me talk to some people. I think we can raise the retainer. But I need some time. Give me a week."

"We don't have a week to screw around."

"Seventy-two hours."

"No."

"Forty-eight hours. Give me forty-eight hours." She hated herself for groveling.

Silence, then: "Forty-eight hours, that's it."

Rita offered profuse gratitude for the extension and started to explain her idea to come up with the retainer when she realized Sandra had already hung up.

8

*C*ade and Rita leaned against the hood of the Green Flash across the street from Our Lady of Seven Sorrows. The cab's radio was tuned to the Nats game. The requiem mass for Father Gus was scheduled for four o'clock. Hundreds of people had been gathering on the church lawn since noon. Some sat in lawn chairs while others reclined on blankets with picnic baskets. Many in the crowd still wore their yellow *Save Chapelita* T-shirts. When the doors opened, the people closest to the front steps swarmed the entrance.

Ten minutes before four, Cade observed a black Cadillac Escalade SUV pull up to the curb. An older man dressed in a black liturgical robe with a purple stole exited the vehicle. Well into his seventies, the man radiated apostolic authority. Three men in black suits, with white clerical collars and earpieces, cleared a path through the crowd for Archbishop Patrick O'Malley.

Eager congregants sought to touch the hem of the archbishop's robe or any available appendage. The crowd jostled the cleric. The black suits closed ranks, creating a no-fly zone as the entourage plowed swiftly ahead toward the church.

Cade watched the archbishop turn and bless the onlookers before quickly being ushered inside the heavy wooden doors. The vibrato of the pipe organ whistled through the cracks and summoned a reflection of fallen brothers—empty helmets propped on carbine rifles stuck into boots, dog tags hanging down, chaplain colonel in combat camo muttering something about sacrifice and honor and country.

Rita checked her watch. "Any idea how long this could take?"

Cade shook off the memory. "No idea. An hour, two, who knows."

"Christ."

"Exactly." Cade fingered buttons on his cell. "I'll text Luis. Maybe he'll know."

"Just curious if everything is good to go."

"Oscar is ready as soon as the funeral procession moves out."

Cade leaned toward the driver's side window to catch the announcer call a double play on the Nats to end their hopes for a win with the bases loaded.

"Since you love baseball so much, did I ever tell you about my namesake?" Rita asked with a sly smile.

"You have a namesake?"

"Ever hear of Saint Rita?"

Cade laughed. "There's a Saint Rita?"

"Yeah, smart guy. It so happens Saint Rita is the patron saint of baseball."

"Get outta here."

Rita crossed herself. "Swear to God."

Cade closed one eye to better see if she was bullshitting. "Next, you'll be telling me the twelve apostles were a baseball team. So how would I know Saint Rita if I saw her?"

Rita pointed to the middle of her forehead. "Easy, she's got a big red wound right here." She pulled out a chain that hung below the neckline of her cotton blouse. At the end of the chain dangled a sterling silver medal. On one side, the medal displayed a man on the cross zapping the forehead of a woman with a laser beam or something. "The legend goes," Rita explained, "that a thorn from the crown worn by Jesus struck the nun. It's called stigmata."

Cade brought his eye close to the medal like a jeweler's loupe. On the reverse side of the medal was a profile of a slugger with a bat over his shoulder. "But I don't get what Saint Rita has to do with baseball."

"It's an article of faith, man. Don't question it."

"It's weird if you ask me," Cade said, checking his watch for the third time in the last ten minutes and starting to doubt the soundness of his own idea for a second memorial service.

Rita sipped a diet soda. "Speaking of weird, have you thought any more about Wimberley?"

"I try not to." Cade recalled his unease in the man's presence. "What about him?"

"The hundred-thousand-dollar retainer for FRED."

"Sure, I got it right here in my glove compartment. What do you think?"

"I think FRED is our only hope to beat this eminent domain scam."

"Did you ask the Kaplan brothers for the money?" asked Cade.

"I talked to their attorney, Sandra Howell. In so many words, she basically said the path of least resistance is to let the city use eminent domain to take Glebe Valley off their hands. Play the victim card to the media. Smaller profit, but less hassle."

The church doors reopened, and Cade noted how the trio of clerics in black suits formed a blockade to deter anyone else from attempting to enter.

"I talked Sandra into giving us forty-eight hours to come up with the retainer ourselves. If we do, then the Kaplans will allow FRED to represent them. Otherwise, no deal."

"A hundred thousand in forty-eight hours! No way."

Rita rubbed sunblock on her face and arms, a beachy fragrance of cocoa butter. "Don't give up so easy. I've crowdfunded legal defense efforts before. Although the short time frame on this one might be tight. You know what they say: when one door closes, another one opens."

Cade snapped his fingers. "That's it."

"That's what?" Rita asked.

"I'll be back in time for our meet-up with Oscar." Cade got into the cab and turned on the ignition.

"Where are you going?"

The cab inched forward as Cade leaned out the window. "I've got to see a man about a door."

* * *

Inside Our Lady of Seven Sorrows, Luis, his wife Angie, and Javier sat in the fourth pew from the front. The family of Father Gustavo

Romero, the mayor, the chief of police, and various VIPs occupied the first three rows.

Fresh flowers festooned the altar in summer pastels and greenery. Archbishop O'Malley presided over the mass in a high-backed throne chair, flanked by two altar boys in black cassocks and white surplices.

After the last organ chord had reverberated to silence, Archbishop O'Malley delivered the first reading from the Book of Job at the same moment Luis received a text from Cade: *How much longer?*

Luis replied: *Unknown.* Angela frowned at Luis, and he put the cell away.

A baby cried, triggering other babies to wail in commiseration. Luis gazed at the casket. Father Gus had forgiven him, but now the absolution lay in the coffin along with the priest. Maybe the forgiveness had expired along with Father Gus.

At the podium, Archbishop O'Malley recited platitudes about Father Gustavo's service to the Lord, cut short by a bullet. The bishop recounted the years the young priest had spent ministering to the *campesinos* in El Salvador. At the mention of *campesinos*, Luis glanced around at the gathered congregation. He didn't believe the bishop's mumbo-jumbo, but he did understand solidarity, and he was smack in the middle of it—grim-faced men in their Sunday best standing next to wives in cotton dresses, teenage boys in baggy basketball shorts, and young girls in sparkly tops. These were the hardworking families of Chapelita seeking solace, and perhaps an explanation, for the murder of their beloved Father Gustavo Romero. Not so many years ago, when he'd served with the Salvadoran Army, the practice had been if the rebels took one soldier's life, they would take ten *campesino* sympathizers in retaliation. *Campesinos* who looked just like the neighbors crammed into this sweatbox of a church. Luis closed his eyes and swore: somehow, somewhere, someone would pay for killing Father Gus.

When he reopened his eyes, the archbishop had raised a chalice of wine to his lips and spoke the words of consecration. Parishioners filed out of the pews to receive the Eucharist. Despite Angie's scowl, Luis texted Cade: *Almost done.*

Archbishop O'Malley concluded the mass with a few words of forgettable remembrance, and then the organ pipes revved up. Six pallbearers rose, three on each side of the casket. An altar boy handed the archbishop a wood-handled aspergillum with a perforated silver ball topping one end. The archbishop sprinkled the casket with holy water. Each pallbearer grasped a handle and moved slowly down the center aisle and out the front door to a hearse waiting at the curb.

As the casket passed by, parishioners exited the church, pew by pew. Luis's family was among the first to follow the pallbearers out the doors. Outside, news anchors spoke solemnly into cameras and spoke of healing and closure. Luis spied Rita across the street and nodded discreetly. He whispered to Angie to take Javier and follow the funeral procession to the cemetery.

Javier objected. "I'm staying with you."

Luis balked, then pulled Javier close and crossed the street to meet Rita. "Where's Cade?"

"He said something about a door and split—wait, there he is." Rita pointed to the Green Flash parked down the block, Cade walking toward them.

"Where did you go?" Luis asked. "Everything all set?"

"Yep," Cade said. "Oscar is waiting for my signal."

They watched the archbishop climb in the Escalade, followed by the three black suits. The hearse and Escalade pulled out, turned right on Washington Avenue, then waited for the funeral procession to form up.

Cade thumbed a text to Oscar. A few moments later, a Ford pickup with signage for Oscar's Excellent Landscaping parked in the spot vacated by the hearse. Flowers from the yards of Oscar's clients cascaded from the cargo bed like a Rose Bowl float.

Propped up in the back was Father Gus's nine-foot four-inch Dewey Weber Performer longboard. Several cans of Mr. Zog's Sex Wax lay near the board. A T-shirt with a digitized photo of Father Gus covered the nose of the board. Underneath, painted in white letters: *MURDERED by URP.*

Oscar's CD player floated a brassy dirge over the heads of curious onlookers. The music drew churchgoers closer to see what was happening. Cade stood in the pickup bed and waited for the mourners to gather. He signaled Oscar to cut the music. "Folks, I know what a sad day this is for all of us. Father Gus died standing up for the people of Chapelita. And now we must stand up too, so his death will not be for nothing."

Cade jumped down from the cargo bed and hooked arms with Rita, Luis, and Javier. He waved to Oscar, who pulled the truck forward at a walking pace. Mourners fell in behind. Camera crews continued to shoot the unexpected event and followed the silent procession, step for step. Reporters thrust microphones in Cade's face, but he swatted away their questions and pointed to the longboard.

Customers in the Waffle Shop gaped from behind the glass windows. A couple ran out and joined the silent march. At the Git 'n Go, the procession picked up a few day laborers. The truck rolled onto the access road leading into the Glebe Valley complex of thirteen brick buildings.

As the marchers passed, heads poked out of windows. Past each building, the cortege grew in numbers. The last apartment building dead-ended next to a patch of protected wetlands. Oscar drove over the curb and onto a rutted path that led to the tributary of the Potomac River called Cub Run. Across the mud flats, Cade noticed abandoned grocery carts poking up like chrome icebergs. The shoreline was a favorite spot where he occasionally fished for bluegills and crappie.

He jumped into the cargo bed and slid the longboard down to Oscar and Luis. He watched as the two men eased the board over to the edge of the stream and set it down on the muddy bank. The crowd huddled on the path. He pulled out the leather-bound notebook Father Gus had given him on the day of their first meeting in the basement of Our Lady of Seven Sorrows.

"Look, folks, I don't want to make another speech, and you don't want to hear one. I'm just going to read a line from something Father Gus gave me. He said I might find a use for it someday. I guess today is as good as any. It says here it's from the Book of Revelation. Cade coughed and began, "Then the angel showed me the river of the water of life, bright as crystal, flowing from the throne of God and of the Lamb through the middle of the street of the city." The reading finished, he placed a foot on the longboard's tail and, with a mighty shove, sent the board southeastward on its journey to where Cub Run emptied into the Potomac river, then onward to the Chesapeake Bay, and eventually the Atlantic Ocean.

Oscar carried flowers from the truck and tossed them in the longboard's wake. The crowd drifted back up the rutted path to the apartments. Luis and Javier rode back in Oscar's truck. Cade and Rita stood alone on the muddy bank.

"Mind if I ask you something?" Rita asked.

"Go."

"Earlier, when you said you had to see a man about a door? What did you mean?"

Cade's eyebrows shot up. "Ah, thanks for the reminder. *Un momento.*" He held up a finger and keyed his cell. He looked at Rita while he spoke to Luis. "Hey, man, one more piece of business. Grab Grif and meet Rita and me at the Waffle Shop in ten minutes. I know, it's been a long day for me, too." He stuffed the cell into his jeans.

"Tell me, now," Rita insisted, inching closer, her chin tilted to meet his eyes. She leaned in and kissed him hard on the lips. Her tongue searched his mouth. After seconds that seemed like minutes, he broke it off.

"To be continued. We gotta be at the Waffle Shop in ten minutes."

"Tell me, dammit. What is it that's so important?"

"To believe it," Cade smiled, "you'll have to see it."

29

Cade had to endure Rita pestering him nonstop to reveal his secret on the drive to the Waffle Shop. Her hand slid between his thighs with a smile that tested his willpower. Inside the diner, he found Luis slouched on one side of a booth, Grif on the other, legs sprawled over the length of the seat. Four iced tea glasses sweated on the table. In his arms, Cade carried a white fire safe.

"Is that the piece of business that can't wait?" Luis asked.

Cade nudged Grif to move his legs. "I'll get to that," Cade said, sliding next to Grif, "but first you need to hear about our meeting with FRED." He caught Rita's eye. "You go first."

Rita ran down the meeting with Charles Wimberley.

"That's it?" Luis asked. "FRED will fight eminent domain?"

"Not exactly," said Rita. "The Kaplans' attorney said the brothers were *willing* to let FRED represent their interests in court until they found out FRED wanted a retainer of a hundred thousand—up front."

"Cheap bastards," Grif said. "The Kaplans have boatloads of money."

"They do," Rita said, "but the Kaplans are also sick of the whole deal, the shooting, the bad publicity from kicking tenants out. Their attorney said the brothers would just as soon take whatever the city gives them and move on."

"Forget it," Luis said.

"Maybe not," said Rita. "The Kaplans' attorney also said if we could raise the retainer, they would agree to let FRED represent them."

"A hundred thousand dollars?" Grif said. "You kidding me? What are we going to do, pass a hat?"

"Maybe not a hat," said Cade. He unlocked the fire safe and withdrew a composition notebook with a marbled black-and-white cover. "Check it out." Cade fanned the notebook's pages, revealing pen and ink sketches of birds, lizards, and mythical creatures. Many pages contained fragments of poems and song lyrics.

"A high school notebook," said Grif. "Big deal."

Cade flipped to the inside cover and pointed to a name in faded pencil.

Luis peered at the inscription. "Who's James Morrison?"

"Try Jim Morrison," Cade said, "lead singer for the Doors."

Grif whistled.

Rita grinned.

Luis stared.

"Before my time," Cade began, "but a lot of geezers think the Doors are one of the greatest bands in rock-and-roll history."

Grif tried to help Luis understand. "Somehow our friend here has managed to cop a notebook of songs and poems of a rock-and-roll legend. It could be worth millions!"

"At least a hundred thousand," Cade said.

"How did you get your hands on it?" Rita asked.

"Interesting story," Cade began. "Back in the sixties, Jim Morrison's father was in the Navy, stationed at the Pentagon. The Morrisons rented a row house in Warwick Village for a short while, just up the street. Same area where Lisa and I lived after we got married. One day I was remodeling the basement, and I reached my hand up between some joists, and lo and behold, what have we here, a notebook and a packet of aluminum foil."

Luis appeared lost.

"Don't you get it?" Cade said. "Lisa and I were renting the same house the Morrisons had once rented. While his father worked at the Pentagon, Jim attended George Washington High School in Alexandria—a few miles from where we are sitting."

Grif leaned over the table. "What was in the aluminum foil?"

Cade winked. "Sadly, just seeds and stems."

Grif slammed the table. "Story of my life. But goddamn! The Lizard King himself. How are you going to prove the notebook is the real deal?"

"Don't have to prove it," Cade replied. "Christie's already did."

"Who?" Luis asked.

"Christie's," Cade said. "Big-time auction house in New York. When I found the notebook, I figured it could be worth big bucks. I showed the notebook to a Christie's agent. Examiners agreed it was authentic. Offered me a contract on the spot to put it up for auction."

"How much did they think it was worth?" asked Rita.

"I'll put it this way. Christie's sold the handwritten lyrics to 'L.A. Woman' for $95,000. I figured the notebook had to be worth more than that. But I decided not to auction it."

"Why not?" Grif asked.

"I thought Christie's was low-balling what it was worth. I'd planned to check with some other auction houses, but I never got around to it. I put the notebook away for a rainy day."

"Didn't Lisa deserve half as part of your divorce?" asked Rita.

"I found it around the time things started going sour between us. I never told her about it."

"So why are you telling *us* about it now?" Luis asked.

"Because I'm going to contact Christie's again and see if they will take the notebook for auction or arrange a private sale. There's gotta be a lot of rich hippies around who would love to own a piece of rock-and-roll history. Hopefully, it will be enough to cover FRED's retainer."

"Are you nuts?" Grif said. "Putting up your money to defend the Kaplans from eminent domain? You're going to need that money."

"Actually," Rita said, "if I may suggest, he can structure it like a contingency loan. Wimberley is fairly confident the Kaplans will prevail in the eminent domain suit against the city. When they do, the Kaplans will file to recover their legal costs and Cade gets his money back."

"*Fairly* confident," Grif said. "What if the Kaplans lose?"

"Life is a risk," said Cade. "Besides, Cassandra says I have good vibes."

"Wait," Rita broke in, arching an eyebrow at Cade. "Who's Cassandra?"

Cade instantly regretted bringing her name up. "Uh, she runs a hair salon a few doors down."

Grif shook his head. "A good vibe won't buy you a cup of coffee."

"All I know about doors is how to open one," Luis said. "But if you would do this thing, you are a true friend of Chapelita." He paused. "Not that you haven't already put your life on the line."

"All of us did, if I recall," Rita said.

"Hey, that reminds me," Cade said with a smile. "Rita has something to show us too."

Rita scowled at the lewd sounding remark.

"The medal." Cade laughed. "Show 'em the medal of Saint Rita, the patron saint of baseball."

Reluctantly, Rita pulled out the medal from under her blouse and repeated the legend of Saint Rita, the wound in her head, and her cryptic connection to baseball.

"The Nats could use her about now," remarked Luis. "How many they lost now?"

"Hell, they need more than a saint, they need a goddamn pitcher." Grif raised his glass of ice tea. "To Father Gus, Jim Morrison…and Saint Rita."

"And the Nats!" added Luis.

Cade lifted his glass. The other two quickly followed, and for the first time in many long days, they enjoyed a laugh.

30

The Northeast Regional deposited Cade at ground zero in Penn Station—a mad hive of harried passengers scuttling across platforms and concourses. He headed for the first men's room in sight. Standing at the urinal, duffle bag at his feet, he threw his head back and unleashed a long, bladder-relaxing stream. Behind him, a stall door slammed, and two beats later, a hard press of metal jammed his head.

"Hand me your wallet." The gun barrel pressed harder, tilting Cade's head forward against the tiled wall. He heard the click of a cocked hammer.

Cade reached into his front jeans pocket and proffered the billfold. A hand grabbed the wallet, then reached for the duffle bag.

"Move and I'll blow your fucking head off."

The restroom door opened and swung shut. Cade zipped and turned around. He heard the urinal's automatic flush—a fitting coda to his short-lived hopes and dreams.

* * *

Rita had dropped Cade off at Union Station. He'd graciously allowed her to drive the Green Flash back to Glebe Valley on the condition she'd pick him up when he returned. She poked a plate of cold eggs. The Waffle Shop was jammed on a Saturday morning. A couple with an infant waited at the door while giving Rita the evil eye for hogging a booth. She was ready to leave when the cell buzzed.

"What are you doing?" Cade said.

"Polishing my nails. What are you doing?"

"Hanging around Times Square. I saw a guy playing a guitar wearing nothing but a cowboy hat, underpants, and snakeskin boots. Weird."

"Get to the point. You've only been in New York for an hour or so. Did you sell the notebook already?"

Dead silence.

"I fucked up, Rita. Big time."

"What are you talking about?"

"I got mugged." Cade's voice rose in anger. "I'm taking a piss at the train station when a punk puts a gun to my head while I'm holding my you-know-what. He took my wallet *and* duffle bag."

Rita struggled for words. "Did you call the police?"

"Of course I reported it. But I didn't see his face, no description. Not a whole lot the police can do."

"I can imagine how you feel."

"I doubt you can. That notebook was going to fund my retirement one of these days. I don't know why I thought auctioning the notebook was a good idea. Anyway, I called an Army bud who lives on Long Island. He's driving into the city to pick me up. He'll loan me a few bucks to get back. I'm staying overnight and plan to get stinking drunk at his place. Pick me up tomorrow at Union Station. I'll be on the Northeast Regional. Gets in around six-twenty."

"Hold on before you go. Wimberley called. Wants me to show him around Glebe Valley, get the lay of the land, that sort of thing."

"No retainer, not sure it makes sense now, do you?"

"Let's not give up on the retainer that fast. I have an idea. So, can I borrow the Green Flash?"

A pause, then, "Sorry, I don't lend out the Flash. Liability issues."

"Bullshit, I already drove it back from the airport and you asked me to pick you up."

"Don't you have a rental?"

"Not on my budget."

"Take Wimberley's car."

"Can't. He's flying in from Atlanta. He asked me to pick him up at Reagan. Don't worry; I'll take care of your precious cab."

Cade relented. "All right, all right. But *just* to Glebe Valley. And Rita—"

"Yeah?"

"Cool it on the rhetoric while you're with Wimberley, okay?"

"Don't worry. I'll be on my best behavior."

"That's what I'm afraid of."

31

*R*obert Oliver raised a snifter of Rémy Martin as he perused the brochure for the Great Reno Balloon Race. When URP Board Chair Boyd Rollins said the current CEO was on sudden sabbatical, he'd assured Oliver that the interim job would be a piece of cake.

"Beam in once a month," Boyd said. "You will still have plenty of free time for your little hobby."

Little hobby, Oliver sniffed—as if he was a philatelist instead of the world's top hot air balloon pilot *and* the defending champion of the largest race of the season coming up in four weeks. Instead of taking practice runs over the frost-kissed peaks in northern Nevada, Oliver was stuck in London babysitting Finn to make sure he didn't screw up the Glebe deal.

His cell chimed Pachelbel's "Canon in D." The readout identified Ashpole, the attorney who had tipped him to the protest by the Chapelita Coalition on Justice—*before* Finn got around to it.

"Bill Ashpole," Oliver answered with good cheer. "How the hell are you, old man?"

"I'm fine, Mr. Oliver. You?"

"Never better. To what do I owe the pleasure?"

"As you know, I'm representing Saint Anthony's on URP's purchase of the shopping mall, part of the Glebe deal."

"Of course, Bill. How are things proceeding?"

"That's why I'm calling. Have you got the Glebe property locked down?"

"I understand that the city is moving ahead with eminent domain. Finn mentioned something about quick take. Why do you ask?"

"I have friends, other developers. They hear things."

Oliver straightened a silver-framed photograph of his balloon crew toasting a win at Albuquerque last year. "Pray tell, what kind of things?"

"Like the Glebe is going to be tied up in court for a long, long time." After a few seconds, Ashpole said, "Hello, Mr. Oliver? Are you still there?"

"Who told you that?" Oliver straightened in the club chair; his elbow jerked outward, knocking the snifter off the side table.

"I just need to know if it's true."

The snifter lay in shards on the hardwoods; the Rémy splashed across the hardwoods. Oliver gritted his teeth. "I honestly don't know what you're talking about, Bill. Please enlighten me."

"Let me ask you something," Ashpole said, pausing for a beat. "Have you ever heard of FRED?"

32

Mick Finn ate lunch at his desk with the door closed, not wanting to be disturbed. Oliver's constant nagging for Glebe updates had pushed him to the breaking point. He'd lashed out in an email to Oliver, telling him to back off, then deleted it before sending. Finn confided to CFO Beth Daniels that he'd had enough of Oliver's micromanagement. He harbored thoughts of punching Oliver in the nose for the sheer satisfaction before resigning and walking away. Worse yet was the threat from Earl Everhard. After being personally assaulted by Cade at the protest, he warned that he would withdraw support from the chamber of commerce if Finn didn't do something about that violent agitator. Adding to his mountain of aggravation were the three calls a day from Soul Patch demanding a job—all the while running up a huge tab for a depleted minibar and adult movies. He didn't want to hear one more goddamn thing about the Glebe.

The cell phone buzzed. The caller ID soured his face. "Yeah, what is it?"

"Are you sitting down?" said City Attorney Stephen S. Slegg.

Finn closed his eyes. "Just spit it out, Slegg."

"I got a call from Charles Wimberley, an attorney with FRED. He's representing the Kaplan brothers in the eminent domain proceedings against Glebe Valley."

Distracted, Finn scrolled his email on a computer monitor. "Who the hell is Fred Wimberley?"

"F-R-E-D," Slegg enunciated each letter. "Federalists for the Repeal of Eminent Domain. A lot of juice."

"What the hell," Finn said. "I thought the Kaplans decided to sit this one out?"

"So did I, but I guess they had a change of heart. FRED will fire up public sympathy for the residents. And the litigation is going to get expensive, fast."

"Eminent domain was your idea!" Finn shouted. "I'll go to Oliver if we need a legal team to back you up. Tell me what you need."

Slegg huffed. "I don't know what I need, yet. I need to talk to the mayor and city council. Oh, and one more thing. Wimberley mentioned a friend of yours connected to the case."

Finn ran a hand through his hair. "And who would that be?"

"Jack Cade."

Finn pounded a fist on the desktop, upsetting a sixteen-ounce cup of hot coffee onto his lap and over the papers. "Goddammit!"

"I knew you'd be excited."

Finn jumped up and found a napkin to wipe off his trousers. "A goddamn mess."

"Maybe not as bad as all that," said Slegg.

Finn lifted the coffee-stained documents. "Huh? What the hell are you talking about?"

"I'm talking about Cade. What are you talking about?"

"Never mind. I'm coming over." Finn ended the call and buzzed Ann.

Ann walked into the office, eyeing the coffee mess with a look of distaste.

Finn motioned at the brown puddles, brushing past her. "Do what you can, will you?" At the elevator, Finn waited impatiently when the receptionist called out, "Oh, Mr. Finn?" She put her hand over the receiver. "It's Mr. Oliver."

"Tell him I just left."

"He said it's urgent!"

He motioned to a vacant office. "Put it through in there, will you?"

As soon as Finn said hello, Oliver barked, "I hear we've got a new problem."

"Hey, Mr. Oliver, I was just on my way out. Can I call you back?"

"No, you can't call me back. I hear the Kaplans got FRED to fight your brilliant eminent domain idea."

Christ, how could he possibly know so fast? I just got off the phone with Slegg ten seconds ago. Was his office bugged? "Well, nothing is certain at this point."

"Rubbish. And I hear Cade is mixed up somehow. Helping the Kaplans raise cash for the retainer. Cade is everywhere. The courthouse protest. The touching ceremony at the river. Got a lot of news coverage. Not that you passed any of it on to me. He went from cowardly vet to local hero."

"Well, I'm looking into it."

Oliver broke in. "That's all you do—look into things. If I wanted a private investigator, I'd hire one."

Finn inhaled deeply. "I understand, Mr. Oliver. I'm on my way to meet—"

"You don't get it, do you?" Oliver said. "I want this settled—*out of court*. Now!"

"Yes sir. I'll talk to Slegg."

"I don't want *you* talking to anyone," Oliver said. "Just get word to Cade that *I* will meet with him, personally. I've wanted to meet one of these agitators face to face for a long time. *I* will work out the deal. And I guarantee he'll withdraw FRED's retainer."

"But, I think—"

"Do me a favor, Mick, and don't think anymore. You've underestimated Cade. Frankly, I'm not sure you're in his league. I'm catching a flight tomorrow. Just set up the meeting." The connection ended.

Finn stormed out of the office. He pushed the elevator button repeatedly, willing the elevator to arrive quickly. After the door hissed shut, he banged on the mahogany veneer wall and screamed, "Local hero, my ass!"

* * *

The glass-enclosed elevator stopped at the twenty-third floor above a cavernous atrium lobby. Distant bar chatter and piano notes drifted up as Finn headed for URP's corporate suite. A "Do Not Disturb" sign dangled from the latch. A room service cart revealed scraps of steak and lobster tail. Finn swiped a pass card and entered the spacious suite.

The French doors to the balcony deck opened to a hazy vista of foothills west of Leesburg. The deep carpet muffled Finn's steps across the room. Outside, a man clad only in soccer shorts and wireless headphones relaxed on a chaise longue, eyes closed. His lean torso gleamed with perspiration. In repose, the young man looked harmless, until he reached under the chaise and whipped out a large handgun.

"Jesus Christ!" Finn said, stepping back. "Take it easy. I just came to see how you're doing."

"Motherfucker, don't ever come up on me like that."

"Sorry, but we need to talk."

The man pointed inside with the gun. Finn grabbed a chair, while Soul Patch draped his frame over the sofa. "Job or no job?"

"Almost there. Need to tie up a few loose ends."

"I got a loose end sitting in front of me right now." The barrel aimed squarely at Finn's crotch.

Instinctively, Finn crossed his legs. "We're opening an office in Toronto next month. I think I can get you on as a consultant, cybersecurity, something like that. You'll need a new identity, passport, etc. I figure you know how to do that."

Soul Patch uncoiled from the sofa, stood behind Finn, and screamed in his ear, "No way I hang here for a month waiting for the cops to find me."

Finn cupped his ear. "Okay, okay. We can revisit that."

"I ain't visiting nothing. We have a deal. I want a job and out of this hotel."

"Absolutely, you will have a job." Finn stared cross-eyed at the gun barrel. "But a problem has come up that, if it were to go away, well, it would accelerate your...uh... promotion."

"What kind of problem?"

"Cade," he said. "The guy who grabbed your gun in the courthouse. He's throwing up more roadblocks, slowing down the Glebe deal."

"Like what?"

"It's complicated."

"Try me." Soul Patch racked the slide of the handgun.

Finn gulped and hoped he didn't piss his pants again. "The Kaplan brothers own the Glebe property. They've changed their mind about selling. Bad PR from the…" Finn paused, then continued, "uh, priest shooting. The city commenced eminent domain proceedings. They plan to turn the property over to URP for development."

Finn waited for the question: What is eminent domain? When none came, he continued. "The Kaplans want to wash their hands of the property, accept the city's offer. From what I hear, Cade convinced the Kaplans to fight the proceeding by retaining a firm specialized in fighting eminent domain. Could tie up the property in litigation for years."

Soul Patch paced the floor. "Kelo v. City of New London."

Finn stared, dumbfounded.

"I took an elective in real estate law," the gangbanger explained nonchalantly. "So, let me see if I got this. Cade disappears, no retainer for FRED, no roadblock for eminent domain. The city pays the Kaplans for the property, and the Kaplans get rid of a PR disaster. The city turns the property over to URP, who makes millions on the project. The apartments are razed, forcing my gang to move out—and in the process, the city gets a shitty neighborhood cleaned up and a bigger tax base. Is that about it?"

Soul Patch was back on the sofa.

"Yeah, that's about it."

"That's not *it*. I get a cut and one for my homies, so they forget about looking for me when I take the new job you're going to get me."

Finn groaned. "How much?"

"Let's see." The gangbanger pulled at his tuft of beard. "Compensatory damages, lost revenue, pain and suffering, broker fees and commissions. I'd say seventy-five thousand should do it, in advance."

"Seventy-five thousand?" Finn blurted. "I can't bury that in my expense account."

"Bullshit. You have at least two percent contingency built into a project budget of this size. Seventy-five thousand is a rounding error."

Actually, contingency was three percent, but still, Finn could not believe he was having this conversation with a thug. Then again, he recalled the textbooks in the maintenance room. Maybe there was a place for him in URP after all. As long as it was far away.

Soul Patch patted the sofa, gesturing to Finn. Finn tottered over to the couch. Soul Patch threw his left arm around Finn, keeping the gun trained at his crotch. "What was that concept again? Oh yeah, emotional communion. I Googled Oliver's Cambridge thesis. The holistic integration of architecture and archetypes. Some heavy shit, man. You should read it sometime."

The words stung. A punk throwing Oliver's thesis in his face. He drew back, but the gangbanger's arm held tight. The gun barrel bounced on Finn's kneecap. "A lot of people are going to make a lot of money. And that's why you're going to get me a job right after I take care of Cade. No more delays. *Comprende?* Now get the fuck out and bring me the money."

Finn was headed toward the door when he heard, "And if you ever come around here again without calling first, I'll bust a cap in your ass."

33

$\mathcal{B}$ ehind the wheel of the Green Flash, Rita idled in the cell phone waiting lot at Reagan Airport. Wimberley's flight from Atlanta was due any minute. After a short wait, she received a text: *I'm at baggage claim.* When she pulled up, Wimberley opened the passenger door but quickly surmised his three-hundred-pound-plus bulk would be more comfortable in the backseat. The shocks sagged as he maneuvered into the cab.

"Whose car is this?"

"Belongs to Cade," Rita said, pulling away from the curb.

"Kind of flashy for a cab."

"Exactly," Rita said, noticing Wimberley listing to starboard.

Wimberley dabbed his brow with a handkerchief. "Would you mind turning up the AC?"

Rita checked the dash. "It's up all the way."

"How far are the apartments?"

"Don't worry, the meter's off."

"I didn't mean that," Wimberley said. "I just—"

"Relax, we'll be there in fifteen minutes."

They passed a dollar store, nail salon, and ethnic takeout joints. Multilingual signs advertised cell phones, money orders, and DVDs. "Small businesses," Wimberley said, more to himself than to Rita, "the backbone of the economy. Yes, indeed, entrepreneurs. They see a need in the marketplace, and they fill it. That's the spirit."

Rita slid over to the right lane. "Well, these shops won't be here much longer. The Glebe development includes this retail strip."

Wimberley said, "Creative destruction, nothing to be alarmed about."

"Is that what you call it?" Rita cried. "These shops are worthless debris to be tossed aside so upscale boutiques can move in?"

"Figure of speech, that's all. New businesses replace the old ones. All part of the business cycle. Quite natural."

Rita half turned her head toward the backseat. "Natural? Sounds like cannibalism if you ask me."

"Pardon me?" Wimberley's tone conveyed annoyance at the crude metaphor.

"Money and power gobbling up the small prey." She twirled a finger in the air. "That's the *real* business cycle."

Rita felt Wimberley's stare as she drove. "Capitalism is not on trial here, Ms. Castro. The city is embarking on a gross violation of the Kaplans' property rights. It has nothing to do with the accumulation of capital." Wimberley leaned forward, his breath warm on Rita's neck. "Speaking of which, when did you say Cade would return with the retainer?"

In the rearview, Rita eyed Wimberley—a pit bull when it came to defending private property from racketeers and politicians. But deep down, past the layers and layers of subcutaneous fat, lay a rotting capitalist heart, one infarction away from a final spastic clutch and collapse.

"I didn't," Rita snapped.

"Very well. Important to get the retainer taken care of immediately so we can proceed with filing an injunction." Wimberley undid his collar button and loosened his tie. "As I was saying, private investment of capital is crucial to our notions of freedom and liberty, just not in the misguided case of the Glebe."

"Bullshit. Capital is simply recirculated in the hands of the few at the expense of the poor. That's what's really driving these residents from their homes."

Wimberley rested his forearms along the bench seat. "I see, and where do *you* think the capital should reside?"

Rita knew exactly where the capital should reside—in the hands of the Glebe Valley tenants, of course. They should be the ones negotiating with investors—not speculators. The same ploy she tried with the public housing tenants in Miami, the one she had bragged about with Cade and Luis. But she hadn't told the whole story. The developer had been a hard case. He refused to negotiate despite efforts to exert maximum pressure. Time was short. She'd called Tomás. The next day, police found the developer in his BMW, engine running, with a hose from the tail pipe into the passenger cabin. Headlines proclaimed: Suicide! The poor man couldn't withstand the opprobrium coming at him from all sides. A note in his suit pocket expressed regret over the pain and suffering he had caused the community. His briefcase contained the latest offer that Rita had drafted, duly signed by the developer, and properly witnessed—a final gesture to redeem his humanity. Suspicions were aroused, but no evidence was found to link the death to nefarious interests.

"I think I've made that clear," Rita said, her voice tight. She pulled the cab into the Glebe Valley complex. Without central air, the residents opened windows, hoping for a breeze. Families in lawn chairs grilled meat on small cookstoves. Young men waxing muscle cars blasted speaker systems, competing for the most annoying asshole award. As the cab approached, kids playing in the street parted to make way for the stunning sparkle of a vehicle. Rita killed the ignition.

"If you don't mind me asking, where exactly do you fit in, Ms. Castro? You said you're not from around here."

Rita turned to face Wimberley, one elbow propped on the bench seat. "I'm from Miami. I'm helping the community get organized. I've fought URP before in Houston, Boston, all over. In Oakland, Oliver bought the Holy Redeemer Mission, a shelter for homeless men down by the docks. Oliver sent them packing with a voucher and a grocery cart. Then he gutted the place, built million-dollar lofts and restaurants. Now it's boho chic. Don't forget to bring your Visa card."

"Ha!" Wimberley laughed.

Rita threw it back in his face. "It isn't funny."

The car waxers paused and stared goggle-eyed at the shimmering metal-flake taxi. They moved in for a closer look. A kid ran up to wipe his hand over the car's gleaming surface. Rita watched Wimberley huff his way out of the backseat. He leaned against the cab, out of breath from the brief exertion. Rita walked around and stood next to him as he surveyed the decrepit surroundings. A knot of teenage boys pointed at Wimberley and laughed and joked in a derisive tone. Rita overheard their comments and figured Wimberley had heard them as well.

Wimberley backpedaled. "Quite right. Not funny at all. Speaking of a mission, are you on a mission of some kind, Ms. Castro?"

Rita smiled to herself. Wimberley would drop their case in a heartbeat if he knew her true mission. "The point I'm making is that it's a pattern with Robert Oliver. He buys a parcel ripe for development, pays off the local officials, and forces people out. Then he puts up another one of his faux urban villages, makes a bundle, and moves on to the next city. His latest marketing scam is emotional communion."

"Emotional communion, eh?" Wimberley mused, looking around to keep the teenagers in sight. "I don't believe I've heard of that."

"It's a concept."

"Yes, I see. Tell me, what happens to Glebe Valley after we win this case? Everybody goes home happy?"

The sarcasm lit Rita's short fuse. "Assuming we can convince the Kaplans to transfer Glebe Valley over to the tenants—let them decide what happens next. Instead of handing over tax breaks to URP bloodsuckers, give it to the tenants."

"Just like that?" Wimberley's lips twisted in a dubious pout. "The Kaplans turn over Glebe Valley to the tenants and the city transfers tax credits over to whom exactly?"

"A tenants' co-op."

"Of course!" An upturned mouth formed an unmistakable smirk. "A transfer of wealth. A grand idea! And what do the Kaplans get out of it?" A pink tongue slid across his lips, imparting a moist sheen. His eyes slipped down to Rita's cleavage.

Rita caught the glance and wanted to bash Wimberley's extremely large head on the cab's hood. "What do you think?" She glared at him. "A charitable write-off."

"Amazing." Wimberley clapped. "You've got it all figured out."

Off to the side, the teenagers, emboldened with macho cruelty, now hurled insults in Spanish toward Wimberley, who reacted by obsessively dabbing his brow and checking his watch.

"You know, I think I've heard—er, seen enough. Can you take me back to Reagan?" He turned toward the backseat and commenced an arduous reentry.

Rita slid behind the wheel. "You got another flight? I thought you wanted to look around, get the lay of the land?"

Wimberley donned reading glasses as he scanned a *Wall Street Journal*. "Yes, I think I got it just now. I need a cab to take me to my office."

"I'll give you a ride," Rita said. "Cade won't mind."

"No, no, that won't be necessary," Wimberley mumbled, his eyes fixed on the paper. "Just take me back to Reagan. I'll catch another taxi there." His tone suddenly brusque, chilly.

Rita's ears perked. Maybe she'd said too much. "Well, how about a quick walk-through? Chat up a few tenants. Get some personal stories. Might help with the—"

"Please just do as I ask," Wimberley snapped, his face hidden behind stock listings.

Rita's face hardened. She turned the ignition, backed the Flash out of the space, and nosed slowly past the gawkers who jeered and whistled in the cab's wake.

They rode back to Reagan in silence. She stopped across from the cab stand. Wimberley squeezed out of the backseat. "Please ask Cade to contact me as soon as he gets back."

"Don't worry. You'll get your retainer."

"I'm not worried about that."

"What then?"

Wimberley handed Rita a twenty. "Gas money."

Rita pushed the bill away. "Forget it. We're on the same team."

Wimberley bent at the waist to gaze eye level with Rita. "I wonder if we are, Ms. Castro."

* * *

205

Once out of the airport loop, Rita turned south on Jefferson Davis Highway and headed back toward Chapelita. She passed the wastewater treatment plant and halted at a traffic light. A black Dodge Charger pulled up to her side, a seismic bass pounding out an indecipherable gangsta rap: *BA-BOOM! BA-BOOM! BA-BOOM!*

From the corner of her eye, she saw two Latino men in the Charger pass a bottle back and forth. The passenger's elbow on the windowsill was inked solid to the neck. The men eyeballed the cab's iridescent paint job, then her. The passenger taunted her in Spanish and made lewd lip-smacking sounds. She stared straight ahead, careful not to make eye contact. These were not the car waxers from Glebe Valley.

BA-BOOM! BA-BOOM!

When the light changed, Rita eased forward slowly, hoping the Charger would pull ahead. Instead, the car swung in behind, bass thumping, the driver wagging his tongue. A sudden jolt whiplashed Rita into the headrest as the Charger rammed the cab's bumper. She swerved, but the Charger stayed right behind, its turbo growl reverberating in her ear. There was a half-mile flat to the next light. Rita floored it. The Checker's engine whined, but gradually accelerated. The Charger was on her tail. The traffic light blinked yellow, then red. Rita raced through the intersection, glancing in the rearview. No sign of the Charger. She'd lost them.

In that split-second of relief, a Buick T-boned the Green Flash, flipping the cab over, spinning on its roof, before slamming to rest against a guardrail.

34

*A*mtrak's Northeast Regional arrived at precisely six-twenty. Cade shuffled behind a knot of college students with backpacks headed toward the glass entranceway into the Union Station terminal. Over their heads, he spotted Rita's tangle of curls, now a frizzed-out supernova of extensions and braids. She wore oversized sunglasses and white skinny jeans. As he cleared the students, he noticed she also wore a large cervical collar and a long brace on her left leg. She was propped up by a crutch under each arm.

"My god, what happened?" Cade asked.

"I had a run-in with some jerks."

"Are you all right?"

"What's it look like?"

"Did you call the police?"

"Oh, yeah, the police responded big-time."

"Give me the keys. I'll drive you back to your hotel, and you can tell me the whole story. Where did you park the cab?"

She handed over the blue carabiner key ring. "It's at the Chapelita Center."

"Why didn't you drive it here?"

Rita moved the crutches about a foot or so, swung her legs forward, and made her way slowly toward the main concourse under the soaring barrel-vaulted ceiling. Tourists and shoppers thronged the restaurants and boutiques. Beleaguered travelers bustled toward the trains and the Metro station.

"Does it look like I can drive? Anyway, the Flash was in a slight accident," Rita said. "Not my fault."

Cade laid his hand on Rita's shoulder, eyes wide with alarm. "Slow down. Tell me what happened?"

"Can we find a place to sit, first?"

Cade spied an open seating bar in the concourse and gently guided Rita to a table. She lowered herself into the chair. "My entire body hurts like a son of a bitch."

A waiter glided over, and Cade ordered two Coronas. "Tell me exactly what happened."

After the waiter returned with the beers, Rita took a long pull before giving an edited version of her conversation with Wimberley before dropping him at the airport and how the gangbangers had rammed the cab.

"They were trying to kill me." Rita closed her eyes. "They pushed me through a goddamn red light."

"Why didn't you pull over?"

"And let them rape me? I don't think so."

Cade doubted gangbangers would have done that in broad daylight on a busy highway, but who knew anymore. "So how bad is it?"

Rita sipped the beer. "Me or your cab? I had it towed to the Chapelita Center. I didn't know where else to dump it. Luis said it would be okay to leave it there for a few days. It's not drivable if that's what you're asking."

Cade covered his eyes with the heels of his hands. "I thought I was screwed when the punk snatched Morrison's notebook. But if I can't drive, I can't make a living."

"How about driving for another cab company?"

Cade glared at her.

"I meant until you get the Flash fixed." Rita shifted uncomfortably in the chair. "I've got to get back to the hotel and take a painkiller."

Cade escorted her to the cab stand. He stowed her crutches in the taxi's trunk and waved as the car moved out onto North Capitol Street. An hour and a half later, a bus dropped him across the street from the Chapelita Center. He walked around to the back alley. His pride and joy totaled—a crumpled roof, the entire right side smashed. The grill grimaced as if in unspeakable agony. If he had a gun, he would've put the miserable beast out of its misery. He saw a light in the office, but the door was locked.

After a couple of knocks, Luis answered. "Come in. Rita told me about the notebook and your car. Bad day, huh?"

"I don't see how it could get any worse."

"I can't do nothing about the cab, but the retainer ain't completely lost," said Luis, pulling out a hand-painted skull of KAH's tequila. He poured generous portions into two coffee mugs. "Rita set up a fund-raising website. I don't understand how these things work, but she said something about hooking up with a bunch of tenants' organizations around the country. Fifty-three thousand dollars in pledges already. Rita is amazing."

Cade felt the tequila burn all the way down his gullet. Rita had destroyed his prized possession, his source of livelihood crushed like a cockroach. Maybe it had been an accident, but her story about being chased by gangbangers sounded bogus. All that money invested in the cab down the drain. He cursed himself for letting her drive the car. "Yeah, amazing," he said, pushing buttons on his cell phone.

"Who are you calling?" Luis asked while topping off their mugs.

"Wimberley. Fifty-three thousand dollars is halfway to the full retainer and a good-faith down payment. I'll ask him to cut us some slack. It's worth a shot."

After a few ringtones, he said, "Hey, Mr. Wimberley. It's Jack Cade. I wanted to give you an update and see if you might...uh-huh...uh-huh...she said what? I see...uh-huh...California?" After a few more grunts, he hung up.

"Let me guess," Luis said, "he wants the full retainer."

"There isn't going to be *any* retainer," Cade said. "Apparently, Rita laid a bunch of crap on him about transferring wealth from the rich to the poor. Now suddenly he has a big case in California with priority over ours. He's not taking our case."

Luis slugged back the drink. "Now what are we going to do?"

Cade poured another round and shook his head. "Hell if I know."

35

*T*he pounding echoed in his cranium. Cade opened one eye. On the coffee table, he spied a tab of oxy and a half-empty fifth of Jack Daniel's. How much did he drink last night? He crushed the pillow over his head to muffle the pounding. What time was it? The brightness behind the closed window blinds suggested daylight. Definitely daylight.

The thumping continued, loud, insistent. Where was it coming from? Go away! He reached for the tab and washed it down with a swallow of JD. No more pounding. No more pain. Just sleep. Peaceful and quiet and glorious sleep.

The pounding returned, this time, accompanied by a voice. "Open the goddamn door!"

What the hell! Frigging neighbors. No respect for people sleeping. I'm going to say something this time. Cade pulled himself from the sofa and wobbled over to the door. He peered out the peephole and saw a fishbowl view of a face and a fist banging on *his* door!

He latched the chain and cracked the door. "Who is it?"

"Who the hell you think it is?" responded Grif. "Open the goddamn door!"

He closed the door and unlatched the chain. Grif elbowed past and surveyed the living room: the vial of oxy, a bottle of Jack Daniel's, scattered clothes, an empty pizza box. "What the hell are you doing?"

"Catching up on some sleep."

"Yeah, I can see that. Come on, sit down." Grif went into the kitchen and brought back a mug of instant coffee nuked in the microwave.

Cade sipped, made a strange face, and raced to the bathroom. His body shuddered and heaved, arms hugging the porcelain bowl for dear life. He looked back and saw Grif standing in the doorway. Grif threw him a towel and walked him back to the sofa. Cade lay prone, one arm over his eyes, stinking of pepperoni vomit.

Grif pulled up a chair. "Luis called and filled me in on the Flash. Said you practically finished off an entire fifth of tequila by yourself last night. From the looks of things around here, that's not all. I tried calling but no answer. You gave me a scare, bud."

"I'm screwed," Cade moaned. "My insurance company is all over my ass about the accident. They may cover some of the damages, but I could be liable for the rest."

"You've hit a rough patch, that's all. You can work something out with the insurance company. We do it all the time at the dealership when a customer wrecks a loaner."

"Rough patch?" Cade grunted. "Did also Luis tell you about the Morrison notebook? Stolen from me while standing at the pisser."

"He mentioned it."

"Remember the construction workers who fucked up my ribs and gave me the black eye?"

Grif cocked an eyebrow.

"Well I returned the favor and gave them an asskicking at the Waffle Shop and now they're pressing charges."

"I hope you have witnesses."

"There's more. Ever since the *Post* ran the article on my court-martial, reporters are hounding me for an interview. They're talking to the soldiers who claimed I was faking PTSD. They want to do a follow-up, hear my side of the story."

"Maybe you should give it to them. Set the record straight."

"I want the story to go away, not drag it out. I can't right now, even if I wanted to, which I don't." Cade held his head in both hands. "I'm too messed up, man."

"Well, not *right* now. After you sober up."

Cade rubbed his face. "I started to tell you something at the Waffle Shop before Rita showed up. About the IED attack. I never told you, or anyone, about what happened *before* we went on patrol."

Grif leaned in closer, elbows on his knees.

"It was during a field exercise when I had the jundi team trying to find mock IEDs hidden in the scrub," Cade began. "I yelled at two jundi who were not paying attention. A couple of knuckleheads. That kind of inattention could cost someone their life. I made them run laps while holding a sandbag. It was fucking hot. They dropped like flies. We got them over to the medic, and they were okay. But the next day, both men quit, just walked out of camp."

"I vaguely remember that," said Grif.

"Yeah, well, Malik was really pissed about how it went down. He came into my hooch while I was getting my gear together before patrol. I could tell right away he was upset about something. Said I seriously dissed his brothers and almost got them killed. He said he was going to report me when we got back from patrol."

Grif folded his arms across his chest, lips pulled tight.

"When we finished our sweep, Malik found the truck with the melons and decided his men needed a break. Started slicing up the melons and passing them out. Right away, I get a bad feeling. I started to order the men away from the truck, but I was as pissed at Malik as he was with me. So, I said *fuck it*. He's gonna report me, anyway. Fine. Eat your fucking watermelon. I ate mine behind a wall."

"You had no way of knowing," said Grif.

"I was counter-IED, man. Trust nothing, remember? Plus, I was on painkillers at the time."

"Aw, man, that's ancient history. You gotta get your head right. Talk to a doc at the VA. Come on, I'll drive you."

Cade rose on one arm. "Bad conduct discharge, remember? I got no VA benefits. You got all the answers. Do this. Do that. Well, here's something for you to do. Go fuck yourself. Leave me alone." He flipped positions on the sofa and turned his back to Grif.

"Okay, buddy," Grif said, standing. "I'll leave you alone. Have yourself a nice pity party."

The door slammed, and Cade turned back to face the empty chair. His fingers searched for the oxy. He swept the coffee table, scattering cups and magazines. The vial was gone.

"Goddammit, Grif. Motherfucker!"

* * *

Sunlight leached through the blinds, and salsa music thumped in the apartment below. Cooking smells drifted in under the door. Hungry, he rose from the sofa to look in the fridge. Something brown in a plastic container, a hunk of cheese with blue mold, and two beers. He heard a muffled whirring sound and traced it to the rumpled sheets on the bed. The cell phone buzzed like a damn insect. "Hello."

"Is this Jack Cade?"

"Who's this?"

"Mick Finn. I work for Urban Renaissance Partners."

Cade recognized the name of the developer he'd first sighted at the gymnasium meeting, and briefly at the courtroom protest. "Yeah?"

"Robert Oliver would like to meet you."

Cade played dumb. "Who?" He heard a snort of impatience.

"The founder and CEO of Urban Renaissance Partners."

Cade lay crossways on the bed and stared at the water-stained ceiling. "Why's he want to meet me?"

"What do you think? He wants you to stop the protests and drop the retainer for FRED. Work something out."

A smile crossed Cade's lips. Finn obviously didn't know Wimberley had already dropped their case.

"Well?" Finn said.

"Well, what?"

"Meet with Oliver tomorrow afternoon. Our offices in Tyson's Corner. Five o'clock."

Before Cade could respond, a tone beeped in his ear, ending the call. Back in the kitchen, next to an empty carton of moo shu pork, he found two fortune cookies. The only edible things in the apartment. Inside the first cookie was a slip of paper: "A chance meeting opens new doors to success and friendship." Cade opened the second cookie: "When hungry, order more Chinese food."

* * *

After a shower and lunch at the Lucky Dragon, Cade felt semi-human again. He walked the three blocks to the Chapelita Community Center. When he stuck his head in the door, the sole occupant was Javier, his nose stuck in a textbook.

"Hey, Javier," Cade called, "is your dad around?"

The boy glanced up with a quizzical expression.

"Your dad. Where is he?"

"Oh, they walked over to the Waffle Shop."

"They?"

"He and Rita."

Cade turned to leave, then said, "Hey, look, I know things got kinda messed up at the protest. But your soccer team did a great job. I just want to say how much I appreciate your help." He extended his hand.

Javier smiled and shook Cade's hand.

"I gotta go." Cade waved on his way out the door.

Cab drivers and locals packed the Waffle Shop. Bacon sizzled on the griddle. Miguel refilled cups, rang up checks, and cleared plates. Luis and Rita sat in the last booth along the window bank, finishing platters of enchiladas and refried beans. Cade slid next to Luis. Rita still wore the cervical collar, and the foot with the leg brace jutted out of the booth. Her crutches stood propped in the corner.

"Thought you'd be long gone by now," Cade said to Rita.

"Just stopped to say good-bye to Luis before my flight tonight." Rita's affect was flat as a tortilla.

Cade looked sideways to Luis. "How are you doing?"

"A few more donations trickled in. Not much." A look of alarm crossed Luis's face. "You okay? Grif was looking for you."

"Yeah, yeah, he found me. I'm fine. Well, I've got news. Oliver wants to meet me to negotiate on Glebe Valley."

"Meet with you?" Luis almost sprayed his iced tea. "Why would Oliver negotiate with you and not the Kaplans?"

"Because he wants *me* to stop the protests *and* call off FRED. Work out a deal of some kind and take it back to the Kaplans."

"Did you tell him Wimberley already canned us?" Luis asked.

Rita opened her mouth as if to ask a question when Cade explained, "Oh, that's right, you didn't hear about that? Apparently, your little talk with Wimberley about a transfer of wealth gave him heartburn. Now he's got another case with higher priority."

A pained expression crossed Rita's face.

Luis nudged Cade with an elbow. "Ease up, buddy. Rita's only trying to help."

Cade glanced at Rita. "Sorry." He paused, eyes cast down in a show of contrition, then continued, "But for right now, let Oliver think FRED is still on our side since it makes him eager to negotiate."

Rita moved her neck stiffly, trying to find a comfortable posture. "Did Oliver contact you personally?"

"Not exactly. Finn called to set up the meeting tomorrow at URP's office."

"What do we get out of it?" asked Luis.

Rita broke in. "The question is what do you *want* to get out of it?"

"I want the city and URP to leave Glebe Valley alone," Luis said.

"Not that simple," Rita said. "Oliver is not going to walk away with nothing."

"Well, what then?"

"I have an idea." Rita looked at Cade. "But it may give *you* heartburn."

"I eat at the Waffle Shop. I already have heartburn. Let's hear it."

Rita laid out the scenario that Wimberley had apparently considered an affront to his capitalistic sensitivities. URP agrees to drop the eminent domain takeover of Glebe Valley. The Kaplans transfer the property to a tenants' co-op in exchange for a charitable write-off. The city transfers tax credits that would have gone to URP over to the co-op to be used to renovate the apartments. Then the co-op sells the apartments to the tenants at below-market rates with loans guaranteed by URP.

"Sweet deal for us," Cade said. "But what does Oliver get out of it?"

Rita checked herself in a compact mirror and dabbed powder on her nose. "What does Oliver love more than money?"

Cade lifted his shoulders. "I give up."

"He loves Robert Oliver." Rita snapped the compact closed. "The man's ego is the size of Manhattan. We agree to put his name on everything: the renovated apartments, the Chapelita Community Center, a new soccer field. Make a list. He'll get so much adoring publicity, he won't be able to resist. Particularly if the alternative is endless litigation."

"Wait," said Luis. "You think Oliver will go for that?"

"He will if it's pitched right." Rita stared at Cade. "Have you ever done any actual negotiating?"

He glanced out the window at a black man wailing a saxophone—a regular who played under the overpass—bebopping the blues while diesels rumbled overhead. Groovin' high, the dizzy riff soared into the upper altissimo and carried Cade back to a time when his squad had received a tip about a man rumored to have information about a suspected bomber. Cade spoke to an old man through the screen door of his house. The interpreter conveyed Cade's questions about the suspect. The elder glanced warily at the nine-millimeter on Cade's hip. Sullen young men gathered in the yard, any one of whom could've been the bomber.

A jundi whispered to Cade that the old man was the deputy mayor of the village. Cade offered food and medical supplies to the village. Nothing. While Cade tried every inducement and bribe he could think of, a tsunami of dirt—a thousand meters high—swept across arid plains that stretched east toward the Zargos Mountains. A monster sandstorm pelted the soldiers' helmets and stung their faces. The young men in the yard ran for shelter. The elder slammed the door in Cade's face. Visibility near zero, an orange scrim descended over the terrain as Cade ordered the squad to fall back—empty-handed.

"Earth to Cade," Rita said. "Do you have experience negotiating or not? You can't just walk into a negotiation with Oliver without knowing what you want and how to get it. You'll wind up thanking him for kicking your ass."

Cade turned from the window. "I know an expert in negotiating. I'll be right back." He left the diner, threw a buck into the saxophonist's case, and walked north on Washington Avenue.

A queasiness overcame him a half mile down the road. The hot sun boiled the alcohol toxins still percolating in his bloodstream. He rested on a bus shelter bench, dropped his head to his knees, and sucked in deep breaths. His fingers found a forgotten oxy hidden in the folds of his jeans pocket. He chewed the tab to hasten the effects.

After a few minutes' respite, he walked the remaining blocks to Ken Brown's Volvo, a sprawling dealership with a tall rotunda and a glass wave wall of modest elegance. An ecclesiastical palace for car worshipers.

Centered in the entrance plaza, a 120-foot-high tapered steel pole stabbed the sky. Attached to the pole was a giant US flag, fifty by eighty feet, hanging limp in the July doldrums. Ken Brown had appealed to the zoning commission to approve a variance for the oversized flag to show his support for the troops. Cade imagined that if the halyards snapped, he would suffocate in a last gasp of patriotism.

He entered the glass showroom gleaming with the newest models. Overhead, a giant digital screen as big as an NFL scoreboard played split-screen images of glam couples cruising beachfront boulevards, snowy passes, and desert flats.

The customer lounge featured HD TVs, a barista serving up skinny lattes, and a putting green. A nineteen-bay service garage hummed with diagnostic computers and monitoring devices more typically found in an intermediate care unit. Cade was greeted by a sales associate attired in the Volvo uniform of country club casual: dark blue polo shirt, khakis, and Docksiders.

"Is Grif here?" Cade asked.

The sales associate pointed to an office off the showroom floor. Cade knocked on the glass panel. "Can I talk to you for a minute?"

Grif remained focused on the monitor. "Close the door."

"I'm an asshole, and I apologize for what I said, you know, at the apartment."

Grif twisted a rubber band on his finger. "Yes, you are an asshole, and you need serious help. Sober up, man."

"I am sober," Cade said, even as the oxy numbed his senses. He wondered if Grif could tell.

"I'm busy right now."

Cade looked around the office and saw certificates naming Grif as the top sales associate—three years running. His Army bud had to be pulling in six figures, while Cade's income was stuck in the low fives, and depleting fast. "I need a small favor."

"Do *yourself* a favor, and go see a doctor." Grif started to stand.

"Wait, wait." Cade pressed his hands down in a gesture for Grif to sit. "Give me five minutes." He laid out the conversation with Finn, and Oliver's offer to work out a deal to end the protests and litigation over eminent domain.

"Get to the point."

"The point is that I could use a few tips on negotiating." Cade smiled. "I figure you know as much as anybody about screwing people out of their money."

Grif shot the rubber band at Cade.

"A joke. I'm joking." The old Grif would have laughed and thrown an insult back in his face. "Look, Luis and Rita are in on this, too. You helped at the protest rally. Just one more time. What do you say?"

Grif moved a mouse and made a few clicks. "I have to get back on the floor." He brushed past Cade on his way to the showroom. Alone in the office, Cade noticed another frame on the wall—this one a congratulatory letter from Ken Brown—commending Grif for outstanding customer service.

Outside the dealership, Cade looked for something to kick. Grif, his best bud. First on the scene after the IED ambush. Stood by him during the court-martial and through his bitter divorce with Lisa. Practically busted the door down to check on his welfare and all got in return was a fuck off.

Cade gulped a bottle of carbonated water that he'd liberated from the customer lounge. With the afternoon temperature in the upper nineties and a lingering hangover, he didn't feel up to retracing his steps two miles back to the Chapelita Center. He boarded a Metro bus and sat on the bench seat in the rear.

Seated in the row ahead was a kid, eighteen or nineteen years old, with stringy hair, a neck beard, and a forearm tattoo of a flaming skull.

Slovenly appearance. Wouldn't last five minutes in a firefight. Probably crap his pants. Cade wanted to slap him for no other reason than he probably deserved it.

A few rows up, a teenage girl yakked on her cell phone loud enough for every passenger to hear every inane thought springing from her empty head. Disrespectful and rude. He imagined grabbing the phone and crushing it under his heel. This is what his life had come to. Riding the bus with society's dregs. Soon, he'd be like the guy slumped over in the front row with piss stains on his chinos.

The bus dropped Cade a block from the Chapelita Center. Inside, he saw Rita staring at her cell phone. Luis hovered over a young man at a workstation studying an English language tutorial.

"You look like your dog just died," Rita said. "What did you find out from your negotiation expert?"

Cade collapsed on a folding chair. "Zip, zilch, nada."

Rita touched Cade's arm. "The conference I attended in DC had a seminar on eminent domain challenges and settlements. I can prep you. And I've got a fat file on Oliver. All his likes and dislikes. Even his hobbies. He's big into hot air ballooning."

"I'm sure *that* will come in handy." Cade closed his eyes, the nausea making a comeback. "Honestly, I don't feel so good right now. Not sure I'm up for it."

A chair scraped on the linoleum floor as Luis pushed back. He stood in front of the window, back to Cade, hands balled into fists. "Father Gus took a bullet for us, *amigo*. And now you're not *up* to it?" He turned and fixed Cade with a stare. "What's the matter? Hitting the tequila too hard give you the shits? Tell Oliver *I'll* meet with him."

First, Grif told him to *man up*. Now the throwdown from Luis. Cade just wanted to pop another oxy and forget the whole mess—except Grif had pocketed his stash when he stormed out of the apartment. Rita tilted her head, observing him closely.

A calendar on the wall from a travel agency showed a white cruise ship docked at a picturesque seaport village. Manifests on cruise ships always referred to the number of "souls" on board—not simply the number of passengers and crew. He recalled Father Gus saying that the soul is the immortal life breath that connects us to our ancestors and all of God's creation. The destruction of the Glebe Valley apartments would be reckoned not by the number of displaced tenants, but by the loss of five thousand souls.

Cade brought his hands together in a sudden handclap, startling Rita. "I'll do it."

"In that case, my friend," Luis snapped, "I suggest you get over whatever is eating you, and listen up to what Rita has to say. Finish what you started. Stand with Chapelita, *remember?*"

Over the next hour, Rita downloaded a crash course on the nuances of challenging a "blight condemnation" of Glebe Valley. It would not be easy or cheap to litigate (don't worry, she said, the crowdfunding will pick up). The thing to do now was to convince Oliver they had the resources to play the long game. Drag out the proceedings and hope for a judicial review and a sympathetic judge.

"I don't get it," Cade asked. "What can a judge do?"

"Order an abatement," Rita said. "Most jurisdictions already have the authority to regulate a public nuisance. A court could force the Kaplans to remove the offending blight conditions at Glebe Valley. Abatement is our countermove to condemnation. It buys us more time."

Cade pulled his beard as if in deep thought. "Arthur wrote that delay is costly to developers and is a good negotiating tactic."

Rita smiled. "Excellent. Glad to hear you read Arthur's book. But abatement is a last resort. Our ace in the hole. Whatever you do, don't tip Oliver about abatement. Now, let's go over one more time the terms of the negotiated settlement." She reviewed the terms she'd described earlier at the Waffle Shop. "Are you getting this down?" Rita said, spearing Cade with an ice-cold gaze. "Or do you want to me to write it out?"

"You're wasting your time," a voice boomed from the front of the room.

"Son of a bitch!" Cade shouted.

"Figure you all could use some *professional* advice," Grif said. "If you know what I mean."

The two men fist-bumped. "I didn't think you would—you know, after what I—"

Grif waved off the explanation. "We all have bad days. You just seem to be having more than your share lately." He lowered his voice. "What's *she* doing here?"

"Rita is helping out."

"Even though she totaled your cab? Something about her I can't put my finger on."

"She's from Miami. They're all a little weird down there. Rita's cool."

Grif grunted. "So, what's the plan?"

Rita overheard the question. "The plan is to prep Cade for meeting with Oliver tomorrow."

"Yeah, fine," Grif said, ignoring Rita, and speaking directly to Cade. "But getting the best deal is about knowing your opponent's strengths and weaknesses. Reading between the lines. Sometimes what is unsaid means more than what is said. It's like poker."

Great. Cade thought of how often he'd lost his paycheck to the stud sharks at FOB Scorpion.

"Knowing the legal options is one thing," Grif said, "but you also need to know the gambits to get the most out of them: like the Red Herring, See-You-in-Court, the False Deadline. The list goes on. My favorite is the Russian Front—two alternatives, one worse than the other."

"They teach you all this in Volvo school?" Cade asked. "Remind me never to buy a car from you."

"Stick with your Green *Flush*," Grif retorted. "Oh, that's right." He eye-rolled toward Rita. "It bit the dust."

"Screw you," Rita said to Grif. "Now can we get going here? We don't have much time. And another thing"—she looked to Cade— "demand that Oliver comes to you for the meeting. Don't go to his offices; that automatically puts you in a weaker position."

Grif stepped in front of Rita. "Always negotiate on your home field. Just like at the dealership. Tell Oliver the meeting will be here, at the

Chapelita Center. He'll balk, but since he asked for the meeting, he'll probably go along."

Luis pulled up another folding chair for Grif. Rita continued to interrupt Grif to get her two cents in. Grif and Rita argued over every negotiating tactic and bargaining strategy. Cade sensed Grif was losing patience and called a time-out. "Just let Grif talk, okay?" he said to Rita. "I want to hear what he has to say."

Rita grabbed her crutches. "I get the message. Anyway, I need to get going." Her chill frosted the room. She leaned over, the cervical collar restricting her movement, pressed a piece of yellow-lined paper into his hand, and awkwardly kissed Cade lightly on the lips. "After you finish negotiating Glebe Valley," she cooed, "maybe you can sell Oliver a Volvo."

* * *

After leaving Cade and Grif, Rita taxied back to her room at the Howard Johnson motel. The thin walls barely muffled the thrum of traffic noise in the room where Rita lay on a bed watching *Wheel of Fortune* with the sound muted. The puzzle was a phrase.

She loosened the straps of the cervical collar and elevated the braced leg upon a stack of pillows. Shock waves of pain rolled across her body. From a small bottle, she withdrew a white pill and swallowed it with a sip of diet soda.

Next to her, a laptop was opened to a document by an anonymous writer. Only a small circle of radicalized apostles knew that Arthur A. Arthur wrote the paper and exchanged lengthy emails explicating a moral principle that Arthur referred to as *homeicide*. The apostles posted scholarly references, historical precedence, formulations of conscience, and a legal defense for those spurred to action. Arthur cited case after case of the capitalist profiteers behind the destruction of the homes of city dwellers in the name of economic development. The litany of examples personifying greed and exploitation went far beyond the vignettes Arthur had presented at the Washington Hilton conference. It was a searing indictment.

On the muted TV, Rita watched the game show hostess reveal five E's.

Arthur avowed that our least advantaged citizenry could not rely on established institutions to uphold their right to remain in their homes. And just as there is the ultimate penalty for individuals who commit murder, so too should there be a capital punishment for corporations that destroy the homes of low-paid urban dwellers. Rita recalled how Fidel dealt with the leaders of the Baptista regime who conspired with American businessmen to line their pockets. The blood-splattered walls stood as mute witness to where the criminals once faced the carbines. She grabbed her cell phone and hit speed dial.

"Yeah?" said Tomás.

"I need you in DC, now. Oliver's meeting with Cade tomorrow."

"Short notice."

"I just got the word."

"Where's the meet?"

"I'm pretty sure we'll get it moved to the local community center. I'll call back and confirm."

"Will Oliver be alone?"

"We'll figure it out when you get here. One more thing. Make it look like a gang hit."

"Local?"

"*Hermanos de Sangre.*"

"Brothers of Blood? Cute. How do I do that?"

"Use a machete, and get some spray paint while you're at it so that you can leave a tag."

"What about your lover boy, the cab driver?"

"Cade? Not my type, leave him out of it. Call me with your flight info." Rita started to end the call. "Oh, one more thing. When you get here, keep your eye out for a black Charger with Virginia plates and a tatted-up Latino driver."

"Why?"

"So you can run the motherfucker off the road. You'll get a bonus."

Three S's appeared on the puzzle board.

She hung up and shifted to a more comfortable position, but the movement sent an excruciating jolt through her neck and limbs. She cried out in physical agony, but also anger at the gangbangers who'd caused her accident—and at Oliver for the countless lives he'd ruined. Tomás had come highly recommended. He would make them *all* pay.

She wiped away the tears, and when her vision cleared, she saw that the puzzle board had lit up all the letters of the phrase: TIME IS OF THE ESSENCE.

* * *

The negotiating tactics, gambits, and ploys that Grif had crammed in Cade's head amounted to information overload. Too much, too late. In the end, Grif had said you'll be fine, just trust your gut. Yeah, easy to say. Except right now his gut roiled with ulcer pains. He craved fresh air to clear his thinking. Halfway down the block, he detoured toward Cassandra's Unisex Hair Salon & Psychic Palm Advisory. A chance to find out once and for all why she wasn't returning calls. Cassandra was his anchor—a steadying, grounded influence. Without her support, he feared a drift deeper into opioid oblivion.

When he entered the salon, Cassandra stood at the counter wearing a long black tank-top dress with Rasta stripes of red, yellow, and green. Bangles of copper and gold circled her wrists. Seeing no stylists or customers in sight, Cade strolled up to the counter and leaned in for a smooch. Cassandra turned herself away.

"Whatsamatter, babe?" asked Cade. "Is it what you read about me in the newspaper?"

Cassandra studied her nails. "I knew you felt guilty about something. Why didn't you trust me?"

"I don't know," he muttered and moved in for another kiss, but again Cassandra pulled back.

"Yes, you do. You have feelings for someone else. The woman in the newspaper, the one photographed with you at the protest."

"Aw, babe, Rita was just helping out, that's all. We had to confer."

"Confer? Is *that* what you call it?"

Cade sighed. "I've been under a lot of pressure. Rita started out being friendly, but she moved on *me*. Honest."

"Honest, huh? Let's see." Cassandra led Cade to the back room. She pulled her chair around to face him. Her fingertips searched his eyelids, lips, and forehead. She held his right palm, studied the lines, and then, with eyes closed, brought it to rest on her high cheekbone. He considered an ambush kiss but held back. As if sensing his intention, Cassandra's eyes fluttered open. She stroked his neck lightly with both hands. "You are very conflicted. Not sure if you should follow your head, your heart"—she nodded toward his lap—"or your—"

"Hey, hey," Cade protested.

"Seriously, your aura is going crazy. Strong vibrations of red indicate strength and anger."

"The lawyer we were going to hire bailed. But then I got a call that Oliver wants to meet with me. Sounds like he might be interested in an out-of-court settlement."

"Yes, those are positive signs, but I also see indigo, a sign of obstacles to overcome. Possibly a betrayal by someone you trust."

Cade knew better than to question Cassandra's intuition. But a betrayal? By who?

Her brow furrowed. "There's something else—"

His hand slid onto her knee. "C'mon, Doc, I can take it."

She slapped his hand away. "Knock it off, if you don't want to listen."

Cade backed off. "I'll behave."

"There's blockage in your throat chakra as if you want to say something but can't quite get it out."

The transparency of his aura was as disconcerting as if his fly was down. He did have *something* to say to Cassandra. He wanted to tell her about his pain and his love. She was throwing him a life preserver. If he didn't grab it soon, she'd write him off as a lost cause. But the time for *the talk* would be after the business with Oliver was settled. "You could do the Heimlich," he deflected.

Cassandra frowned, waving her hand around Cade's head, not quite touching hair, beard, or skin. "One more thing. There are black spots around your vital layer. Vibrations of danger, threats. I'm a psychic not a doctor, but I know that certain medications cause chemical imbalances and can trigger wild aura fluctuations. Are you taking something?"

"What?" Cade said with unintended emphasis. "Medications? No. Nothing. Maybe an occasional aspirin for migraines, but that's it."

She shot him a sideways glance. "You're *still* not telling the truth about something." She reached for her handbag and keys. "I have to go pick up some supplies."

"How about I swing by tomorrow after my meeting with Oliver?"

Cassandra hesitated, mulling a response, when she smiled.

Cade pulled her chair toward him. "And I'll be bringing lots of *positive* vibration, mon."

36

*D*espondent, chin in hands, Cade wondered how things had gone from bad to worse so fast. Everything was unraveling. No hope on the horizon. Might as well end it all right now, quick and painless. Don't drag out the misery any longer—and that was just from reading about the latest loss in the Nats' record-breaking losing streak.

He had gotten up to nuke his cold coffee when the idea struck. He typed the name into the browser, and up popped hundreds of hits from all over the country: California, Texas, Florida, even Anchorage. He scrolled down until he found a posting closer to home: 1968 Checker Station Wagon. 300k miles. No rust. $9,000 OBO.

The owner lived in Timonium, Maryland, north of Baltimore. He googled the Amtrak connections and discovered it was possible to get to Timonium, check out the car, and be back in time for the meeting with Oliver at 5 PM. He called the owner and made an appointment.

He knew a guy who could rebuild the engine on the cheap and give him a discount on a new paint job. With a little spit and polish, it might just be the son of Green Flash. And with all his newly acquired negotiating skills, he could probably get the price down several thousand dollars.

On the screen was an opportunity to start earning money again. With luck, he might cut a deal with the insurance companies clamoring for his hide. It was a big risk, though, assuming he could even get insurance again. If the insurers and personal-injury lawyers filed lawsuits, he'd be bankrupt with ruined credit—although not such a big leap from his current situation. At least buying the car felt as if he was taking charge of a bad situation, moving forward, not sitting around waiting to be sued.

And since money was going to be tight for a while, he'd been thinking of asking Cassandra to move in together, cut down on expenses for both of them. Not marriage, exactly, at least not right away. Maybe down the road. His mind wandered to who their kids would resemble. He, with his Irishman's red hair and fair skin, she with her exotic African-East Indian bloodlines.

In fact, the thought of living together had been on the tip of his tongue at the very moment Cassandra had been diagnosing the blockage in his throat chakra. As soon after the meeting with Oliver as possible, he resolved to take Cassandra out to a nice dinner and have a serious talk about their future together. Until then, he'd have to swing by the bank and draw out enough cash from his dwindling savings account to buy the used Checker. What the hell. It was worth a shot. Like the Nats, things could hardly get any worse.

* * *

From his top floor office overlooking the Tyson's Corner mega-mall, Finn sighted thousands of cars arrayed in endless rows across acres of steamy asphalt. Super-heated sheet metal glinted in the noonday sun. Back at the desk, he read a soil testing report for the second time, and a third, and still couldn't remember a word of it. He tossed it aside.

On the bright side, it hadn't been difficult to get Beth Daniels to increase the budget for the contingency fund. He told her the money would backstop the city in its eminent domain legal battle. Which was partly true. So what if the money went to Soul Patch instead of a lawyer? It was the result that mattered.

Finn picked up a stress ball embossed with the Washington Nationals logo and squeezed it ten times. He had to find a way to get Soul Patch a job in the Toronto office. He switched the stress ball to the left hand. And he had to bring Oliver up to date about his call to Cade. He pitched the stress ball against the glass wall and then dialed the hotel and asked for the corporate suite. The phone picked up, but no voice answered.

"It's me, Finn."

"You got my job yet?"

Momentarily stress-free, Finn replied, "Yes, and the money."

"All of it?"

"All of it, for the little job we talked about, remember?"

"I'm talking about a permanent job."

"I'm talking about both. I got a line on a job at our Toronto office. But first, the other job we discussed."

"When?"

"Today at 5 PM. Cade is meeting Oliver at our offices. Make it look like he never showed. Can you do that?"

"Cash up front." The line went dead.

Next, Finn needed to brief Oliver before he met with Cade. Oliver had flown in on a red-eye overnight, went directly to the CEO suite, and had not been seen or heard from all afternoon. Finn walked briskly to the suite and told the executive assistant he needed to see Oliver right away.

The young woman, smartly dressed in a black suit and a white silk blouse, replied, "Mr. Oliver is not available."

"It's urgent." Finn placed his hand on the inner door.

"Mr. Oliver is *not* in his office," the assistant insisted, her voice rising a notch.

"Where is he? I said it's urgent."

She wrinkled her brow. "Mr. Oliver is having dinner at the Ritz Carlton—"

Finn spun on his heels as she called after him, "And he doesn't want to be disturbed!"

* * *

The MARC train pulled out of Union Station, the cars jammed with commuters and tourists. Cade sat by a window and watched the dregs of the Washington-Baltimore rail corridor flash by: abandoned warehouses, razor wire strewn over chain-link fences, dilapidated tenement houses, junkyards. His face reflected amidst the wreckage.

Bored by the depressing landscape, he slid another CD from his *Don Quixote* collection into a portable player and listened intently to Quixote's duel with the Knight of the White Moon. As he lay vanquished, Quixote realized he must now fulfill his promise to the Knight: abandon his fanciful quest and return home.

A wry smile crept across Cade's lips. He wondered if his upcoming negotiation with Robert Oliver might also be a fool's errand. Would a triumphant Oliver stand astride his broken body and bid Cade return home and live happily ever after? The tall tale implanted fantastical thoughts in his head. Unproductive thoughts. Cade removed the earbuds and let the rocking train lull him into a fitful sleep.

An hour later, the train arrived at Baltimore's Penn Station. Cade transferred to a light rail line that deposited him at the Timonium Business Park Station. He found the owner behind the wheel of the Checker in the parking lot, an older gentleman with a white goatee and wearing a linen driving cap, a metal cane by his side.

After a visual inspection of the engine and the undercarriage and a short test drive, Cade made a low-ball offer on the car. A shrewd opening bid. Grif would be proud. The man tugged his goatee, and responded that he hated to sell the car, but he needed the money to pay for prostate cancer treatments. The hard luck story moved Cade to peel off nine thousand dollars in cash, the full asking price. The old man handed over the key and the title. The two men exchanged back slaps. Cade slid behind the wheel of his "new" 1967 Checker Marathon station wagon. As he pulled out of the Timonium Business Park Station, the rearview showed the old gent hustling over to the passenger side of a white Mercedes Benz. Pretty spry, Cade noted, for an elderly man with a glob of rotten tissue clogging the plumbing.

When he floored the gas pedal to merge onto I-70 back to DC, the Checker shook, rattled, and stalled. Dead in the water in the right-hand lane of traffic. Drivers honked and swerved around the vehicle. He switched on the emergency flasher signal. On the highway shoulder, Cade noticed a historical marker for Timonium, Maryland. The final resting place of Spiro T. Agnew—the corrupt vice president of Richard Nixon. May the bastard rest in peace—which was more than Cade could say for the geezer who sold him this worthless piece of shit.

* * *

A tow truck had hauled the Checker to a garage. Cade pushed call back on the cell.

A voice answered, "Finn."

"Slight problem with my cab. I can't make the meeting at five."

"Oliver's flying to London tomorrow morning. Rent a car, ride a bike, take a bus. Just get here."

"Hold on. Lemme see how long it's gonna take." He muted the cell and checked with the mechanic. "They gotta order a part."

"How long?"

"A couple of hours. I'll keep you posted." He recalled Rita's insistence that the meeting take place on the home field. "Oh yeah, one more thing. Tell Oliver I'll meet him at the Chapelita Center."

Finn hedged. "No way. It has to be at our office, so we can draw up any papers that might be needed."

Cade glanced at the mechanic's butt bent over the engine compartment. "Chapelita Center. That's the deal." The Russian Front ploy—two bad alternatives. Chapelita Center or no deal.

Finn chose the least bad option. "All right, unless you hear back from me, Oliver will be there. But I need an assurance from you. Actually, it's Oliver's condition."

"What is it?"

"He will only negotiate with you. Not Charles Wimberley. Not the Kaplans. None of your tenant friends. Just you."

* * *

The mechanic broke ninety minutes for dinner. To kill the boredom, Cade popped in the last *Don Quixote* CD wherein the knight errant falls ill for six days but wakes on the seventh day, having returned to sanity. In a moment of lucidness, Quixote disavows his past acts of chivalry, then keels over and dies. Great, Cade mused, after all the drama and fighting with imaginary villains, when clarity finally dawns on the hero, it is too late in the game to make any difference.

When the mechanic returned, the critical thingamajig had been delivered to the garage. The parts and labor were going to eat up most of whatever savings he had left. Three hours later, Cade rolled out of the garage, but not very far. Traffic on Interstate 70 toward Washington sat immobile on the highway in both directions. In the distance, flashing blue lights signaled an accident. He heard a driver in the next lane say something about an overturned tractor trailer and a spill. At this rate, he'd be lucky to make the Chapelita Center by midnight. The Checker came to a halt behind a minivan. Two young kids in the van made faces at Cade, then ducked below his line of vision. He called Finn.

"Where the hell are you?" Finn barked.

"On my way, sort of. I'm in a jam on I-70, looks like an accident. If I'm lucky, I might get back around eleven or twelve."

"Midnight!" Finn screamed. "Are you out of your mind?"

In the minivan, the kids' heads bobbed up and repeated the facial contortions. Cade flashed the peace sign, and the heads disappeared. "Look, you said yourself Oliver is flying back tomorrow morning, so if he wants to meet, this is the best I can do, under the circumstances."

Finn grumbled, "I'll get back to you and confirm."

Next, Cade called Luis and relayed the news to him. "And get this. Oliver agreed to meet me at the Chapelita Center. Call Rita and let her know. And thank her for the idea."

"Tell you what," Luis said, "how about I meet you at the center, open it up, and keep you company."

"Sorry, buddy. Oliver only wants me at the meeting. One of his conditions. Leave a key for me at the Waffle Shop, will ya?"

"But—"

"Gotta go. Traffic's moving. Later."

Up ahead, the minivan jolted forward and then braked again. This time, only a pair of tiny fists rose above the bench seat and slowly unfurled two middle fingers.

* * *

The Ritz Carlton hotel adjoined the Galleria Tower, where URP North America maintained its offices. Oliver arrived early to place wine selections with the sommelier. The Ritz private salon was the only dining establishment acceptable to Oliver within a ten-mile radius of the mega-mall dystopia. White linens dressed the dining table accompanied by place settings of fine china and stemware. Fresh-cut flowers sprouted from a carved planter atop a marble-topped sideboard. The cozy warmth of a gas blaze in the fireplace buffered an air-conditioned chill.

The maître d' opened the door to admit a striking woman of indeterminate age. Oliver smiled to see her again, resplendent as ever in a saffron linen blazer, pencil skirt, and heels. She offered Oliver her cheek. "Good to see you again, Robert. A delightful surprise when you called."

He pulled back the chair for Deidre Moon, CEO of the Monterey Group, a marketing firm headquartered in Carmel-by-the-Sea. Early in her career, Deidre had pioneered the LIFEMAP typology—an integration of census demographics with consumer lifestyles. LIFEMAP eventually became the marketer's bible for a generation of MBAs. Groundbreaking research for its time.

Oliver had read that Deidre had recently taken on real estate clients. Fortuitous timing. He'd flown to Carmel to meet with her, and briefed her on PULSE *tec*, the breakthrough brain-computer interface.

"Psycho Unified Life Style Environment!" Deidre squealed with delight. "I love it! Well done. A tremendous advance over LIFEMAP." Within minutes, she'd brainstormed an integrated, multi-channel marketing strategy—a grand alignment of mind and body connectivity across the urban landscape. A complete immersion experience for a new generation of urban renaissance pioneers. On her iPad, Deidre diagrammed a lifestyle segmentation plan for Fast Trackers, Uptowners, and Beltway Boomers. Impressed, Oliver had his fountain pen ready as the contract slid off the printer.

"Yes, well, I'm returning to London tomorrow."

The sommelier presented Oliver with a bottle of 2008 Blanc Fumé de Pouilly.

"And you said you had news for me? Good news, I hope."

He approved the label and nodded the okay to pour. Then he directed the maître d' and wine steward to leave the room. When they were alone, he briefed Deidre on the complication posed by the protest and with FRED entering the eminent domain litigation. "I'm meeting the instigator behind the opposition later today. I'll have the mess cleaned up, and we'll be on our way."

"By 'on our way,'" Deidre asked, "do you mean we'll be ready to roll out the Glebe campaign? I can't put off other clients indefinitely while waiting for a court decision."

Oliver swirled the wine, sniffing notes of ripe pear and peach. "Deidre, my dear, there isn't going to be any litigation. We'll settle out of court. And then it's full speed ahead." He tapped his wineglass against Deidre's.

A soft knock on the door and then André reappeared. "Are you ready, sir?"

Oliver waved him off. "Not now, André."

Deidre sipped her wine. "I've got an idea for an emotional communion marketing campaign I think you're going to like."

A few moments later, another rap on the door. Oliver bellowed, "André, I said not now!"

This time, Finn stuck his head in the room. "Excuse me, Mr. Oliver. Could I talk to you for a minute? It's urgent."

He threw down his napkin. "I'll just be a minute." Once outside the salon, he confronted Finn. "What the hell is it?"

"Cade's changing the time and place of the meeting. I told him you were leaving tomorrow and could only meet today."

"And?"

"And Cade said he could meet you tonight at the Chapelita Center, near the Glebe Valley apartments."

"When?"

Finn hesitated. "Not sure exactly—he said somewhere around eleven or twelve tonight. He'll let us know."

"Bloody hell. What kind of rubbish is this?"

"He had car trouble. He wants to settle, Mr. Oliver. Let's get it over with. Throw in some sweeteners, bump up the relocation bonus, whatever it takes for Cade to think he drove a hard bargain. Once he goes away, he'll take the protesters and FRED with him. And the Glebe moves forward on schedule."

Oliver glanced through the door at a sliver of Deidre in the salon. "All right. Tell Cade I shall meet him tonight. Have a car ready—I'll drive myself." Before Finn could respond, Oliver slammed the door.

"Problems?" Deidre asked, fixing her lipstick.

"No, just a slight change in arrangements." Oliver raised his glass. "Now, where were we? Ah, yes, a toast. Let's see, to emotional communion!"

Pink frosted lips nuzzled Oliver's earlobe. "And to us."

37

S oul Patch crouched in the shadows of a narrow strip of dusty trees and shrubs separating the Chapelita Community Center from Lucinda's Lavandería. Finn's last-minute change in location had been a pain in the ass. Headlights swept the shrubbery as a car pulled into the lot. A black Lincoln Town Car stopped in front of the mural under the security light. An interior light snapped on as the driver exited the car. Oliver's groomed silver mane spilled over the collar of a tailored suit that bespoke money. Finn had promised he would delay Oliver long enough to make sure Cade arrived first and allow him time to dispose of the body. Another change, another complication. He tightened his grip on the Glock with the suppressor barrel and waited.

* * *

In the humid darkness, Tomás flattened against the back wall that ran the length of the alley, becoming one with the stucco and concrete, a unified mass of form and substance. The machete melted into his hand and arm, and reconstituted as an extension of his being. Deep breaths and controlled exhales focused the mind on its singular mission. The sound of tires crunching gravel alerted him to the target's arrival. Slowly, he inched his way along the wall toward the corner entrance. As he drew closer, he raised the machete overhead, like a scorpion's tail, poised to strike a deadly blow.

* * *

Off to his right, Soul Patch sensed movement. A shadow alongside the building crept toward the corner, holding what appeared to be a long-handled blade. A local punk, no doubt, sizing up the driver as an easy mark. A threat to Oliver, but also to his plans. Finn had mentioned a job in Toronto, but URP also had offices in Tokyo, London, and Rio.

He could definitely picture working in Rio. But not if some dumbfuck shanked the CEO for his cash and credit cards and threw the company into chaos. He pulled back the slide and chambered a round.

He crept along the tree line, parallel with the shadow approaching the corner. One more step and the shadow would round the corner. Another car pulled into the lot as he took a two-handed aim. The car swung wide, headlights blinding, just as he squeezed off a muffled shot. A spray burst from the shadow's head as it crumpled to the ground. Soul Patch bent low, ran to the body, and dragged it to the tree line. Inside the man's jeans, he found a can of spray paint and a Delta ticket voucher to Miami in the name of Tomás Flores.

He stuffed the spray paint in the backpack, but kept the machete within arm's reach. The cop car pulled up next to the well-dressed gentleman aside the Lincoln. Soul Patch hurried down to the corner to overhear the conversation.

* * *

"Can I help you, sir?" said the female officer. "The center is closed."

"Thanks, Officer, uh, I just pulled over to take a call. Wouldn't want to drive and talk on the phone at the same time."

"Good idea, sir. But I wouldn't park here at this hour. Just up the block is an Exxon station. Better lighting, if you get my drift."

"Yes, Officer," said Oliver. "I believe I do. Thank you."

Soul Patch watched the cruiser back up a quarter turn, then merge onto Washington Avenue. Oliver got back in the car just as an old yellow Checker cab pulled up to the Lincoln's driver's side so the men could talk side-by-side. The Checker driver's red beard and hair were unmistakable.

Cade said something Soul Patch couldn't hear. Then Oliver exited the car and followed Cade inside the community center. Soul Patch ran back up to the tree line and thumbed a text. A minute later, a black Charger whipped into the lot and stopped next to him.

"Pop the trunk."

"Is that Cade?" Butcher asked.

"Pop the goddamn trunk."

Soul Patch spread out a tarp, and together they stuffed the body in the trunk.

"Who is it?" asked Butcher.

"A punk," he said, sliding into the passenger side.

Butcher nestled a can of beer and a .45 Magnum in his crotch. He grabbed a plastic six-pack ring and handed it to Soul Patch. "What do we do now?"

Inside the darkened Chapelita Center, the lights suddenly flicked on. "We wait."

* * *

Cade flipped the light switch, bathing the room in a harsh fluorescence. He sat behind the metal desk. Across from him sat Robert Oliver, legs crossed, hands clasped around one knee. A study in poise and confidence. Cade remembered Grif's first rule of negotiation: Wait him out. Make Oliver talk first.

Uncomfortable seconds dragged into a full minute before Oliver finally said, "Well, you invited me here, Mr. Cade. What is it you want?"

"You asked for the meeting. I only specified the place."

"Ah yes, so I did." Oliver looked around the sparsely furnished room. "Is this your office?"

Cade held Oliver's gaze but did not respond.

Oliver uncrossed his leg and slapped both hands on his creased trousers. "I see. Very well. Let's get to it, shall we? As I understand it, you, or should I say the Kaplans, have retained Charles Wimberley of the Federalists for the Repeal of Eminent Domain to oppose the condemnation of the Glebe Valley apartments. What you should know right off the bat, Mr. Cade, is that in ninety-nine percent of all cases in which a community opposed an eminent domain action, the government won."

Cade smelled a bluff. The intimidation gambit. A bogus statistic, designed to put fear and doubt into the opposition's head.

Oliver shifted in the metal chair. "Admittedly, you and your little band of protesters may delay the inevitable, but make no mistake, we will win. Also, be prepared to cough up more money for Wimberley. No doubt he told you that benefactors support the FRED Foundation. But the truth is, FRED's donations have been drying up for years. Wimberley may have to sell that historic townhouse on Capitol Hill to stay afloat. Pity."

Another gambit. Feign empathy for the opponent's weak hand. Cade moved imperceptibly in the chair. The corner of his right eye registered a jagged white flash—a migraine onset.

Oliver thrust out one arm, then the next, and shot his cuffs to the requisite half-inch below the sleeve. "Perhaps Wimberley has already advised you of this jurisdiction's quick-take law. We can be in and out of court with the property rights to the Glebe before you know what hit you. So please dispel any thoughts of a prolonged legal fight. While we *could* litigate and win, I am prepared to offer a resolution that will benefit all parties." He leaned forward, forearms resting on his knees, hands clasped. "But I don't have much time, Mr. Cade. We need to meet certain obligations and timelines. Tonight. Otherwise, any deal we might entertain is off the table."

The urgent deadline ploy. "Your contract deadlines are not my concern."

Oliver tented his fingers under his chin. "Tell me then, what exactly are your concerns, Mr. Cade?"

"You know my concerns—the residents."

"Hmmm. Yes, I see. May I remind you, the Glebe Valley apartments are private property. The tenants are renters. As such, they have no claim."

A stab of pain ripped through Cade's legs, a tingling like pins and needles. For a moment, he felt dizzy.

"Are you all right, Mr. Cade?" Oliver asked. "You appear a bit flushed."

Cade wiped his brow with the back of his hand. "Tenants have as much a claim to their homes as anybody else."

"Yes, well, I'm afraid the courts see it differently. Your so-called coalition is attempting to prevent legally entitled parties from developing a property for public use."

A pinprick of pain stabbed Cade's eyeball. "Since when is destroying homes a public use?"

"An admirable but misplaced sentiment, Mr. Cade," Oliver said, "as you will soon find out. Economic development *is* a settled issue in the courts."

Cade rubbed his face.

"Tired, Mr. Cade?"

"Yes, tired of your bullshit. Public use ain't as settled in Virginia as you think." A stone-cold bluff, but two could play this game. "Or didn't Finn mention that?"

Oliver's expression remained impassive.

"And you needn't worry about the retainer for FRED," Cade continued. "We can keep your lawyers busy for years to come. In the meantime, there's a city council election next year. We'll make Glebe Valley the top issue in the campaign. Trust me, every politician on the ballot will want the votes of five thousand tenants. Then we'll see who has rights. You'll never break ground."

Oliver examined his hand-stitched oxfords. "You sure they can all vote?" He coughed. "Never mind. A small jest. I'll double the affordable unit set-asides and the lease termination bonus. That's the best I can do."

Cade's crossed arms signaled rejection.

"You know what I can't figure out?" Oliver said. "Why are *you* the one leading the protest? I read about your unfortunate accident in Iraq. A tragic loss of life. What were you doing in the Army? Oh, yes, training Iraqi soldiers to take back their country. I imagine that must have felt like a thankless task." Oliver's eyes bloomed. "Is that what this is all about? Trying to help residents hang onto some run-down apartments so you can feel better about your, uh...shall we say *abortive* efforts in Iraq?"

Cade blinked twice; a searing arc of pain flashed across the temple region. "You know, I saw some ruthless bastards in Iraq," he managed to say. "You'd fit right in."

Oliver brushed imaginary lint off his lapel. "Name-calling is not going to get us very far, Mr. Cade. Now, let's get back to—"

"I need some air," Cade interrupted before walking out the door.

* * *

"There he is," Butcher said, pointing a beer in the direction of Cade standing by the door of the Chapelita Center, cell phone to his ear. The Charger was indistinguishable in a darkened corner of the lot. "Ready?"

Soul Patch drained a can, tossed it in the shrubs, then texted Finn. A few seconds passed. The reply came back: *Wait until Oliver leaves.* There were two cans left in the plastic ring that Butcher handed him.

* * *

Grif picked up on the first tone. "I've got you on speaker. How's it going?"

"I'm ready to punch Oliver in his goddamn face," Cade said.

"That good, huh?"

"He doesn't give a shit about FRED and says we'll lose anyway."

"He's bluffing," Rita broke in. "He's losing on two fronts. His reputation is getting trashed in the press, and the threat of litigation will drag out the project longer than he is willing to admit. Stick with the plan. Remember, Oliver is an egomaniac."

"Take me off speaker," Cade said to Grif.

"You're off."

"Oliver brought up the IED ambush. Asked if I'm leading the protest to relieve my guilt. I wanted to rip his throat out. And now I've got a major migraine."

"Easy, buddy, relax, just breathe," Grif said. "It's a diversion tactic to get under your skin. He'd love for you to throw a punch so he could have you arrested. You can do this, man."

"All right, all right. I gotta go." Hands on knees, Cade sucked in deep breaths. Training Iraqis to reclaim a hellhole country had also been a diversion tactic, and as far as he was concerned, a miserable failure. Six jundi dead on his watch. A thankless mission, sure, but Oliver had no right to throw it in his face. Cade chewed an aspirin and reentered the room just as Oliver ended a call.

"Feel better?" Oliver asked.

Cade ignored the question and returned to the desk. He leaned back and sized up Oliver as if for the first time. The distinguished gentleman in the custom-tailored suit seemed miscast in the cheaply furnished room. Oliver glanced at a stainless-steel timepiece on his left wrist and smiled.

Fingertips steepled, Cade locked eyes on Oliver. He reached into a pocket, retrieved a piece of yellow-lined paper, and gave it a quick glance. Then, in a calm, deliberate tone, he laid out the terms Rita had thoughtfully scribbled for him.

Oliver stood, hands behind his back, and paced the small room.

"How about it, Mr. Oliver?" Cade asked. "Your name in lights all over the city. The community center, a soccer field, a new job training center." He spread his arms wide, heaping on the flattery. "Just think, every event will be a grand photo op. Fanfare and hoopla. Ribbon cuttings and proclamations. Your name, your legacy of generosity and community spirit, will live on forever."

Oliver stopped pacing in front of the map pinned above the coffeepot. "Is that all? Are you sure you haven't forgotten something, Mr. Cade? An important detail, perhaps?"

Cade gritted his teeth. Had Rita overlooked something?

Oliver walked over to the window, his face reflected on the blackened glass. "Did you actually think you could intimidate me with your puny threats of litigation and delay?"

Perspiration ran down Cade's collar. Hammer blows pounded his head. Any second now he might leap across the desk and crush Oliver's windpipe. "Well, if that ain't enough, we can always get a judge to order an abatement." As soon as the words were out of his mouth, he remembered Rita's admonishment not to tip Oliver about abatement. Too late now.

"Abatement, eh?" Oliver sniffed, then turned to the map. He placed a finger on a blue line, indicating the access road to the Glebe Valley apartments. He half-turned, lips twisted in a semblance of a smile. "Plus, rename this Oliver Street."

* * *

"Check it out," said Soul Patch, nudging Butcher in the driver's seat. Cade appeared at the community center door, Oliver a step behind. The men stood by the Lincoln Town Car, talking. After several minutes, Cade climbed in the Checker and headed down Washington Avenue in the direction of the Glebe Valley apartments.

"Go," he said. "Stay behind, out of sight." Butcher cranked the ignition, and the Charger rumbled to life. He swung into the traffic flow. When Cade turned into the apartment complex, Butcher drove past and entered the complex from Jefferson Street. Soul Patch ordered him to park the Charger in front of Cade's building and wait.

* * *

As usual, Cade parked the Checker in the space furthest from any other car in the lot. Exhausted, he craved an oxy and whatever else he could find to tamp down the migraine before calling the others with an update on his successful negotiation with Oliver. Rita had been right. The threat of prolonged litigation delaying groundbreaking of Oliver's emotional communion prototype had its desired effect. The messianic urgency to bring the concept to market had spurred Oliver to cut his losses, accept a face-saving offer of community praise for his generous philanthropy, and look for easier pickings elsewhere.

A measure of self-satisfaction blossomed that his effort tonight, combined with the tenant rally at the zoning hearing, the sacrifice of Father Gus, and the teamwork of Grif, Luis, and Rita, had managed to save the homes of thousands of neighbors.

And further back, in the darkest corner of his soul, stirred hope that his small part in the win against Oliver might somehow make amends for loss of the jundi lives in the IED ambush. A stretch maybe, but a step in the right direction.

And another step on the long road to redemption was to make a quick call to Cassandra and apologize for not swinging by the salon as promised. He'd make it up to her. Take her out to a nice dinner, perhaps a little wine before easing into a conversation about moving in together and pooling their resources so they could make a down payment on a house. One advantage of being a cab driver was that Cade knew all the neighborhoods like the back of his hand. He'd had his eye on a fixer-upper in a fringe area—a bungalow that backed up to a sound barrier wall for Interstate 95, which was probably the reason why the property had sat on the market for several months. But where others saw a money pit in a marginal location, Cade envisioned an affordable starter home—a place where he and Cassandra could raise a family. The thought prompted a wide smile to spread across his face. But he was getting too far ahead of himself. One step at a time, but things were looking up.

"Hey, man, can you help a brother out?" A slender man with a tuft of beard under his lower lip had stepped out from between two cars directly into Cade's path. "I need three dollars on my Metro card. Got to get to Rockville. My mother's real sick."

Cade knew the scam. "Metro's not running this late, pal."

"Really?" said the man, bringing a gun up to Cade's nose. "My mother wouldn't like that."

Laughter erupted a few cars away. A door opened, and a whiff of Colorado Kush wafted in the humid air. Two young Asian couples exited the car, giggling and coughing. One man looked in Cade's direction and then turned back to his friends, gesturing wildly. The foursome seemed in no hurry to go anywhere.

Soul Patch lowered the weapon. "Okay, we're going to take a little ride." He whistled through his teeth, and a black Charger pulled up. "Get in front."

When Cade climbed in, he felt an object against his neck, followed by a high voltage shock of incapacitating pain.

* * *

Slowly, feeling and control returned to Cade's arms and legs. The migraine was back with a vengeance, pinpricks of pain stabbing the right side of his head. He tried to rub the pain but discovered both arms tied to the back of a chair. A drop cloth was spread beneath his feet.

"Pay attention, sucker," said the man with the soul patch and sick mother in Rockville, "or my friend here will zap you again."

Cade grunted. "What's going on, man?"

"You hear that, Butcher? My man here wants to know what's going on." Soul Patch squatted on his calves in front of Cade. "*You* what's going on, sucker."

Cade twisted and saw a large-muscled man with a shaved head and tats on his arms and neck. "You got my money and my car. What the hell else you want?"

Soul Patch said, "I got what I want right in front of me."

"What are you talking about?"

Soul Patch crumpled the flyer for the Chapelita Coalition for Justice and threw it against Cade's chest. Cade recognized the maintenance room as one of several in the Glebe Valley complex. Textbooks and a weight bench cramped the space. "The protest? That's what this is about? Why do you care if people are trying to save Glebe Valley from being torn down?" Then as soon as he said it, the fog in his brain lifted, and he remembered. "Finn, of course, that rat fuck."

Soul Patch flashed a tight smile. "At first, but not now."

"Then who?"

In response, the slender man turned a laptop screen toward Cade with a headshot of Robert Oliver.

"You're working for Oliver?" Cade snorted. "I don't believe it."

Soul Patch backhanded Cade across the face, flipping the chair over sideways. Cade's head hit the cement floor. "Fuck you, motherfucker. I don't give a shit what you believe."

Butcher righted Cade like a rag doll. His split lip dripped blood. "Whatever you think you're doing with Finn will fuck up the deal I just made with Oliver. I doubt the CEO will like that."

Soul Patch swung again. Cade flinched, but the slap never came.

"Look at that," Soul Patch said to the man he called Butcher. "Bitch is afraid of getting hit."

The rope binding Cade to the chair bit deep into his arms, constricting the blood supply. The prolonged application of tourniquets in combat field dressings could lead to permanent nerve damage. If he didn't get loose soon, his hands would be useless. Soul Patch he could handle, but Butcher presented a larger problem. He scanned the small room for anything that could be useful as a weapon. "Let me go and I can pay you. I got money."

Soul Patch studied Cade for a moment. "How much?"

"Thirty thousand dollars," he lied.

"Cash money?"

"Untie me and I'll take you to it."

The slender man laughed. He tapped on the laptop keyboard. "My man has a concept that's going to make a lotta people rich for a long time." The screen displayed the rendering of The Glebe at Cub Run.

Cade threw his head back and brayed with derisive laughter.

"What so funny, motherfucker?" Soul Patch snarled.

Cade tried to regain composure. "News flash, pal. Your man's concept is pure bullshit. Besides, *I* just made a deal with Robert Oliver. The Glebe will never be built."

The gun barrel moved to Cade's left eye. "Doesn't matter to me if the Glebe gets built or not, sucker. Investors are lining up to give equity to URP for a lot of other projects. But I wouldn't expect a dumbass cab driver like you to know that."

With his left eye closed tight, Cade's right eye fixated on the wrist holding the gun. That's when he noticed the U-shaped bite marks on a reddened patch of skin—and in that instant, the chaos in the courtroom returned when Rita bit the gunman on the wrist.

"You shot Father Gus."

Soul Patch didn't miss a beat. "No, you shot him when you grabbed my fucking arm. And, you also got suckers killed in Iraq."

Cade's eyes flashed.

"Yeah, I read the paper. And you calling out Oliver's bullshit? You're the biggest piece of loser bullshit I've ever seen." He shoved the barrel in Cade's mouth. "You got something to say about that, bitch?"

The gun barrel broke a tooth. Cade tasted a metallic tang of blood. His mind raced. How long before Grif and Rita would worry they hadn't heard from him? They'd call, then come to his apartment, find the Checker in the lot, and wonder where in hell he was. He imagined Grif busting through the door and spraying the punks with a .45 automatic.

From behind, Butcher yanked Cade's head back, the throat tendons taut in sharp relief. Soul Patch reached behind the cinder blocks and drew back the machete. Instead of fear, anger raged inside. His arms strained against the rope. He hoped an adrenaline surge would snap the binding so he could unleash his fury on these thugs. Cade hocked up a glob of saliva and blood and spat on the concrete floor. "While you're at it, shave that fucking cunt under your lip. You look like a goddamn pussy."

* * *

Luis sat solo in the Waffle Shop booth. Grif said he would wait for Cade's next call at home. Rita said she had an errand to run but to call her if anything developed. The late shift cook fried eggs and hash browns for two cab drivers at the counter. A salsa riff emanated from his shirt pocket. Luis punched his cell. "What're you doing up?"

"I just got a call," said Javier. "From Enzo. He asked me to meet him. You told me to let you know if I heard from him."

Luis flashed to the order by Officer Corrine Rodriguez and Detective Nichols to contact them immediately if Javier heard from Enzo.

"Meet you where? What time?"

"In a half hour. Said he had a few things to clean up first." Javier gave Luis the number of the apartment building. "Meet outside the maintenance room in twenty minutes."

Luis checked his watch. "You did right by calling me. Stay where you are. I'll handle it from here."

"Are you going to call the police?"

Luis replied, "Eventually."

* * *

Luis squatted on his haunches, ready to spring. Fragments of canned laughter spilled through open windows in the apartments above. A heavy door slammed, followed by a soft scrape on the concrete steps. Luis peered around the corner as a figure emerged at the top of the stairwell. A handle protruded from a backpack slung over one shoulder, the face obscured by a hoodie drawn up over the head. The figure paused and scanned the courtyard in all directions. The man turned, and for the first time in three years, Luis laid eyes on Enzo.

He stepped out of the shadows. Enzo was taller by several inches, although much slimmer. At five-nine, Luis packed over two hundred pounds on his frame. Soft around the middle, but enough soccer muscle remained to not fear being overpowered.

Momentarily surprised, Enzo quickly recovered. "The fuck you doing here? Where's Javier?"

"Homework."

"It's summer."

"Summer school."

"Fuck you."

Luis recognized the blue carabiner key ring in Enzo's hand. "What are you doing with Cade's car keys?"

Enzo moved to step past, but Luis blocked him.

"Where's Cade?"

"I don't know any Cade. Get the fuck out of my face."

"I did everything I could for you. I worked three jobs to save enough to put you and Javier through college."

"Step aside, or I'll cut your fucking balls off."

Luis squared up, his barrel chest inches from Enzo.

Enzo smiled. "And I'll chop off Javier's feet. Then we'll see how good a soccer player he is, eh?"

Luis shoved Enzo in the chest. Enzo stumbled. His right arm reached for the blade. Luis charged like a mad bull and pushed Enzo down the stairwell. Moans erupted from the twisted body. Enzo's leg contorted in an unnatural position. He struggled to rise. "I'll kill you, motherfucker!"

Luis flew down the stairs and straddled Enzo's chest. "Where's Cade?"

"Fuck you!"

Luis grabbed Enzo by the hair and slammed his head on the concrete. "Where's Cade?"

Eyes clenched in pain, Enzo muttered through gritted teeth, "You'll never find him, motherfucker."

Sweat from Luis's brow dripped onto his son's face. "First, you hacked a kid to death with a machete. Then you killed Father Gus, and I bet Cade. Now you threaten the brother who visited you in prison. You are one evil SOB."

"I guess I take after you," Enzo sneered through bloodstained teeth at the surprise on Luis's face. "Yeah, lots of Salvadoreños in Portsmouth know about you in the death squad. Too bad if that word ever got out."

Luis grabbed a can of spray paint from the backpack. He tagged the wall of the stairwell with the symbol for the Four Mile Kings.

Enzo struggled to rise. "What are you doing?"

"Gang retaliation, for the kid you butchered."

"Wait a minute." Enzo's voice quavered, no trace of bravado now. "Leave now. Call it quits. I won't touch Javier. I swear."

Luis picked up the fallen machete.

"No, no! Wait!" Enzo held his hands up in supplication. "*Mi padre! Soy tu hijo!*" He curled in a tight ball and folded his arms over his head.

Luis raised the blade overhead, his face darkened by shadows. His arm trembled. The blade quivered, unsteady. He looked down at his *hijo* cringing in the stairwell. The son who had crayoned a Father's Day card that he kept in a sock drawer. The boy he had once snuggled in bed, his breath like the puff of an angel's wing.

The machete weighed heavy in his hand. He felt the full measure of the countless *campesinos* who had cast their last pleading look upon his own merciless eyes. And then, there it was, with crystal clarity—Enzo's eyes. The same pale green as Luis's. The cool translucence of an executioner. The blade steadied, and with a downward tilt of his head, Luis pronounced sentence upon the boy sobbing at his feet:

"I am the angel of death.

God have mercy on your soul.

Because I will not."

Two Months Later

38

The live feed from the news chopper reminded Officer Corrine Rodriguez of a compound of religious zealots in a stand-off with authorities. Police had cordoned off the streets. A large crowd watched the drama unfold from behind barricades. Officers in the breakroom with Corrine huddled around the TV. On-the-scene reporters said that an unknown number of former tenants had broken into a condemned apartment building, locked the entrance, and refused orders to vacate.

A camera panned the complex. In the background, a yellow demolition crane stood idle, dangling a four-thousand-pound steel ball. A banner strung from the apartment roof proclaimed, *Glebe Valley Is Our Home*—the same banner displayed at the city hall protest several months ago. Just then, Corrine's cell buzzed. Police Captain Jensen told her that one of the tenants, evidently the leader, had been identified as the owner of Oscar's Excellent Landscaping.

"He says he'll only talk to you," Jensen said. "Get down here right away."

When Corrine arrived, the captain briefed her on the situation. "Oscar is believed to own a shotgun," Jensen said. "He may be armed. We don't know how many people are in there. Talk him out, Officer Rodriguez." He handed her the cell phone. "Nice and peaceful."

She sucked in a deep breath and greeted Oscar. "*Hola*, Oscar. This is Corrine. What's going on, *amigo*?" A long pause, then, "How many in there with you?" Corrine flashed five fingers, then two more. "Oscar, we need you and your friends to come out peacefully. Nobody gets hurt." She locked eyes with Jensen. "You have my word." She listened for a few moments and then handed the cell phone back to Jensen. "They're not coming out. He says they have a right to remain in their homes."

"Tear gas?" asked an officer in body armor and a riot helmet.

Jensen waved it off, clicked a radio, and barked a command.

A few minutes passed and then a massive police tow truck wheeled onto the scene. Police snipers covered the driver as he attached a steel cable to the front door of the apartment building. The crowd howled and shouted curses. A teenage boy broke through the barricades and flung himself in front of the tow truck. A roar of solidarity rose from the onlookers until four officers each grabbed an extremity and carted the kid away.

As the truck inched forward, the cables pulled taut. Suddenly, the door exploded off its hinges. A phalanx of police officers with riot shields rushed the entrance. Within minutes, Oscar and his seven-member crew of excellent landscapers appeared, cuffed and smiling, to deafening applause and whistles. Trumpet blasts from a trio of vuvuzelas greeted the heroes as the police led them away.

Two hours later, the crowd had mostly dispersed. Only Corrine Rodriguez and a partner remained stationed in a cruiser parked at the entrance to the construction site. Movement inside the fence shifted her focus to another man, this one thickset and muscled, wearing a hard hat and an orange safety vest. He climbed into the cab of the demolition crane. Black smoke spewed from the exhaust pipes as the hydraulics chugged to life. The crane rotated on its base, sending the steel ball into a high arc. With a deft touch, the operator whiplashed the demolition ball and brought it crashing against the apartment wall, dead center on the banner proclaiming *Glebe Valley Is Our Home.*

After her shift ended at the construction site, Officer Corrine Rodriguez stopped by the Chapelita Community Center. Inside, she found Luis stooped over a box with a tape dispenser. Stacks of cartons lined one wall. Squares of a lighter shade of paint revealed spaces where soccer posters had once papered the office.

"Hey, Luis," Corrine said. "What's going on?"

Luis set down the dispenser. "Moving day came early. URP paid to rehab a new job training center, and they finished ahead of schedule.

More computers, classroom space, even child care." He jerked a thumb toward his chest. "And I'm going to be the director—with a raise to boot. I'm waiting on the landlord to check me out before I leave. I'd offer you coffee, but the pot is in a box somewhere."

"Sweet deal," Corrine said.

"That's not all," Luis said. "I'm moving to Woodbridge. I got a larger apartment for less rent, but the commute is a hassle. URP doubled the relocation bonus, *and* they're paying for all moving expenses, *and* the first month's rent at my new place."

"Great," Corrine said. "I got a new apartment, too. URP is paying the subsidy for a police liaison to live in the Kent Gardens apartments. And, get this, I have AC and a pool now."

Luis smiled.

Corrine walked around the room, peeking into boxes. "Just curious, whatever happened to that lawyer you guys were hiring to fight eminent domain? I mean, it's too late now."

Luis wagged his head. "The FRED guy changed his mind, and well, after Cade disappeared, things kind of unraveled."

Corrine stared out the window. A man wearing a wifebeater T-shirt leaned in the doorway of Renaldo's barbershop smoking a cigar.

"Are the police going to arrest the Four Mile Kings?" Luis asked. "I mean, they killed Enzo, right?"

Corrine leafed through a *Sports Illustrated* on the desk. "Maybe." She paused at a two-page photo spread lampooning the Nats' historic losing streak. "The graffiti tag looks fishy. We'll know soon." Her eyes remained on the magazine. "How's Javier doing at UVA?"

Luis stacked a box on a pallet. "Pretty messed up. All that crap about Cade faking PTSD. He never believed it. He thought he was some kind of hero fighting city hall."

Corrine moved next to Luis as he loaded a shipping carton with office supplies. "I got an anonymous tip yesterday. A guy said he smelled something bad coming from the garage next door. We found a black Dodge Charger that belonged to BOB. Must have switched cars when they split. Left a body in the trunk."

Eyes wide, Luis asked, "Was it—"

"We don't have a positive ID yet. Definitely male, though."

Luis snorted and resumed loading the carton.

"And I found this in the car." Corrine thrust a cell phone under his nose. "Our digital forensic team hacked it. Enzo's last call was to Javier, around the time the coroner says Enzo was murdered. You know anything about that?"

Luis stared at the phone as he recalled Enzo trembling at his feet, pleading for his life. He turned away from Corrine.

"Yeah, I didn't think so." She headed for the door. "We'll be in touch, *amigo*."

* * *

Luis watched Corrine's cruiser leave the lot and then broke for lunch. He grabbed the sports section, and headed across the street to the Waffle Shop. He claimed an empty stool and spread the paper on the counter. Miguel poured him coffee without asking.

On a second cup, his cell chimed. He recognized the Miami area code.

"*Hola*," Luis said.

"*Hola*, Luis. It's me, Hector."

It took a moment for Luis to recall Hector as the public housing director in Miami. "Hey, Hector. What's happening, bro?"

"Thought I'd call to personally give you the news."

"Yeah, what news would that be?"

"Remember a few months back you asked me about Rita Castro?"

"Of course, I remember. You recommended her as a hotshot tenants' lawyer."

"Right. So, Rita ran into some trouble down here."

"What kind of trouble?"

Hector hesitated. "Rita and her father were victims of a double homicide."

"What!" Luis stammered. "She was just here helping us to fight a development deal. What the hell happened?"

"Police are still trying to sort it out. Looks like a break-in gone wrong. But word on the street is it's an execution."

"An execution? What are you talking about?"

"Her father, Cesar Castro? Half-brother to Fidel, served in the Army with Raul. Real revolutionary. Power to the people and all that shit. Until he split with a suitcase full of casino money. Settled in Miami, opened a couple of restaurants. Did pretty well from what I hear. Unfortunately, the Castro regime has a long memory. Took a while, but operatives finally tracked him down. Rita must have been visiting her father—wrong place at the wrong time. Thought you'd like to know."

"Uh, if you don't mind me asking, how did, I mean, was she—"

"Murdered? Thirty-eight, right between the eyes."

It took Luis a moment to process the image of Rita with a gaping wound in her forehead, just like Saint Rita, the patron saint of baseball. "When did this happen?"

"Yesterday, it's all over the news."

On the deli counter, the *Washington Post* screamed in a font size not used since Nixon resigned: *Nats Crush Marlins. Losing Streak Ends at 42!*

Hector asked, "You still there?"

"I'm still here. Thanks, buddy. Let me know if you hear anything else."

Miguel refilled his mug. "Bad news?"

"Tell the truth, Miguel, I'm not sure." He sipped the hot brew. "Who are the Nats playing today?"

* * *

The third day of the Sussex International Balloon Festival began on a pinkish dawn breaking over acres and acres of grassland and forest once inherited by Aelfweard Lovegod, the Lord Chamberlain for Henry VI. The mass ascent of one hundred hot air balloons was a remarkable sight to behold. Kaleidoscopic burps of gas rose heavenward amidst undulating currents of air and propane, rising, dropping, rising again.

Through binoculars, Deidre Moon picked out the purple and gold stripes of Robert Oliver's balloon, suspended as if in amber. She waved, knowing he could not see her. She strolled back to URP's sponsor tent. An array of serving stations offered omelets and Atlantic salmon.

At this insane hour, Deidre needed sleep more than the flute of mimosa a waiter presented, but she graciously accepted it. Guests with lanyard badges adorned with purple and gold ribbons mingled and noshed. Crewmember families sported polo shirts and ball caps in URP's team colors. A chamber group entertained the guests with her favorite Schubert quartet.

A fabric wall displayed framed pictures of Oliver and his crew from previous balloon races. A glass case contained an exhibit of trophies and medals. At the end of the wall, a raised platform exhibited a scale model of The Glebe at Cub Run. Guests took turns wearing the virtual reality headset to tour the latest evolution in urban living.

A waiter offered Deidre a fresh mimosa. She and Robert would have plenty to celebrate when he returned to terra firma. They'd inked a deal to accelerate the emotional communion campaign in ten more urban villages, including one in London. PULSE *tec* beta testing exceeded all expectations and had now moved into full product release and distribution mode. Industry buzz boosted URP's share prices to an all-time high.

A burst of laughter drew Deidre's attention to a young woman chattering to friends about the virtual tour. Deidre raised her flute, yawned, and toasted the rising sun.

* * *

Exhausted from soccer practice, Javier trudged back to his dorm room at the University of Virginia. With two papers due by tomorrow, it figured to be a long night. Fortunately, his roommate had opted to study with a girlfriend for the evening, so at least he could work in quiet.

As he ate a sub sandwich, he fingered a small leather journal with a gold cross on the cover. A re-gift from Cade via Father Gus after the longboard ceremony at Cub Run. Tucked inside, like a bookmark, a photograph of Cade and two Iraqi soldiers standing in front of a military-type vehicle—all three flashing wide grins. On the reverse side, inscribed in ink: *FOB Scorpion, 2005.*

Many of the pages contained handwritten passages, some with a date or a note in the margin. He flipped a page and read:

Shame on you who make unjust laws
and publish burdensome decrees,
depriving the poor of justice,
robbing the weakest of my people of their rights
despoiling the widow and plundering the orphan (Isaiah 10:1:2)

Javier flipped back to the photograph. At the zoning rally, Cade had said if things worked out, the U-9 soccer teams might attract a big sponsor. Soon after Cade disappeared, the Glebe condemnation sailed through the expedited quick-take process. The city flipped the property to a nonprofit development corporation, coincidentally headed by Robert Oliver. A few days later, a package arrived at the Chapelita Community Center containing new soccer uniforms, the Nike swoosh emblazoned on the sleeve underneath the URP logo. The following week, crews installed new sod and lights at the field. Oliver and the mayor cut a yellow ribbon in front of cameras. The whole deal stank.

Javier brushed away crumbs and picked up a day-old university newspaper. An article next to a dating advice column reported the sale of a student apartment complex located a few miles off campus. Curious, he Googled a search and brought up the Charlottesville Planning and Zoning Commission. Another link connected to the Edgemore zoning application. A developer sought a special exception for the height of the new condominium as per a section of the zoning code: *Zee 9*. The applicant: Urban Renaissance Partners.

* * *

Mick Finn busied himself setting up the laptop projector. The digital jocks had finished the latest animated transformation just in time. He could hardly wait to see the audience's faces as the dilapidated apartments morphed into an exciting new dimension in urban living: the Arbors at Albemarle. Deidre Moon had performed a marvelous job of bundling the emotional communion concept with Jeffersonian aesthetics of art and architecture. A mirror to reflect a customer's desired persona of a city dweller in a forward-looking renaissance community. PULSE *tec* was a money-making machine.

Tonight's sales meeting at the Red Roof Inn was Finn's first since the turnover of The Glebe at Cub Run to the construction division. When Cade and his scheme for fund-raising FRED's retainer disappeared, so did the Kaplans' interest in litigating the eminent domain takeover of Glebe Valley. Leaderless, Cade's coalition fell apart amidst infighting and finger-pointing. With Glebe demolition underway, Finn was awarded this plum project. A new CEO had been hired, and Oliver was last seen in a hot air balloon somewhere over Albuquerque. Even better, Soul Patch had met an unexpected, but well-deserved fate.

Invitees filtered into the ballroom—university academics, medical school professionals, software techies, and retirees flush with pension funds. Ten minutes ahead of schedule, and a packed room. Finn stepped up to the podium and threw out the first pitch. "Good evening, my name is Mick Finn. Welcome to The Arbors at Albemarle—the next generation in city living."

The crowd loved the transformation video. Finn asked about interest in pre-construction financing, and twenty hands shot up. It felt great to be back in the game with a roomful of hot prospects and open checkbooks.

During a question on HOA fees, the ballroom doors quietly opened, and a silent parade of college-age men and women filed into the room. A young man in a UVA soccer shirt directed the students to stand along the walls. Each student held a sign, hand-lettered with their first name, and below: *Edgemore is my home.*

"Excuse me," Finn said. "This is a private meeting, folks. I must politely ask you leave."

No one moved. No one spoke.

The audience gawked at the intruders. The young man in the soccer shirt held a sign that announced his name was Javier. He nodded, and the students flipped over the cards: *No Zee 9.*

Finn groaned.

A middle-aged man in a pinstriped suit stood up. "You heard him. Get out. Leave."

A tastefully dressed woman with spiked hair and a nose stud scolded the students. "You are being extremely rude. All of you. Go home."

Just then, the hotel security chief and a stocky bell captain stormed the ballroom. "You are trespassing on private property," the security chief bellowed, his blazer stretched tight over a bouncer's physique. "If you don't leave immediately, I will call the police, and you will be arrested."

No response.

"Last chance," the security chief said. "Exit the premises now or be arrested."

Off to the side, the bell captain ripped a sign out of the hands of a male demonstrator. The student grabbed for it back. The two men locked arms and grappled like wrestlers angling for a takedown. The bell captain managed a headlock on the student and swung him to the floor. The security chief ran to break it up, but a linebacker-sized student yanked him backward, toppling him to the floor.

The pinstriped man tried to exit the room but found the door blocked by several students. Attempting to create a wedge, he threw an elbow and caught a young woman on the chin. She screamed, then pepper-sprayed the man in the eyes. The man howled and clawed his face.

The security chief scrambled off the floor and threw himself into the melee. A tangle of arms and legs and teeth mashed and bit and punched. The student leader leapt onto the chief's back, landing wild punches to his head. Two more students pinned the chief's arms while a third threw body blows to the man's gut.

Finn watched in sickened amazement. Memories of the shooting disaster at the Glebe hearing flooded back. Suddenly, a squad of Charlottesville police officers swarmed the room. The protest leader shouted, "Die! Die!"

On cue, the demonstrators collapsed to the floor like marionettes with cut strings. A mock death protest. Police officers hauled off the limp bodies. Two cops lifted the student leader under each arm. His bloodied nose dripped onto the ballroom carpet. He turned toward Finn. "We're leaving, but we're not going away."

* * *

Cassandra felt emotionally drained. Back-to-back appointments all morning: a spiritual energy evaluation, followed by a chakra reading, then an aura cleansing. Plus, her psychic stock prediction business was picking up subscribers at an incredible pace. She had parked her growing portfolio in money markets and Treasuries. Steady work kept her mind off the grief. She'd tried to warn Cade of the danger signs in his aura. Maybe she should have tried harder.

She remembered the blockage in Cade's throat chakra. It had made it hard for him to express what was in his heart. Cassandra carried the same blockage. A love lost before it was found. She checked the lock on the back door and heard the bell on the front entrance door.

"We're closed," Cassandra called out. "Come back tomorrow."

"Girl, I could use a dusting," the voice answered, "but that ain't why I'm here."

Cassandra recognized the voice and entered the salon. "Well, pray tell, why are you here?"

"Don't you know?" Shavonne teased. "*You're* the psychic!"

Cassandra cocked her hip. "I've had a long day."

"Okay, okay, but you gotta see something. It's the damnedest thing. It just showed up overnight. Nobody knows who did it."

"What are you talking about?"

"Across the street."

"I'm tired, Shavonne. Just tell me."

Shavonne grabbed Cassandra's hand. "C'mon girl, you have to *see* this for yourself!"

Holding hands, Shavonne and Cassandra dashed across Washington Avenue and up the block to the Chapelita Center, closed since Luis moved to the new training center. They walked around to the side entrance, where the colorful mural covered the exterior wall. Cassandra had seen the mural so often that she took it for granted, like a backdrop in a play—the peasant woman confronting a military man, white crosses on the brown hills, factory workers, women of all nationalities holding hands across a brick wall.

Shavonne pointed to the left corner of the mural. "Right there." Then her finger swung to the right. "And over there. Not here last night, then all of sudden—it shows up this morning!"

In the left-hand corner of the wall, almost hidden by an overgrown hedge, was a portrait of Father Gus. An excellent rendering of the priest killed during the zoning protest.

But the portrait in the right corner shocked her. An uncanny likeness. Shadowing and cross-hatching brought out the sharp nose, unflinching eyes, and the ragged red beard of a guerilla fighter. An overall effect of tightly wrapped intensity.

And underneath the portrait, written in cursive, *Victory or Death*.

She placed her palm over Cade's forehead. From deep within the bricks and mortar, an aura of golden light warmed Cassandra's hand.

HISTORICAL NOTE

My version of *Cade's Rebellion* was inspired, in part, by an event in medieval history. In 1450 England, an ex-soldier by the name of Jack Cade led a rebellion against a corrupt king intent on imposing heavy taxes and other hardships on shopkeepers and laborers as a means to seize land and pay off war debt.

Cade and his accomplices also make an appearance in William Shakespeare's play, *Henry the Sixth*, when Cade declares, "For our enemies shall fall before us, inspired with the spirit of putting down kings and princes." To which Dick the Butcher replies with one of Shakespeare's most memorable lines, "The first thing we do, let's kill all the lawyers."

Cade's rebels achieved victory in several skirmishes against the king's men. However, during one encounter, he suffered mortal wounds. Jack Cade died on July 12, 1450, in Heathfield, England. After death, he was drawn and quartered and decapitated. His head was placed on a stake as a warning to other would-be traitors.

Depiction of the English rebel Jack Cade, as represented in Shakespeare's Henry VI, Part 2. Painting by Charles Lucy, entitled "Lord Saye and Sele brought before Jack Cade 4th July 1450"

Discussion Guide

1. Cade blames himself for the death of the seven Iraqi soldiers killed in the IED blast. Do you think Cade is solely to blame for the soldiers' deaths? Can guilt be a positive force for change in a person's life? Was it for Cade?

2. Eminent domain is a legal process whereby the government can take private property with just compensation and turn it over to another private party for development that is deemed to be in the public interest. After his attempts to buy the Glebe Valley apartments fail, Mick Finn works with the city to use eminent domain to take control of the Glebe Valley apartment complex. Although upheld by the Supreme Court, opinions differ widely on the constitutionality of taking private property away from one owner and giving it to another owner even if the reason is claimed to be in the public interest. Was the use of eminent domain, as applied to the Glebe Valley apartments, in the public interest?

3. Father Gus tells Cade about how Jesuit priests preached liberation theology to the peasants during the civil war in El Salvador—a philosophy that asserted it was justifiable for the poor to fight a corrupt government (even one supported by the United States) that was stealing the farms of the peasants in the name of land reform and murdering the resisters and protesters and sympathizers. Biblical citations in support of the philosophy are mentioned throughout the novel. Liberation theology was condemned by critics as thinly veiled Marxism in its aim to redistribute the wealth of the country in a socialistic manner. Accordingly, the United States considered the spread of liberation theology in Central America as a threat to free-markets and democratically-elected governments. Is there a moral argument to be made against capitalism as a root cause of oppression and income inequality?

4. Arthur A. Arthur's book *Urban Rebellion: A Call to Action* is based in part on the philosophy of Henri Lefebvre, a French Marxist intellectual who postulated a philosophical framework that demanded a "right to the city," i.e., a right by city dwellers to not be displaced from the place they inhabit. Lefebvre's call for a right-to-the-city later became a foundation for a global social movement. Among the principles of the RTTC movement is that individuals have a right to housing that is free of market speculation and that housing is a basic human right. Aside from who holds legal title to the property and the constitutionality of eminent domain, did the tenants of the Glebe Valley apartments have an *intrinsic human right* to their apartment homes?

5. The inscription "Victory or death" appears three times in the novel. Must death always be the only alternative to victory in a war or battle? Was Cade's death in the fight to preserve the Glebe Valley apartments a wasted sacrifice or a victory?

6. Robert Oliver has a vision to construct urban villages based on a concept articulated by Lewis Mumford as the aspirational destiny of cities: the *emotional communion* of mankind's consciousness. The magnification of all dimensions of life—from technological advancements to civic engagement to creative expression. The unification of mankind's inner and outer life. Oliver intends to achieve that *emotional communion*, in part, through the application of smart technologies (brain-computer interface) in his new urban village project, The Glebe at Cub Run. Is it realistic to believe that smart technology can truly improve the bonds of community relationships and further humankind's progress in artistic and scientific endeavors and civic engagement?

7. Protecting turf is a recurrent theme throughout the novel. Enzo and the Brothers of Blood want to protect their turf from encroachment by other gangs. The tenants of Glebe Valley apartments want to preserve their apartment homes from a take-over by a developer. Salvadoran peasants were forced off their land by the government in the name of land reform. Robert Oliver and Mick Finn want to construct a residential enclave for wealthy condo owners by booting out the existing tenants. Cade trained Iraqi army soldiers to protect their country from the insurgents. Protecting one's turf is a primal instinct of humankind. Does your personal turf extend beyond the four walls of where you live? How far would you go to defend your turf? Are there examples of turf issues in your neighborhood and/or community?

Acknowledgments

I wish to give a shout out to all my fellow writers, editors, and teachers who supported me throughout the long journey that resulted in this novel. A big thank you to my writers group that patiently and constructively workshopped multiple drafts over the course of several years: Emily, Brian, and Bill. My outstanding copy editor and proofreader, Erica Ellis. The cast of excellent teaching artists at the Loft Literary Center in Minneapolis, including: Brian Malloy, Mary Gardner, Kevin Fenton, Mary Carroll Moore, Robert Voedisch, and Kate St. Vincent Vogl. Also, the published authors who read early drafts and provided sorely needed critiques: Erin Hart, Hugh Cook, Stanley Trollip, and Mary Logue. The entire production team at Dog Ear Publishing. And a final word of thanks to Mary Gilroy for her support and encouragement.

CPSIA information can be obtained
at www.ICGtesting.com
Printed in the USA
FSHW04n1005060418
46614FS

9 781457 560248